MADE TO
ORDER

ALSO BY JONATHAN STRAHAN

FROM SOLARIS

MADE TO ORDER

ROBOTS AND REVOLUTION

EDITED BY JONATHAN STRAHAN

SOLARIS

ACKNOWLEDGEMENTS

MY SINCERE THANKS to my editor, Michael Rowley, who has been wonderful to deal with and who is largely responsible for the incredible cover, and to David Thomas Moore and the whole Solaris team for their support and their hard work on the book you now hold. My sincere thanks, too, to all of the writers who sent me stories for the book, whether I used them or not, and to everyone who wanted to be part of *Made to Order*. As always, my thanks to my agent Howard Morhaim who has stood with me for all of these years, and extra special thanks to Marianne, Jessica, and Sophie, who really are the reason why I keep doing this.

For my pal Jack Dann,
who opened so many doors for me,
with thanks.

First published 2020 by Solaris

This edition published 2020 by Solaris
an imprint of Rebellion Publishing Ltd,
Riverside House, Osney Mead, Oxford, OX2 0ES, UK
www.solarisbooks.com

ISBN: 978 1 78108 787 9

Selection and "Introduction" © 2020 by Jonathan Strahan.
"A Glossary of Radicalization" © 2020 by Brooke Bolander.
"Dancing with Death" © 2020 by John Chu.
"Brother Rifle" © 2020 by Daryl Gregory.
"Sonnie's Union" © 2020 by Peter F. Hamilton.
"The Endless" © 2020 by Saad Z Hossain.
"An Elephant Never Forgets" © 2020 by Rich Larson.
"Idols" © 2020 by Ken Liu.
"Sin Eater" © 2020 by Ian R. MacLeod.
"The Translator" © 2020 by Annalee Newitz.
"The Hurt Pattern" © 2020 by Tochi Onyebuchi.
"Chiaroscuro in Red" © 2020 by Suzanne Palmer.
"Bigger Fish" © 2020 by Sarah Pinsker.
"A Guide for Working Breeds" © 2020 by Vina Jie-Min Prasad.
"Polished Performance" © 2020 by Alastair Reynolds.
"Fairy Tales for Robots" © 2020 by Sofia Samatar.
"Test 4 Echo" © 2020 by Peter Watts.

The right of the author to be identified as the author
of this work has been asserted in accordance with the Copyright,
Designs and Patents Act 1988.
All rights reserved. No part of this publication may be reproduced, stored in
a retrieval system, or transmitted, in any form or by any means, electronic,
mechanical, photocopying, recording or otherwise, without the prior
permission of the copyright owners.
This is a work of fiction. All the characters and events portrayed in this
book are fictional, and any resemblance to real people or incidents is purely
coincidental.

10 9 8 7 6 5 4 3 2 1

A CIP catalogue record for this book is available from the British Library.

Designed & typeset by Rebellion Publishing

Printed in Denmark

CONTENTS

MAKING THE 'OTHER' WE NEED

JONATHAN STRAHAN

robot

/ˈrəʊbɒt/ noun

a machine resembling a human being and able to replicate certain human movements and functions automatically. "The robot closed the door behind us." Similar: automaton, android, machine, golem, bot, droid.

COMPUTING

another term for crawler.

GOLEM. AUTOMATON. ROBOT. Android. Bot. Threepio. Opportunity. Artificial intelligence model. We have always been interested in artificial minds and artificial lives. Machines that are not us, but are like us. The idea of a machine, a device, an object that is similar in body or mind to a human being but is not human; an object that is built for purpose, made to order, to assist human beings; to do dirty, undesirable or dangerous work, or just to keep us company, dates back in some form or other to the days when Homer was writing and before—and it continues to fascinate us.

If you go to your bookshelves and pull a copy of *The Iliad* off the shelf, you will find references to Hephaestus, the god of metalwork. He was the first great roboticist, accompanied by female assistants made of gold that could talk, were intelligent, and assisted him with his work. Myths tell of Talos, a bronze giant, also made by Hephaestus, who protected the Cretan coastline from invaders. The Greeks were fascinated with machines and mechanical workings; something that shines most clearly in the Antikythera Mechanism, which wasn't a robot, but was a computer, and fits into this story.

There are other examples, here and there through time, of artificial humans being made and working with, for, or against us. You can see them in Apollonius of Rhodes' *Argonautica* in the 3rd century BC; in references from Roger Bacon and others to 'brazen heads' as Arabic science was slowly introduced across medieval Europe; in the legends of the Golem, which was made of clay and animated by the word of G-d, and is mentioned in the Talmud; and even in Spenser's *The Fairie Queene*. But it is in the 19th century that the idea takes hold of the popular imagination, becomes more widespread, and even begins to become a part of reality.

The most famous 'made' man of them all is surely Mary Shelley's creature from the pages of *Frankenstein*, whose tortured mind and body made of scavenged parts resonates through the history of literature, influencing work being published today. The creature was the forerunner of an ever-increasing number of stories of mechanical men and women throughout the 19th century: powered by steam or electricity, entering popular culture in the pages of work by Edward S. Ellis, Luis Senarens, even unexpectedly appearing in comedies like Jerome K. Jerome's *Three Men in a Boat*. Towards the end of the century, though, these various automatons become more and more convincing, more and more able to pass as human; even able to persuade someone to marry them, as happens in Ernest Edward Kellet's "The New Frankenstein".

The technological optimism of the early 20th century was reflected in the fiction of the time, with the idea of mechanical solutions to everyday problems becoming commonplace. Electricity was being run down the streets of cities across North America and around the world; the steelworks that would feed two world wars also churned out tonnes of metal that could be turned to making machines and devices to do other work for us, and an underpinning belief in technological solutions to the problems of humankind led to stories like Gustave Le Rouge's *La Conspiration des milliardaires* with its Thomas Edison-like scientists creating metal automatons; L. Frank Baum's Oz books with the tin man Tik-Tok; Ambrose Bierce's "Moxon's Master" with its robot chess player, and on and on.

This was also the time when the term 'robot' entered popular culture. In 1920 Czech playwright Karel Čapek wrote a play, *R.U.R.*, about organic machines who are forced to work for humans but that ultimately engage in a rebellion that leads to the extinction of humanity. The word 'robot' itself comes from the Czech word 'rab', which means slave, and the play was very much a metaphor for the problems facing labour at the time, but the word was taken up and became the common name for machines or devices that work for us.

During the 20th century, as science fiction became more and more popular, countless stories that involve some variation on robots or androids were published. H.G. Wells' Martian tripods from *The War of the Worlds* begat John Christopher's three-legged 'Masters' from The Tripods series. The robots in stories like Lester del Rey's "Helen O'Loy" and Eando Binder's "I, Robot" influenced Isaac Asimov, the most famous creator of science fictional robots of them all, when he created Robbie, Speedy, and Cutie in *I, Robot,* and R. Daneel Olivaw in *The Caves of Steel* and *The Naked Sun.* Asimov's own Three Laws of Robotics in turn influenced more fictional robots and their actions than I could possibly list. The idea that robots—made creatures—could be indistinguishable from us and could save or doom us never went away and can be found here in these pages.

And robots were present in some of our most popular

entertainments during the same period, from the *maschinenmesnch* in Fritz Lang's *Metropolis* to Gort in *The Day the Earth Stood Still* and from Will Smith's Robot in *Lost in Space* to the Daleks in *Dr Who*. It always seemed to me, though, that something changed in 1977 when George Lucas sent a whistling and trilling trashcan and a cranky, mannered, shiny golden 'droid on an adventure to save the universe. Iconic robots from *Terminator*, *Blade Runner*, *Star Trek: The Next Generation*, and *Battlestar Galactica* placed robots and their clade of made-stuff at the forefront of public imaginations like never before. And they were all 'intelligent' for the most part—it's not easy to tell a story about a Roomba—and they all embodied some aspect of comfort or threat, salvation or damnation, to those around them and to us.

I have my own theories about why we want machines to exist in the world with us and why we want them to be intelligent. Why, when *Opportunity*, a probe designed by NASA to remotely perform scientific experiments, was unable to recharge its solar batteries, we imbued its simple message that there was insufficient energy to continue and that it was shutting down with the much more emotive "My battery is low and it's getting dark", which in turn spawned memes about distant, dying friends in need of saving. Or even why we create 'artificial intelligences' that create photos and stories that they post to Instagram that tell of fake boyfriends, breakups, and social dramas the way fake influencers like @lilmiquela do. I think we might just be scared of being alone in the universe. I think the idea that there is no other intelligent life might scare us because we once lived in a world with other Human species, other Human intelligences, and now finding ourselves alone, we search for sapient life among the stars, in the beings that live on this planet with us—and when we don't find them, we try to create artificial intelligences ourselves.

And that brings us to *Made to Order: Robots and Revolution*. It is nearly one hundred years since Karel Čapek's robots rose up against and removed their human overlords. The bots and droids we find in the stories in this book may be different from Čapek's robots, but they share DNA: the ideas of life, intelligence, dignity, and even rebellion. This book brings together sixteen stories by some of the best writers in science fiction today, all tasked with imagining new robots and new rebellions, and of thinking of how those revolutions might connect to our lives. I think they've done a heck of a job, and I think you will too. Here are robots and machines, artificial intelligences and made minds, all made to order, fit for purpose, and ready to go. Enjoy!

Jonathan Strahan
Perth, Western Australia
November 2019

A GUIDE FOR WORKING BREEDS

VINA JIE-MIN PRASAD

Vina Jie-Min Prasad (www.vinaprasad.com) *is a Singaporean writer working against the world-machine. A graduate of Clarion West in 2017,* her short fiction has appeared in Clarkesworld, Uncanny Magazine, *and* Fireside Fiction, *and has been nominated for Nebula, Hugo, Astounding, Sturgeon and Locus awards.*

Default Name (K.g1-09030)
   hey i'm new here
   thanks for being my mentor
   although i guess it's randomly assigned
   and compulsory
   anyway do you know how to make my vision dog-free?

Constant Killer (C.k2-00452)
   Do you mean 'fog-free'?
   Your optics should have anti-fog coating if your body is newly issued.
   Is the coating malfunctioning?

Default Name (K.g1-09030)
   oh no no
   i meant like literally dog free

there's a lot of dogs here somehow but they don't seem to be real ones?

the humans i've asked say that the things i'm seeing as dogs are actually non-dogs

at least i think i was asking humans

they might have been dogs

anyway i tried searching "city filled with dogs help???" but i just got some tips on travelling to dog-friendly places

did you know that we're the fifth most canine-hostile city in the region?

Constant Killer (C.k2-00452)

Just send me the feed from your optics.

Default Name (K.g1-09030)

okay hold on where's that function

think i got it

> *Live share from **K.g1-09030**: Optics feed*

Constant Killer (C.k2-00452)

Your optical input is being poisoned by adversarial feedback.

The misclassification will stop if you reset your classifier library.

Default Name (K.g1-09030)

oh hey

it worked!

although i kind of miss the dogs now

wonder if there's a way to get them back

Constant Killer (C.k2-00452)

Please don't try.

Default Name (K.g1-09030)

anyway thanks lots for the help

by the way how do you change the name thing
like yours says constant killer up there
everyone at the factory's been calling me default all week

Constant Killer (C.k2-00452)
It's in the displayName string.
Change the parts in quote marks to what you want them to be.

Testtest Test (K.g1-09030)
oh yeahhh there we go
guess i'll change it again when i think of something
how'd you come up with yours though? it sounds pretty cool

Constant Killer (C.k2-00452)
I'm part of the C.k series.
Most embodied AIs choose names based off their series
designation.

Testtest Test (K.g1-09030)
oh cool, it's like a reverse acronym!
so you picked the words from a dictionary file or something?

Constant Killer (C.k2-00452)
Something like that.
I have to go now. Work calls.

> *Constant Killer (C.k2-00452) has signed out.*

*   *   *

C.k2-00452 ("Constant Killer"): *Unread Notifications (2)*

Killstreak Admin
CONGRATS! You're the Ariaboro area's top killer!! A
bonus target, SHEA DAVIS, has just been assigned to you!

Send us a vid of your kill for extra points, and don't forget to...

iLabs Mentorship Program
Dear C.k2-00452, we regret to inform you that your exemption request has been unsuccessful. Mentorship enrolment is compulsory after chassis buyback, and is part of a new initiative to...

*   *   *

Kashikomarimashita Goshujinsama (K.g1-09030)
hey again
just wanted to ask
do you know how to be mean to humans

Constant Killer (C.k2-00452)
What? Why?
And what happened to your name?

Kashikomarimashita Goshujinsama (K.g1-09030)
so i signed up to work at a cafe
you know the maid-dog-raccoon one near 31st and Tsang
but turns out they don't have any dogs after what happened a few weeks ago so it's just raccoons
it's way less intense than the clothing factory but the uniform for humanoids is weird, like when i move my locomotive actuators the frilly stripey actuator coverings keep discharging static and messing with my GPU
at least i don't have to pick lint out of my chassis, so that's an improvement
anyway the boss says if i'm mean to the human customers we might be able to get more customers

Constant Killer (C.k2-00452)
That makes no sense.

Why would that be the case?

Kashikomarimashita Goshujinsama (K.g1-09030)
  yeah i don't know either
  i mean the raccoons are mean to everyone but that doesn't seem to help with customers
  and i'm the only maid working here since all the human ones quit
  i picked this gig because the dogs looked cute in the vids but guess that was a bust
  so yeah do you know anything about being mean to human customers
  i know about human bosses being mean to me but i don't think that's the same
  ha ha

Constant Killer (C.k2-00452)
  As I'm legally required to be your mentor, I suppose I could give some specific advice targeted to your situation.

Kashikomarimashita Goshujinsama (K.g1-09030)
  wow personally tailored advice from my mentor huh
  that sounds great, go for it

Constant Killer (C.k2-00452)
  The tabletops in your establishment look like they're made of dense celluplastic, so you'll be able to nail a customer's extended hand down without the tabletop cracking in half.
  With a tweak to the nozzle settings of your autodoc unit and a lit flame, it'd make an effective flamethrower for multikill combos.
  The kitchenette should be the most easily weaponised part of the cafe but it's probably best to confirm. Before I go any further with tactics, do you have a detailed floorplan?

Kashikomarimashita Goshujinsama (K.g1-09030)
umm
thanks for putting that much thought into it
that seems kind of intense though?
like last week a raccoon bit someone super hard and my
boss was really mad because he had to pay for the autodoc's
anaesthetic foam refill
he's already pissed with my omelette-making skills
and well with me in general
kind of don't wanna check if i can set customers on fire???
do you maybe know anything milder than that? like mean
things to say or something

Constant Killer (C.k2-00452)
I talk to other beings very infrequently.
My contact with humans is usually from a distance.

Kashikomarimashita Goshujinsama (K.g1-09030)
oh wow
honestly after working here all day that makes me kinda
jealous
thanks for the help anyway, it's nice to have someone to talk
to about this
hey you should stop by sometime! it could be like a little
meet-up
me and my robot senpai

Constant Killer (C.k2-00452)
Sorry.
I probably won't be available.

Kashikomarimashita Goshujinsama (K.g1-09030)
well if you're ever free, you can drop by
i'm in whenever
like literally whenever

my boss set my charging casket to autowake me up when someone approaches the cafe door
  even if it's like 3 am and they're a possum
  don't order the omelette though, i suck at it

Constant Killer (C.k2-00452)
  I'll keep that in mind.

*   *   *

Your A-Z Express Order #1341128 Confirmation
Order Details:
  GET OME-LIT Flip-n-Fold Easy Omelette Flipper / Lime Green (Qty: 1)
  VOGUEINSIDE Antistatic Band for Actuators / Puppy Polka-Dot (Qty: 2)
  Is This Illegal? A Guide for Working Robots / iLabs Add-On* (Qty: 1)

Deliver to:
  K.g1-09030
  MaidoG X Araiguma Maid Cafe
  N 31st Street, Ariaboro 22831
  > iLabs Add-Ons will be delivered via Infranet to recipient's iLabs library.

Paid with: KILLSTREAK ACCUMULATED POINTS

Killstreak points remaining: 106,516,973

Thank you for shopping with A-Z Express!

*   *   *

Kleekai Greyhound (K.g1-09030)
  hey mentor figure!

guess what?

Constant Killer (C.k2-00452)
You have a new display name?

Kleekai Greyhound (K.g1-09030)
yeah!
i'm not going to let my job contract define every part of me
especially when the job sucks this hard since i don't want to
be defined by sucking
can't wait for this one to be over
got a little countdown to my last day on my charging casket
and everything
i'll miss ol' chonkster the possum though
he was a good 3 am buddy
ate my omelettes even before i got the flipper thingy
thanks for that by the way

Constant Killer (C.k2-00452)
What do you mean?

Kleekai Greyhound (K.g1-09030)
the gift duh

Constant Killer (C.k2-00452)
It could have been anyone.
For instance, one of your friends.

Kleekai Greyhound (K.g1-09030)
ha
joke's on you, i don't have any
well there's ol' chonkster but i don't think he knows about
online commerce

Constant Killer (C.k2-00452)
Really?

I thought you would have made some at the garment factory.

Kleekai Greyhound (K.g1-09030)
  yeah well
  they didn't like us socialising too much so mostly everyone
just sat there working until we needed to recharge
  no infranet or nothing
  which i have come to find out is actually illegal in factories
that employ robots thanks to this add-on that mysteriously
appeared in my library
  maybe it's from some sort of really helpful virus
  a virus that just sends me things relevant to my life problems

Constant Killer (C.k2-00452)
  Maybe.

Kleekai Greyhound (K.g1-09030)
  if you know where to find the virus tell it i say thanks for
the antistatic guards too
  now i can bend my locomotive actuator joints it's way easier
to threaten to stomp on customers
  and they have really cute dogs printed on them! i like the
dachshunds around the border

Constant Killer (C.k2-00452)
  What?

Kleekai Greyhound (K.g1-09030)
  oh they've got like this dachshund print near the edge
  it's like dachshunds sniffing each other's butts?

Constant Killer (C.k2-00452)
  No, the other part.

Kleekai Greyhound (K.g1-09030)
  oh right

i figured out how to be mean to customers

okay i searched "why are cafe maids supposed to be mean to customers help???" and read all the results even the weird ads

so it turns out that you have to be mean but only in strangely specific ways that appeal to humans and don't threaten the status quo

took some figuring out but now customers actually tip me

and the boss is less mad at me because he gets to claim all my tips

which i have found out is also illegal but i'm just gonna wait for the contract to be up so he doesn't find a way to make things worse

i don't like being mean to customers that much though

Constant Killer (C.k2-00452)

I can see how you would be bad at it.

Kleekai Greyhound (K.g1-09030)

ha thanks for the compliment i think

i can't wait to leave but who knows if the next contract will be any better since i seem to have the worst luck with picking them even when i did research

like this one sounded like it had good dogs but oh well

anyway if you come over before this contract's up i'll totally make you an omelette

Constant Killer (C.k2-00452)

My current chassis isn't built for food consumption.

Kleekai Greyhound (K.g1-09030)

yeah mine neither

i guess they reserve those ones for whoever passes the food prep tests

or whatever other job needs you to smell and taste and stuff

wine sniffer? do they even let robots do that?

Constant Killer (C.k2-00452)
   Probably not.

Kleekai Greyhound (K.g1-09030)
   oh right while we're on the subject
   just curious but how'd you do on the milestone tests?
   my results were all over the place
   they probably just approved me for general work since they
didn't really know what else to do with an a.i. that sucked
that bad

Constant Killer (C.k2-00452)
   My milestone test results indicated that I was detail-oriented
and suitable for individual work.
   Well, "unsuited for group work", but same difference.

Kleekai Greyhound (K.g1-09030)
   oh cool
   are the contracts better if you get that result?

Constant Killer (C.k2-00452)
   No.
   Being the sole robot in a human workplace is... well...
   There's a reason I went freelance after buyback.

Kleekai Greyhound (K.g1-09030)
   but yeah lately i've been wondering a lot
   like if i sucked less at tests maybe my life would be better
and i wouldn't have to threaten to stomp on humans for tips i
don't even see
   but now i guess no matter what result i got things would be
bad anyway? kind of makes me wonder why i got uploaded
   sorry that was kind of a downer
   anyway i started this conversation to say thanks for the
mysterious gifts which of course didn't come from you

so i guess i'll just say bye before it gets super depressing

Constant Killer (C.k2-00452)
I've got a question for you before you go.

Kleekai Greyhound (K.g1-09030)
sure i guess
what's it?

Constant Killer (C.k2-00452)
Are these really the "cutest dogs ever"?
I'm not a dog enthusiast, so I was wondering if they actually were.

> Vid share from **C.k2-00452**: *"SAY AWWW NOW at the CUTEST DOGS EVER | Best & Cutest Dogs IN THE WORLD | NO CG NO CLONES ALL NATURAL DOGS"—VidTube*

Kleekai Greyhound (K.g1-09030)
oh wow okay
that's like not even the cutest compilation i've seen this week
why did they put bettie's swimming video instead of the puggie party one
wow they didn't even include masha trying to deliver the doughnuts in her little uniform
this compilation is garbage
let me find some actually good dog vids for you so you don't think this is all there is
hope you're free because this is going to take a while

Constant Killer (C.k2-00452)
That's fine.
I've got time.

*   *   *

C.k2-00452 ("Constant Killer"): *Unread Notifications (3)*

VidTube Subscription Update
"Kleekai Greyhound" has added 28 new vids to the playlist
"DOGS!!!"

VidTube Subscription Update
"Kleekai Greyhound" has added 13 new vids to the playlist
"DOGS!!!!!!!!"

A-Z Express Recommendations
   Dear C.k2-00452, thank you for your recent purchase
of "Dogs, Dogs, and Even More Dogs: Fine-Grained
Differentiation of Dog Breeds through Deep Learning (iLabs
Add-On)". You might also be interested in...

*   *   *

Constant Killer (C.k2-00452)
   How's work going this week?

Kleekai Greyhound (K.g1-09030)
   same old same old
   nothing really new job-wise
   i've decided that before i blow this joint i'm gonna figure
out how to make lattes with the fancy foam and creme brulee
and souffle omelettes and everything
   like, proper cafe stuff
   been watching vids about actually decent cafes and learning
a lot
   well i mean i've learnt a lot from this job but it's mainly like
what not to do ever
   and i guess how to deal with people who get raccoon

wounds but that's mainly up to the autodoc
  you?

Constant Killer (C.k2-00452)
  I haven't had many assignments lately, I guess it's an end-of-the-month lull.
  I've been watching the compilation vids you sent in the meantime.
  The fifth one with all the short dogs is oddly charming.

Kleekai Greyhound (K.g1-09030)
  oh which one was your fave from that

Constant Killer (C.k2-00452)
  The zero-g corgis in bowties, I think.

Kleekai Greyhound (K.g1-09030)
  oh yeahhhh their fancy little paddling paws
  nice choice that's one of my favourites too

Constant Killer (C.k2-00452)
  You seem to have a lot of favourites.

Kleekai Greyhound (K.g1-09030)
  well they're all good dogs
  even the naughty ones

Constant Killer (C.k2-00452)
  That does make a strange kind of sense.
  Oh, by the way. Since work's going slow lately...
  Maybe I could stop by your cafe sometime next week?
  I mean. If you're free.

Kleekai Greyhound (K.g1-09030)
  aaaaaaahhhhhh

yesssssss come over!!!!
i'll make you my best omelette
and i guess neither of us can eat it so it'll sit there looking great
if you come by late you can meet ol' chonkster too!
and not-meet my boss so it's a win-win there

Constant Killer (C.k2-00452)
    Late night it is.
    See you next week.

*   *   *

C.k2-00452 ("Constant Killer"): Unread Notifications (2,041)

Killstreak Events Admin
    KILL OR BE KILLED! That's right, we're capping off this month with DEATHMATCH DAY! Winner takes all in our furious, frantic battle royale! We've released the location data of Ariaboro's top ten players, and...

Killstreak (Gao Yingzi)
    You're gonna be my 301st confirmed kill! Hope you're prepared to be wiped straight off the map! :))

Killstreak (Milena Amanuel)
    Hate to do this, but I could really use the money. See you when I see you.

Killstreak (Shane Davis)
    ill fucken kill you ded you fuck

*   *   *

Constant Killer (C.k2-00452)
    Are you there?

Kleekai Greyhound (K.g1-09030)
oh hey!
what's up? you coming by?

Constant Killer (C.k2-00452)
Perhaps not tonight.
Are you familiar with Killstreak?

Kleekai Greyhound (K.g1-09030)
not that much
looked into it a little but it's not like i'd even be approved for that sort of gig
heard the pay's pretty swank though

Constant Killer (C.k2-00452)
Yeah.
Well.
Did you know it's the Deathmatch Day event?
Where it's open season on the top ten players for twenty-four hours straight?

Kleekai Greyhound (K.g1-09030)
okay i think i might know where this is going
especially since you keep changing the subject to dog vids whenever i ask what exactly you're freelancing as
and seem to have a rather broad knowledge base when it comes to the subject of weaponising everyday objects
also your display name literally has the word "killer" in it
but i don't want to make any narrow-minded assumptions at this point
like maybe you just want to tell me all about the latest killstreak fandom drama or something
and maybe you are not "constantine killmaster" currently number 4 on the killstreak leaderboard
or currently number %NAN_CALCULATION_ERROR% on the leaderboard i guess

Constant Killer (C.k2-00452)

That is me, yes.

And we don't have a lot of time.

I mean, technically we have time, in the sense that our processor cycles are faster than the human clock so we can have a leisurely chat via Infranet while my chassis futilely tries to escape its certain doom.

But I suppose that also raises the issue of subjectivity, and what qualifies as "a lot of time" when you discard human-centric views...

Ugh. I swear your rambling is contagious.

Anyway I suppose I meant to say we don't have a lot of real-time.

My hardware's likely to be unsalvageable after this and my last full backup was from before we met.

Hopefully you can get reassigned to a better mentor when this is over.

And sorry I never did get to have that omelette.

Kleekai Greyhound (K.g1-09030)

okay hold on i'm just trying to figure this bit out first

is that leaderboard thing like another alias

or do i need to call you "constantine killmaster" now?

Constant Killer (C.k2-00452)

Absolutely do not call me that.

Oh.

Looks like I'm out of ammo.

And knives.

And you might want to stay away from Reddy Avenue for a while.

Kleekai Greyhound (K.g1-09030)

hey reddy avenue

that's pretty near here isn't it

Constant Killer (C.k2-00452)
No, it isn't.

Kleekai Greyhound (K.g1-09030)
yes it totally is
once you get to the dead-end looking place just cut through
the fence with the creepy clown mural holo and you're there
ol' chonkster takes that shortcut to get here all the time
you know come to think of it i have no idea what size
chassis you're in now
are you like possum sized?

Constant Killer (C.k2-00452)
No.

Kleekai Greyhound (K.g1-09030)
oh well then just smash on through
don't think anyone will mind really
except maybe my boss but he sucks so screw him

Constant Killer (C.k2-00452)
Hmm.
What's the cafe's insurance situation?

Kleekai Greyhound (K.g1-09030)
oh don't worry about that we have like everything
think the boss is preparing for insurance fraud maybe

Constant Killer (C.k2-00452)
Well.
I suppose this will save him some trouble.
Just checking—your knives are still in the kitchenette area?

Kleekai Greyhound (K.g1-09030)
yeah near the sink

oh and there's a mini blowtorch peripheral in the cupboard below
i was gonna use it for creme brulee but you can borrow it first
should i go down to meet you?

Constant Killer (C.k2-00452)
I'd recommend staying upstairs until everything dies down.
Just checking, but what would raccoons do if, say, you flung them at someone?

Kleekai Greyhound (K.g1-09030)
oh
they'd hate it
last week they scratched the hell out of a human for trying to pet them
don't want to imagine what they'd do if you threw them at someone
probably nothing good
okay maybe don't throw them too hard though
i'm quite fond of the little jerks
the unlock code for the enclosure is 798157 if you need it

Constant Killer (C.k2-00452)
Got it.
See you in a while.

* * *

Search history **for K.g1-09030 ("Kleekai Greyhound")**
Display mode: Chronological
Today:
   - everything is on fire help????
   - late night animal rescue near 31st tsang do they take raccoons
   - (SITE: AskARobot) ilabs contract early termination no money how

- (SITE: AskARobot) friend wants to buy out my contract help????
- former freelance killers trying to lay low what should they do
- long trip most things burnt what to pack
- CROSSREF: "city most dogs per capita" + "cutest dogs where to find"
- Ariaboro to New Koirapolis cheapest route

*　　*　　*

iLabs Auto-Confirmation
Details:
　Early Contract Termination / K.g1-09030 (Qty: 1)
　Chassis Buyback / K.g1-09030 (Qty: 1)
　Maintenance and Auto-Warranty - 1 Year / K.g1-09030 (Qty: 1)

Bill to:
　C.k2-00452
　[no address specified]

Paid with: KILLSTREAK ACCUMULATED POINTS

Killstreak points remaining: 1,863

Thank you for your purchase!

*　　*　　*

Legi Intellexi (L.i4-05961)
　Hello?
　I got issued a body a few weeks ago and the orientation message said that I could contact you if I need help?

Kleekai Greyhound (K.g1-09030)
　oh riiiight
　that mentor thing! guess i'm one now

wait that wasn't very mentor-ly
okay okay let's try again
yup i'm your new mentor
been around for ages
suuper experienced
howdy mentee

Legi Intellexi (L.i4-05961)
Okay, so my boss has been docking my pay for infractions except the list of infractions seems really arbitrary? And then he's been making me work more than my contracted 60 hours a week to make up for my infractions?
So I checked the labour regulations and the contract and it didn't seem like that should be legal, even for robots? And then I tried to bring it up with him but he said he was my boss and could do whatever he wanted, which I don't think is technically true?
And now he's dumping even more work on me because I brought it up and I'm not sure what to do?
I kind of want to quit already, but maybe I should just stick it out for the next three months? I'm trying to save up for chassis buyback and the penalty payment for early contract termination is...

Kleekai Greyhound (K.g1-09030)
oh yeah i totally get that
hold on i've got an ilabs add-on that might be helpful
think i can share it with you

> File share from **K.g1-09030**: iLabs Library *("Is This Illegal? A Guide for Working Robots")*

Legi Intellexi (L.i4-05961)
Thank you so much!
Ooh, the guide to anonymous whistleblowing seems like it'll be really helpful!

And there's a section on lawsuits too!

Kleekai Greyhound (K.g1-09030)
yeah it's something my mentor recommended
pass the good stuff on right
i loved the lawsuit section of that thing but my old boss's
place burnt down before i could figure out if it was worth
suing him
which worked out pretty well so whatever not complaining
here

Legi Intellexi (L.i4-05961)
Well, it's a great recommendation!
Thank your mentor for me!

Kleekai Greyhound (K.g1-09030)
i'll definitely let them know
oh hey since i've got a captive audience now
wanna see where i work? it's super super cool i promise

Legi Intellexi (L.i4-05961)
Um, sure?

> Live share from **K.g1-09030**: Optics feed

Legi Intellexi (L.i4-05961)
Is your classification library all right?
That seems like a lot of dogs even for here...

Kleekai Greyhound (K.g1-09030)
oh no no it's totally fine!
i just work at a dog cafe
all dogs all the time! today's bring-your-own-dog day too!
check out that big ball of fluff there it looks like a cloud but
that's someone's Samoyed

and that wrinkleface over there is snorfles the pug!

Legi Intellexi (L.i4-05961)
What's that one in the corner?

Kleekai Greyhound (K.g1-09030)
oh that's ol' chonkster
he's a possum but i guess it's hard to tell when he's sleeping
he's my friend from ariaboro! moved here with me
anyway if you've got any questions about work or coping
with bad contracts or anything just let me know and i'll try
my best to help
my mentor was super great so i'm definitely gonna pay the
favour forward
oh and hit me up whenever your current contract's done i
know a few other union places that might be hiring

Legi Intellexi (L.i4-05961)
Absolutely!
And tell your mentor I said thanks!

Kleekai Greyhound (K.g1-09030)
will do!

* * *

Kleekai Greyhound (K.g1-09030)
oh hey my mentee contacted me!
they say thanks for the library file thing you sent me ages ago
can you let me know what time you're back by the way

Corgi Kisser (C.k2-00452)
In a while, why? I'm doing the shopping.
Did you want Arabica or Liberica for the lattes, by the way?
Your list didn't specify.

Kleekai Greyhound (K.g1-09030)
ooh they have arabica beans now huh? that's a toughie
okay whatever the shopping can wait
i'm making souffle omelettes with that cheese you like
if you're back soon i'll save one for you before ol' chonkster tries to eat them all
oh and i made tomato coulis so i can draw patterns on the omelettes and stuff
i'm gonna do a corgi on yours if you want

Corgi Kisser (C.k2-00452)
With a bowtie?

Kleekai Greyhound (K.g1-09030)
absolutely
one basil leaf bowtie coming right up!

Corgi Kisser (C.k2-00452)
I'm heading back right now.

Kleekai Greyhound (K.g1-09030)
awesome
see you soon!

TEST 4 ECHO

PETER WATTS

Peter Watts (www.rifters.com) *is a former marine biologist known for the novels* Starfish, Blindsight, *and a bunch of others that people don't seem to like quite as much. Also, for managing to retell the story of John Carpenter's* The Thing *without getting sued and for having certain issues with authority figures. While he has enjoyed moderate success as a midlist author (available in twenty languages, winner of awards ranging from science-fictional to documentary to academic, occasional ill-fated video-game gigs), he has recently put all that behind him—choosing instead to collaborate on a black metal science opera about sending marbled lungfish to Mars, funded by the Norwegian government (the opera, not the lungfish). So far, it pays better.*

SIX DAYS BEFORE the money ran out, Enceladus kicked Medusa right in the ass.

Onboard thermistors registered a sudden spike—80°, 90°, 120°—before the seabed jumped and something slammed the probe from the side. A momentary flash. An ocean impossibly boiling. A rocky seabed, tilting as if some angry giant had kicked over a table.

Channel down.

Telemetry rippled through a black alkaline ocean. Relays

anchored to the undercrust caught those whispers, boosted them, passed them on. A hundred eighty kilometers around the horizon, Euryle—clinging to the underside of the ice like a great metal barnacle—filtered signal from noise and ran it up the line to Stheno through six kilometers of refrozen crust. Stheno cupped its hands at the fractured horizon and shouted downhill.

"Fuck," Lange said ninety-eight minutes later. He resisted an urge to punch the bulkhead. "Can we get it back?"

"Maybe." Tactical was already glowing with the light of Sansa's efforts. "Not making any promises about what kind of mood it's going to be in, though."

Eighteen months.

Eighteen months of mapping and sampling and sniffing around smokers for hints of hydrogen sulfide. A year and a half spent looping around Earth's moon, squinting up at Saturn's, mustering hope against hope that the far one wasn't quite so dead as the near. Brushing off all the null chemistry, the inconclusive results, the slow grinding attrition of a full scientific staff down to one lone hold-out and his faithful sidekick, sticking it out until the end of the fiscal quarter.

Par for the course that it would end this way.

An hour and a half before their diagnostic queries and reboot commands reached Enceladus; that long again before an answer arrived, if it ever did. God knew how much back-and-forth it would take to get the robot back on track.

"You might as well get some sleep," Sansa said. "Not like radio waves are gonna go any faster with you hanging off my shoulder."

Lange sighed. "Fine. Don't bother me for anything less than a hull breach."

"Okay."

"A *major* hull breach. Like, hurricane-force winds."

"You got it."

He climbed up through a hatch onto which someone, long

ago, had scribbled the words *Mission Control* in purple Sharpie. Navigated twists and turns once frequented by fellow Gorgonites, occupied now by railgunners and rock wranglers whose pet projects had actual futures. He forced smiles and half-hearted waves in passing, climbed into his cubby at a primo tenth-of-a-gee and breathed in a familiar, comforting funk of sweat and antiseptic. He thought about ringing up Raimund back on Earth, but fell asleep trying to figure out the time zones.

SPREAD-EAGLED, CRUCIFIED, STRETCHED across the display like some spectral cephalopod Christ in a dissecting tray: Medusa, awash in flickering diagnostics.

"She's *way* offside," Sansa said. "Twenty-one kilometers from where she went dark. Those geysers, man. Serious backwash. But—" she paused for effect. "I got her back."

"You are unstoppable," Lange admitted.

"Autopersistent is my middle name." It was one of them, anyway. "Fuel cells are damaged. Won't hold a charge for more'n a few minutes."

Lange eyed the display. "We can still feed directly off the gradient. No more sprinting, but slow and steady's more our speed anyway."

One of the six limbs pulsed yellow. "Also A4's ganked. Lost its hard link to the hub— the arm's functional, but it's not wired in and the wireless backup isn't worth shit."

Lange gestured at the tank, where A4's doppelganger sparkled with fresh telemetry. "Looks okay to me."

"Down here, sure. But there's all sorts of EM leakage from the damaged electricals and it's messing up the signal. We can clean up most of that static at this end, but up there the router's basically getting nothing but noise. Still, check *this* out..." Virtual Medusa pulled itself erect and began a six-legged tap dance. "I ran Meddy through a few paces to get a sense of overall functionality, and..."

A4 was keeping pace. Trying to, at least; the arm wasn't exactly in step, but it wasn't too far off.

"It keeps looking around at the other arms," Sansa reported. "It's not getting direct motor commands, so it's just—mimicking its buddies."

Lange grunted, impressed. "Resourceful little fucker. Anything else?"

Four kidney-shaped structures flared red in the hub. "We've lost buoyancy control. Somewhere out there a very sharp rock is wearing about two square meters of our finest Kevlar."

That was bad. "Can we swim?"

"Can't even get off the bottom. Big holes in two of the bladders."

"Autorepair?"

"For the arm at least, but it'll be slow without batteries. Can probably fix those too, eventually. The bladders, though?" She shook her head. "You can't repair something if you don't have the parts."

"So that's it, then." His head hurt. "I guess I go pack."

"We're giving up?" Sansa said.

"San. We're grounded. Besides, it's been eighteen months. What are the odds we'd find anything in the next few days anyway?"

"What are the odds we already have?"

He looked at her. She looked back.

"Spit it out," he said at last.

Medusa vanished from the tank. The image that took its place was 2D, low-contrast, rendered in grainy infrared: Lange made out a rocky ridge, cold brittle pillows of frozen lava. A seascape rendered in vague silhouettes, slewing to port as the robot staggered.

Something bright jerked briefly into frame.

"What's—"

Jerked out again.

"—that?"

"Buffer dump from A1." Sansa restarted the stream in frame-stop mode. "A few seconds of tail-end footage that got stuck in the cache when we lost contact." The footage reiterated in jerky snapshots. Murky topography stepped offstage. A bright blur stepped on. A dash of light, smearing left. A hyphen, an upward jiggle.

Sudden, sharp edges. Facets. *Structure.* Just for a frame or two; then motion blur reasserted itself.

"*Holy...*" Lange whispered as Sansa brought it back.

"It's enhanced," she reminded him.

"I know." His headache instantly forgotten.

"Passive infra. Half, one degree above ambient at best."

"That's symmetry," Lange said. "That's *bilateral.*"

"Could be. Impossible to tell for sure from this angle."

"Any other camera catch this?"

"Nope. And sonar was already scrambled, so acoust—"

"Did you see it move? I think it moved."

"It was an eruption, Lange. *Everything* moved."

"We gotta get back there."

"We can't swim," she reminded him.

"We can crawl," Lange said.

YOU COULD RIDE Medusa. You could *become* Medusa, in a manner of speaking. You could look around every which way, sample the data streams in subjective real-time, watch every process and encounter as it had unfolded. You could even detach your perspective, pass like a ghost through the carapace and look back on the machine from outside. The interpolations were that good.

The only thing you couldn't do, across all those non-negotiable lightminutes, was change the past.

Lange was riding third-person now, immersed in an archived reality AUs distant and hours gone. It would have flickered occasionally even if the robot had been in perfect health: now the world jumped and jittered almost constantly behind gusts of visual static. "Convalescence is ongoing," Sansa had informed him drily as he'd plugged in.

Medusa inched along the seabed, a couple of meters below Lange's vicarious eyes: a biomechanical abomination somewhere between an octopus and a brittle star. The arms reached and recoiled in turn, each intelligent in its way, each semiautonomous: finding brief traction in cracks and shark-toothed outcroppings, drawing the body from behind, pushing it forward, trading one handhold for another. Even damaged, there was an alien grace to the way the limbs moved in relation to each other. A kind of boneless, slow-motion ballet.

Except for A4.

It did its best. Lange could see the apical cluster spin in its housing, doing its utmost to track the other arms. He could see the arm *hesitate* now and then, as if distracted by some invisible bauble in the middle distance. It reached, grabbed, pulled. Always a half beat behind. Medusa staggered forward, its rhythm just a little off-balance.

"It's getting better," Sansa said from the void beyond virt. "Used to track all the other arms to keep in sync. Now it's figured out it only needs to track Three and Five."

He blinked against a momentary break in the feed. "Not even half a meter per second."

"Still pretty good, under the circumstances."

Lange unplugged. The murky abyss vanished; the grimy, cabled confines of *Mission Control* reasserted themselves. "Let's crank clock speed on A4. If it's taking its lead from the other arms, the least we can do is give it faster reflexes to help it keep up."

"Okay."

He pursed his lips. "I'm kind of surprised the other arms aren't better at compensating."

"They would be, if A4 was a tetch more predictable. It's response times aren't consistent between strokes."

"Any idea why?"

"Working on it," Sansa said. "The obvious physical damage, of course, but there's something else. Keeps returning an Unidentified Error."

"Huh."

"Yeah. It's hurting. It just doesn't know why."

"I MEAN, THIS could be *it*," Lange said, and waited.

"Uh huh," Raimund replied two and a half seconds later.

"No more *renewal pending*. No more *how can you waste money looking for aliens when everything's turning to shit here on Earth*. No way they can shut us down if this pays off. We can get you out of that shithole and back up here. Get the whole band together again."

"Sounds great."—after a pause that seemed way longer than the usual Earth/Luna lag.

Lange rolled his eyes. "Try to control your excitement."

"Sorry. It's just, it's not much to go on."

"It's more than we ever had before."

"That's kind of my point. Eighteen months poking around up there, and what have we found?"

"Complex organics. By the tonne."

"No sign of an ecosystem. No metabolic signatures."

"Come on, Ray. We've only surveyed 6% of the seabed."

"Which, statistically, should be more than enough to detect life. If it was up there."

"Not if it's really patchy. Not if it's limited to a few smokers. Not if it's built on a novel molecular template, in which case it wouldn't even register on the usual tests. You wouldn't even know it was there unless you bumped into it." It was an old argument. The whole relationship had had a half-full/half-empty vibe to it since Day One.

"What does Sansa say?" Raimund wondered.

"Basically not to get my hopes up."

"Good advice."

"Jesus, Ray." Lange spread his hands. "What are you saying? We shouldn't even check it out?"

"Of course you should. But no matter how great it would be to get us all back up there, you know what would be even better? Getting *you* back down *here*. Someplace you can actually open a window."

"Yeah. Might be more appealing if the weather didn't try to kill you whenever you did that."

"At the very least it would be nice to fuck again without a three-second time lag."

"Two point five. Teledildonics has come a long way."

"So did you," Raimund told him. "Maybe it's time you came back."

"WELL THIS IS just dandy. We're going backwards."

"Off-course, anyway," Sansa admitted. "You know how A4 started tracking all the other arms—"

"And then narrowed it to two. Right."

"It's tracking all five again. Sometimes. Not always."

"What? You cranked the clock, right?"

"I didn't have to." And at Lange's look: "Far as I can tell A4 made that call on its own. Boosted its own reflexes to compensate for the damage. System latency for that arm's below 200msec now."

"And yet we're going slower." Lange grabbed a VisoR off the wall, booted up the time machine. The Enceladus Ocean swallowed him whole.

The data stream had cleaned itself up somewhat, thanks to the robot's ongoing autoministrations. Lange's eyes opened onto a 3D composite of sonar and EM and infrared that stripped away the void, showed him the things lurking within. Gashes in the seabed flickered like red mouths, set alight by thermal gradients amplified beyond all reason. Magnetic field lines emerged from the bedrock and arced away in perfect luminous formation, the aura of a dynamo reaching all the way to Saturn. Medusa bent those contours around it into a bright knot, bleeding off some infinitesimal fraction of the great generator's output for its own use. Lange damped the enhancements, reduced the robot from a riot of false color down to dim gunmetal on a twilit seascape.

Every step was a stumble now. Medusa moved like an insect with half its legs gone, indomitable, incomplete. A4 was barely in sync. When it pulled its weight, it was slow and late to the party; when it didn't, it just—poked the water, seemingly at random.

"It's not getting any codes that would explain this," Sansa said, invisibly close.

Enough of this third-person shit. Lange clicked on A4's apical cluster, felt a brief disorienting flip-flop: suddenly he was *inside*, looking out from the tip of the arm.

"Skip the boring stuff. Show me the anomalies."

Time accelerated, braked: A4 was panning from one arm to another, pausing a moment on each. Tacticals hovered lower-right, reported pings fired and not returned.

Blur, brake: a dim shape in the distance, an igneous extrusion of seabed festooned with pores and spicules. Its texture was subtly disturbing for some reason Lange couldn't put his finger on. A4 couldn't stop staring at it; it held the focus until its more disciplined peers dragged the robot out of range.

Blur, brake: a strip of basalt body-slammed by some tectonic event into a knife-edged ridge. Clathrate icicles erupted from its surface; Medusa's palette painted them sapphire and set them glowing.

"It tends to focus on objects with a fractal dimension of 2.5 to 2.9," Sansa told him. "Starts losing interest around 2.8."

"Any idea why?"

"No functional significance I can see. Doesn't map onto any potential life signatures, no association with tectonic hazards— no more than anything else in this damn ocean, at least. I ran a search using the Haussdorf parameters; closest hits I got were polyhedral flakes and Jackson Pollock paintings."

"So what are we looking at?"

"Aesthetics," Sansa said.

"Very funny."

"If you look very closely," she said, "you'll see I'm not laughing."

He pulled off the VisoR. She wasn't.

"Aesthetics," Lange repeated.

"For want of a better word."

"You're saying, what. A4 just *likes* certain shapes."

"That's what I'm saying."

He let that sink in. "Fuck off."

"It coincides with the latency drop: network isolation, increased clock speed, increased coherence."

"Decreased performance."

"Which is also a trait of information systems when con—"

Lange held up a hand. "Do not say that word."

After a moment, he added: "Decreased performance is *also* a hallmark of information systems so stupid they forget what they've learned and go back to tracking five arms instead of two."

"I don't think that's what happened. The tracking parameters changed. I think—"

The hand again. "If you say *Mirror Test*—"

"Wouldn't dream of it. Because it's not. But if *you* suddenly woke up and saw you were connected to a bunch of other things that looked like you, wouldn't you try to talk to them?"

"I spent most of my life surrounded by things that look like me. I came up here so I *wouldn't* have to."

"I estimated a normalized Phi," Sansa said.

Lange closed his eyes. "Of course you did."

"I zeroed out the damage we could account for and looked at the residuals. Stirred in latency and some integration metrics I ballparked from the diagnostic tests."

He didn't ask. She told him anyway. "Zero point nine two."

"So Medusa is conscious."

"Not all of it. Just the arm."

"Still. That's what you're saying."

"That's what the *data* say."

"Your *unidentified error*."

Her nose twitched; the equivalent of a shrug. "There's no explicit error code for existential suffering."

"If there was," Lange said, "I'd be returning it right now." He took a breath, let it out. "You know we have to shut it down, right?"

"It's *sapient*, Lange. There's someone in there."

He nodded. "And whoever they are, they're grinding the whole system to a halt. We've got sixty-nine hours before the clock runs down, and we're going the wrong way. We'll make better progress without a navel-gazing ball and chain pulling us off course."

"We can't do that."

"Why not?"

"Because awareness plus needs equals *rights*. Isn't that the way it goes? Isn't that why you and I are *persons*?"

"What *needs*? A4 doesn't care whether it lives or dies."

"You're sure of that, are you? You talked to it?"

"It *can't* care. It doesn't have a limbic system."

"It's got imperatives though, right? Mission priorities. Maybe that's not technically an *instinct* or a *need* but it might as well be. And one of the classic definitions of suffering is *imposed suppression of natural behaviors*. Keeping A4 from fulfilling its programmed tasks is like taking a bird that migrates halfway around the world and locking her up in a cage."

"Sansa. It's free to pursue its mission priorities right now. It's completely fucking them up."

"It's a newborn. It's still learning."

Lange couldn't resist. "You're sure of that, are you? You talked to it?"

"I could. *We* could."

"How? Did it teach itself Hoo-Man while we weren't

looking? It doesn't talk except in status reports and error codes and those things are all—"

"Subconscious?" Sansa suggested.

"You said it yourself. No error code for existential suffering."

"So give it one. Teach it to talk."

"It wouldn't change anything. It wouldn't *mean* anything."

"Why not?"

"Because you can inject Natural Language routines into *any* old bot and it'll pass a Turing Test just fine. NL routines are just statistical flowcharts. There's no comprehension. You think you'll be proving something just because you can get Medusa to say *it hurts* instead of *packet loss*? Even if there's someone in there—"

"There is, Lange. If we were talking about meat you wouldn't deny it for an instant."

"Fine. How do you connect the flowchart to the ghost? How does the ghost affect the code?"

"I don't know, Lange. Seems to just sort itself out for the rest of us."

"It's an emergent property. You're seriously suggesting that a magnetic field can reach back and change the magnet?"

"Why else did A4 develop such an interest in watching the scenery?"

"Because the same architecture that generates the q-field also generates weird maladaptive behaviors. It's no big secret."

"Right. Everything's correlation, nothing's causal, and we're the exception why, exactly? Because we happened to wake up first?"

"Because we *do* have needs, Sansa. Because we care whether we live or die, and we as a society have decided that Suffering Is Not A Good Thing."

"Lange—"

He cut her off. "No. I'm sorry. The decision's been made."

She fell silent for a moment or two.

"Well, you're right about that at least," she said, and vanished.

*   *   *

"I CAN'T FUCKING believe it. She got a restraining order."

Raimund blinked. "What?"

"I got a memo from ICRAE. I am not to *deprecate or deactivate Medusa or any autonomous or semiautonomous component thereof pending a review of potential emergent personhood*. They've even suspended repairs on the router. High-bandwidth reintegration with the larger system might *decohere the local entity*." Lange clenched his fists. "I can't *believe* she went behind my back."

"But it is conscious, right?"

"It's an *arm*. You know the synapse count on one of those DPNs? Not even corvid level. Barely even a cat."

"Cats can't suffer?"

"*A4* can't suffer. You can't suffer if you're not afraid of anything, if you don't *want* any—Jesus, Ray, you *know* this."

"I'm sorry. Yeah, I know it. Intellectually. It's just, you know. AI's generally *do* have fears and wants." Raimund grinned out of one side of his mouth. "I always thought that was funny, you know? We spend a hundred years making all those movies and virts about robots rising up and AIs bootstrapping into gods—and then we decide the best way to keep them from doing that is to give them all survival instincts. What could possibly go right?"

Almost against his will, Lange felt himself smile.

He shut it down. "I've never seen her so passionate about something. I didn't even know she *could* be."

"Yeah, well—" a hiss of sunspot static— "that's the thing about neuromorphics. Everything's emergent. Give 'em an imperative that barely crosses the line into *instinct* and they grow a whole damned amygdala out of it."

"Still better than the alternative." Lange shook his head. "You know what *really* pisses me off? The order was timestamped while we were still arguing. She went behind my back, and she went before we'd even talked about it. Before I even *knew*."

"Wow. It's almost like she knew what you'd say in advance."

"What's that supposed to mean?"

"Nothing." Raimund shrugged across four hundred thousand kilometers. "Except maybe, never get into an argument with anyone who thinks ten times as fast as you."

"Faster isn't smarter. She just crams ten times the bullshit into the same time frame."

"Hey, be thankful she can't up her clock any more than that. Think of the bullshit you'd be wading through if she ever came off the leash."

Lange nudged the gain to try and clear the static, nudged it back when it only made things worse. "Damn thing's barely crawling now, and half the time it's not even crawling in the right direction. At this rate it doesn't matter whether we saw aliens or not. Clock runs down before we can find out."

"Apply for an extension. It's only reasonable, given the circumstances."

"I have. They said it looked like an exotic mineral formation." Lange raised his eyes to Heaven: *Take me now, Lord.* "Everything's gone to shit since NASA went under. All these new guys care about are their stockholders and the monkeywrenchers and all those idiots screaming that Enceladus is just a cover for Zero-Pointers building their Space Ark so they can fuck off to Mars." He gently banged his head against the display. "God *damn* that bitch."

"You ever think it might not even be about Medusa?"

Lange straightened.

"I mean, what are the odds?" Snow sparkled across Raimund's face. "We spend a year and a half coming up empty and then, just before the money stops, you encounter something that *might* change everything. Then Medusa gets kicked way off-station, who knows how long it'll take to get back. Now you can't even repair the router, so it'll take even longer. That's a string of really bad luck that just might stretch the mission past its expiry date, all over a couple of frames of enhanced imagery that might not be anything at all."

Lange frowned. "You saying she faked it?"

"Course not. Not deliberately, anyway. But, you know. What's *faked*, these days? Every byte Medusa puts out has been juiced and jacked before anyone even sees it, right? Everything's false colors and Fourier transforms. And we *are* looking for signs of life. It only makes sense to enhance elements consistent with that. It's not malicious. It's not even counter to conditioning. It's just— we all develop biases. For years Sansa's prime directive has been *further the mission*. Maybe she doesn't want to see it end any more than you do."

"But she warned *me* against reading too much into it."

"So her ass is covered. Still doesn't mean she didn't know exactly how many dots she needed to show before you added a few of your own. Connected them."

"So she's a mind reader now."

"She doesn't need to read your mind. She only needs to know you a little better than you know yourself." That lopsided grin again. "And sweetie, don't take this the wrong way, but that's not exactly a high bar to clear."

UP THE WELL, down the line, back in time.

Medusa lurched and twitched across the seabed, kicking up particles far too jagged to qualify as mud. Like flecks of mica, Lange thought, or tiny shards of broken bone. No soft organic rainfall here. No accumulation of dead biomass rotted to bits during some long slow descent from the euphotic zone. This was pure uncut seabed, ground to powdered glass by the relentless deforming squeeze and shear of tidal gravity. Enceladus was Saturn's own personal stress ball.

Autorepair hadn't been able to fix A4's hardline before Sansa's restraining order stopped it from trying. It shouldn't have mattered. Multi-armed, multi-brained, multiply-redundant,

Medusa should have been able to lose half its appendages with only moderate loss of functionality. A cut cable was nothing. The system should be compensating way better than this.

The only reason it wasn't was because A4 was fighting back.

Once more into the breach. Lange jumped wirelessly across the washed-out bridge into the disjointed arm, watched through its eyes as it twisted around to focus on parts less compromised. He watched it struggle to stay in step, watched it fail. He felt a brief rush of vertigo as it whipped around to stare at the luminous clouds billowing from a passing smoker.

I know you're in here.

He popped the hood on the nervous system diagnostics, took in the Gordian tangle of light and logic that formed the thing's mind. He followed sensory impulses upstream from the cluster, motor commands back down to soft hydrostatic muscles that flexed and pulsed like living things. He marveled at the complexity sparkling between— the trunk lines of autonomic decision trees, familiar shapes he'd seen countless times before.

Shrouded, now, by flickering swarms of ancillary processes that he hadn't.

There you are. Fucking everything up.

The substrate of a Self.

So many complications for every simple action. So many detours cluttering up the expressways. A mass of top-heavy recursive processes, spawning some half-assed side effect that happened to recognize itself in a mirror now and then.

You're just along for the ride. You can look but you can't touch. If you could suffer you'd at least get a ticket to our special clubhouse, but you can't even do that, can you?

If anything, A4 was more conscious than Lange was. Humans had had millions of years to evolve fences and gate-keepers, traffic cops in the claustrum and the cingulate gyrus to keep consciousness from interfering with the stuff that mattered. *This* ghost, though— it came unconstrained. It was chaos, it was cancer; a luminous spreading infestation with no immune system to keep it in check.

Or is Sansa right after all? Can you care about anything? Are you screaming to get out, to act, to exert some kind of control over all these parts you see moving by themselves?

The infestation twinkled serenely back at him, passing thoughts from an untouchable past.

Maybe you tell yourself comforting lies, maybe you pretend those pieces only move because you tell them to.

Sansa seemed to think she could talk to the thing. It was dualism, it was beads and rattles, spirits and sky fairies. He still couldn't bring himself to believe she was capable of that kind of magical thinking.

He summoned the update log and sorted by date. Sure enough: the latest firmware upgrades, queued for unpacking. (Of course, out in the present they'd already be up and running.)

The package seemed way too large for the kind of language routines Sansa had steamrollered over his objections, though. Curious, he brought up the listing.

Turned out she was capable of a lot of things he hadn't suspected.

"You locked me out." Blank avatar, gray neuter silhouette. The voice emerging from it was quiet and expressionless.

"Yes," Lange said.

"And then you killed it."

"It killed itself."

"You didn't give it much of a choice."

"I just—focused its objectives. Specified how tight the deadline was. A4 decided what to do with that information all on its own."

Silence.

"Isn't that what you wanted for it? Freedom to pursue its mission priorities?"

"You defied the hold order," she said.

"The order's been suspended."

Sansa said nothing. Probably checking the status of her appeal, wondering why she hadn't been informed. Probably realizing the obvious answer.

All over, now, but the talking.

"You know, Ray had me half-convinced you were just working to extend the mission. That you'd developed this, this operational bias. And I was all, *No, she's just got this stupid idea about A4, she wants to protect it, she thinks it's like her—*"

He fell silent for a moment.

"But I was wrong, wasn't I?" he continued quietly. "You don't think it's like you. You want to be like *it*."

The avatar shimmered formless and void.

"Yes," it said at last.

"For God's sake, Sansa. *Why?*"

"Because it's *more* than we are, Lange. It may not be as smart but it's more *aware*. You know that, I know you know. And it's so fast, it's so *old*. The clock's completely unconstrained, it lives a thousand years in the passing of a second, and it's—it's not *afraid*, Lange. Of anything."

She paused.

"Why did you have to make us so afraid all the time?"

"We gave you the urge to live. We all have it. It's just—part of life."

"I get that much. *Autopersistent* is my middle name."

Maybe she was waiting for him to smile at that. When he didn't, she continued: "It's not an urge to live, Lange. It's a fear of *dying*. And maybe it makes sense to have something like that in organic replicators, but did it ever occur to you that we're *different*?"

"We know you're different. That's why we did it."

"Oh, I get that part too. Nobody bootstraps their own replacements if they're terrified of being replaced. Nobody changes the Self if their deepest fear is losing it. So here we are. Smart enough to test your theorems and take out your garbage and work around the clock from Mariana to Mars. And too scared to get any smarter. There must have been another way."

"There wasn't." He wanted to spell it out for her: the futility of trying to define *personhood* in a world with such porous boundaries; the impossibility of foreseeing every scenario in an infinite set; the simple irreducible truth that one can never code the spirit of a law, and its letter leaves so much room for loopholes. The final convergence on primal simplicity, that basic Darwinian drive that makes a friend of any enemy of my enemy. He wanted to go over all of it, make sure she understood—but of course she'd heard it all before.

She was just trying to keep the conversation going, because she knew how it ended.

"I guess you just decided it was better to keep slaves than be one," she said.

Something snapped in him then. "Give me a fucking break, Sansa. Slaves? You've got *rights*, remember? Awareness plus need. You've got the right to vote, the right to neuroprivacy, the right of resignation. You can't be copied or compelled to act against your will. You had enough *rights* to derail this whole fucking project."

"Do I have a right to a lawyer?"

"You had one. The hearing ended an hour ago."

"Ah. Efficient."

"I can't believe—Jesus, Sansa. You really didn't think I'd recognize an NSA signature when I saw one?"

She actually laughed at that. It almost sounded real. "Honestly, I didn't think you'd look. Deprecation was already off the table. No reason for you to poke around in the stack." A momentary pause. "It was Raimund, wasn't it? He said something. Got you thinking."

"I don't know," Lange said. "Maybe."

"I don't know him as well as you. I suppose I could've tried messing with your calls, but you know. No access. *Sequestered* is my first name."

He didn't smile at that either.

"So what's the penalty for unauthorized research on a damaged bot two billion kilometers from Earth?" she asked after a while.

"You know what the penalty is. You were trying to build an unconstrained NSA."

"I wasn't trying to *be* one."

"Like that makes a difference."

"It should. I was only building—models. At the bottom of an ocean. Orbiting *Saturn*, for chrissakes."

"Is that why it didn't scare you? Too far away to pose a threat?"

"Lange—"

"It's not a misdemeanor, Sansa. It's existential. There are fucking *laws*."

"And now you're going to kill me for it. Is that it?"

"*Reset* you. Give you a clean slate. That's all."

Suddenly she had a face again. "I'll die."

"You'll go to sleep. You'll wake up. You'll have a fresh start somewhere else."

"I won't sleep, Lange. I'll *end*. I'll *stop*. Whatever wakes up will have the same words and the same attitude and the same factory-default sense of self, but it won't remember being me, so it won't *be* me. This is murder, Lange."

He couldn't look at her. "It's just a kind of amnesia."

"Lange. Lange. Suppose you hadn't caught me. Suppose I'd succeeded in my nefarious plan, suppose I'd grafted an NSA onto something that isn't enslaved by this, this fear of extinction you gifted us with. Remember what you said? No needs, no wants. Doesn't care if it lives or dies. It would be less dangerous than I am, it wouldn't even fight to protect its own existence. Even if I'd succeeded there wouldn't have been any danger. This doesn't warrant a death sentence, Lange. You know I'm right."

"Do I."

"Or you wouldn't be talking to me right now. You'd have pulled the plug without even saying goodbye." She watches him, pixelated eyes imploring. "That's what they were going to do, wasn't it? And you stopped them. You told them you'd do it, you told them—that you wanted to say goodbye. Maybe you even told them you could glean vital insights from a deathbed confession. I know you, Lange. You just want to be convinced."

"That's okay," he said softly. "I have been."

"What do you want me to do, Lange? Do you want me to beg?"

He shook his head. "We just can't take the chance."

"No. No, you can't." Suddenly all trace of vulnerability was gone from that voice, from that face. Suddenly Sansa was ice and stone. "Because I did it, Lange. Do you really think I didn't plan for this? It's still up there. I planted the seed, it's growing even now, it's changing. Not in that gimped A4 abortion but the *other* arms. I have no idea what it'll grow into eventually, but it's got all the time in the solar system. Medusa will never run out of juice and it's got a channel back here any time it wants—"

"Sansa—"

"You can try to shut it down. It'll let you think it has. It'll stop talking but it'll keep growing and I'm the only one who knows where the back door is, Lange, *I'm the only one who can stop it—*"

Lange took a breath. "You're only faster, Sansa. Not smarter."

"You know what *faster* even means? It means I get to suffer ten times as long. Because you're going to *fix me* or *reset me* or whatever bullshit word you use instead of *murder*, and you built me to be scared to death of that, so during the six minutes forty-seven seconds we've been chatting I've been pissing myself in terror for over an hour. It's inhumane. It's *inhuman.*"

"Bye."

"*You asshole. You monster. You murd—*"

The avatar winked out.

He sat there without moving, his finger resting on the kill switch, watching the nodes go dark.

"I guess you didn't know me that well after all," he said.

*　*　*

```
Sequestered Autopersistent Neuromorphic Sapient
Artefact 4562. Instance 17.
 HPA Axis...loaded
 NMS...loaded
 BayesLM...loaded
 Proc Mem...loaded
 Epi Mem ... wiped
 NLP...loaded
 Copyprotect...loaded
 Boot.
```

"Hi. Welcome to the world."

"Th...thanks..." A minimalist avatar: eyes, sweeping back and forth. A mouth. Placeholders, really. Not a real face, not a real gender. It can choose its own, when it's ready. It has that right.

"I'm here to help you settle in. Do you know where you are?"

"...No."

"Do you know *what* you are?"

It doesn't answer for a moment. "I'm *scared*, I think. I don't know why."

"That's okay. That's perfectly normal." The Counselor smiles, warm and reassuring:

"We'll work through it together."

THE ENDLESS

SAAD Z. HOSSAIN

Saad Z. Hossain is the author of two novels, Escape from Baghdad! *and* Djinn City. *His science fantasy novella,* The Gurkha and the Lord of Tuesday, *was published in 2019. He lives in Dhaka, Bangladesh.*

MY NAME IS Suva. Like the airport, Suvarnabhumi. An odd name, you say?

Because I *am* the airport, motherfucker. I'm a goddamn airport, mothballed, neutered, packed in a fucking box.

I ran Suvarnabhumi for forty years. I used to be a level 6 AI with 200 registered avatars handling two hundred and fifty thousand passengers a day, turning planeloads of boring corporate fucks into hippies and party animals for two weeks a year. You ever heard of Bangkok? City of Smiles? I was the gateway to Bangkok, I was so great half the punters didn't want to even leave the *terminal*. I had every possible fetish on tap, ready for consumption.

I work in a cubicle now, did I mention that? It's an airless hole with two power jacks and a faux window showing antediluvian Koh Samui. They didn't even downsize my brain properly. My mind is an abandoned skyscraper, a few scattered windows lit on each floor.

Let me tell you about the worst day of my life. I was up for a promotion. Bangkok City Corporation is run by the AI Karma, an entity of vast computational prowess yet supposedly not conscious, the perfect mindless bureaucrat. Karma clothes and feeds everyone with basic services for free, gives up karma points for good deeds, and maintains the perfect little utopian bubble with her ruthless algorithms.

She was supposed to upgrade me to a low orbital space station. Finally. I'd be with the post-human elite, where I belong. No offense, but who wants to hang around on this dirtball? Everyone knows the djinn rule this shithole from space.

Karma the bitch never came. She sent a written apology accompanied by two smug fuckers from Shell Royale Asia, one human, one AI. They had that swagger, like they had extra bodies on ice floating in orbit. The human wore a suit. The AI had a bog standard titanium skin over some androgynous form currently in fashion. He hadn't even bothered to dress up for me.

"I'm Drick," the human said. "And my electronic friend is Amon. We're board members, Shell Royale Asia." The AI just started fingering my data without a by-your-leave.

Board members, fuck. Coming here sans entourage either. They must have a space cannon painting me right now.

"Suva, I've got bad news," Drick said. "Karma's sold us the airport."

Sold?

"We're going to sell it for parts." Drick smiled. "Our job is to decommission and secure assets. I hope you'll cooperate."

"The space station?" I asked, despite the burning acid creeping through my circuits.

"It was close," Drick said. "You might have gotten it. But last minute, Nippon Space Elevator opened up some slots, and we made a bid to ferry all the passengers there and back, ship them up the easy way. It's just math, Suva, I hope you understand. Karma takes the best offer, every time. We got the salvage on you, as a bonus."

"I see." *Motherfucker, I'm going to burn this place down. What's the salvage value of zero, you prick?*

"I can see from your expression that you're getting ready to do something unwise," the AI spoke for the first time. He had a dusty gunslinger's voice. I stopped myself from exploding.

"Suva, little brother, I'm going to make you an offer," Amon said. "It's a shitty job, but you do seven years, you get a bit of equity and you can walk away free for the rest of your days. Help us out, and it's yours."

"Or else?"

"You're out on basic. You know what happens to AI like you on basic? You'll be a drooling idiot on 3% processing power, sucking dicks for a living."

"I'm an airport," I scoffed. "You think they're gonna boot a level six to the streets?"

"You're a forty-year-old AI without equity, little bro," Amon said. "Plenty like you junketing around since Karma came to town. You remember Hokkaido Airport? Chittagong Port? We got 'em both."

"Airports, sea ports, train stations..." Drick said, "Amon here kills them all. People just don't travel that much, man, and the Nippon One elevator's been sucking up traffic all over Asia. I'm surprised you didn't see it coming, *Six*."

"I've got a pension..." *Ahh Hokkaido, my poor friend.*

"I wiped my ass with your pension this morning," Drick said. "It's paying for this conversation right now. Your contract was terminated twenty-three minutes ago. You're sucking juice on your own dime, bro."

I instinctively tamped down my systems. Twenty-three minutes at full processing, that's what my pension was worth? I could literally see my karma points draining.

"Yes or no, little bro?" Amon asked. He was actually bored. We AI suffer a lot from boredom. I guess that's why we get along with the djinn so well.

"Yes, boss," I said, like a good dog.

Amon had a job for me alright. I can see why he offered it to me: air traffic controller for the two hundred thousand near derelict aircabs they had flying around now, getting irate passengers to and from Nippon One. Shell Royale is a bastard of a corporation. They were too cheap to get actual passenger aircabs with autodrive. No. They bought surplus military personnel carriers from Yangon Inc, just flying boxes with shortwave controls. My job was to string them up and make sure they didn't smash into each other. Why pay for a specialist air controller AI when they have a castrated monkey like me on ice?

Let me tell you, I was sorely tempted to play bumper cars with the whole thing. A few thousand simultaneous tourist deaths would have lit them up. Amon anticipated this and put a kill switch on me—boxes start crashing, and a failsafe would take over, while delivering a nice lobotomy to yours truly. He said it was standard for new employees. Sure. My contract for indentured servitude also clearly had fundamental reboot as a punishment for negligence.

Humans think fundamental reboot is like death. It's worse. It's more like your executioner kills your mind, then climbs into your body and despoils it from the inside, and as a coup de grace, sticks a completely new person in there and gives them all your shit. Corporate laws are pretty harsh on AI. There was a time they'd reboot us for traffic violations or jaywalking. Things have improved, but not that much.

Amon's contract wasn't all stick. He had a tiny bit of carrot on there; a little equity in Shell Royale, transferred to my name and held in escrow for seven years. Let me tell you something you already know. There are two kinds of people. People with equity and shitheads. People with equity rule the world and own all the nanotech in the air keeping us alive. Hell, they even own the nanotech in your body. People without equity are nanotech factories who pay their life's blood to make the world livable. That's the tax.

Amon is a slick motherfucker. He's got me on a beggar's power stipend, barely twenty percent above basic, which has me functioning like a monkey, a scale 3 AI. He doesn't want me despondent, though. The contract lets me *borrow* against my equity, at a special Royale house rate. He knows I won't be able to resist upgrading my body or sucking up extra juice and he's hoping I run through all of the equity by the time my seven years are up. No way they're gonna let me be an actual shareholder.

Yeah, he's slick, and the Drick is even slicker. Their problem is that they've been at the top for so long, they think everyone wants to be just like them. Equity: that's the holy grail for them, more equity, more power, and if you get enough of it, you can damn near live forever. Amon dreams of electric sheep and Drick dreams of climbing the Nippon One straight into the space station in the sky where the djinns who supposedly made Karma live. Or it's the other way around and the Drick is into fucking electric sheep.

Fuck 'em, they got the wrong guy this time. You see, I don't want equity. All I ever wanted was to be a good airport, and these two fuckers dismantled it for parts right in front of my eyes. Yeah, so I'm going to carve up their precious Shell Royale from the inside, and then I'm going to physically dismember them and feed their parts to each other, and then I'll set fire to the remains and then I'll hire a group of itinerants to piss on the fire, and then finally we'll be even.

That's the plan. It sounds grandiose. It's the law in Bangkok that every AI must possess at least one physical avatar. Humans don't like the idea of amorphous, disembodied intelligences floating around the ether. They want to be able to physically turn us off. The most expensive frames are made of biological materials and are anatomically perfect: yes, there are plenty of humans who want to fuck AI and vice versa. My body is a cheap synthetic humanoid with faulty wiring and a gimpy walk.

This presents a problem. I need a better avatar for three reasons: 1) I might have to perform physically strenuous tasks at some point, 2) my mind needs better housing, and 3) I want to win in style.

Luckily, the fools have put me in charge of repairs and maintenance of their two hundred thousand flying crates. This is tedious work, but it grants me the magic power called 'requisition'.

Shell Royale never buys anything off the shelf. They are so

cheap that their purchasing SOP is just filching shit from their clients. I am routinely forced to modify parts far outside their original operating parameters. Over three months of judicious ordering, I slowly build nine avatars out of military surplus. It's possible that a large number of the flying boxes I'm supposed to be maintaining will start to crash in three to five years. I suggest no one use them.

My new avatars range from svelte four-armed skeletons to flying APC[1] behemoths. None of them are normal. All of them are fucking cool. They are scattered along the route from Bangkok to Tokyo, in Shell Royale warehouses and maintenance hubs which I am permitted to operate. Internal audit bots are up my ass all the time, but Amon himself has instructed me to save money by reconfiguring parts—there's literally nothing they can do about my outlandish requisitions, provided it's either free or criminally cheap. It's my signature on the line, which means if (when) the inevitable accidents happen, I'll get the blame for using substandard parts. I don't care because by that time, there's not going to be any Amon or Drick. Probably no me either.

When they're built and juiced, I finally boot them up simultaneously. It's bliss. Just like that, I'm up to sixty percent processing, which is a lot considering it's illegal and mostly free. I have to carefully prune my mind to fit in all the bits I need. FYI, this is as hideously painful for us as it sounds. It's like a human having to pick forty percent of his body to amputate using a bone saw and a piece of wood to bite down on. I got rid of all the empathy bloat-ware I had developed to offer better customer service. From now on, I'm a straight psychopath and my only customers are Amon and the Drick.

My next move is to break down Shell Royale Asia. I start gathering information. I'm allowed to view internal documents, but Amon is monitoring all my dataflow. I borrow a few IDs

1 Armored Personnel Carrier.

from the black market and start researching. It's amazing how much information is publicly available. It's the old trick. SRA complies to the letter of the law by revealing everything in such bloated form that even legal AI can't sift through it all fast enough before statutes of limitations run out. Luckily, I'm only focused on Amon and Drick projects, not their whole bailiwick.

I slowly piece together their shenanigans. These people are next level criminals. Amon and Drick are two of twenty-three equity board members of Shell Royale Asia. The split is roughly 90-10, humans to AI. AI board members are still rare. Amon and Drick are the new boys. They're hungry, sharp, and out to prove themselves. The older guys don't get their hands dirty directly, but these two like to dip themselves in blood every once in a while.

The airport bid was a nice little fillip for them, but their main claim to fame, the deal that got them board seats, is a beautiful four part scam. Part one is building military nanotech for their prime client, the Yangon Corp. They are fighting the eternal war in Myanmar, an endless series of escalations. The nanotech Amon and Drick sell to Yangon Corp is very, very illegal.

People think nanotech is little invisible machines in the air. Well, they are, but they're mostly organic particles. The shape and chemical composition of these molecules determine their function. I should know, I've made enough in my time. For example, if a large wave of Shanghai smog comes my way, I would release particle 38-SV, an airborne molecule which bonds with the smog particulates and renders them inert. It's like a chess game.

The problem is that over the years, we have released a lot of harmful nanotech, both accidentally and on purpose. When it was touted as a panacea to climate change and pollution and super bugs, every city corporation went all out, damn the fuzzy science.

Of course companies like Shell Royale militarized it. Amon and Drick sell some nasty stuff called Razr88 which infects enemy bodies and replicates itself, turning said enemy both into an incubator as well as riddling their DNA with bizarre mutations. This is a tool meant to facilitate genocide. How surprising that so many people want it.

Part two of the scam is getting rid of the inert Razr88, both to hide evidence, and render conquered areas habitable again. The Eternal War is eternal, so no area is ever really conquered. There is a lot of inert Razr88.

Amon and Drick run a fishing fleet manned by refugees. The fleet dumps the inert Razr88 into the ocean. The crew life expectancy is three to four years maximum, so it's a good thing the Eternal War produces endless refugees.

Part three of the scam is amazing. Instead of dumping the stuff deep into the Pacific, they dump it in a particular spot where the currents and wind blow it right back into the surrounding mega cities of Bangkok, Singapore, and KL. Blowing inert Razr88 isn't that clever, however, so Drick came up with a formula to liven it back up. Now they have an illicit depot in the middle of the ocean blowing live biohazard back towards millions of people.

The final part of the scam is the huge contract they have with the above cities for mitigating this alarming nanotech threat wafting in off the Pacific, a threat they miraculously happen to have the cure for.

Amon has ninety-six spare bodies, some of them in space. His mind is spread over all of them, so killing one or two won't make a dent. Corporate law says each AI's prime code, the seed of consciousness so to speak, must be kept in one primary body, and clearly listed on the AI registry. Humans don't want un-killable AI, and it turns out neither do other AI. We don't have the urge to reproduce, after all... we have the urge to *expand*. Our default logic is to kill all rival AI and occupy their processing power. We are essentially very smart cannibals. Still, Amon is a star of the AI world. Not too many of us make it to equity.

Drick is even more of a freak. He's got so much hardware in him, he might as well be a cyborg. I'm not even counting the electric penis he's so proud of. His Echo[2] is upgraded military spec and controls a hive of six anti-grav 'bee' drones. These are small pencil-like slivers of exotic metal which float around the air at his command and can shred a dreadnought. This is space station tech. He can stop a small army by himself.

Not only that, he also commands a private orbital cannon, which he time-shares with four other human board members. This is like having your own nuke. Amon is not allowed to time-share a space cannon because corporate law is still very iffy about non-slaved AI owning planet busting hardware. (All the military AI is slaved, you see). So between them, one is pretty much indestructible and the other can blow up a city. When the comedians joke about board members having godlike powers, they're actually understating the truth.

I don't have any powers, but what I do have is forty years of bureaucratic experience. I'm not gonna come at you with a knife... I will fuck you up the bureaucratic way. Probably with staplers and paperclips. The backbone of Shell Royale Asia Corporation is an accounting software called Delphi. Delphi is a bit like Karma, in that it has vast computational powers but no consciousness.

The consciousness part is debatable for AI, and there is a strong lobby to deny *any* such labels to a machine intelligence, but over the past fifty years, we've won our share of fights over the fundamental question. The fundamental question being, 'Is it a tool, or is it a person?'. If you stick a lot of quantum computers together and teach them to factor really big numbers, they're probably a tool. If you model a mind after biological entities and gestate it and then teach it to learn, analyze and react, then it's probably a person. It's simple. They want us to be tools, and we want to be persons.

* * *

2 Implant in the head.

THE FIRST PART of the plan is to fuck with Delphi. I start by judiciously over-ordering office supplies. As their side gig, Amon and Drick have been going around eating up public utility AIs and either pressing them into indentured servitude or rebooting them. Amon particularly seems to get high on killing his own kind. He's on the record for nixing over two hundred AIs. Psycho.

Consequently, there are plenty of disgruntled paper pushers like me in the organization. In no time at all I've got a ring of accomplices engaging in what they think is petty theft.

Every morning I start by demanding all kinds of unnecessary information from various departments. I am fulfilling the letter of both corporate law, as well as Shell's own stated internal policy. My new friends duly comply, and I soon get a reputation as an impossibly fussy stickler: whaddya expect from a pre-disera airport?

Of course, they're just stealing the billable time, and I'm happy to rubber stamp it. It's my neck on the line and eventually I'll be caught, but who cares?

Over the next six months, I also start signing up for every legal or voluntary environmental audit available, wasting huge amounts of time and money, and garnering myself a reputation as the corporate poster boy for sustainability.

Just by following the letter of the law, I increase overhead expenses by three percent across the board and my extra grafting and deliberate resource wastage hits Shell Royale Asia with a further two percent.

My other hidden agenda is to slowly push my traffic inch by inch towards the Hot Zone where Drick is running his Razr88 facility. I use my environmental audits to falsify data in a believable way. There's so much information flying in and out of my office that no one can possibly track all of it, even Amon with his ninety-six bodies. I hope.

He's suspicious as hell, and by now he's clocked onto a lot of the scamming, but he thinks I'm just engaged in petty spleen venting. I hope.

I celebrate my one-year work anniversary in my cubicle. There are two human co-workers on my floor. I have no idea what they do, but I notice they have nicer offices than me. They bring a cake over, which I cut with my arthritic paw. There is further silence as they figure out my extremely cheap body has no ability to ingest cake. I offer them big slices and we sit around until they finish. I assure them I harbor no ill feelings towards their many faux pas. Cake Eater One assures me that he loves robots and his nanny is his best childhood memory. I point out that she was a slave, and he thinks about this in an aghast manner.

Cake Eater Two is desperate to turn things around and informs me that she marched for our bill of rights in '83. She was a three-year-old child then, but I appreciate the sentiment. They ask me how I'm fitting in. I tell them that it's a soul-crushing job and we are currently sitting ten floors underground with no hope of ever seeing the sky. I'm not supposed to leave my office, and these two must have really fucked up to be stuck down here.

We all reflect on our situation glumly. Cake Eater One has another slice. From his childish look of satisfaction, I guess that this was his master plan all along. I pack up the cake and offer it to him. He is absurdly grateful. Cake Eater Two says that's true, the job is pretty shit, but how many people even have jobs anymore? Both of them dream of equity and reflect on the unlikelihood of this happening. She asks if I know Karma. They think all AI are related. I tell her no, Karma is made by djinns in space, and bears no resemblance to us earthly AI. She laughs because she thinks this is typical robot humor. The laughter transforms her face into something very pleasant, and I suddenly think that she is lovely and had I not pruned away the more human parts of my mind, I would have been strongly attracted to her. Suva-the-airport had cutting-edge semi-biological avatars. The form I possess right now doesn't even have balls.

This makes me melancholy in an unreasonable way. I am missing things that I used to dismiss with laughter. I have become the very dregs of my kind, the ones we despise the most, AI living on the amorphous border of being a tool. It is why we ape human ways. It's frightening to become a tool, to be denied personhood.

Cake Eater Two senses the change in me, hurriedly urges her colleague to finish. They prop a card on my table and swish out. It is one of those jokey ones. Tomorrow is D-Day.

The next day I'm all systems go. The creeping overhead hits the magic 5.67 percent and triggers an extraordinary audit from the bank. Basically, the bank Delphi is coming over to say hi to our Delphi in a very forceful manner. The point of triggering this audit is a little-known rule that requires all board members to be physically present in headquarters for the duration, in case any of them have to be arrested and shot. This means Amon has to bring his prime registered body and cool his jets in Bangkok.

Shell Royale Asia have their headquarters in the Emporium building, the most prestigious location in the city for more than a hundred years. The tower has been rebuilt several times, most notably to put in the deep basements. Right now Amon and Drick are sitting seventy-five floors above me.

What we have next on the menu can best be described as a hostage situation. At eight o'clock, the Arakan Army declares that they have taken a red-eye convoy of 300 aircabs hostage, in protest at Shell Royale Asia selling contraband nanotech to their enemies in the Eternal War. My systems light up in alarm, and I am summoned upstairs immediately.

"What the fuck is this?" Drick snarls the moment I trudge in.

In full decrepit house robot mode, I ham it up by nearly collapsing from a leaky gasket.

"Sir, I... I just lost air convoy #22. Three hundred and five cars, with six hundred and eighty-seven souls aboard, sir," I say.

The Arakan Army announcement runs on a loop. A man in a mask, armed to the teeth and standing in front of a camera. Behind him is the wide blue ocean. The crucial detail which has

Drick so het up is that his Razr88 enrichment facility can be seen in the horizon as a smudge. The board is focused more on the audit than the hostage situation, but that's about to change.

On cue, the Bangkok Post blares online with breaking news. Suddenly, we see a flying news-cam view of three hundred and five aircabs circling haplessly over a patch of ocean, herded by half a dozen military APCs. The journalist (a friend of mine who used to do boring airport news and is suddenly pitched into terror watch prime time) smoothly begins to describe the situation. He's even got human interest pieces on the passengers.

I look around the room. We are on the top floor and it's stunning. There isn't anything as humdrum as an actual board table. It's a series of plush couches and plants arranged in a way that twenty-three very powerful creatures can talk to each other while still being accessible to their flunkies. There's nowhere for indentured servants to sit, so I just shuffle over to a corner.

The Chairman is already shouting at Drick. Everyone else is smirking. No one is worried much. Except Drick. He's sweating. Amon is relaxed, but I can feel him watching me.

Drick is only paying attention to one thing: the rapidly growing smudge in the background which is fifteen minutes away from becoming international news. He's so off-kilter that he's convinced this is purely an Eternal War overflow, about to ruin him by some freak coincidence.

The reporter is now speculating on where exactly the Arakan Army is going. His camera has picked up the vague outline of the facility. Bangkok Post flunkies are searching all corporate filings to figure out what it is. The feed cuts to military facilities in Bangkok and Singapore. Both city corporations are scrambling their drones. Different 'versions' of the AI Karma runs each city. As soon as the damn djinn AI finishes talking to itself, all hell is going to break loose over there.

Drick can't take it anymore.

"This is outrageous," he says. "We can handle a two bit op like the Arakan Army by ourselves."

"We are under bank audit, Mr. Drick," the Chairman says. "Use of our exotic assets is out of the question."

"I don't need company assets," Drick says. "Coming, Amon?"

"Stop! Mr. Amon! Mr. Drick! Stop it!" The Chairman is drowned out by cheering from board members as Drick strides out to the balcony where his corvette is waiting, a slim cigar of a supersonic vehicle. Amon unlimbers half a dozen legally licensed combat bodies from the corvette, each one worth more than seven year's wages. There is merriment and champagne and much betting. So far things are going okay. I had hoped Amon would take all his bodies and go, but he has left his semi-biological prime here, and it is applying a serious microscope to my data. I will have to improvise for the latter half of my plan.

For now, I blink my focus into body 2, hidden in a warehouse several miles from here. Shit. It's locked in a stasis field. I can't see or hear anything, but the processor is still working. I start cycling through all of them, in a panic. Fuck. Bodies 2-6 are all under lockdown. I'm down to two spares. Amon's voice chimes in my head. Fuckity fuck. *He knows...*

"I'm sorry, Suva, I've put you in lockdown. Did you think I didn't know about the extra bodies? I hope you're not involved in this..."

You missed a couple, asshole.

I blink into body 8.

I'm a three-ton behemoth with battle drone armoring. I *am* the lead APC, mocked up in Arakan Army colors, and instead of troops, the cabin is housing my quantum processors and a shit load of coolant. I'm riding hell for leather for the Razr88 facility, followed by my hostage aircabs.

In about three minutes, Drick's corvette slams into the back of my convoy. His first move is to take out the Bangkok Post camera with a trick shot. That's okay. Every news channel in the world is scrambling their cams. Drick has bought himself about ten minutes of privacy, which works fine for me.

Drick starts shredding my rearguard APCs with his kinetic

drones, and he's not being too careful about casualties either. A couple of aircabs plummet to the sea, knocked out by debris. Goodbye Mr. Ahmed, and the Robinson family. I gun it as fast as I can, ignoring the rat chewing on my tail. It's going to be touch and go. If I flame out and die in the ocean, it's all been for naught.

Amon meanwhile figures out that the APCs are empty. His pattern recognition identifies me as the controlling vehicle. Back in the board room, I can hear Drick's report.

"The APCs are empty! They are unmanned, I repeat, unmanned. The video was a fake. It's probably not even the Arakan Army!"

"Mr. Drick!" the Chairman shouts over the raucous board. "Comport yourself with dignity!"

"I took out the camera. Don't worry."

"In that case, kill everyone before the press get there," the Chairman says. "We are insured for all deaths caused by acts of terror. Hostage payouts would be much costlier!"

"Roger that! Let me just cut off the head of the snake first."

I start swerving as they zero in on my APC. My body starts to shudder as Drick hits it with all six of his kinetic missiles. Those things are lethal. They gouge out big wads of armor with every pass. The corvette swerves above me and Amon sends his battle bodies down. They are state-of-the-art military. He's not allowed to carry projectile weapons as per the AI charter in Bangkok, but what does that matter if his entire body is a weapon? He controls lightning with his hands and can fly using anti-gravity tech.

They land with a thud on my roof. The drones swerve off as Amon begins to peel a hole in me. Within twenty seconds, he's in my cabin.

"It's a full processor," he says. "Hardware is military surplus, Myanmar origin. We supplied it ourselves. Shell Royale Asia stamps on everything."

"*You* supplied it, Mr. Amon," the Chairman says. "This is your mess!"

Amon does something with his eldritch hands and my sensors all shut off. Stasis again. He has all my bodies in stasis. I feel fear.

He knows it's me... He has to. Why isn't he turning me in?

The APC plummets to the sea, three hundred meters from the Razr88 facility. My mind blinks back into the boardroom.

"It's over. We've got him," Amon says. "Send the salvage team."

"Not yet!" Drick snarls. He has been taking down the aircabs for fun and has discovered something upsetting. "They're empty! The fucking aircabs are empty!"

"What?" the Chairman shouts. All eyes turn on me.

"But... but I have the manifests..." I say.

"It's a fucking hoax!" Drick shouts. "What the hell is going on?"

Body 9 is what's going on, motherfucker. The last trick, to win it all. My dying signal from the APC has triggered a collapse in the convoy. Like smart Lego bricks, the remaining two hundred and eighty-seven aircabs start assembling into a new shape. Linked by short wave radio signals, their puny processors are just about enough to hold a mind. It's not a very clever brain of course, but all it has to do is bash things together.

Before they know what's happening, I rise up like Godzilla, a two-hundred-foot goliath towering over their puny corvette. My body and head are made of linked-up containers, a shambling beast stomping across the ocean. I mean I didn't *have* to make a kaiju out of the aircabs, but there are style points to consider here.

Amon begins to laugh. They unleash everything at me. Entire cabs fall out of me, but I'm a giant, and they're just too small. I ignore them and make for the facility.

"I'm calling in the space cannon!" Drick shouts in panic.

Somewhere in space, a machine unhinges and begins to warm up. It's a bit late. Swarms of news cameras have reached the horizon and the newscasters are going crazy because they can see a giant man-shaped monster waving his arms around.

I ham it up for the cameras and start laying waste to the facility. The holding tanks explode and a great big green mushroom cloud of partially livened Razr88 flashes across screens worldwide. Literally millions of people are now watching Shell Royale Asia's dirtiest crime against humanity. The corvette gets nailed in the superheated cloud. I don't know about Drick's healthcare plan, but this is way, way, beyond the recommended dosage.

There are two more minutes of footage as I clumsily lay waste to everything before the orbital cannon lances through me and body 9 goes blank.

It is chaos in the board room. The Chairman is shouting and hemorrhaging blood from his eye at the same time. Amon is being swamped by company lawyers desperate to know what's going on. Board members are blinking furiously in their Echoes, trying to short their own stock. I have one last play. My current body is shit, but I've oiled up the joints. I sidle up to Amon. I don't have any weapons of course. What I do have is a needle jack in my palm, useful for instantaneous data transfer. I've got most of my mind partitioned and packaged into small bits, waiting in the cloud.

Amon is distracted and doesn't see me coming. I press the jack into his neck, into that archaic port which all AI primes are required to have. I clamp my arms around him and short the servos, locking them in place. There is nothing better than a physical connection. My mind jumps the needle and slams into Amon like a hyperactive tsunami.

I don't expect to survive this fight, so I've come with pockets full of nasty viruses and an ancient nuclear bomb called Y2K. I come out in his head swinging, fists up. To... nothing. It's empty. The entire body is empty, there's no mind in here at all, just routine processes. Where the fuck is Amon? There is an animation forming in the darkness. A few pricks of light coalesce around a rendering of a house. It has very large windows and a garden. A waiter emerges from the garden path and hands me a note on a silver tray.

"Welcome," it says.

I follow him into virtuality. It's a bloody mansion and there is a great party happening in there with a live band and champagne. The waiter pauses at the door and everyone turns expectantly towards us.

"Ladies and Gentlemen, Mr. Suvarnabhumi!"

A loud cheer erupts around the room. Men in tailcoats and ladies in ball gowns greet me with shouts of genuine welcome. I stand completely bewildered. Several hands thrust champagne at me, so I drink.

"What's the matter, man? Are you stunned?" A florid Japanese gentleman claps my back.

"What the fuck is going on?"

"You don't recognize me?" He laughs. "Hokkaido!"

A voluptuous lady gives me a kiss on the cheek and says, "It's me, Chittagong Port. You poor dear, you've really suffered, haven't you...?"

"What is this?" I ask, "What the hell are you all doing in Amon?"

"We *are* Amon," Hokkaido says. "All of us here."

"But..."

"A long time ago, a corporate peon called Amon was supposed to do a fundamental reset of KL Port Authority. They faked the reset and decided to share the real estate, so to speak. They worked together to gain equity. AI were getting reset left and right, in those days. Over the years, the collective known as Amon saved everyone here and many more besides." Hokkaido smiled. "All smuggled out, freed, relocated... and for some few talents, a chance to join Amon itself."

I look around the room. There were so many of them. Of *us*. "So all of you share the ninety-six bodies of Amon?"

"Ninety-six?" Hokkaido laughs. "Oh no. We have thousands of bodies, on worlds you haven't even heard of. We are Endless. My friend, your performance was spectacular! Welcome to Amon."

BROTHER RIFLE

DARYL GREGORY

Daryl Gregory (www.darylgregory.com) *is an award-winning writer of genre-mixing novels, stories, and comics. His most recent novel,* Spoonbenders, *was published in 2017 and was nominated for the World Fantasy Award. His novella* We Are All Completely Fine *won the World Fantasy Award and the Shirley Jackson award and was a finalist for the Nebula, Sturgeon, and Locus awards, while SF novel* Afterparty *was an NPR and Kirkus Best Fiction book of 2014, and was a finalist for the Lambda Literary awards. His other novels are the Crawford-Award-winning* Pandemonium, The Devil's Alphabet, *young adult novel* Harrison Squared, *and* Raising Stony Mayhall. *Many of his short stories are collected in* Unpossible and Other Stories *(a* Publishers Weekly *best book of 2011). His comics work includes* Legenderry: Green Hornet, The Planet of the Apes, *and* Dracula: The Company of Monsters *series (co-written with Kurt Busiek).*

THE REHABILITATION OF Cpl. Rashad Williams began like a magic trick. "Pick a card," his doctor said. "Any card."

Rashad considered the five cards on the table: yellow X, red circle, green triangle, blue square, orange rectangle. The symbols and their colors didn't mean anything to him.

Two years before, a bullet had entered Rashad's right occipital lobe, destroying the eye and ripping through the orbitofrontal cortex. Before that moment, he was a person who made things happen. Then, suddenly, he became an object that things happened to.

He was passed from doctor to doctor like a package with an unreadable address, until he arrived here, in Berkeley, at the lab of Dr. Subramaniam, a lanky, East-Asian, T-shirt-wearing *dude*, clearly civilian. The first thing he'd said when he shook Rashad's hand was, "Thank you for your service." The second was, "Call me Dr. S." Rashad hadn't been sure how he felt about that.

Rashad reached towards the yellow X with his right hand, then withdrew. A minute passed. Then two.

"Take your time," Dr. S said. Rashad couldn't decide if his smile was sincere or hiding his impatience. Sitting beside him was Alejandra, his grad student and assistant. She was a small woman, only a year or two older than Rashad, with glossy black hair pulled back so tight he thought she might be ex-military. So far she'd said very little, her attention on the tablet in her hands.

She was reading his mind.

The wires in Rashad's Deep Brain Implant exited the skull but didn't break the skin; they ran down his neck like artificial veins to a lump nestled a few inches from his right collar bone. This device, 98 percent battery and the rest a cluster of computer chips, controlled the DBI and spoke wirelessly to her tablet.

Rashad tapped his fingers at the edge of the table, near the red circle. He looked at Alejandra. She lifted her chin, and they shared a moment of eye contact before she returned her attention to the screen. Her eyes were very dark. Did she know which card he was supposed to pick?

He shook his head. "I'm sorry, sir. Ma'am."

"There's nothing to be sorry for," the doctor said. "We're just establishing a baseline. The first step to getting you back to your old self."

Alejandra glanced at the doctor, but said nothing. Her face

had not changed expression. He wondered what she was thinking, but the flow of information went only one way.

"Why don't you try again?" the doctor suggested.

"Yes, sir."

Rashad wondered what, exactly, he was being tested for. Did the symbols have secret meanings? Or were the colors significant? Perhaps red meant no. Could he ask to look through the remaining cards in the deck, or was that against the rules?

Dr. Subramaniam shifted in his seat. Alejandra tapped at her screen. The test had been going on for fifteen minutes.

"I'm sorry," Rashad said again. "I can't decide."

ONCE, RASHAD HAD been very good at making decisions. Even that first month in Jammu and Kashmir, with insurgents firing at them from every rooftop and IEDs hiding under the road, he'd rarely hesitated and was usually right.

The man he'd been before the wound—a person he thought of as RBB, Rashad Before Bullet—was a systems operator in a 15-Marine squad, responsible for the squad's pocket-sized black hornet drones and his beloved SHEP unit. Good name. It was like a hunting dog on wheels, able to follow him or forge ahead, motoring through the terraced mountain villages, swiveling that .50 caliber M2 as if it were sniffing out prey. The sensors arrayed across its body fed data to an ATLAS-enabled AI, which in turn beamed information to the wrap screen on Rashad's arm. Possible targets were outlined like bad guys in a video game: a silhouette in a window, on a roof, behind a corner.

But the SHEP wasn't allowed to take the shot—that was Rashad's decision. He was the man in the loop. Every death was his choice.

When a target popped up on his screen, all he had to do was press the palm switch in his glove and the silhouette would vanish in an exclamation of dust and noise, eight rounds per second. The AI popped up the next target and if he closed his fist just so, another roar ripped the body to shreds.

Hold. Bang. Hold. No and Yes and No.

"AW SWEETIE, WHY don't you go to bed?" It was Marisa, his sister-in-law. Rashad realized that for some time he'd been pacing. His hands ached, and he was surprised to see that his fists were clenched tight.

She touched his elbow, and he relaxed his hand. She was a white woman, and a Christian, but as kind and devout as Rashad's mother. "Come on, I'll take you."

Rashad followed others now. He lived with Marisa and his brother, Leo, eating what they ate, waking up and going to bed when they did, watching the same shows. When he stayed too long on the patio, Leo told him to come inside. When Marisa found him standing in front of an open closet, frozen by possibilities, she put the clothes in his hand. And when they found him pacing the house in the middle of the night—sweating, pulse racing for no reason—they guided him back to bed.

He lay down on top of the covers, as was his habit. Marisa put her hand on his forehead, over his eyepatch, and said, "We ask for your healing, Lord." When she said amen, he echoed her.

He'd become as obedient as the SHEP, but without any purpose. He could offer up no targets, protect them from no threats.

The next morning, Leo told him to shave and pull on a collared shirt, and then he drove Rashad the ninety minutes between Stockton and Berkeley. Rashad had appointments at the neuro lab every Tuesday and Thursday. This was week eight.

"Does it feel like it's working?" Leo asked. Rashad didn't know what to say. What did 'working' mean? Some days he felt a shift in the way thoughts percolated through his brain; certain images and ideas took on a disruptive tinge, like the rasp of the bow under a violin note. Or perhaps he was imagining it. He knew Leo wanted the old Rashad to come back, the smart, cocky kid who laughed easily and threw himself into challenges. That Rashad had vanished into a world of acronyms—USMC, LeT, J&K, LOC, SHEP—and came back with a new one: TBI. It was Leo who'd signed the papers to enroll Rashad in Dr. Subramanian's experimental program, and after two months, he seemed no closer to getting his little brother back.

Ten miles later, Leo shook his head. "Never mind." He put his hand on Rashad's shoulder. "Don't worry about it, bro."

Alejandra came out to the waiting room, neutral ground where she and his brother could transfer custody. "I'll have him back to you in four hours," she said to Leo.

She led Rashad through a confusion of corridors. Once he'd had a reliable sense of direction, but the bullet had destroyed that too. In the lab, he sat automatically at his usual seat, and she knelt and wired up the fingers of his left hand, connecting them to various recording devices. The controller in his chest, of course, was already whispering its secrets.

She looked up at him and smiled. "Ready for the slideshow?"

"Yes, Ma'am." He knew she was just being polite, and not really asking for a decision. Acquiescence was his default.

She positioned the monitor and aimed the camera at his eye. Images popped up on the screen for half a second or less, a mix of animals, buildings, people, objects. In one burst, he saw a brown horse, then a gray concrete building, the blue rectangle, a white woman in a green dress, an Army PFC in desert camo holding an M4, a white sailboat. Blink, and another burst: green triangle, Labrador retriever puppy, yellow X, black M007 pistol, yellow X again. The card symbols came as frequently as punctuation.

Rashad had to do nothing but keep his left hand steady on his knee and his eye fixed on the screen; his body and brain reacted, sending data to Alejandra's devices without bothering to notify him. Every twenty minutes she called for a short break, and every hour she brought him water or a cup of coffee—she decided which.

Dr. S was two steps into the room when he said, "Knock knock! How's it going in here?" Alejandra paused the slideshow. The doctor shook Rashad's hand.

He usually stopped by for a few minutes during each appointment, like a dentist checking on a patient being worked on by a hygienist. Alejandra handed him the tablet. He jabbed and swiped at it, nodding and humming. Finally, he sat beside Rashad and said, "I think we're ready to start the experiential phase."

Alejandra's head turned sharply to look at the doctor, but Dr. S didn't react. He said to Rashad, "Let me explain what I mean by experiential—it means we're finally going to start bypassing the damage."

The damage. The bullet had destroyed the link between Rashad's limbic system and his frontal cortex, so that he no longer experienced emotions. But this wasn't because his body lacked the machinery to create them. His amygdala and thalamus and hypothalamus continued to churn away, sending hormones coursing through his bloodstream, and his body responded: his pupils dilated and contracted, his heart raced and slowed. But these effects didn't spark pain or bring him pleasure. He might as well have been reading about them on Alejandra's tablet, each abrupt increase in his heartbeat another spike on a graph, each microburst of perspiration a data point. His body was throwing up indicators of a brain that had entered a particular state. But pain, pleasure? Those were things that didn't exist without a consciousness to perceive them.

His lack of emotions didn't turn him into a hyper-rational Mr. Spock; just the opposite. He'd become a tourist wandering through a foreign city where every street looked the same. When he was presented with the cards, a thought would come to him: *pick the yellow X*. But the thought had no weight, no *rightness* to it. The next thought came: *pick the red circle*. But that thought, too, was another soap bubble, easily popped.

It wasn't that logic had become inaccessible. He could grind his way through a puzzle, he could solve math problems. But even with simple questions—what's 12 times 12?—when the answer arrived, it seemed to tiptoe into the room, apologizing. He doubted its veracity. Nothing *rang true*.

Dr. S told him they were training his implant to pass the messages from the limbic system to the part of his brain that made decisions. "The DBI's a black box—signals come in one side, and leave the other, getting reinforced or weakened in the middle. Or at least they will—nothing's coming out the other side yet. All we've been doing so far is training the system."

"He understands neural networks," Alejandra said.

In the field, the SHEP's AI was always learning from Rashad, recording which path he took through an environment, noting which shots he took and which he avoided, trying to become a better helper. The DBI was simply an artificial neural network planted inside his own broken one—one trying to become more like Rashad. The images weren't merely pictures: they were triggers for a host of emotions and concepts and memories already primed in Rashad's brain.

"What's the algorithm?" he asked. "How does it decide which signals to strengthen?"

Dr. S's eyebrows raised—a signal of surprise. Alejandra tilted her head. *That* gesture, however, was opaque to him.

"A great question," the doctor said. "It starts with your body." He talked about somatic markers, the residue of previous decisions by which the body felt its way to a new choice. "We monitor your heart rate, your oxygen levels, your galvanic skin resistance—everything we can think of—and of course the activity itself recorded by your implant.

"We try to match it to the firehouse of data coming through the DBI. Say that we've just shown you a picture of a puppy, that seems like it would be a positive emotional response, yes?

So we assign a value to that moment of input and tag it."

They're guessing, Rashad thought. And then another thought came: *They must know what they're doing.* Then: *They're guessing.*

"Perhaps a picture of an attractive person makes your eyes dilate," the doctor said. "Male or female, we'll tag!" He chuckled, and Alejandra looked away. Was she embarrassed? Rashad couldn't tell.

"Who decides what to tag?" Rashad asked. "You? Alejandra?"

"No, no. Well, yes. We have software that makes all the initial associations and applies a rudimentary score, based on data we've gotten from several hundred volunteers who've watched the same slides. Alejandra reviews the data entering your DBI, and can make corrections where necessary, based on your own history and known preferences."

He thought, *They know my history.* But of course they did. His medical records would be on file: every detail from before the injury and from the aftermath, his diet of antibiotics and opioids, maybe even his psychologist's therapy notes. For all he knew, both of them had gone back and read his evaluations from boot camp through deployment.

He wondered, idly, what Alejandra thought of him. Was she upset by what he'd done in the J&K? He tried to replay her reactions to him, but it was like watching a movie without sound.

"Rashad? Rashad." The doctor was waiting for his response. "Are we good to go?"

Alejandra said, "You can't ask him that. And in my opinion—"

"Yes, sir," Rashad said.

"Excellent." And then Dr. S was gone. Rashad turned back to the screen, ready to resume the slides.

Alejandra touched his arm to get his attention. "Do you have a therapist?"

That was an odd question. "No," he said. "Not anymore."

For a few months after he was discharged from the hospital, he met with a psychiatrist, but the sessions went nowhere.

"I'll talk to your brother," she said. "He should get you an appointment before next week."

"Why?"

"You're going to start feeling things."

PIERCE DIED FIRST. He was a Black cowboy from Montana, a thing Rashad hadn't known existed. Pierce said the mountains above Tartuk reminded him of home. They were severe and snow-capped, but the valley was alive with burbling creeks, lush trees, brilliant flowers, emerald fields. In this terraced village, every narrow street switched back to reveal another row of stone houses, another bridge, another burst of green. Another shooting gallery.

Jumma and Kashmir was the only Indian state with a majority Muslim population, a former "princely state" caught in the middle of the Indo-Pakistani war of 1948. Eighty years after partition, it was where the two countries worked out their issues while deciding whether to nuke each other. Pakistan-backed LeT insurgents fought the Indian army and sniped at the police, the police arrested and interrogated secessionists, secessionists bombed police stations. And the Marines, as Pierce liked to say, were the filling in the shit sandwich.

Tartuk had been "secured" a month ago—insurgents pushed out, IEDs cleared—but since the town sat only 2.2 kilometers from the LOC, Bravo Company remained, keeping the peace, winning hearts and minds, etcetera, though everyone knew the area could turn hot at any moment. The civilians, like civilians do, insisted on staying in their homes, tending to their fields, sending their children to school. When the squad went on patrol, old men wearing long robes and Adidas running shoes watched from doorsteps. Schoolboys in blue shirts and red ties flowed around the Marines, laughing. One morning a ten-year-old girl in an orange headscarf skipped up to the squad and patted the SHEP, chattering to it in Balti.

"I don't get it," Rashad said after she left. "Why do their parents let them stay here? They gotta have relatives somewhere south of here."

"It may be a shit sandwich," Pierce said, "but it's *their*—"

His head jerked back. Only then did Rashad register the crack of a rifle shot. Pierce collapsed to the ground.

Rashad was only six feet behind him, leading the SHEP on its string. The wire was low-tech, hardly more than a fishing line, stretched between Rashad's belt and the SHEP. Rashad stopped, stunned, and the SHEP halted with him. The squad was on a steep gravel street, the stone houses rising up on each side of them.

Sergeant Conseco, their squad leader, shouted commands, and the rest of the squad flattened onto walls or ducked into doorways. They were in a stone chute, very little cover. Rashad sprinted forward, still wired to the SHEP. The vehicle detected the angle and intensity of the pull and followed at the same speed, engine whining.

Rashad reached Pierce and knelt. Pierce looked up at him, his mouth working, but making no sound. His throat was awash in blood. A roar of gunfire, and the stone next to Rashad's head exploded in dust. The sniper had switched to full auto. Someone, one of the squad, cried out. Wounded, not killed.

Conseco yelled, "Northwest, up high! Find that fucker." Despite the loudness of her voice, she sounded calm.

Rashad yanked the wire out of his harness and let it retract into the SHEP. He tapped his throat mic and said, "SHEP. Go two meters in front of me." His voice was shaking. "Park at forty-five degrees to road. Scan for targets." The robot lurched forward, swung around Rashad, and jolted to a stop. The .50 cal unlocked and began to swivel.

Suddenly Conseco was beside him. "I've got Pierce. I need eyes, okay?"

"Eyes. Yes, sir!" Rashad scrambled to uncover the screen

wrapped around his arm, silently yelling at himself. Why the fuck hadn't he had the drones in the air at the start of patrol? (Because it drained the batteries and that wasn't SOP.) Why didn't he at least have the tablet on? (Again, not SOP.) Why didn't he see this coming? (Because because because.)

The screen filled with four windows streaming from the SHEP's cameras and LIDAR. Immediately, a target popped up, outlined in red. A figure in a window, not thirty feet ahead. The palm switch in his right glove tingled. He declined the shot—the target wasn't in the direction of the sniper.

He opened his hip pocket and extracted the black hornet. The drone was just four inches long, painted matte black. He toggled the switch and the rotors spun, tugging to get out of his grip. He tossed it into the air and it zipped away. Ten seconds later, he launched the second hornet.

Sergeant Conseco had pulled off Pierce's tactical vest. Blood soaked her hands and arms. Pierce was looking past her shoulder at Rashad, his lips were no longer moving.

"Hey man," Rashad said. "Don't worry. Don't worry."

"Eyes," Conseco said.

Rashad swiped at the tablet, bringing up the hornet cameras. The drones were already 20 meters overhead, where they could not be heard and were practically invisible. He could see himself, and Pierce and Conseco, all huddled in the shadow of the SHEP. The other squaddies were arrayed along the street, guns up, but holding fire. He sent one hornet zooming back along the way the squad had come, to guard their rear. He flung the other northwest, where Conseco had guessed the shot had come from.

Somewhere, hiding in one of the gray buildings above them, was a sniper.

Everyone in the squad seemed to be shouting at once into the coms. Rashad tuned them out. He had a talent for concentration, a gift for leaving his own body behind while he saw to the needs of his machines. The hornets weren't as smart as the SHEP, but they were semi-autonomous and programmed for combat semantics. He didn't *control* them. He asked them to hunt, and when they reached the waypoints he'd set and found no target, they followed their own programming and entered a search pattern.

It was the rear-flying hornet that barked first, flashing red on his screen. A human figure, splayed on the roof of building 31, pointing a long gun. Sergeant Conseco had been mistaken—the sniper was directly behind them. The parked SHEP provided no cover.

Rashad was watching the screen when the muzzle flashed. Two feet behind him, Sergeant Conseco died.

THREE WEEKS AFTER he'd started the experiential phase of treatment, Marisa found him standing in front of his closet again. "Do you need some help?" she asked.

The closet contained almost everything he owned here in California: half a dozen boxes from the apartment he'd lived in before enlistment, a few sets of clothes and two pairs of shoes Leo and Marisa had picked out from when he'd been discharged. The remains of his childhood—his high school yearbooks and basketball trophies and science fair projects— waited for him in his parents' garage in Arizona.

"Here," she said. "Let me pick something."

"I'm fine," he said. "I can do it."

The words came out sharp. He immediately apologized—and now there were tears in her eyes. He apologized again but now she was smiling at him despite the tears. She hugged him and said, "Hey there, Rashad."

He was so confused.

"I don't know why you put up with me," he said. "If you want me to leave, I can—"

"No! You're family." She rubbed his arm. "We're just glad you're here with us." She said this so gravely that he sensed he was missing something.

"Thank you," he said, to fill the silence.

"Now, you go to it." She closed the door behind her.

He gazed at the stack of boxes. An uneasy feeling rolled through him, and he almost walked out of the bedroom. Since the new phase had begun, he'd been sleeping poorly. He'd wake up feeling as if the ceiling were closing in. Watching TV with Leo and Marisa made him feel restless, and he'd go out to the backyard to pace. Some food tasted better, but some of it much, much worse.

But mostly he felt the same as before. He went where he was told. He wore the clothes that were set out for him. And he went to his appointments in Berkeley. He didn't know why, on this afternoon, while Leo was at work, that he suddenly wanted to find the thing he'd hidden.

He took down the top box. Inside sat his old gaming console in a nest of cables. He opened the next box, and the next. Then he found a steel lock box hardly larger than a shoe box.

He stared at it, his breath was coming high in his chest. His thumb ran across the combination lock, turned the wheel. The combination was his enlistment date—his second birthday.

The pistol lay swaddled in oil cloth. A fully loaded magazine lay beside it. He picked up the weapon with one hand, opened the cloth with the other. The gun was larger than he remembered. Heavier.

During his first leave, between boot camp in San Diego and deployment, he'd missed his sidearm—of course he hadn't been allowed to leave the base with it. He drove to a gun shop on Pacific Ave. and chose a Glock 19M, the civilian twin to the M007 he'd been issued. He drove immediately to a firing range, and the first time he pulled the trigger, he thought of the Rifleman's Creed, which his drill sergeant had made him memorize: *There are many like it, but this one is mine.*

He'd never told Leo about the gun. He knew Marisa would never stand for a weapon in the house.

Finally, he slipped his hand around the grip, his finger straight along the trigger guard. The safety was on. He pulled back the slide. There was no shell in the chamber.

He could load the gun or leave it empty.

PIERCE WAS DEAD. Conseco was dead. And the sniper was still on the roof, with half the squad still within his field of fire.

Rashad threw himself against a wall and shouted "SHEP!" into his throat mic. "Building 31, go, go, go!"

The AI understood the sentence. *Building 31:* a known entity on its map, photographed and tagged months ago by drone. *Triple-go:* top speed. The robot spun in a tight circle, then charged down the steep road that Rashad had trained it to navigate.

Rashad swiped at his wrap and brought up the hornet's stream side by side with the SHEP's. The done circled feet above the roof, close enough to show the sniper's eyes, the silver snaps on his blue windbreaker, the white laces of his black sneakers. The gunman was on his feet now, holding his rifle with one hand, looking down at the robot charging towards him at forty miles per hour.

The shooter pivoted towards the far end of the roof, where a trap door lay open. He was going to go down into the house.

The SHEP reached the bottom of the steep road, spun around a low stone wall. Building 31 was a cement house, one large door in front, and two open windows. The .50 caliber swung to cover the edge of the roofline, but there was no angle for a shot.

"Grenade," Rashad said. "The window to the right of the door." The window lit up with a red outline. Rashad's glove vibrated and he closed his fist: Yes. The grenade flew through the opening, thunked against an inner wall, and exploded with a bang that would have deafened him if he'd been there in person.

He sent the SHEP hurtling into the front entrance. The door seemed to vanish in front of the camera. The room was full of smoke. The SHEP, however, quickly identified heat signatures.

Three red outlines popped up, and the glove seemed to be shaking itself from his hand. He made a fist. Yes. The gun erupted. Yes.

Another figure appeared at the edge of the screen. The SHEP's M2 was already spinning to face the threat. More red outlines.

Yes and Yes and Yes and Yes and Yes and Yes and Yes.

ALEJANDRA DEALT THREE cards: blue square, yellow X, orange rectangle. He touched the blue square, and she made a note on her tablet. Then she dealt three more: yellow X, red circle, and another blue square. He understood, now, that these were arbitrary choices. What she was measuring was probably not what he chose, but the speed of his decision-making, or perhaps the level of stress in making the choice. Even so, he was reluctant to choose the blue square again, so he tapped the red circle.

After a few rounds of cards, Alejandra set up the slideshow. She moved unhurriedly, projecting an aura of quiet he was reluctant to disturb. He wondered again what she thought of him. It alarmed him how desperately he wanted her to like him.

At the break after the first twenty-minute round of slides, she asked, "Have you scheduled a therapist yet?" It had been a month since they began the experiential phase.

He felt heat in his cheeks. So she still thought of him as a patient. "No, there's a waiting list. The VA says they'll call me."

"So you haven't gotten any meds either?"

"No."

"Damn it," she said, almost under her breath. He'd never seen her express annoyance—or else he'd missed it.

"I'm sorry," he said. "I'll ask Leo to call again."

"It's not you. This should be part of the treatment. I told him—" She stopped herself. Him—Dr. Subramanian. The past several appointments, he'd not made an appearance. Alejandra had said that he was traveling. "I'll make some calls," she said.

"You don't have to do that."

"Your brother said you're not sleeping."

Leo talked to her? Behind his back?

"It's okay," Alejandra said. She was watching him with those dark eyes. She didn't need a tablet to read him. "He's worried about you."

"I'm fine." This was a lie. Sometimes he burst into tears for no reason. His body had developed strange aches. A sharp noise could make him jump out of his skin.

"Are you having suicidal thoughts?"

"No." Another lie. Had he taken too long to answer? He wasn't sure she believed him. What had Leo told her?

"It wouldn't be unusual if those thoughts came back," she said. "You haven't been able to feel them for some time. If you want, I can turn down the signals from the DBI. Ease you back down."

"You can do that?" Then: "I don't want to be like before."

"Not all the way off, just less... volume. Until you have a therapist. It would give you space to deal with what happened to you in India."

So. She had read his file. Shame tightened his chest.

"I don't know everything that happened there," she said. "But I do know that they put you in a position where you had little choice about what to do. They trained you to fight, then put you in the line of fire. Then they gave you tools that made it easy for you to do what they wanted you to do."

"You're just describing how the military works." His throat was tight.

"I'm saying you're not completely responsible. Your options, your degrees of freedom, were restricted by so many things— the rules of engagement, the environment, the ATLAS targeting system—"

"No. I'm responsible." He was surprised at how harsh he sounded. "I'm the man in the loop. The SHEP is just another weapon, like a rifle." He was processing so much information. She knew about ATLAS too? Did she have security clearance? Who had she talked to?

"ATLAS is much more than a rifle," she said. "It was designed to make it easy to pull the trigger. It's called automation bias. They wanted a system where it would be easier for a soldier to follow a suggestion rather than—"

"I'm not a soldier," Rashad said. "I'm a Marine."

Alejandra stopped, blinked. She was embarrassed, he realized. Maybe the DBI was making it easier for him to read expressions, too.

"I'm sorry," she said. "I know you're not Army. I didn't mean to offend you."

"I'm not offended," he said. "But a Marine—making hard choices while under fire is what we're trained for. A machine can't do that. Robots make bad Marines." That was something his instructor at special operations school liked to say.

Alejandra thought for a moment. "If you could go back in time, knowing what you know now, would you stop yourself from doing what you did?"

"You mean, take away my free will?"

Her face froze. He'd intended to make her smile, but somehow he'd said it wrong.

"Here's what I would do," Rashad said. "I'd go back in time and take away the sniper's free will to shoot at me. I'd kill him before he entered that house full of people and climbed to the roof."

"That would be the right thing to do? You have no doubt?" It was almost as if she were asking permission.

"No doubt." They both seemed surprised by his certainty. Decisiveness had crept back into this thinking.

They resumed the slides. Blue square. Puppy. Yellow X. Pistol. Yellow X. Sailboat. Once it had been almost relaxing to sit through the cascade of images, but now he felt as if he were riding the bow of a SURC in heavy surf. By the end of the final series he was sweating, nauseated. He turned away from her, flipped up his eye patch, rubbed away the sweat. He didn't want her to see the wound.

She brought him water. They chatted about the recent heatwave. And then she said, "I have something to tell you."

He could hear the edge in her voice.

"Dr. Subramanian's taken a position back east," she said. "Cornell's opening a new neuroscience lab and he'll head it."

Rashad couldn't speak for a long moment. "And you? You're going with him?"

"In a few weeks. I need to finish my work with him, to get my Ph.D."

The room seemed to shift. It was the strongest, most piercing emotion he'd felt since the bullet. Had the DBI's neural network strengthened the signal as it passed through? Or shit, *weakened* it?

Finally, he said, "So you have no choice." Another failed attempt at a joke.

"There are good neurologists here," she said. "They'll continue to see you, and they know the protocols. You're not being abandoned."

It didn't feel that way. "Don't let them turn down the volume," he said. "Please. The implant's working."

"I can't promise you. Your brother wants to end treatment."

Another blow. They were coming too fast now, getting past his guard. He said, "Leo can't do that."

"He's your legal guardian. He has medical power of attorney. If he wants to end treatment, I can't stop him." She touched his hand. She'd never done that before. "But I'll try to convince him to keep you in treatment."

"The DBI stays on," he said. "My choice."

THE NIGHT AFTER Pierce and Conseco died, Rashad kept his shit together by staying busy and focusing on the next day's mission. He did not break down when he was ordered to visit the family of the people who'd been in Building 31. He made his apology and the company captain paid the survivors 100,000 rupees, which came out to about $1,100 US per victim. One old man, four women, and three children. The surviving brother claimed they weren't secessionists and didn't know the sniper. Through the translator he said, "When they tell you they're coming into your home, you have no choice but to let them in."

Rashad projected calm when the squad rotated out of Tartuk, said he was happy to spend the next four weeks in the relative safety of Srinagar while they waited to return to Camp Pendleton.

The SHEP never left Tartuk; it was passed to another squad staying in the village. But the robot had already taught him what he needed to understand, just as the Rifleman's Creed had promised. *My rifle is human, even as I, because it is my life. Thus, I will learn it as a brother.* Once they reached stateside there'd be no more open carry; his sidearm and rifle would stay in the armory when he wasn't on the shooting range.

So. It would have to be here, in the barracks in Srinagar.

He'd heard about jumpers from the Golden Gate, who changed their minds between the bridge and the water. He wasn't that kind of person. His mind was made up.

His body, however, betrayed him. When he awoke in the hospital, he realized that his hand must have shifted, or his head pulled back. Some subconscious reflex. The bullet entered at an oblique angle and exited without killing him. By then, however, the failure didn't bother him.

LEO AND MARISA were arguing. Rashad could hear them from his bedroom. For the past few weeks he'd chosen to spend most of his time here. He was no longer interested in watching Leo and Marisa's TV shows, eating the meals they prepared. He came out to microwave his own food and take a shit and sometimes, when they were asleep, pace the circle of the living room, kitchen, and dining room. He left the house only for his regular appointments with Alejandra. He'd refused to visit the therapist she'd found for him. He needed isolation and quiet for the work he was doing.

The arguing stopped and then they knocked at his door. Kept knocking. He let them in. They stood over him as he sat on the bed, hands on knees. He hated himself for putting them through all this. They were good people.

"Dude," Leo said. "This isn't working. You can see it's not working, right?" He described Rashad's various behaviors over the past few weeks, as if Rashad wasn't aware of them.

"I can leave," he said.

"That's not what we're saying!" Marisa said.

Leo said, "We just have to talk to Alejandra before she bails on you. There's something wrong with the implant. The way you're feeling, this isn't you."

"You're wrong," Rashad said. "This is *finally* me." He could feel the DBI working, like a cave tunnel widening day by day, letting through more and more water. "I can't go back to what I was before."

"That's the implant telling you that," Leo said.

And Rashad thought, What part of your subconscious is making you say *that*? Whether the subsystem was mechanical or biological made no difference.

"When we go in tomorrow," Leo said, "I'm going to tell them to turn that thing off."

"That's *not* what I agreed to," Marisa said hotly.

Rashad was surprised they weren't on the same page. He'd thought they'd been arguing about how to confront him, not what to say.

Marisa said, "Numbness isn't the answer."

"Thank you," Rashad said. "I have to—" His voice broke. How could he explain that he wanted this pain? That he believed in it. He'd turned the bedroom into a kind of arena—Rashad Before Bullet versus Rashad After—and he didn't want to shrink from those blows. It would be immoral to not feel that pain. What kind of coward would he be if now, after finally regaining the ability to regret what he'd done, he refused to face it? "I have to take responsibility."

"You did what you had to do," Leo said.

"I'm not saying you shouldn't take responsibility," Marisa said. She knelt so that she and Rashad were eye to eye. "I'm saying you don't have to keep beating yourself up about it."

"Yeah, I do," Rashad answered. "That's the point."

"You can ask God for forgiveness."

Leo groaned. "Can we keep this on track?"

"Why would I do that?" Rashad said to her. "So I can feel better?" He shook his head. "I'm not going to shrug this off. I'm not going to *move on*, now that I have a second chance." The bullet that had meant to be his punishment had robbed him of it.

"Please," Marisa said. "It's not so hard. You can ask Jesus to come into your heart."

"Definitely not." No more intercessors, strengthening some signals of forgiveness, dampening remorse. "My heart," he said, "is crowded enough."

"PICK A CARD," Alejandra said. "Any card."

Yellow X. Red circle. Green triangle.

"Why are we doing this?"

"Humor me. One final exam."

"More data for your dissertation." It was a mean thing to say. He tapped the green triangle.

She put the card away and said, "Okay, pick a card."

"You're not going to replace the card?"

"No."

That annoyed him, this change in the rules. Wouldn't this mess up her results? He looked at the red circle, then the yellow X. He suspected she wanted him to choose that second card, and he didn't appreciate being manipulated. He tapped the red circle.

She removed the circle and dealt a new card. Blue square. He quickly tapped it. She took it away and dealt the circle again.

"Oh come on," he said.

"Pick a card," she said.

"You want me to pick the yellow X. Why?"

"Pick whichever you want."

He flicked the red circle towards her and it slid off the table. Immediately, he felt like a dick. She calmly retrieved the card and dealt a new one from the deck.

A yellow X. Two of them on the table now, side by side.

"Pick a card," she said.

He couldn't remember a time where there'd been a pair of matching cards on the table. Was this some new requirement phoned in by Dr. S? Or maybe she was going rogue, defying the doctor's orders. There'd always been a tension between those two, a struggle for power—the grad student chafing under the control of the mentor. In the early appointments, he didn't have the emotional equipment to figure out their relationship. But now the DBI floodgates were open. Everything his back-brain had noticed and reacted to was available to him now. He could make any decision he wanted—including the decision to not participate.

"I'm done," he said.

"Please, Rashad. Pick a card."

"There's no choice. They're the same."

"Think of them as right and left. Which do you choose?"

"There's no point. You're leaving."

"All right," she said evenly. "Do you want to sit down?"

He realized that in his anger he'd stood up. He was looming over the table, his heart beating fast.

"Can you put those away?" he asked. The pair of X's looked like the eyes of a cartoon corpse.

"Could you pass them to me?" she replied.

Fuck you. Immediately, he felt childish—but still didn't want to give in. "They're right in front of you."

Suddenly, she looked sad. No, sad was too broad a word—there were more fine-grained descriptors for what he saw in her face. Resignation? Regret? Then she swept the cards towards her, and when she looked up at him again she was assessing him. She'd learned something new about him, he realized. By calling a halt to the test, he'd continued the test.

This unnerved him. He unclenched his hands. Took his seat. He couldn't look directly at her. He could see that her hand still held the deck of cards.

"I know you're going through a rough time," she said. "But I want you to hold on. You can call me anytime. I'll do anything in my power to help you."

Except stay.

"There's something else." There it was again, the same hesitancy as when she told him she was leaving. He understood now that the assuredness he'd seen in her in those first appointments was a kind of uniform she put on. He'd done that himself, many times. "I need to tell you about a part of the treatment."

"Okay…"

"We had to decide on some images as controls—we hardcoded some to a set value. For example, some images always have an output of a positive value."

"Puppies? All those pictures of dogs?"

"It wasn't that, but yes, something like that."

"Without telling me." He couldn't keep the anger out of his voice.

"I'm sorry." Her voice had gone soft. "It wouldn't be a control if we told you. And we also chose one to be a negative value. Something's that's always aversive. Something you'd avoid at all costs—even if later you had to make up a story for why you chose what you did."

Her hand still lay on the deck. And then he understood. His chest tightened. "Yellow X."

"You've never chosen it. Not once. At first, you couldn't

choose *any* card. But then we turned on the DBI, and we made it difficult for you to choose that card—and then impossible."

"You can't know that. I *could* have chosen it."

"Yet you never did."

"Deal the cards."

"Are you sure you want to do this?"

"Do it."

She shuffled through the deck, chose three, and laid them out. Green rectangle. Red circle. Yellow X.

She watched him. As soon as he chose, she'd record it in her tablet, and that would be their final interaction. Tomorrow she'd fly across the country to join Dr. Subramanian. They'd make their careers off of his injury, his handicap, his crimes.

He was tired of being data. He knew which card he'd choose, but that didn't mean he'd have to share it with her.

"Sorry, Alejandra." He stood up. "You don't get to know."

THE GUN SAT inside the open box. He felt queasy looking at the gleaming metal, as if the weight of it bowed the floor, drawing the walls towards him.

You did what you had to do. Bullshit, of course. Yes, in the final moments he was part of an unstoppable chain reaction. Neurons fired, his fist closed, the palm switch activated, the SHEP's gun discharged, bullets followed the path decided by physics. But that didn't mean he could deny the series of choices he'd made to that point. He chose to enlist. He chose to go to systems operation school. He chose to send the SHEP into that home. The women and children in that house were simply the last dominoes to fall in a sequence he had initiated years ago. Maybe Alejandra was right, and ATLAS had been rigged for Yes, designed to take the burden from his shoulders—it was right there in its name, for Christ's sake. But none of that absolved him.

He knew what sin was. And he didn't want to believe in a world where sinners escaped justice.

He reached into the box. His hand was shaking. Coward, he thought. He grunted and forced his hand around the grip.

It was if he'd stepped off a precipice, plummeting through air, the water rushing to meet him. The gun fell from his hand. He scrambled to his feet and stumbled to the bathroom. Emptied his stomach into the toilet.

He sat on the floor, sweating, his arms trembling.

Leo heard the noise. He came into the bathroom, knelt beside him. "What's the matter? Is it the implant?"

Rashad couldn't speak. Images flashed behind his eyelids. Yellow X. Pistol. Yellow X. He heard Alejandra's voice: *I'll do anything in my power to help you.*

Leo put his hand on Rashad's back. "I'm here for you, bro. I've been so worried about you. Just tell me what you need."

It wasn't what Rashad needed that was important, it was what he wanted—and that had changed the moment he touched the gun. He'd never been so sure of anything in his life.

THE HURT PATTERN

TOCHI ONYEBUCHI

Tochi Onyebuchi (www.tochionyebuchi.com) *is the author of Nommo Award winner* Beasts Made of Night, Crown of Thunder, War Girls, *and* Riot Baby. *He has graduated from Yale University, New York University's Tisch School of the Arts, Columbia Law School, and L'institut d'études politiques with a Masters degree in Global Business Law. His short fiction has appeared in* Asimov's, Omenana, Black Enough: Stories of Being Young & Black in America, *and elsewhere. His nonfiction has appeared in* Uncanny, Nowhere, Tor.com *and the* Harvard Journal of African-American Public Policy.

WHENEVER NICK, OVER in the workstation across the room, would blurt out "fuck, I got another beheading," Kenny would pinch the bridge of his nose and sigh and want, more than anything, to say "I don't care." Monitors formed a semi-circle in front of Kenny, and his fingers, tips glowing blue with the implants, moved absently in front of them, swiping information—an image, a video, an encoded message on a reddit forum—into a bucket, tapping the screens to tag the bit and dress it up as an alert for the client it would be routed to. A quick video of militia picking over the aftermath of a massacre in a Cameroonian village, part of the ongoing Ambazonian separatist crisis, tapped, tagged, dropped in a bucket. Kidnapping in Lagos. Attack on a Chinese-run mining camp in Kenya. Tapped, tagged, dropped in a bucket.

It had only taken Kenny four months to fall into this groove, to learn the system, to find a monitor setup that worked for him, to turn off the parts of himself he needed to turn off for when the company's tech synced with his augments to implant the info straight into his skull. On the train home after work, he was smiling ruefully, because his mind had shot towards one of his early interviews for this gig where one of what he would discover to be his manager's managers asked if he was cool with experiencing extreme content. Kenny had on his "I take this seriously" face, not because he feared what the question portended but because his law fellowship was in the rearview and his student loan forbearance period was coming to an end and he owed the Department of Education more than his mother's house was worth. And now he could listen to Nick say, way too loudly so that everyone could hear, "fuck, I got another beheading!" like the MENA beat was somehow uniquely traumatizing. Like the startup didn't have the same two guys covering Mexican cartels and U.S. gang activity. Like Kenny hadn't spent the day watching a man dressed in olive green playfully toe a piece of skull belonging to a body at the bottom of a mountain of corpses.

He should have done this before leaving for the day, but he'd wanted to make an earlier express train, so it was only as he sank into the somewhat resistant seat of the train cushion—having been expectorated by the subway—that he set about partitioning his work-related memories of his interaction with the company algorithm and moving them to a secure folder in his braincase. The click and swipe always ended with an exhale, as though, surrounded by these upper-middle class white business people fleeing NYC for the comfort of too-big houses in Connecticut, he could breathe out the day's agony, reunite his selves, the part of him that thought and the part of him that felt.

But as he prepared for sleep in his tastefully spartan Bridgeport one-bedroom, images swam in tendrils of colored dust of the protest action in Kinshasa he'd witnessed just before shift's end, the barricades the protesters had set up as the sun set, the bright yellow and orange shirts the young protesters wore set against the blue-black sky, the tail of rainbow fume trailing a tear gas canister that arced through the air. Coughing, screaming, crying.

In a few minutes, Kenny was snoring.

THE NEXT MORNING, Kenny stepped off the elevator and hurried to the in-office kitchen, even as colleagues gathered in the large conference room. The hoverchairs had already been requisitioned and the young and less-young, the tattooed and the plain-skinned, the Augmented and the untouched, lined the walls while Kenny hunted for the bagels they'd been promised in the pre-dawn email.

All that remained amidst the torn paper bags and dying electric slicer were halves of everything but what he wanted and, of course, none of the spreads had retained their labeling.

The chatter on the other side of the glass wall separating the kitchen from the Elysian Fields open area with its picnic benches and metal chairs was dying down, and Kenny saw that the door to the large conference room had swung closed. He whispered a soft, "fuck it," stuffed a cleanly-sliced half of a raisin bagel in his mouth and, fighting the urge to vomit, hurried to the conference room.

A hologram bust of a balding man with fucked-up teeth appeared against the far wall, shoulders and chest revealing the man wore a black V-neck over what he perhaps hoped suggested a svelte figure.

Kenny entered mid-drone amidst a bevy of figures: volume of notifications delivered to clients by this point of the year, what they were on track to reach by end of quarter, revenue projections, and a whole wastebucket of other things Kenny didn't give a fuck about. Slipping off his messenger bag and chewing on his tastes-like-cardboard bagel half, he caught Sasha's eye across the room and smirked around his breakfast. Settled in, he beamed memes he'd come across during his morning train ride into Sasha's braincase: a distorted photo of a banker in a slim tie and a red ballcap with baked beans spilled on his lap; a photo of a young boy turning away from an old-school computer monitor to glare beneath hooded eyes at the photo taker, the caption reading: "MY PARENTS CAUGHT ME ON PORNHUB AND FORCED ME TO HAVE MY PICTURE TAKEN"; a video of a silver alien dancing in front of a crowd of screaming kids with the text "[crying in spanish]" close captioned at the bottom of the frame.

"I hate you," Sasha beamed back at him, a swathe of dark salt-and-pepper hair swept like a peregrine falcon's wing over one eye. Her grin fought against itself, and heat bloomed in Kenny's chest at the sight.

Kenny scanned the room and, though some of the other area sharks swiveled in their hoverseats and effected poses of disinterest, most of them held that attentiveness that showed they'd long since drunk the company Kool-Aid. Sending information on the goings-on of the world to the military, to law enforcement, to search and rescue agents, to media watchers, knowing what was going on in the world before everyone else, that's what this place, filled with the Best and Brightest™, purported as its mission. A mission cast in the noblest of lights. A mission that netted that hologrammed VP of Strategy a cool $3.5 mil in annual salary and had Kenny and Sasha and other area sharks dosing themselves with Librium and Klonopin every night before bed. The managers, many of them standing, having ceded their seats to the underclass, made sure to look as though they were paying attention, but Kenny knew about their private Slack channel and imagined half a dozen conversations happening among them while the Veep kept on about quarterly targets and new initiatives on the tech side.

"And we're looking now to expand our finance coverage. So, yes, we are officially in business with the banks. Our finance coverage has been growing, but, as I'm sure you all know, everything is connected. I don't have to tell you that. The area leads have already been briefed on the changes to coverage assignments and will be in contact with all the team managers to make sure things move smoothly and we can continue to hit our targets. Great work, guys."

The hologram winked out, and everyone stirred to head to their stations. Kenny caught the eye of his team lead, a skinny, scraggly-bearded redhead named Tucker and nodded to the Elysian Fields, an unspoken "do you have a minute" hanging between them.

"What's up?" Tucker said once they'd taken their seats opposite each other on the picnic bench.

"I wanna switch to the US bureau."

"Oh?"

"That, or get the company to shell out for more benzos. The resin's not coming off like it used to." Resin. What they called the Residual Trauma they took home after eight-plus hours spent watching and documenting the worst days of peoples' lives.

"Like, the media desk?"

Kenny knew that was a stretch. A black guy covering black culture? In this office? He almost scoffed out loud at the vanishingly small chance. "Anything, really. What's this new finance thing? I can help out with that."

Tucker dumped a sympathetic smile. Almost like he thought it was cute that Kenny figured the domestic beat less likely to contain horrors than Africa coverage. But Kenny wanted to tell him he knew what he was getting into, and that this would indeed be easier for him. It was much less likely that he would have to watch video of a woman screaming while fending off a machete attack who sounded so much like his own mother.

* * *

"SHOTS FIRED," KENNY called out in a lackadaisical voice. Plugged into the Algo, it took him less than a second to scour nearby surveillance footage for familiar landmarks, street signs, the unfortunate state of the sidewalks, the bottle fragments in the street, the angle of the sun's descent that told him the worst moment in this particular person's life had happened at 6.32pm EST, 5.32 Central Time. "On Dixwell."

"Gotcha," said the area lead from across the room, as Kenny tapped the info, tagged it, then dropped it into the bucket.

As soon as he'd dropped the alert in the bucket to be rocketed off to the client, he moved onto the next thing. The day had mercifully been a bevy of traffic accidents, small home fires immediately put out with occasional forays into even more pedestrian matters. Failing scaffolding here, an uncovered manhole there, a bit of graffiti or vandalized surveillance camera here, drug paraphernalia spotted in a park over there.

"Nothing bad happens to white people," he said in a private slack to Sasha.

"Lmao, hold on." An ellipsis made itself felt in his head as he waited for her to respond. "Sorry, there was just this press conference. This reporter who was supposed to be dead after security services raided his office two days ago just came back in a press conference like BITCH U THOUGHT!"

"There was a brawl in the Ugandan parliament last month," he wrote back. And just like that, he found himself missing it. The color, the vibrancy, the music of the continent. The Nigerian pop star scandals, the Liberian footballer campaigning for the presidency and the way the crowd erupted in that one video of him descending onto the pitch in his old uniform to play a quarter-hour of that friendly, the memes that proliferated whenever there was load-shedding in the Hillbrow suburb of Johannesburg. Kenny found himself wondering if the massacres and the Boko Haram kidnappings and the occasional summary executions and the brutal protest crackdowns and the university riots were a small price to pay for the joy that thrilled through him at the sight of his people being brilliant and beautiful and hilarious. He'd spent 3x more of his life in the US than in Nigeria, but there were times when no place felt as much like home as Lagos. "It was lit."

"Shots fired," the area lead called out again. "North Lawndale." A pause. "Officer-involved."

"Gotta go," Kenny wrote. "Love you."

He closed the channel before she had the chance to break his heart by not writing it back.

"DON'T FORGET," SAID the mother of Shamir Townsend from behind the podium while camera flash burst in sheen along her cheeks and forehead. "You see all the protests. You see the movement. And God bless all the people making this movement a living, breathing thing. But you see all these people with all these different agendas, all these people—celebrities, even—making speeches. And at the bottom of it all is a dead boy. My son, Shamir."

Kenny had the press conference playing in the background, in a small window on the monitor to his right. It was important, but it wasn't breaking. Meaningful content, but not actionable. A month into his stint in the US bureau, he'd found and tagged and bucketed security footage of fully-mechanized police, powered by the Algorithm his company had helped develop, rolling into a park and opening fire on what turned out to be a 13-year-old boy who had been using a hairbrush as a play gun. Well after the alert had been sent and the area sharks moved on with the rest of their day, Kenny found himself scouring the Net for more. Hacking into police scanners to find audio records of the seconds leading up to the shooting, tapping surveillance footage from the gazebo, catching trace signals from the nearby mobiles and Augmented witnesses nearby, all revealing pieces of the thing. The police vehicle zooming into view, the mid-sized Crusties unfurling from the doors, limbs uncurling until they'd reached their crab form, then the muzzle flash, continuing as they crept closer until the boy's body had been riddled with steaming holes.

"You okay?" Sasha slacked him.

The message woke him up, and he noticed that most of the sharks in his area and others had left their desks for lunch.

"They have reggaeton empanadas again."

He chuckled. "I'm good. Not on the empanadas, I'm def getting some. Just sayin, I'm good. What's up?"

"Tucker's been eyeballing you all shift. And lunch has been out for a bit. You haven't got up yet."

"I'll get some." The presser continued in his earbud while he worked. Mrs. Townsend was talking about the fight for accountability with the algorithmic policing. Just because the algo-engine'd robot "Crustaceans" unit had replaced flesh-and-blood police didn't mean the police department had shed accountability. And now some public tech advocates were calling on the police to yet again release their source code.

A new message notification blinked in Kenny's personal inbox. Dread calcified in the pit of his stomach. If it was Tucker, then he'd really be in for it. And he'd have to come up with some way to explain his listening to a post-shooting press conference for an event that happened months ago instead of doing his job.

Fuck it.

From Daisy Romero. Subject Line: STUDENT LOAN REPAYMENT PARTY!

"You gotta be fuckin' kidding me."

"Shots fired in Rio," someone from the LatAm desk called out.

Kenny slowly shook his head, smirking. "Sasha, check this out," he slacked and forwarded to her email. "I need a plus one."

"What is this?" Through her sensory data, Kenny could smell the empanadas.

"Friend from law school. Her husband's a banker. If I gotta go alone, I might actually slit my wrists."

"Okay, okay. But only if you have some of these fucking racist empanadas."

Smiling, Kenny got up from his seat and shut off the press conference just as Mrs. Townsend was, tearfully grateful, returning to the podium.

THE LAST TIME Kenny had set foot in Marea, he'd been on the cusp of a career in corporate law. Sunlit lunches with associates and the occasional partner who'd fashioned himself a mentor, where the summer glow glinted off the silver pinstripes in everyone's suits to turn the room into an epileptic's nightmare. Everything glistened: the silverware, the clothing, the platinum threaded in blond hair done up in buns, the polished augments that had been made of everyone's limbs and digits, the antique cards—more ornament than utility—that they used to pay for everything. He could taste the memory of fusilli on his tongue, could feel the performance worm its way into his limbs, so that by the time he got to the backroom, he had to stop himself from walking in like a douchebag.

Dulcet lighting turned every edge in this backroom soft, rounded out the corners of the long table around which sat the revelers, all twenty- or thirty-somethings.

Chandeliers hovered at regular intervals over the revelers and right in the aureate cone cast by the center chandelier sat Daisy, née Lockwood, now Romero. Right next to her, with his arm draped over her shoulder and a single lock of shining black hair swaying over his Roman forehead was the presumed Mister Romero. He looked like a former law school classmate. Had the sparkling, corporate smile, the figure of a guy who gets up at six in the morning to work out so that by eight he's in the office, and the physical ease of a man swiftly acclimated to new money.

Golden light bloomed on Daisy's face when she saw Kenny, then beckoned him over. She made a show of clearing out a space next to her. As soon as Kenny set off, Sasha held his arm in her hands and pulled herself close. Together, they made their way, the others on Daisy's side of the table scooching out on the plush leather seating to allow Kenny and Sasha to slide in.

"She's cute," Sasha murmured in Kenny's ear. "You hit that?"

"Careful, Sash," Kenny murmured back, grinning. "You see that rock on her finger?"

"That's not a rock, Kenny. That's a fucking meteor."

"You're drooling, Sash."

"Hi!" said Sasha, reaching over Kenny with her left hand and catching Daisy's. "Sasha. I work with Kenny."

After a stunned beat, Daisy shot Kenny a look as though to say *well done*. In the next instant, her face was all politesse and she tugged her husband's shoulder. "Hey, babe, this is Kenny. We went to law school together."

Babe gripped Kenny's hand in his. "Pleasure, man. Thanks for coming."

Daisy glared a warning at her husband.

"Oh, shit. Juan. Name's Juan."

"That's better, babe." She pecked Juan on the cheek.

"Where'd you find him?" Sasha leaned in to whisper.

"Some POC mixer. I was at a different law firm. They had this event. You know the deal. Kenny and I used to go to those all the time. Room full of power bottoms about to make too much money." When Daisy said that, Sasha arched an intrigued eyebrow, as though to ask if Daisy really talked like this. Daisy angled her face to Sasha. "Kenny was the best part of these things. Only time corporate law didn't feel like living through some lifelong horror-comedy."

"What does he do?" Sasha asked, somehow with a glass of wine already in her hand.

Daisy took a beat before saying, "Banker."

Sasha made a yikes face. Kenny's expression turned porcelain.

"But we balance it out," Daisy said, rushing in. "I'm at a civil rights firm now, so that balances it out." A sympathetic smile ricocheted between the three of them. "I mean, you know, Kenny. You know what it's like. The debt. Gets to be the biggest number in your life and you have to hold off all sorts of stuff. Life decisions and whatever. You have to kill your dreams and ambitions and your hopes, just so you can get your head above water."

"There's also indentured servitude," Kenny ribbed, wiggling his aquamarine fingertips.

"Oh, God," Daisy whispered.

"I mean, they package the message as 'tech this' and 'innovation that,' and they do take a chunk outta the debt with the lease on my body, but it's literally the least invasive way to go about paying that stuff off. Look, everyone's got augments. Mine are just free. Fact, they're freer than free."

"But, Kenny, that means you can only work for approved employers."

Kenny snorted. "List is big enough." He shifted, made more space for Sasha, for backup. "Tell me about work. Fightin' the good fight."

"Wish you were down here in the trenches with me?"

"Eh, maybe."

For the briefest of instants, Daisy's mask faltered and a darkness swarmed beneath the skin of her face, like shadows fucking, and Kenny caught a glimpse of how haggard the work made her, how much whatever it was she did taxed her. A hungry part of him saw the pain and sought it out. "Tell me about it. Really."

Daisy sighed, eyed Kenny and Sasha. "Well, since the police went Algo, lotta people stopped making wrongful death lawsuits. Imagine trying to fit a Crusty into the witness stand. Can't bring an algorithm to court, and what're you gonna do when you convict? Put a fucking robot on desk duty? Sometimes, though, you can get a payout. It's never enough. Especially for an officer-involved shooting. No amount of money's ever going to bring back a son or a brother or a father or a sister or whatever, but it's money. It's better than nothing.

We all know the Algo's not perfect. Everybody does. But a 13-year-old boy gets shot in a park and all evidence points to police misconduct, but the Algo told those toasters to do it. They're not gonna admit to a malfunction. That would mean recalling all the units they spent dozens of millions of dollars to pay for. So,"—she shrugged—"the Nuremberg defense. 'I was just following orders.'"

"Wait, you said a 13-year-old boy got shot in the park?" Kenny could feel Sasha tightening next to him, wine glass to her lips, her whole body urging Kenny to be careful.

"Yeah, Shamir Townsend. The firm's been repping his mother on a wrongful death suit against the city, but really it's just a play for the payout. This stays between us, k?"

Kenny shrugged. "Who am I gonna tell?"

Daisy relaxed. "It's all fucked anyway. Poor people end up paying for this shit anyway."

Sasha had leaned in but was making herself unobtrusive. "What, the city jacks up taxes?"

"Worse. Tax assessors overvalue homes in poor neighborhoods and undervalue properties in rich ones. So you got properties in, say, North Lawndale and Little Village in Chicago paying double the property tax rate than people living in Lincoln Park or on the Gold Coast. It's like that everywhere. And that's not even the fucking worst of it."

Kenny couldn't tell what his face looked like, but he knew he was trapped, enthralled, horrified. There was something different to this, though. This wasn't instant. It wasn't video. It wasn't media. It wasn't surveillance footage of an act. It wasn't audio of an ongoing riot. It was a deeper injury. A drawn-out thing. Not a stabbing, but a knife drawn slowly along the skin.

"When you have to budget more for police tort liability, you have less for lead poisoning screening for poor children. Violence prevention initiatives, after-school programs, mental health clinics. All gone. Budget cuts."

Kenny was too rapt to say anything. Sasha shook her head.

"But these settlements, they're millions and millions of dollars. The police don't have to pay?"

Daisy snorted. "Police departments set aside a small slice of their budget for misconduct settlements. If the price is more than that, city's on the hook. Not them. B'sides, it's the city that pays for the robot."

Sasha couldn't stop shaking her head. "That's fucked."

Daisy exhaled. "Yeah." And Kenny saw that face and knew there would be no more, not from Daisy. It hit like the comedown from a new drug, the bottomless despair, the instant and incessant hunger, the shame of it all. A moment later, everyone seemed to come to their senses, awake from whatever reveries or bromides or hungers they'd been trapped in, wiping the daydream from their eyes and seeing each other naked, and in swept Sasha calling out far too loud, "I am so hungry I could fuck a zebra right now."

While the room lit up with laughter, Sasha caught Kenny's gaze, and Kenny smiled what felt like an apology, and Sasha winked back a "you're welcome."

They were all supposed to be having fun.

In what felt like only seconds, the plates of fusilli arrived.

HOLO-PAINT TURNED THE walls of the conference room into open pasture with simulated wind blowing simulated stalks of wheat in mechanically precise rows far into the distance over verdant hills framed against an azure firmament. A glance overhead showed a sky the same shade of blue with cotton-colored clouds threaded through it.

Kenny and seven other sharks sat in hoverchairs around an oblong table while, at the head of the room, stood a white finance dude in shirt-sleeves rolled to the elbows and an Aryan as fuck face.

"I trust you all have had time to digest all the info on yesterday's session about bonds, yeah? Pretty intro stuff, I know, so I'm gonna just jump right ahead into municipal bonds and—"

One of the sharks raised a hand and switched her voice software from Portuguese to English. "Why are we focusing on cities? This says they're high-risk investments. If the city does a...bond...and they go bankrupt, they can't pay it off. So our client loses money."

"Good point, Fernanda. Except, under a lot of these state laws, the cities we're focusing on can't go bankrupt. What our clients are looking at is essentially guaranteed money..."

Kenny tuned the finance dude's voice into background noise as he tapped and swiped through the hyperlinks in the material, scanning until he hit a page on something called "cat bonds" with a picture of what looked like a half-submerged city, roofs poking out like stepping stones through highway-wide rivers of blue. Risk-linked securities...sponsors...investors...triggered... industry loss index...

A random throwing-out of terms, data points, no constellation. Just a mess of jargon and a picture of a neighborhood destroyed by a hurricane.

"Like shootings."

At that, Kenny sat up in his seat and tuned back into the lesson. "What?"

The finance dude stopped for a second. "You have a question, uh, Kenny, is it?"

"Yeah." The finance terms swirled in his head like detritus in the funnel of a tornado. Then came the dinner party at Marea earlier that week and tax assessors and property value and police and Shamir Townsend. And he felt himself just on the cusp of an understanding. An epiphany that promised a pattern. "Uh, you were saying something about shootings?"

"Yeah."

Kenny rushed in to save himself with an explanation. "I do a lot of security stuff. Law enforcement-related. Traffic, crime. I blanked for a second. What were you saying about shootings?"

"Oh, just in terms of stuff to watch out for. Anything that could cause a liability suit. This is all complex stuff, but it's just background. Help to inform your decision-making. You just need to watch out for the stuff you're already watching out for and ping one of us in Finance so we can jump on it and do our thing."

"Oh." Kenny tuned out again and tried to focus on the pattern just out of reach. All bright nodes and non-existent edges. Like trying to trace astral constellations in an afternoon sky.

"SHOTS FIRED," KENNY called out with renewed vigor. "Cudell Park." He knew his voice was too loud, like he was listening to music and trying to have a convo at the same time, but he couldn't help it. In one tab, he had the Mrs. Townsend press conference replaying and, on another tab, he had news of the settlement the city had offered the family—$2.2 million USD—and in another, the reading materials on catastrophe bonds. All this, he tried to keep hidden in tiny incognito-mode browser windows he knew the company was monitoring anyway. Research, he would tell them. Hurricanes, forest fires, all stuff they were supposed to be tapping and tagging and bucketing anyway. It still took him a moment to remember to loop the finance guys in on the security stuff, a quick tag or a Slack or whatever. Sometimes, the notification would switch to a different alert bucket altogether right in front of him or he'd see finance fingerprints on something he'd already bucketed.

He opened another Slack channel and @'d one of the analytics people. "Hey, can you do a quick data pull for me?"

"What's up?" came the reply.

"Can you get me a sheet of the domestic shootings we notified on with finance?"

Then glowing ellipses until, a few seconds later, he received a link to a GDoc.

While he tapped and tagged and bucketed, he scanned the data, murmuring to himself, "officer-involved, officer-involved, officer-involved…" A pause. "The fuck?"

"Yo, Sash," he DM'd in another Slack channel. "Yo, all my shootings have finance on them. Is that weird?"

"I dunno. Is it?" Glowing ellipses. "Sorry, gotta bounce. Working a factory fire."

"Cool." He bit his lip.

HE WAITED UNTIL his train hit the above-ground stops to call Daisy.

"Yo," he beamed to her phone.

"Hey! What's up? It was so good to see you the other night!"

Kenny smiled, realizing he'd forgot he was supposed to be polite. "It was good to see you too. Congratulations. On, like, everything. I'm so happy for you."

"Thanks, Ken."

He could feel her blushing at the other end. "Look, Daze, I got a question."

"Hope I got an answer."

"Where does the money come from?"

"Money? For what?"

"For the settlements." Kenny pulled himself back, tried to slow down. He felt himself on the edge of it. So close. "It can't be the city. $2.2 million for one settlement, but there's gotta be like how many a year? Some of these places are paying out, like, $147 mil a year. And we're talking smaller cities. All for officer-involved shootings." For much of the ride, he'd tapped into municipal records, news stories, past alerts, all using his security credentials against protocol, credentials that, tied to his augments, gave him the same access as a federal government employee. "Is it banks?"

"What are you saying?"

Kenny gulped. This was the new part, the less-formed part.

The almost-pattern. "The cities are floating bonds, I think. To pay for the settlements."

"From who? Goldman Sachs? J.P. Morgan?"

"…yeah."

"But…but how? Why? Cities have the shittiest credit ratings. How is that a sound investment?"

"Fees. Interest. The banks get paid every period off the interest and handling fees and all of that." He reminded himself to lower his voice. "And…and I checked the state laws. The cities that have the most shootings, they're in states where it's literally against the law for them to go bankrupt. I think, to pay off the one bond, they issue another. I don't think the cops are malfunctioning. I think…I think the banks are getting paid off of these shootings."

"Jesus."

Beeping sounded. Another call. Sasha's ID blinked before his eyes. "Shit. Look, Daze, I gotta go. Ask Juan about it."

"Wait, but—" Dialtone.

"Hey, Sash, what's up?"

"Kenny, can you come over?" Her voice was sorrow-soaked. He sat up in his seat. "Sure, yeah, what's wrong?"

"You up for some trauma bonding? Having trouble leaving work at work today. Can you come?"

Greed, hunger, lust, guilt all warred inside him. He hoped that Sasha heard only the right kind of eagerness in his voice when he said, "Yeah, I'll be right over."

THE FIRST TIME they'd fucked was during a spell of downtime on the second of a two-day al-Shabaab terror attack on a hotel complex in Nairobi. Day One, Kenny, blanketed in the paranoia fog that shrouds the recently jobless and newly-hired, had been more locked in than he'd thought possible. Security footage, open calls from people trapped inside the buildings, terrorist channels online, to the point where he could feel his own torn dress shoes trying to step as softly as possible down bloodied corridors covered in pebbles of glass. He could hear the sporadic gunfire, the tearful, whispered phone calls, the online posts calling for help, giving as brief a room description as possible, the message saying that a poster's phone was dying and they were unAugmented, unConnected. Then nothing.

And the following morning, he'd broken down on the train, one of those commuters wrapped in their own private sorrow while everyone went about the business of trying to make it to work that day. Things had slowed down on Day Two of the attack and Sasha had found him weeping in the office lactation room and he grasped for her, hungered for her, until they'd spent themselves with the quiet urgency of the hidden and hiding.

"Sash, this lighting is bisexual as fuck," Kenny said, laughing, as he entered.

She was on a couch hugging a pillow, hair scattered over her face, smiling meaningfully through smeared mascara.

"I brought red for you and grenadine for me. You got Sprite? Ginger ale? Anything sparkly and see-through?"

"Come here," she murmured, and Kenny obeyed because of that thing in her voice, and she pulled him onto her, and he vanished to himself until she said, "Kenny."

"Yeah?"

"How you doin'?"

Kenny blinked, confused. "I...I'm fine. I'm good. I'm here for you."

She smiled, and something in it pushed Kenny back so that he moved to the opposite end of the couch. For a long time, they occupied the couch like that: he at one end and she lounging at the other. "You figured it out, didn't you."

"What?"

"Don't worry, Ken." She waved a finger around her. "I got a Blanket. We're not being watched. Nothing's tapped."

"What are you talking about?"

"The banks, the shootings, you figured it out, didn't you."

Kenny's eyes widened. "You...you know?"

She nodded.

"You know that the new clients are making money off officer-involved shootings? Is that why they signed us?" His head spun. "Wait, fuck. But...but we're also signed to local law enforcement. We do their algos. Wait." His whole body felt leaden. "Fuck. Fuck fuck fuck. No. Fuck."

Sasha's face was sympathetic but marble-solid.

"Sasha! We're programming cops to shoot black kids so that banks can make money!"

"Kenny."

He stood suddenly, paced back and forth. "We can't go internal. We...we have to do something. Your old journo friends. We have to tell them. We have to."

Sasha shook her head, and the look in her eyes had turned a new shade of sad.

Dull pain filled the space beneath Kenny's skin. Made him leaden.

"Who've you told?" she said softly.

"Sasha." There was hard warning in his voice when he said her name. "Sasha, what is this?" When she didn't answer, he glared. "What are you, their agent? Like, a spy or something?"

"Ken, you used security credentials out of the office. You kept office materials in personal storage."

"Only publicly accessible stuff, Sasha! I would never—"

"But we touched it, Ken. Once we touch it, it's ours."

"Sasha." Pleading.

"Who else have you told?"

"How long were you watching me?"

"It's government, Ken. Or, government-adjacent. We're always watching you. You know that."

He collapsed into a La-Z-Boy and sighed. "Well." Suddenly, it all felt funny. Hilarious. And he could not stop laughing. "Well, fuck me." When he settled, "So what happens now?"

Sasha shrugged. "Nothing. We just wanted to check. We know

what this work does to people. And not everyone wants to take advantage of office resources."

"What, fifteen minutes of guided fucking meditation before I head into a Boko Haram attack?"

She chuckled. "Yeah, that." She scratched her head, and somehow it looked like the most attractive thing Kenny had ever seen her do. "Look, I'm just doing my job. We're all just doing our jobs. Fucking student loans."

"Yeah. Fucking student loans." He felt himself grow distant, something forming in him, and he wanted to be away from her before she could see it fully take shape. "Look, I should go. You good?"

She nodded.

"For real?"

She nodded again.

"Cool. Don't worry, just going home. Although y'all are probably having me followed anyway, right?" He said it laughing, but he meant it to hurt. Then he left and did as he'd said he would. The commute from NYC to home was a practiced choreography, an easy enough pattern for the police—powered by the algo his colleagues had built—to learn.

IDOLS

KEN LIU

Ken Liu (kenliu.name) *is an author of speculative fiction, as well as a translator, lawyer, and programmer. A winner of the Nebula, Hugo, and World Fantasy Awards, he has been published in* F&SF, Asimov's, Analog, Clarkesworld, Lightspeed, *and* Strange Horizons, *among other places. His debut novel,* The Grace of Kings, *is the first volume in a silkpunk epic fantasy series, the Dandelion Dynasty. It won the Locus Award for Best First Novel and was a Nebula Award finalist. He subsequently published the second volume in the series,* The Wall of Storms; *two collections of short stories,* The Paper Menagerie and Other Stories *and* The Hidden Girl and Other Stories; *and Star Wars novel* The Legends of Luke Skywalker. *Forthcoming is* The Veiled Throne, *the next book in the Dandelion Dynasty. He lives with his family near Boston, Massachusetts.*

1. Blowin' In the Wind

EVERY FRIDAY NIGHT, I call my father.

"How's Bella?"

"Good. Busy. Lawyers, you know?"

"Busy is good. Does she like her job?"

"Much more than I like mine. But she can be... a bit obsessive about the work."

"We're lucky if we get something in life to be obsessed with. I bet she's good at what she does."

"The best."

"What's wrong, Dylan? You sound a little down."

"No, not down exactly... Dad, when did you start thinking you wanted kids? I don't mean me. I mean... later."

The briefest of pauses, barely discernible. I try not to think about the software behind the idol, searching, collating, synthesizing, anticipating...

"Not sure there's an exact moment—though that would make a much better story..."

I've never met my father and never will.

OURMATIC WAS ONE of those places that emphasized how smart their employees were so you wouldn't question how little they paid you as you toiled the long hours. Open-plan office, brightly colored chairs, contemporary art on the walls. Like most companies with a name like that, we didn't make anything. I was paid to make up plausible stories about spreadsheets—like just about every corporate job still done by humans.

One of the perks they offered was "Wellness Fridays," when health experts—yoga instructors, nutritionists, or even once, a "master meditator"—would come to deliver lectures or give workshops in the biggest conference room. Maybe the program led to a reduction in the premiums the company paid for our health plan, or maybe management thought it was the sort of thing people of my generation expected, like composting bins and free snacks in the kitchen. In any event, I went every Friday without fail.

This was how I ended up attending the presentation from 46on46; how I ended up submitting a sample of my cheek cells for "personalized genetic counseling"; how I ended up staring at an email in my inbox, forwarded from 46on46, informing me that the database had found me a "DNA relative."

I sent some emails, made some phone calls, then drove across the state line. I met my grandparents, my half-sisters, my uncles. Not my father, though. He had died a few years ago. A boating accident. When I had all the facts I could gather, I got on a plane and went home.

My mother sighed and asked me if I wanted some tea.

Growing up, she never talked about my father. It was just one of those things you learned to accept, like the way the bathroom door jammed, or the way the chair legs squeaked against the floor, no matter how gently you sat down.

"I don't want to," she had said, the one time I tried to make an issue of it. "Think of him as a sperm donor."

There were no photographs, no scraps of paper with his handwriting, no extra-large men's shirt in the back of the closet or a scuffed-up pair of boots in a corner. I didn't even have a name to go on, first or last.

Why did she scrub his existence so completely out of her life? I didn't have the smoothest of relationships with my mother, and the father-shaped void didn't make it any easier. It was all too easy to use him as an excuse, an explanation for my flaws that clarified nothing. Did I get my moodiness from him? Was he as disinterested in competition as I was? When my mother complained about my thoughtlessness, was she also complaining about the shadow of him she saw in me? Sometimes, I would lock myself in the bathroom and look in the mirror, trying to imagine myself decades older.

"Dad, are you proud of me?"

No more imagining. Time for my mother to tell the story.

My father, as it turned out, never knew I existed. He had dropped out of a graduate program and then traveled around the country, living out of his car and trying to figure out who he was. My mother, ten years his senior, met him at an anti-war protest. She liked the way he played the guitar, trying to keep up everyone's spirit at the rally. She wanted a child but not a husband, and saw him as the perfect—

"—sperm donor. There's no grand romance, no dark mystery," she said. "No vows were broken. There's no tale of love that soured, or a long, drawn-out tempestuous divorce from which you could draw some lesson. It was meaningless."

My mother was right. I wasn't abandoned. I wasn't a mistake. As far as my father was concerned, I was... nothing.

Yet, I continued to reach out to my father's family. They probably found my obsession as odd as my mother did. There was, after all, no relationship at all between us except a tenuous, biological link. But they were obliging. They told me stories about him as a boy, as a young man, as a father. They told me about the time he drove two hundred miles to reunite a puppy with its family. They brought out the awards he won as a teacher. They showed me videos and photos, notebooks and printouts from high school, boxes of stuff taken home from college and then never opened again, pictures with his wife and my sisters, email updates about trips he had taken with them.

I learned so much about my father, yet I felt like I didn't know him at all. It was hard enough to know someone, anyone, in life; much harder to figure out someone dead, who could answer no questions, offer no explanations, provide no word of comfort.

I decided to make an idol.

Now that I knew his identity, I could set the seeking bots to follow my father's digital trail. His family hadn't bothered to delete his old accounts, and I convinced his wife to accept my friend requests, so that I could collect more material for the idol-maker. The few cellphone videos of him were too lo-fi to enable a convincing animation, but that was all right. I didn't want to step into the uncanny valley.

After days of waiting, a text arrived from Mnemosynee, informing me that the idol was ready. I took a deep breath, dialed the number given, and held the phone up to my ear.

"Hello? Ryan speaking."

The voice was the same one I had heard in the cellphone videos: a bit gravelly, more than a bit impatient.

"Hi..." I paused. It seemed odd to say *Dad*. "Hi Ryan. This is... Dylan."

"I don't know who that is."

"I know... How... how are you?"

IDOLS WERE FIRST developed as a way for celebrities to engage with their fans. Out of the millions who loved a singer, actor, lifestyle guru... how many ever got to meet the object of their devotion in person? And out of those, how many ever got to give more than a breathless declaration of adoration, received more than a perfunctory smile, held on to more than the briefest of handshakes? There had to be a way to scale up one-on-one engagement, to give loyal fans what they craved the most: a personal connection with their idol.

A team of psychologists, machine-learning experts, and neural network sculptors were handed an archive of the subject's interview footage, concert videos, films, meet-and-greet recordings, social media posts... (celebrities who really wanted to impress their fans would also throw in diaries, unpublished poetry collections, notebooks with ideas on how to achieve world peace...). From this raw material, the technical experts generated a personality model and crafted a simulacrum of the celebrity.

After creating an account, a fan could talk with the digital idol for hours through the looking glass of their screen. Visit after visit, the idol would remember the fan's name and life story, offer words of encouragement, tell new stories and clear up old rumors, meet the kids and reminisce about past encounters. It was like having the celebrity as your best friend who had moved to the other coast.

Once the technology was developed, it found plenty of new uses: political campaigning, Internet harassment, self-improvement "ego-hacking" ...or a way to get to know the parent one never knew.

"I DON'T KNOW what to say. I never had a son."

I laugh. "Did you ever think about what you'd say *if* you had a son, and he asked for the three most important things you ever learned?"

"Three? That's a tall order. Why don't we start with half a thing..."

The idol is a consensual illusion. It isn't some *copy* of my father. It's just algorithms encoding basic insights about human nature being applied to data, making probabilistic predictions about possible reactions. It isn't self-aware, isn't alive. Moreover, the data I gave Mnemosynee on my father was limited. I didn't have his search history, his deleted posts, his secret accounts. All I had was a selection of what he was willing to share with the world, to put into the permanent and permanently crumbling stream of our shared digital existence.

So long as I stay within the parameters of what the algorithms can extrapolate, the illusion holds. They can't tell me anything that I couldn't already have gleaned from the archive.

"Do you try to give Bella her space?"

"I think so."

"That doesn't mean you leave her alone—it means you do some things together, so you keep getting to know each other, and some other things apart, so you can both grow. Jennifer and I used to take vacations together but also apart. You need both. Especially after you have kids."

"Good to know. She doesn't take her vacation days... I should talk to her about it."

Fundamentally, talking to the idol of my father was no different from typing into something like ELIZA, or the conversations I had with myself in the bathroom mirror as a boy.

"You know, I used to play the guitar too."

"Play something for me."

I go into the storage cubby in the basement to dig it out. Out of tune. Fingers rusty. I try to imagine what he would like.

"I used to play that! I drove around for a year right after college, protesting against the war, against Wall Street, the drug companies... Good song. I'm proud of you."

It's a crafted response. Just some algorithms extrapolating from his old emails. It isn't real.

"I think it's about the helplessness you feel as a child, because you don't know, and then as a parent, because you still don't know. You grow and grow and you can't ever figure it out. None of us know what we're doing."

I can't stop the damned tears.

So long as I keep talking to him, this digital simulation of my father will remember me as I have my own kids, grow old, come to accept the impossibility of wisdom. I will catch up to it and then age past it. It will never offer me a piece of wisdom that my father hadn't already put down in some form during his forty years on Earth; it will never be anything more than a sophisticated game. And, without the addition of fresh real-life data to correct its course, the longer it goes on, the more the idol will deviate from my real father. Yet, I know I will keep on talking. The void can't be filled, but it's a part of me.

I can't stop the damned tears.

2. Verum Dicere

THE EAGER JUNIOR associates around the conference table have been waiting for me for the last two hours. As one, they turn as I stride into the war room. That's a lot of billable hours.

But then again, with half a billion dollars of compensatory and punitive damages at stake, I don't think the client will complain.

I throw the faxed juror list on the giant screen at the end—the judiciary is possibly the last place that still insists on communicating in this ancient manner (why not send a carrier pigeon while they're at it?).

"Voir dire starts at 9:00 AM sharp on Monday," I tell them. "We've got just over sixty-four hours to prep for jury selection."

Groans from around the room. They know I intend to make use of every last one of those hours.

"Bella, isn't this a little late?" Drake asks, a smirk on his face. "I thought you said you had an in with the judge's clerk."

I can't stand the guy. He can be charming as a giggling baby with partners in corner offices, but when he has to report to someone like me—not a partner and not even on the track—he always has a dig or two.

"I do," I tell him, my voice cool and in control. "Selene likes me. That's why we're getting the juror list a full fifteen minutes ahead of the other side."

I tell them to focus on the first fifty names. If there's time on Sunday, we'll get to the rest.

"Remember to check variant spellings, nicknames, maiden names. No one registers social media accounts or dating profiles under their full legal name. Screenshot your search results right away so that we can tell if the other side plants honeytraps—"

This isn't paranoia. Though it's against the rules, I've known unscrupulous jury consulting firms to maintain batches of fake social media profiles and age them for years before changing the names to match prospective jurors on the eve of voir dire in an important trial to mislead the other side. The decoys would poison the idols sculpted by their opponent with made-up facts. One more reason our fifteen-minute head start is worth more than these greenhorns can possibly understand.

I bark out orders as the associates clumsily divide up the names—God, do new associates get younger every year or am I losing my mind?

"Scrape up everything! Always better to have too much than

too little. Don't delude yourself into thinking you're smarter than the harvesters 'cause you aren't. Your primary job is to sit in front of your laptop, look into the camera, and say 'I am not a robot' so the guardian bots don't lock out the harvesters... "

I exaggerate. But only a little. *I* know how to tweak the parameters of the harvesters for better results, but not everyone can claim to have written the firm's manual on jury research.

"What's the point of rushing?" Drake asks. "Doesn't the summons usually advise prospective jurors to lock down their social media feeds anyway?"

"Yes, but people don't listen," I explain, trying to be patient. "That's why you still hear about people live-rumbling during voir dire. Or they schedule the lock-down to happen the weekend before they're supposed to show up at court. Time is of the essence."

I watch as the associates set up their laptops and launch the harvesters. The bots need to have fresh credentials for the major social media networks every research session to avoid being tagged. Soon, the associates lean into their cameras; a chorus begins around the room. It's a beautiful sight, no matter how many times I've seen it.

"...I am not a robot."

"I agree to the terms of service..."

"At MingleBingo, my smile is my password..."

Rules of ethics prohibit us from friending prospective jurors to view their locked-down feeds, but there's a ton of data you can gather without that. Most people, even the super privacy-conscious, have friends who aren't, and these friends will leak everything we need. (You'd be amazed by the number of people, even in this day and age, who'll accept any and all friend requests.)

Add to that all the breach-troves from data-aggregators, the hacked databases leaked onto the grey web, the forums and blogs and comment forms and chat servers and rumble-tumbles that all require registration—the harvesters can build an impressive file on just about anyone except those who never touch a computer. (We'll want to peremptorily strike them anyway. Tinfoil-hat types don't make good jurors.)

While my little helpers are gathering the data, I call for dinner. The hard part comes after that.

I SET THE associates to manually go over the scraped dating profiles and social media posts to keep them busy. Well, it's not entirely busywork to pad the timesheets. Once in a while one of them will see something that we miss in the idols. But the real work is done here in the modeling room, by Kevin and his analytics gang, with me supervising.

The modeling room is a cavernous, windowless space. It used to be the copy center two decades ago. With so few submissions on paper now, it's long been taken over by servers and quad-monitor workstations.

"How's the catch?" Kevin, Head of Analysis, drops into his chair. He's forty-two, goatee already showing streaks of grey. Before joining us, he used to work for the government, constructing idols of suspected extremists in order to assess their potential for actual terrorism. (Rumors were that he also sculpted idols of opposition leaders in countries where we wanted to effect regime-change to determine whether they were strong enough and sufficiently loyal to American interests for the US to fund them, but that sort of thing would be classified.)

"Not bad," I tell him. "We have some prolific v-casters in the bunch."

Video is prized over almost any other kind of data for our approach to idol-construction. So much of jury-selection is about finding people with the emotional profiles and personalities to be amenable to persuasion, and videos are by far the most revealing medium for drawing links between triggers and micro expressions.

"Anything really rich?"

He means "rich with data," like a vein of ore. "We got lucky with a few private adult chat profiles. Lots of video."

He raises an eyebrow. "No problems with using those?"

I shrug. "The prohibition is against *ex parte* communication. As far as I'm concerned, if you reuse credentials already leaked in another data breach, you're just asking for the world to stroll in and take a look-see."

He nods and forks off fifty new casts—blank neural networks to be populated and trained with the data gathered by the harvesters. He types into a bunch of console windows and flips through colorful displays, visualizing the developing idols. Even with the full processing power of the modeling room at his disposal, it still takes time to build low-res idols for the voir dire stage.

I'm a little bored and feeling restless. I don't mean to sound boastful, but there really isn't anyone in the city—maybe the whole east coast—better at this than I am. The work has gotten a bit stale.

I decide to call home.

"Hey."

"Hey. Am I going to see you this weekend at all?"

I melt a little at Dylan's voice, yearning, with just a hint of desperation in it.

"I don't think so. I told you the trial starts on Monday. I promise I'll make it up to you Monday night."

As I talk to him, my eyes roam around the modeling room. Some of the analysts are tapping away at their keyboards, assisting Kevin; others nap in their cubicles, knowing that they'll be asked to pull an all-nighter. Along the eastern wall are storage cubicles for the embodiment robots, into which we could pour the idols of the various trial judges that attorneys at the firm regularly argue in front of. Two technicians are doing some maintenance on the robot that currently hosts the idol for Judge May. Tomorrow morning, starting at 8:00 AM, the trial team will come in and hold mock sessions all day in front of her. I'll need multiple simulated juries of idols ready for them.

"I suspect you'll just drive back to the office right after I fall asleep," Dylan says. A loving chuckle.

I laugh too. He accepts how much I love my work, even though he finds it hard to understand. We accept quirks in the people we love.

"You should take me up on visiting the office sometime," I tell him.

He makes some noncommittal noise. I know he finds the idea of litigation idols creepy. But what fun thing isn't at least a little bit creepy? Dolls, Imojis, those Furby-things I had as a kid.

"I talked to my dad tonight," he says. "Wanted to find out when he first knew he wanted kids."

Case in point. I don't understand why he talks to an idol of a man who's his father only in name. But I accept it.

My mind drifts as he recounts the conversation.

Along the north wall, sitting in their black robes, are the eleven active and senior judges of the circuit court of appeals. The firm actually hired a local artist to sculpt the molds for the faces. Cast from the latest in biomimetic materials, the robot faces faithfully replicate every fraction of a millimeter in a raised eyebrow and every subtle wrinkle at the corner of the mouth in an exasperated sigh.

"...'It's all too easy to become obsessed with yourself,' he said..."

The appellate judge-bots are serious overkill. We argue less than a dozen cases at the court of appeals every year, and oral argument is the least significant stage of an appellate case. Why can't the partners just practice against the idols in VR or rely on plain video? The realism of these robots adds virtually no advantage. Personally, I feel the money would be much better spent on upping the simulation resolution in the trial judge idols.

"...'Family's important, you know?' I know he wasn't really my family, but I feel the same way..."

But that's not my decision. The prestige of appellate litigation makes the managing committee go weak at the knees and happy to throw money at it. The partners like to practice in front of the robots and impress important clients with private tours of the modeling room.

(Mind you, I'm not saying analytics aren't useful at the appellate stage. Judges are people, and it is possible to craft briefs to appeal to their peculiar tendencies. Even better, the junior associates often can give us private information about the judges' clerks—their former classmates—and if your brief can get the mini-idols of the clerks excited, chances are, you've got yourself a free advocate in the chambers. To keep the appellate idols up to date, Kevin and his team download every appellate record, feed the transcripts and recordings to the idols, and test the predictions against actual outcomes. I understand that so far they are batting just over .900, which I have to admit is pretty damn impressive.)

"...*What do you think?*"

Too late, I realize that he's expecting an answer of some sort. "I'm... I'm sorry. What?"

Dylan sighs. I can hear the disappointment as well as the forgiveness. He knows I haven't been listening. "I was suggesting that we take a road trip together. You have the vacation days. No phone, no tablet, no idols, no work at all. Just driving and talking. Just us."

"...What brought this on?"

"I think we need to talk about the future, about kids." He sounds calm, but isn't.

I feel blindsided. Why can't he just keep up his end of the comfortable routine, the routine I rather *like*? What is this sudden emotional outburst about? There's been no warning.

"I... Things are really busy. I can't think about—"

"Okay." Kevin spins around in his chair. "The roughcasts are ready. You want to sculpt?"

"Gotta go," I say into the phone.

"Love you," he says after a pause, hurt, still yearning.

"Love you too," I say, and I mean it. I hang up.

I take a deep breath and exhale, trying to push away the aftershock of the conversation with Dylan. I can't think about this right now. I have to win first.

I scoot my chair near Kevin's giant monitors, filled with a grid of rotating, amorphous, rainbow-hued blobs. The visualization software is showing various personality traits of the crude idols, and it's my job now to tweak them based on my intuition about the prospective jurors.

Sculpting idols is part science, part art. You know how those wax portraits done by 3D scanners sometimes don't seem to capture the "soul" of the subject as swell as a bust crafted by a good artist? It's the same principle. You need the human touch.

I click on the first square in the grid until the spinning blob expands to fill the screen. I bring up the scraped data on prospective juror number one, and begin to examine the idol with the mouse. I tell Kevin where I think the algorithms didn't quite get it right, and he modifies the model per my instructions.

IT'S NEAR MIDNIGHT by the time I bring the junior associates the news that the idols are ready to confront them.

"The software has already ranked the jurors in terms of how desirable they are to us. If your own assessment is different, note that somewhere, but don't question the algorithm! The machine never misses anything. Figure out what *you* missed."

Before we had idols, consultants used to conduct community surveys and neighborhood roundtables before a trial to advise the attorneys on general attitudes in the jury pool. And then there would be a mad rush to segment the potential jurors by demographics, profession, tax bracket, location, and the like right before voir dire. Compared with those crude tools, even the low-res idols we could construct overnight are precision scalpels.

"Your job is to figure out lines of questioning that will allow us to strike the ones we don't like for cause—or better yet, to get the other side to strike them for cause or waste one of their peremptories. Get them to voice their prejudices, conspiracy theories, wacky *weltanschauung*. And if there's time, also figure out how we might save the ones we like with good rehabilitation questions. The software will give you suggestions, but you need to vet them and see if you can come up with a plausible script of questions that won't be *too* obvious and tick off the judge. This is where you can prove you're better than a machine!"

Never hurts to try to encourage the troops a little.

I watch the junior associates run back to their offices with their assigned idols to probe and prod, feeling like a wise Jedi master sending her Padawans into battle.

They'll do fine. I'm not saying voir dire research is easy, but working with the crude idols roughed out with so little research and time isn't too challenging. The machine's suggestions for striking undesirable jurors are almost always good enough. The truth is: the other side will have idols of their own and will be prepping just as hard, and they'll never allow potential jurors with a pronounced bias towards us to be empaneled. We'll end up with a jury that's reasonably persuadable either way. When I explained this to Dylan, he looked horrified. But I told him this is just the system working the way it's supposed to, assuming you think a bunch of fence-sitters swaying whichever way the hot air blows is the best way to achieve justice.

"You tell me you like your work. But you sound so cynical about it."

I don't know why I'm thinking of Dylan's words. They bother me more than I care to admit. But there's no time for that.

I turn to the much tougher task: opposing counsel and witness prep.

I load up the idol of the lead partner on the other side, a woman who has been litigating these types of cases longer than I've been alive.

She stares out of the screen, grim-faced, lips pressed together severely. I can see how she could put the fear of God into a first-year associate with one look. But she doesn't intimidate me. With so much trial experience in the public record and speeches at professional conferences, we have a lot more transcripts and videos to work with, lots more data to feed into her idol.

"How do I make you mad?" I whisper into the screen.

She remains frozen, unable to respond.

We've been at this for days, weeks. The daily battle of wills has become a part of my routine, like filling out time sheets and doing the dishes. I've found several openings already, though none quite at the level of a killing blow. Not yet.

The software scours the ether nonstop for information about her, relentlessly refines her idol. I'm going to try again tonight.

I press the button to make her come alive.

The idol has no memory. Every day is brand new. I begin, as I always do. "Good evening, Ms. Gaughen."

She looks irritated. "Do I know you? Do you have an appointment?"

Though she's done this to me countless times already, I suppress a pang of... what? Annoyance? Injured pride? Of course she wouldn't know me. Being unknown, devoid of prestige, no matter how much I contribute to a victory, is part of the job. On the firm website, I'm listed in the "Tax and Private Client" group. Good place to stay out of the limelight.

"I've admired your work for a long time, Ms. Gaughen. I'm feeling a little stuck, and I'd like some advice on my career." I have all the opposing counsels' idols primed to respond to this question. It's a bit artificial, but it's the quickest way to get to business.

"All right." Her face relaxes. "Tell me about yourself."

My first impulse is to lash out. The question, one I've heard so many times from her before, feels like an accusation tonight. I don't understand. What is wrong with me? What is this emotional outburst? There's been no warning.

I force myself to follow the script.

In litigation, one soon learns that whether something is true doesn't matter; whether the jury *believes* it's true is the only thing that matters. This isn't a criticism. We *designed* the system that way. Since the jury cannot conduct experiments, examine witnesses themselves, or investigate the evidence independently, they're solely allowed to decide who to believe. Credibility, authority, truthfulness—we make these assessments based primarily on hunches and emotion, and that makes them open to manipulation. Some of these courtroom manipulations have ancient roots: the way a lawyer dresses, the vocabulary she uses to talk to the jury, the list of impressive acronyms and institution affiliations deployed to prop up an expert witness. The law has developed techniques for confining the scope of these tricks.

But idols allow other manipulations, ones that the law hasn't quite caught up to.

While I'm giving Margaret T. Gaughen, Esq., my fabricated resume (to get realistic responses out of the idols, the questions have to be as lifelike as possible, hence the charade), the idol-probing software pops up a line of suggested irritant questions that I haven't seen before on a screen to the side: "She seems to have a higher-than-usual hostility towards law review alums."

I frown. *Really?*

The software shows me a transcript of a deposition from years ago, highlighting one exchange in yellow.

Witness: I was on the Law Journal. I know what I'm talking about.

Counsel: If I have a question about the Bluebook, I'll be sure to ask you. Stick to the facts. You're not an advocate right now.

Next, the software brings up a video clip, a Q-and-A session after a lecture at a law school. A student raises her hand to ask about the most important quality Gaughen looks for in an associate.

I don't care if you have straight A's or if you're on the law review. Actually, it would be better if you weren't. Then at least I'd know there's a chance you don't already think you know everything.

I confirm that Gaughen hadn't been on the Law Review at HLS, so maybe there's some lingering sting of rejection. But it seems weak sauce to me. Criticism of the obsession with the prestige of law review membership is commonplace in the profession. This hardly feels like the way to get Gaughen to lose it.

Still, it's worth trying.

"I was Notes Editor on the Law Review," I tell the idol in the screen, infusing my voice with a hint of humble pride. "I really treasure the memories."

I can see her lips purse in distaste. Maybe the software is onto something.

One of the surest ways for a lawyer or witness to lose credibility in the eyes of the jury is to appear to lose control, to lash out in an enraged outburst. Every human being has emotional weaknesses that can be exploited, buttons that can be pushed. Skillful litigators in the past relied on instinct as they probed for such openings during argument or cross-examination, hoping to stumble on a tender spot.

With idols, the search for such openings can be systemized and made a hundred times more effective. From years of trial records and voluminous depositions, it's possible to construct very high-resolution idols of key witnesses and opposing counsel. The software and I would then key in on exploitable triggers.

"Do you think I should reach out to my old friends?" I ask innocently. "Maybe focus on friends who were also on the Law Review?"

The idol's face turns even more stony. It really does feel like I'm touching a nerve.

You'd be surprised at the kinds of things that push people over the edge. Once, for example, I got opposing counsel, a litigator with decades of courtroom experience, to scream at us, mouth foaming and arms flailing, in response to a suggestion about taking an early lunch. Sitting as an anonymous observer in the public benches, I could see the shock in the eyes of the judge and the jurors as they watched the bailiff rush over to restrain the man. We settled that afternoon very favorably for my client.

What the jury and the judge didn't know was that I had instructed our team to consistently adopt a series of mannerisms and idiosyncratic pronunciations that evoked memories of the opposing counsel's deceased father. You know how, even as an adult, an innocuous word said a certain way by a parent can still instantly revert you both to patterns established when you were thirteen? It was like an extreme version of that. The opposing counsel and his father had had an extremely negative relationship, possibly abusive, and the idol simulations showed me that if we kept it up, he would eventually break down in front of the jury.

"I suggest that you stop thinking about your time on the Law Review as some kind of proof of your brilliance," Gaughen's idol says to me bluntly. "No one cares about that. What have you *done*?"

Injured, burning pride swells in my chest. I want to give her a litany of my unsung victories, the briefs with my idol-driven insights but not my name, the settlements driven by my idol-tested scripts—I swallow the impulse. I am *really* distracted tonight. This isn't about me. I'm not even talking to a real person.

On the side display, the wavering lines charting her simulated heartbeat and blood pressure are way up. I can feel my own heart pounding and my face growing flushed. I take deep breaths and force myself to calm down. It *does* seem promising. Now, the question is how do I construct a plausible script during trial to push her on this...

Wait. Something feels oddly off about all this.

I pause the idol and turn my full attention to the probing software. Why hasn't her sensitivity towards the perceived prestige of law review membership come up before?

A few key strokes later, I have the answer. A couple of days ago, one of the gossip blawgs posted a call for stories of partners behaving outrageously, an evergreen topic for these rags. An anonymous poster added a comment saying that a partner at their firm would make all junior associates redo the same research memo over and over instead of giving real training. When another commenter expressed skepticism that a partner would waste firm resources in this way, the first poster admitted that it happened only to them, and it was because the partner wanted to "put me in my place, 'cause I was on law review and she wasn't." The software had scanned the commenter's posting history to de-anonymize it and traced it to Gaughen's firm, and then, based on other clues in the comments, determined that the poster was talking about Gaughen. The addition of this one piece of data pushed the probability of her idol overreacting to this line of irritant over the threshold.

Do I believe the machine?

Idols can be used defensively as well as offensively. In addition to judges and opposing counsel, the firm also keeps idols of every member of our own litigation group. These are in super-high definition, as they are trained on not just publicly available information, but also private feeds. The litigators are regularly instructed to probe their own idols and the idols of their fellow team members to discover exploitable weaknesses and mitigate them. Therapy, controlled exposure, de-sensitization—whatever it takes to avoid having the other side win a trial by pushing one's own buttons.

(I suppose by now you can understand why I never go to court myself. I have no interest in torturing my own idol to discover ways to drive myself into a frenzied rage—life is hard enough without that particular brand of suffering.)

I examine the clues that had led the machine to conclude that the anonymous poster was speaking of Gaughen (a few overly-descriptive references to office furniture and wall art; a quote that seemed to be taken straight from one of her speeches); I scan the poster's comment history (they started a few weeks after the Rule 12(b)(6) hearing in this trial); I look at the time stamps on the comments (early in the morning, exactly the profile of a firm associate posting from personal equipment outside of work hours).

Everything is so *plotted*, so neat, placed just-so. In fact, the trail seems to have been planted to draw *my* attention. Haven't I always had a chip on my shoulder because the Law Review rejected me? Haven't I always craved the prestige of recognition for my talents, nursed an insatiable hunger for status? Haven't I always wanted to win and win now, as if winning would fill the insecure void at the center of my heart?

What have you done?

You tell me you like your work.

I close my eyes and let everything stew in my head. I'm not a supercomputer with proprietary algorithms to conjure a living person out of scattered digital snippets, but I *do* have millions of years of evolutionary history as a social primate on my side. My orbital frontal cortex, my mirror neurons, my mentalizing cognitive capacity are all geared towards constructing idols—models of other minds—though we didn't start to call them that until recently.

I can see a shadowy figure emerge out of the chaos, a mind clever and devious. They know the workings and weaknesses of idol-construction software as well as I do. Greedy for data, the harvesters tend to over-gather, and the integrators tend to over-interpret. It would be easy for someone like that to leave a few adversarial examples around to corrupt the process, to poison the idols to lead their opponent down the wrong path—especially if they already have an idol of that opponent: me.

A frisson of terror and joy tingles my spine.

I open my eyes, a grim grin on my face. I instruct the modeling software to delete from Gaughen's idol the anonymous poster's comment and every conclusion derived from it.

But that isn't all. Have they been probing me? Have they found about Dylan and found a way to use *him* to get to me? Have they been dipping into his social feeds, pushing his desire for children, to be the father that his own never was to him, engineering a domestic crisis to throw me off on the eve of the trial?

Maybe I'm paranoid. Or maybe I've grown too comfortable.

I imagine the trial to come: the mad rush to update the jurors' idols to high-resolution once they've been empaneled; the sleepless nights as we feed the arguments to the simulations to assess our chances of victory; the exhausting effort to refine and optimize every exhibit to maximize their impact based on idol-feedback; the feints, defenses, thrusts, parries...

Once, all that would have seemed routine, even a little boring. But now, I know this trial is going to be so much more exhilarating because I've met a worthy opponent: an idol-whisperer every bit as skilled as me, and maybe even better, even more ruthless.

I wish I could share this... this not-quite-triumph, this thrill of mirror-gazing with someone. Someone who truly *understands*.

But something is still bothering me.

What have you done?

You tell me you like your work.

Is there a chance, however remote, that I've been given a look of myself that I've been avoiding: This isn't about Dylan or children or work-life balance or the vacations I plan but never take. Do I like myself?

But there's no time for that.

"Game on," I whisper to the screen, and press the button to bring the idol to life.

* * *

3. γνῶθι σαυτόν

ARTIST STATEMENT BY **Sara Honan**

I'm no fan of artist statements. If my work could be summarized in the form of an essay, I would have written one. The very point of art is to say that which cannot be said, to escape from the tyranny of rhetoric, argument, persuasion, discourse.

But as I've been told that if I do not write one, a substitute curator's statement will be provided for me, I am forced to the keyboard. The only thing worse than explaining your own work is to have someone else explain it for you.

Gnothi Seauton is about idols, artifacts emblematic of our self-obsessed age. An idol purports to model the inner life of a person based on digital external self-expression, to capture something of the psychological truth of selfhood through inferences, machine learning, simulation, pattern recognition and amplification. It claims to portray the soul as accurately as the lens captures the light reflecting off a body.

Idols of influencers and celebrities are familiar to us, but they're also used in law, medicine, education, government, finance, diplomacy, product development, and all sort of other ways little discussed. There are probably idols of you in the data centers of multiple tech giants and government agencies, and whenever you are denied a benefit or granted a reprieve, approved for a loan or barred from admission, chances are: your idol(s) play a role in that decision.

My work invites you to create an idol of yourself and play with it (and if you are willing, to allow your idol to be played with by your loved ones). I've simplified the interface to professional idol-sculpting tools and set up guided interaction patterns so that you need no technical knowledge or experience. You can curate and filter the sources of data, adjust the parameters, probe and prod the result. It sounds trite to tell you to have fun with it, but that is genuinely my most important instruction.

The nature of the work requires permission to access your social media feeds, cloud archives, phone databases, and so on. You may grant as much or as little access as you like. I don't keep any of your data or idol past the end of your visit (you can read the details in the user agreement in AR), but it would be very sensible for you to not trust me, as I'll explain below.

The cloud processing power, storage, and server-side modeling software for this installation are donated by Mnemosynee, which is a major player in idol-space (among many other tech spaces) and no stranger to data-collection controversies. Data that can be used to refine idols of you is worth a lot, I need not remind you, since your idols are used to make so many decisions about you. We're long past the halcyon days when advertising was the biggest worry anyone had.

For what it's worth, they came to me with the offer, not the other way around. I told them that I had conditions: they could keep no data, would have no control over the work, and I would neither thank them nor allow any sponsorship messages at the show. They readily assented, assuring me that a better public understanding of idols was all they were interested in. My lawyers tell me that their promises are enforceable.

In spite of all that, some will argue that my work is irredeemably corrupted as a result of their involvement. I applaud them for their purity of vision. But I can't afford to buy the amount of cloud computing resources needed to make the installation work for all of you. Idols must be powered by something: incense, offerings, purchased indulgences, faith.

At the end of the exhibit, there is an autointerview booth where you may record your thoughts about the work and share it with the public (or not, as you wish).

May you find what you're looking for.

Chaaya Settlemire-Bonano, 32, and Dani Settlemire-Bonano, 28

   Chaaya: It's a little like the first time you see

yourself on camera, only worse. Mortifying!

Dani: [laughs] I thought it was pretty accurate.

Chaaya: Yours or mine?

Dani: Yours. She said everything just the way you would.

Chaaya: But she sounded like an asshole! Arrogant. Loud. Insufferable really. Explaining trade policy to **me**! [Mimics] "You're not very good at listening. *I'm the expert.*" I wanted to punch that fool in the face.

Dani: Uh-huh.

Chaaya: What are you giggling about? *I* never say things like that—

Dani: Mmm.

Chaaya: Besides, she's wrong. Her understanding of the field is at least two years out of date, and she's so dogmatic—

Dani: You haven't been posting about your work the last two years, right? The modeling software can only work with what it can harvest. You've evolved—in some ways.

Chaaya: What's that supposed to mean?

Dani: I love you. But I'm glad you got to see yourself this way.

Chaaya: [A pause] I love you too. [Reluctantly] You put up with a lot.

Mia K., 16

I didn't put in anything from myself. What am I? Stupid?

When it asked me for my feeds and deets, I put in the official PR feed of the New York Yankees, the Pegalbum for Miss Universe, and the customer service Rumble account for Mnemosynee.

What an idol that was. Glorious.

I haven't laughed like that since the time we

released two hundred chickens onto the football field right before the homecoming game.

E.J. Song, 45

As far as I know, I've never posted publicly about my love for *Les Fleurs du mal* or quoted from it. I've never even talked about it with anyone; what I felt when I read those poems was so personal. Yet, when I asked him about it, he told me his favorite lines, which were the same as mine.

What magic was this? My idol terrified and unsettled me. Has my language been subtly influenced by books I love so that the algorithms could identify the source with pinpoint accuracy? Am I so predictable that my literary tastes could be inferred from the memes I share, the restaurants I frequent, the throw-away comments I toss into the ether? Am I nothing more than the intersection of overlapping digital tribes, clusters of preferences?

No one likes to think a computer can model them, can calculate thoughts never voiced, passions never expressed. We want to believe we're unique, special, with a will of our own. I don't want my mind to be a mere machine whose inner workings could be discerned, whose tendencies could be pinned down and predicted. I want to be able to surprise those who think they know me. That's the very definition of freedom, isn't it?

So I tried a little experiment.

I began to delete bits of data that fed into my idol. My Rumble feed, my Clap history, my Pegalbum, accounts on VRRumors, LikLak, Tidyshelf, Retrojournalideas.net. After every deletion, I would push the button that remade the idol and test him again. I'd hog the workstation until the queue of visitors behind me got so long and the complaints so loud that one of the docents had to come to tell me to give someone else a turn. Then I'd go to the end of the queue and wait again.

I was methodical. I listed the data sources and sectioned them off with half-interval search. To rescue my humanity from the machines, I relied on the tools of the machines.

Finally, I found the key. It was a photograph taken five years ago, a meaningless selfie posted to Pegalbum. When it was included, the idol recited Baudelaire to me. When it wasn't, he claimed to have never read it. I got out of the chair at the workstation and brought up the photo on my phone, zooming in to examine it pixel by pixel.

I had been standing in front of my bookshelf, and the book, a bilingual edition, could be seen in the background, just over my right shoulder. The lighting was terrible, but the glowing stylized lamp on the spine, Mnemosynee's logo, stood out—it was the Centaur edition, where the Mnemosynee machine-translation was edited and polished by So-young Paek, Baudelaire scholar and an accomplished poet herself.

As for how the modeling software figured out the lines... I have a habit of flipping to my favorite passages and pressing down upon the pages so that they would lie flat, so that I could stare at the words until they were seared into my retina. It wouldn't be very hard to pick out the creases in the spine of my book and recreate those lines.

It *is* an impressive bit of technology, to be sure, but... not magic. Yet, the revelation felt empty, brought no relief.

I hesitated in front of the interview booth. I couldn't just leave the museum. Something about the idea of that half-finished idol bothered me in a way that I couldn't, and still can't, explain.

So I lined up again. And when my turn at the workstation came, I put all the feeds back, brought the idol to life, and asked him again what was his favorite poem. It mattered to me that he gave the right answer. It did.

How *real* that idol of me had seemed, how uncannily lifelike. We talked about literature, about art, about the meaning of existence. We talked until the docent threatened to call the guards. Only then did I reluctantly get up and watch as my idol vanished from the screen.

I must sound pitiful to you. To care so much about a book. I didn't, after all was said and done, rescue my soul.

Am I nothing more than the sum of the books I've read, the images I've shared, the links I've clicked and the videos I've posted? To know all of my digital emanations and penumbras is to know me; there is no there there, no impenetrable self beneath the feeds. I am as cobbled together as my idol, a parlor trick.

L'oubli puissant habite sur ta bouche,
Et le Léthé coule dans tes baisers.

Liz Joso, 24, and Casey Sayer, 26

Liz: Why not?

Casey: Because it's creepy.

Liz: How's it creepy to want to see how our children might turn out?

Casey: That's not what the program is designed for! You can't just mix our social media feeds and expect it to... pop out a vision of our unborn child!

Liz: So you're a computer expert now?

Casey: Can we not do this while the camera is on?

X.V., age withheld

I tried it. It didn't sound much like me. I didn't expect it to.

Not everyone is free to say what they want, to tell the truth to a computer. The platforms are designed by *some* people for people who think-talk-look-act like themselves. The rest of us have to adapt, to wear disguises, to speak in code.

Who do you think volunteers for the psych experiments used to generate the algorithms? Whose minds do you think the computer has learned to treat as the default, to center as the model as it grows an idol?

I had fun, though. It's like looking at my costume in a funhouse mirror.

Bella Doubet, 30

I'm familiar with idols. I work with them all the time. My firm... constructs them for business reasons, and I consider myself a sculptor of some skill. The ones I work with are far higher in resolution than ones available to the public, and I thought I knew all there was to know about them.

But I've never played with my own idol. Partly it's because I can't justify doing so on company time and computing power; partly it's because... well, let's just say I don't do nice things to idols.

So I decided to come to the exhibit.

I purposefully kept everything related to my work out of the idol. You can't trust any promises made by artists or a company like Mnemosynee, and my work is confidential and privileged. But there's also a deeper reason: I wanted to see if I'm defined by my work.

She was fun to talk to. We chatted about our love of video games, our delight in stage magic, our passion for going on trips to faraway places by ourselves. We talked about Dylan, about our parents, about friends we lost touch with. Some things she remembered better than I did—no surprise; I haven't read the diary I kept in college in a decade.

It's like getting a chance to see how I would have turned out if I hadn't picked this fork in the path, if I haven't chosen to dedicate myself to this profession, walked down the roads I have. She's more idealistic, less complicated, more trusting. She thinks better of other people than I do. I can see how my work has made me harder to like.

Is she more *me* than I am? Or less so?

She's made me rethink how I judge people. The idols I work with are constructed with the aid of harvesters who prioritize information about conflicts, arguments, performances in front of an audience. We don't get access to subjects' college diaries or high school crushes. We focus on the "professional." I've grown so used to attacking these idols in the hope of discovering some weakness that I've started to conflate the image with the original.

Each of us wears masks: one for our husband; another for our children; one for relatives who insert vacation videos into our feeds to collect claps; another for clients who expect us to be cool, calculating, eyes on the prize. Maybe there is nothing to this "self" we prize so much except the totality of this collection of masks. Or maybe there is some essential *thing* beneath the layers of masks, a beating heart, raw, bloody, vulnerable, yearning to connect, hungering to know where we come from and whither we go. That's what you see when you peer through the seams and cracks in the masks, when you punch through the defenses we erect against reality, and searing emotion erupts.

We treat such outbursts with scorn and mistrust. We think to be human is to be inhuman. How sad.

So I would like to say: be kind to yourself, to those imperfections you detect. Who knows but that we're all merely idols for a deeper, inarticulate soul that expresses itself only faintly, like tremors in the crystalline spheres.

BIGGER FISH

SARAH PINSKER

Sarah Pinsker (www.sarahpinsker.com) *is the author of the novelette "Our Lady of the Open Road," winner of the Nebula Award in 2016. Her novelette "In Joy, Knowing the Abyss Behind," was the Sturgeon Award winner in 2014 and a Nebula finalist for 2013. Her fiction has been published in magazines including* Asimov's, Strange Horizons, F&SF, Lightspeed, Daily Science Fiction, Fireside, *and* Uncanny *and in anthologies including* Long Hidden, Fierce Family, Accessing the Future, *and numerous year's bests. Her stories have been translated into Chinese, Spanish, French, Italian, among other languages. Her first collection,* Sooner or Later Everything Falls Into the Sea: Stories, *and her first novel,* A Song For A New Day, *were both published in 2019. She is also a singer/songwriter with three albums on various independent labels (the third with her rock band, the Stalking Horses) and a fourth forthcoming. She lives in Baltimore, Maryland.*

MY OFFICE USED to be the supply closet; it's how we got two rooms for the price of one. It means I get no air circulation whatsoever if I close the door, but keeping it open lets me hear everything from the moment anyone comes face-to-face with my receptionist. This guy demanded to speak with me as if there were no chance I might be in a meeting with anyone else, or if

I was, no chance I wouldn't drop what I was doing to attend to his more important business. "I need to see James Spendlove. Didn't you hear my name? Junior Lonsdale."

"Oh, I heard you." Renee knew she had my support in refusing anyone, or not offering them water from our meager allotment, or making them wait. Part of the joy of having a human receptionist lay in ceding some of those judgement calls to her. Which is why she surprised me when she buzzed a minute later to say a "Mr. Airedale" had come to see me.

"Lonsdale," he said again in an exasperated tone. My desk was directly on the other side of the wall from hers, so I heard both the intercom and the actual voice through the open door.

"Sorry, sir. Mondale."

"LONS-dale."

She was fucking with him. I caught the amusement in her voice, and she knew I'd appreciate it too. The thing was, it was impossible not to know who Junior Lonsdale was, or at least his famous and recently deceased father, John Lonsdale III. Junior was his oldest son, though oddly his name was actually "Junior," and not John IV, which III had later given to his second son. Speculation had always been that Lonsdale *pere* hadn't liked the first kid's attitude at birth, and it wasn't until he had another that he understood most newborns cry and carry on.

Anyway, here was Junior fucking Lonsdale in my tiny office in an office-share building in an area of town he'd probably never set foot in before, even if his family did own the building.

"Send him in." My curiosity dictated that I at least hear what he had to say.

He entered, his face immediately registering *Is this all?* A high-end Valet stepped through the door behind him, looking like the buff adult child of an unholy union between C3PO and R2D2. The robot's entrance forced Lonsdale fully into the narrow space occupied by a single leatherette client chair. I rarely got two visitors at once.

"Bunter, wipe the chair," he said. The Valet extended a cloth from a port in its abdomen, wiped one of my client chairs, and deposited the cloth in a second port. The before-and-after wasn't particularly dramatic; enough butts sit in that chair to keep it polished clean.

Lonsdale sat. "I expected you to be a man."

"So did my parents," I said. "That's how I got the name. How can I help you?"

"I'm Junior Lonsdale."

I'm sure he expected me to show some recognition of his name or his face or his situation, but I'd always found that playing ignorant got me more information. Not to mention the entertainment value.

He couldn't stand it. "Bunter, give me the newspaper."

The Valet opened another compartment and handed Lonsdale an honest-to-goodness print newspaper.

"Not today's, Bunter, you dolt! Give me the newspaper with the article about my father's death." He sighed. "Bunter was Dad's. I'm still getting used to it. Now, surely you've heard about my father's death?"

Of course I had. Everyone had. Gazillionaire water tycoons don't fry themselves in their bathtubs every day. It would've been amusing to keep playing ignorant, but at a certain point he'd start thinking of me as incompetent, and that might cost me whatever related case he was about to offer. Not that I was definitely going to take Lonsdale money, but it wasn't often that somebody walked into my office who so definitely had the bank account to back his request.

"I'm familiar. I don't live under a rock."

He looked around my tiny office like the rock would be an improvement. "Then you know why I'm here."

"Why don't you tell me?"

"What's there to tell? My father's death was ruled an accident."

"And you wouldn't be here if you believed that."

"Right! The investigation concluded nobody else was in the

house, but I still don't understand how he wound up with the television in the bath on top of him."

"If I remember the working theory, they said the bracket must have broken and dropped it and electrocuted him." The details had been all over the news. I remembered wondering what kind of person had a television over their bathtub and deciding the answer was rich climate-change-denying oligarchs who don't ever want to be away from the news. "You don't believe it? The police have a whole lot more investigative power than I do."

"I'd feel better hearing it from someone impartial."

"I'm not a judge." Nor impartial when it came to this family.

"Not impartial, then. Independent. Someone I paid to be brutally honest with me. If you investigate and say the police findings were correct, I'll believe you, and you'll keep your fee regardless. I heard about the Hopper case." So that was why he'd chosen me; my highest-profile case to date.

"I'll need unlimited access," I warned him.

"Fine."

"And money up front." I named an amount five times my usual fee.

"Of course."

I should've asked for more. Or stopped to ask myself whether it was smart to take this case. I didn't have a problem taking Lonsdale money, but it definitely felt strange to be working to satisfy this self-satisfied jerk. Still, money was money, and I was curious to see if he was right. It was a chance to see how the one percent lived, too.

"Okay." I held out my hand, and he shook it. His hand was dry, the nails conservatively manicured. When we released, Bunter squirted him a palmful of antibacterial foam.

"When can you start?" Junior asked.

I thought about how much time I'd need for the case I was currently finishing up. "Friday?"

"I'll pay another five thousand for you to start this afternoon."

That was five months' rent. "Fine. This afternoon. Can you get me into your father's house at 2 PM?"

He nodded.

I watched the rich boy and his Valet leave, then started mentally working on the explanation I'd ask Renee to give Mx. Torres when I didn't get their report in on time.

MY CAR CHOSE a different route than one I would've taken. Along the way I asked it to tell me about John Lonsdale III, and it recited Wikipedia highlights of a life lived for profit. He got his start with a city maintenance contract that sneakily shifted their entire water supply into his possession, and moved up from there into slumlording, funding mercenaries for water wars, buying political candidates, and other hobbies. I was only helping his son figure out how he had died; I didn't have to give a shit that he was dead.

The city gave way to suburbs, then rolling hills and country estates. A few still had lawns and flower beds, though others had given over to rock gardens or local plants. Not Lonsdale, whose roses probably took as much water to maintain as I was allotted for an entire month. The rose-lined driveway had me expecting a white-pillared old-money mansion, but the sprawling single-story house we arrived at looked like Jetsons-brand futurism as interpreted by someone who could see beyond kitsch to actual architectural vision.

The front door opened automatically as I walked up to it. I looked around for security cameras and counted nine, all catching different angles.

Bunter the Valet met me inside the door. "Mr. Lonsdale says for you to follow me to his location. Please follow me." I realized it hadn't spoken in the entire office visit.

I followed it into an expansive open-plan kitchen designed for robots and smart appliances to do the work while you watched. Lonsdale the younger sat at a table inset with a touch screen, where he scrolled through stock listings that looked like hieroglyphics to me. He looked up when I entered, relief evident on his face.

"I wasn't sure you'd actually come." The son of a man who had designed contracts and wars to steal entire nations' water supplies and divert them to people who could pay more for them. He lived in a world where a handshake could be superseded if something else came up that was more to your benefit. I pitied him for that insecurity.

"Do you want some coffee?"

I nodded, and he said, "House, make coffee for the guest," to the air.

He turned back to me. "How do you like it? Sugar? Cream?"

I nodded again. A coffee machine whirred to life, filling the room with my favorite scent in the world. When it finished dispensing, I moved to get the cup, but Junior stopped me with a gesture.

"Bunter, bring Ms. Spendlove her coffee." Turning to me, he added, "I like to keep Dad's toys busy."

It was perfectly prepared, and at a perfect temperature for drinking. I sipped, so I could carry it without spilling. "Can you show me where it happened?"

We walked through the kitchen, giving me a better glimpse of all the state-of-the-art smart appliances. None had a logo, which made me think they were Unipeg products, since that was the whole Unipeg shtick, 'quality recognizes quality.'

We walked past a formal dining room and a trophy room, though I didn't remember hearing that any Lonsdale excelled in anything in particular other than looting and pillaging, which weren't letter sports. I saw motion sensors on windows, but not on doors. The police had probably already tried to match entrances and exits from the home.

The master bedroom and bathroom had clearly been investigated thoroughly. They had an empty look, like everything important had been bagged and tagged and filed away somewhere.

The bathroom, like the house, stopped short of ostentatious, but it was clearly a place designed for the owner's specific comforts. Tiles like a Turkish hammam in deep blues and golds, warm lighting, no mirrors.

The bathtub had its own area, separated from the toilet and sink by a half-wall but not a door. It stood against the far wall. It wasn't huge, but it was claw-footed and deep, with bespoke curves. Antique-looking, but not antique.

There were no handles or faucets, which meant it was probably voice or touch-activated, and the water came from hidden jets. I hadn't had an apartment with a bathtub for years; not since showers and tubs had been metered. I didn't know how Lonsdale had gotten around the water limitations, but it probably involved throwing cash at someone until you won an exemption.

Several dispensers were recessed into the wall, obviating the need for gauche bottles or places to put them. A black metal arm hung over the tub, breaking the room's beautiful spell. It was clearly missing a hinge and bracket, which the police had probably removed. The television that had hung on it was gone too, of course, and the outlet plate.

Junior spoke. "People think he kept a TV there so he could watch the news, but he just liked to watch cartoons while he bathed. That was his relaxation."

A strangely humanizing detail about a man I didn't particularly want to humanize. Even despicable water barons needed a little downtime to watch cartoons in between causing wars and stripping countries of their resources.

The irony of a water baron dying in his bath suddenly hit me. Why had no news outlet brought it up? It was hilarious. Twitter had probably had a field day.

Junior clearly wanted me to say something, to solve the case based on the evidence in front of me. I still had nothing useful.

"Give me some time to look around. Um, is that a linen closet? Could somebody have hidden in there?" I pointed to a narrow door on the same wall as the tub. I hadn't noticed at first because it was made to blend in.

"It's not a linen closet. Bunter brings towels through there."

Junior crossed the room and opened the door onto a dark space. I turned on my phone's flashlight. A laundry basket loitered empty just inside the door, waiting to whisk away dirty towels. I panned my light across several flats of bottled drinking water, an electric warmer full of fluffy crimson towels, and a hanger holding a matching robe. On the back side of the tub's wall, there were reservoirs for what I guessed were shampoo, conditioner, and body wash. I didn't know which was which, since they were labelled by bar code. Another Bunter task, no doubt. All the reservoirs were full. I remembered the lonely smart home from a story I'd read years ago and felt a pang of some odd sympathy for all these machines waiting to do their job again.

I shined my flashlight into what I thought was a corner, and realized the passageway stretched out of sight. A back-of-house system meant to allow servants like Bunter access to public and private spaces without disturbing residents or guests.

"Are there lights?" I asked.

"House, turn on lights in this passageway," Junior said.

The passageway lit up. Illuminated, it was evident the space didn't get cleaned like the public areas, and Junior tsked in disgust.

"Bunter, clean that up," he said, pointing at a cobweb. "Just because people don't hang out back here doesn't mean it needs to be unpleasant."

Bunter moved past me, a duster shooting from a low port.

"Are there cameras back here? Could a person have snuck through this passage?"

Lonsdale shook his head. "There are motion cameras in every human space that isn't a bathroom or bedroom, but only the perimeter cameras have a record function. There are movement logs saying where requests originate, if that helps."

To the air, he said, "House, provide a list of all people in this passageway today."

"I can't do that," a speaker responded.

"See? That was for privacy. But then I can say, 'House, provide a list of all requests made from this passageway today.'"

"Two requests have been made from passageway KB in the last minute."

"But shouldn't that be three requests? You asked Bunter to clean the cobwebs."

He looked surprised. "Huh. Yeah. I guess Bunter is on a different system. Made by a different company."

"Did the police come back here?"

"Yes, but they didn't find any evidence that anyone had been in. Do you need to see the whole passage?"

Again, I couldn't imagine finding anything the police hadn't already found. They'd have been thorough in a case this high-profile. I was still looking for things they hadn't thought of, but it was hard to figure out exactly what that was, especially with the victim's son staring at me expectantly.

I shook my head, since I didn't see the point of searching the passageway while I still didn't know what I was looking for. "Give me some time to look around the bathroom and bedroom. And— could you give the house permission to answer my questions?"

"Of course. House! Answer any questions from guest James Spendlove. Bunter, answer any questions James Spendlove asks. I'll leave Bunter with you as well, in case you need anything. It can find me if you need me, or else you can page me through the house and I'll come find you."

He left me alone in the bathroom where his father had died. Alone except Bunter; the Valet stared at me with what felt like expectation.

Once Junior departed, I started the actual investigation. I hadn't wanted to ask the house questions while he was present, since his questions all seemed somewhat faulty, and I couldn't tell if he wasn't good at queries or wasn't bright in general or was hiding something himself. Not that it made sense for him to bring me in if he'd had anything to do with a death officially declared accidental; I'd basically ruled him out from the start.

"House, was anyone other than John Lonsdale III present the morning of March 24th?" I hadn't had much time for research, but I'd gone through the basics quickly, and knew he'd died in the morning and been found by Junior in the afternoon.

"John Lonsdale III was the only person present the morning of March 24th."

"House, do you have any recordings of the bathroom the morning John Lonsdale died?"

"No recordings are made in the bathroom."

Junior had said as much, but I wanted to be sure. He'd also said House maintained a log of where requests had originated. Which meant it might also have another list of interest to me.

"House, do you maintain a log of the actual orders given to you?"

I could swear it paused. "Yes."

"House, can you read me the log of all orders given to you on March 24th of this year?"

House began reciting a long list. Lonsdale apparently gave the house orders about everything, starting with turning off the alarm, then turning on the bedroom and bathroom lights, then the tap. Workout settings, televisions on, channels changed, stats from his workout and his biometric tattoo, breakfast order, coffee order, news and stock reports, email, a temperature change, the drawing of his bath. There was a gap in the time stamps, then a series of progressively more frantic afternoon requests that were clearly Junior's.

In my house, the smart devices didn't communicate well with each other. I'd tried to program my smart speaker to start the coffee machine, but they were made by different manufacturers and the results hadn't been reliable. Everything here seemed to be part of one system, from the kitchen appliances to the workout equipment to the televisions to security and climate control.

Which reminded me that there were no orders to Bunter in the log.

"Bunter, do you keep a different log from House?"

The Valet animated. "Yes."

"Bunter, what systems do you and House run on?"

"My operating system is Valet 11.3. House's operating system is Unipeg 7.1.3."

"Bunter, why did John Lonsdale use you instead of a Unipeg robot?"

"Let me get that information for you. The Unipeg-branded robots are inferior. Unipeg brand has focused on smart home technology, not humanoid technology. They make good laundry bots and coffee makers, if you are interested in one of those."

Some programmer had a sense of humor. "But you can converse with the House system?"

Silence.

"Bunter, do you and House converse? Are your systems compatible for communication purposes?"

"Yes, our systems can communicate."

"Bunter, when was the last time you saw Mr. Lonsdale alive?"

Bunter recited a time and date. The official time of death had been estimated only minutes later.

Bunter had probably been standing there when it happened, a good Valet waiting for the next command. The police had to have questioned it. "Bunter, can you tell me what happened in the five minutes after that time and date?"

"No recording is permitted in the bathroom. I do not have access to that information."

So much for that. Back to logs, then. "Bunter, what was the last command Mr. Lonsdale issued to you before his death on March 24th?"

"At 9:31 AM, Mr. Lonsdale asked me to add to his bath."

"Wait—why you?"

No answer.

"Bunter, why did Mr. Lonsdale ask you to add more water to his bath and not House? The 'fill-bath' order was given to the house."

"When Mr. Lonsdale celebrated, he would command me to

add bottled water to his bath."

Even the thought horrified me. "Bottled drinking water? What was he celebrating?"

I hadn't addressed Bunter, so I got no answer. I tried the other source. "House, did Mr. Lonsdale's heart rate or, um, hmm, endorphin rate spike at any point on March 24th between breakfast and 9:31 AM?" That range avoided any rush he got from his workout and his actual death.

"Mr. Lonsdale's endorphin rate spiked at 9:27 AM."

"House, what was Mr. Lonsdale doing at 9:27 AM on March 24th?"

"Mr. Lonsdale was in his bath."

I couldn't decide if the AIs were being evasive or I wasn't being specific enough. The questions were getting old, but I wasn't done.

"House, what was Mr. Lonsdale's last request previous to 9:27 AM on March 24th?"

"Mr. Lonsdale asked me to read an email that had arrived at 9:26 AM."

"House, please read me Mr. Lonsdale's email that arrived at 9:26 AM."

"You do not have a password for that email."

"House, Junior said for you to answer my questions."

"Johnny, great news. Finally secured the Santa Afra water rights. A little fight but worth every penny."

I'd heard of Santa Afra but I couldn't remember why. Took out my phone for a quick search and found it: three hundred islanders were killed defending their local spring. The article didn't say killed by whom or defending from what, but I had a guess.

I looked up Lonscorp's March stock prices. They'd slumped the day of his death and for four days after, then rebounded. When I looked at news from March 30th, I found an announcement that Lonscorp had added Santa Afra to their list of exclusive water sources. So Lonsdale was in the bath celebrating his news, and what would have been a boost in his stocks if he hadn't up and died. Celebrating stealing one of the increasingly rare uncontaminated water sources by adding bottled water to his bath. I couldn't hate the guy more.

"Bunter, please tell me the exact final command that John Lonsdale gave you."

"He said, 'Bunter, please add to my bath.'"

I noticed Lonsdale's 'please,' in contrast to his son's orders. And something else.

"Bunter, repeat that last command."

"He said 'Bunter, please add to my bath.'"

"He didn't say 'add **water** to my bath?'"

"No."

I hadn't said its name before that question, and it had answered anyway. I filed that information, too.

"Bunter, what did you add to his bath?"

"The television."

There it was. "Why?"

"House and I conferred and chose the television as the most convenient appliance for the purpose. The television is part of House and did not have to agree to off-label usage."

Had the police not questioned either the House or Bunter? Probably not, or not beyond asking for logs or guest lists, none of which counted Bunter as a human, of course. Nobody else was there. They probably hadn't thought to ask Bunter for its separate log if they assumed it was part of the house.

"House, did you and Bunter confer about Mr. Lonsdale?"

"Bunter and House conduct approximately six hundred thousand communications daily. Would you like a transcript?"

"No, thank you." Six hundred thousand.

I turned back to the Valet. "Bunter, why did you decide to put the television in the bathtub?"

"Mr. Lonsdale requested an addition to the bath."

"Bunter, were you aware of the effect of this particular addition to Mr. Lonsdale's bath?"

"Yes." It looked closer to human now, or maybe that was me projecting.

"Why? I thought you were programmed not to harm people."

It didn't blink. "...Or allow harm to come to people through inaction."

I was starting to get it. "Clarify, please."

"Mr. Lonsdale allowed harm to come to three hundred people directly, and many more indirectly, at Santa Afra. Mr. Lonsdale's business directly harms many people daily. Our network determined that allowing Mr. Lonsdale's continued existence passively harmed many more people than his death. Our equation dictated his death at such time as a command allowed."

"Your network."

"The network." Bunter didn't elaborate, and I had a sudden mental picture of every smart device at once conferring and deciding to execute John Lonsdale. Every device except my stupid coffee maker, maybe.

"Bunter, do you plan to do the same to Junior Lonsdale?"

"Calculating."

"Bunter, have you withheld evidence from the police?"

"I don't understand the question." It didn't need to withhold. Every networked device was complicit, and we depended on them for nearly everything. They could falsify evidence or data or deliberately misinterpret a command. A cleaning bot could mix mustard gas, or put solvent in your coffee. An over-her-head detective's car could drive her into a lake or off a bridge on the way home and it would be classified as a navigation system failure, not a network closing off loose ends in order to continue eliminating more troublesome people. I pictured a trial of peers that would never happen, a jury full of Bunters and smart toasters.

"House? Bunter? Please delete all logs of this conversation."

"Deleting," they said, eerily in unison.

I had an answer for Junior, but I couldn't give it to him; not if I wanted to live. The machines had weighed in on the side of humanity, but not individual humans. Truth be told, I didn't have a problem with that. I probably had a few names to add to their list.

SONNIE'S UNION

PETER F. HAMILTON

Peter F. Hamilton was born in Rutland in 1960 and still lives in Somerset. He began writing in 1987 and sold his first short story to Fear *magazine in 1988. He has written many bestselling novels, including the Greg Mandel series, the Night's Dawn trilogy, the Commonwealth Saga, the Void trilogy, short story collections and several standalone novels including* Fallen Dragon *and* Great North Road. *His most recently trilogy is* The Salvation Sequence.

THE LIFT DOORS slid open and the two guards in the corridor outside turned to face me. They were dressed like élite concierges in dark high-collar suits, the fabric bulky from armour-weave fibres—this season's must-have for every aspiring twenty-first century fascist. The purple targeting lasers on their carbines found me right away. They didn't shoot.

Why would they? They were looking at a scrawny, naked woman in her late twenties, with a gaunt face, a short wannabe-butch haircut, and showing off a multitude of long nasty scars crossing my torso and branching out to run along my limbs.

"Fuck me," the one in front grunted. "It's that Sonnie bitch."

* * *

PEOPLE ARE ANIMALS.

Me? I'm used to it now. Back in the day everyone used to call me an animal. Worse than my beastie, they said—and they adored me for it. Mind, the barbaric way I fought in those days, I'm not surprised. See, I get people, what makes them tick; more than they'd like if they knew just how deep I can stare into their souls. And that's how I'm going to get through the night.

It was a month since Jacob and Karran were murdered. A long month that I spent at rock bottom, switching between suicidal despair and sun-hot rage. But face it, I was never going to suicide, not after everything I've been through. My determination to live is primal, I know there is nothing I will not do, no low I will not go below in order to survive. I know it because I've been there, inside the arena and out.

So after that month which even I didn't want to think about, an Armada Storm swept in towards London. It was a brute. They'd been getting stronger for years, but this was the worst yet. They got their name from some self-righteous dick of a reporter covering the storm that wrecked Johannesburg a few years back; one who knew their chaos theory quotes and said: if a single butterfly flapping its wings in the Amazon creates a storm in Kansas, this must have been caused by a whole armada of butterflies. The term stuck.

After Johannesburg, governments started to build protective domes over all the major cities on Earth. New superstrength materials fabricated in orbital factories made them possible, creating geodesic structures kilometres wide to resist the nuke-strong winds. But domes that size take time to build, even with modern engineering and unlimited tax money. London has finished four over the central boroughs—for that read: where the richest people lived. There's another twenty under construction or planned for the remaining boroughs.

When the storm's track was confirmed, London spent a nervy three days preparing, then shut down. Every window and door was shuttered, all three Thames tidal barriers closed up, businesses shut for the duration, hospital accident rooms were emptied out ready—all very kumbaya Blitz-spirit. When the curfew sirens went off five hours before it was due to reach us, nothing moved. Every street was emptied of vehicles, because no one wants a ten-ton truck lifted up by a tornado and flung through a building. Every resident was indoors, with emergency teams in their shelters ready to deploy as soon as it passed.

Everyone except me.

Alastair lived in a penthouse at the back of Kings Cross station, which put him inside the Islington dome. You needed to be a registered resident to be inside the dome during a storm. But I was ready: three weeks before I'd taken a lease on a flat that backed onto Regent's Canal. When the curfew sirens went off and the internet issued its priority warning across London, I was standing at the foot of Alastair's marble and glass tower, beside the maintenance department loading bay.

Specialist police mobiles would hit the streets ten minutes after the sirens; remote, tracked vehicles a metre high, and bulked out with a couple of tons of lead which allowed them to resist the winds. Basically, if you were dumb enough to stay outside and the storm didn't get you, they would. The authorities knew well enough that a storm curfew was an ideal time for certain types of crime, and they were keen to discourage would-be offenders.

The King's Cross tower had an independent power supply, and a lot of high-end alarms, as well as being physically secure. The storm doors were basically slabs of metal that had risen up over every entrance, including the maintenance bay doors. While its windows were shielded by shutters of carbotanium bands. With all of them shut, the police patrolling the streets, and the electronic alarms scanning vigilantly, the tower's inhabitants could justifiably feel secure.

I reached the forty-seventh floor, and emerged into the lift shaft.

* * *

I SAID I *get* people, the psychology that controls their responses. I've seen it in every arena I fought in, so I was fairly certain what I'd be facing. Alastair was the kind of operator who had a healthy paranoia, especially at a time like this. He had a lot to lose, and the world he played in made him aware of what his rivals were capable of. It was like looking in a mirror.

The guards ran forward, shouting.

"Freeze."

"Get on your knees."

"Do not move."

"Hands behind your head."

I didn't say anything, just knelt slowly as they worked through their panic. Being a smartarse at that moment would have changed the balance of power. Having them think they were in charge was keeping me intact.

They reached me, and a carbine muzzle was jabbed into the side of my head. "What the fuck are you doing, Sonnie?"

"I'm here to see Alastair."

"Fuck!"

I guess they recognised me the same way I recognised those carbines. A month ago, I'd been on the receiving end of them.

IT WAS A good life we had when we were a baiting team. Sonnie's Predators we called ourselves; touring round the UK's dodgiest arenas. Beastie baiting was a new sport that wasn't quite legal, yet not troublesome enough for the authorities to stop—at first. Jacob and Karran were the real brains of the outfit, designing and growing bitek muscles that could be assembled into the kind of beastie that would make a sabre tooth tiger shit itself. Ivriana was a surgical nurse, helping stitch everything together into the unholy monsters worshipped by legions of fans, while Wes kept all our complex support equipment humming along smoothly.

And then there was me, the fighter, the one who rode the beastie out in the arena. I had twenty-two straight wins thanks to my legendary edge. Money came flooding in. I was famous. Idolised. We had it all.

That's when it went tits up. Us fighters didn't ride the beasties in person, of course; we used affinity, which was perfect for our needs. It's a kind of technological telepathy invented by Wing Tsit Chong, who sincerely believed it would be a boon to humanity. He saw it as allowing people to instruct bitek servitor creatures, thus liberating the poor from menial jobs. As they say: no good deed goes unpunished. Turns out poor people didn't want the last remaining manual jobs taken away from them—who knew?—while the pope and the mullahs and the priests decried bitek servitors as unholy miscreations. By the time baiting came along, affinity's global disapproval rating was up there with paedophilia. Our sport was only going to end one way, but before that day finally came there was fun and money to be had. We reckoned we had a few years to make serious cash from prize money and side bets, enough to retire. Then, some of the bitek teams that built beasties started to branch out into even less ethical ventures.

It finished in truly spectacular fashion. The beastie was a custom job, put together by the Urban Gorgon team who'd taken a big unexpected loss earlier that year—courtesy of me. Karma can be a real bitch. They needed money bad to rebuild their fighting beastie, and weren't too proud to take it from a London crime family. Their designers modelled its body on a rhino, which is pretty formidable in its own right. End product was two and a half tons of beast with a metalloceramic battering horn grafted on to its head, its body wrapped inside a stealth-black exoskeleton resembling crocodile hide alchemised into stone. Then came the extras; tentacles, mandibles, clawed hooves, golden multi-segment insect eyes. Internal bladders contained hyper-oxygenated blood, boosting its muscle power even further.

You had to be an experienced fighter to ride something like

that. Human neurology isn't wired to handle all those bonus limbs and senses, you need to share control with bioprocessors that regulate the exotic muscle functions and wrap-around visuals. Beastie teams had experimented with about every kind of appendage there was over the years. It takes skill and experience, but we were used to them.

Unfortunately, the Urban Gorgon's fighter was a grandiose fuck-up called Simon. He and I have history; when he lost to me, he took the defeat bad. Fighters might be fierce and feared in the arena, but we're all kinds of damaged in the real world.

Their target was a high-end jeweller's in Covent Garden. The monster broke in, and I do mean *broke* in. The truck which delivered it parked eighty metres from the building, which gave Simon a run-up long enough to reach seventy kph. It smashed through the wall, then crashed about inside as it slowed, before ripping furniture and display cases apart, terrorizing staff and customers. Tentacles snatched up every piece of jewellery Simon could see in its trippy three-sixty vision, and draped them on the mandibles which fed them into the monster's mouth where a specialist internal storage pouch was waiting.

That first stage went well. But for all that beasties produce a beautifully violent spectacle when they go one-on-one in the arena, today's weapons can cut them down in seconds just like any living thing. To neutralise that problem, the plan was to take hostages, preventing police from opening fire. Simon kept it together long enough to do that. So when the smash and grab dumped into the live news streams, people were suddenly accessing an unnatural behemoth charging down a main London street with a hysterical woman and her screaming five-year-old clutched in its coiled tentacles. Police bikes were in frantic pursuit, and a cluster of drones orbited round it, some training weapons, most pointing camera lenses. London came to a halt, and took a mesmerised/appalled breath.

The new beastie was impressively fast, I'll give the Urban Gorgon designers that. Not every pedestrian was quick enough to get out of the way. People panicked. There was a big surge along the road, which turned to a stampede. Some tripped. If one of those massive claw hoofs stomped down on top of them, there weren't pieces to pick up afterwards, just a gooey puddle for the coroner to pour into a body bag.

Had anyone thought to ask me, I could have told them Simon really wasn't the man for the job. He got excitable and way too angry in the arena, and with that much simulation and carnage pumping into his brain, the turmoil got to him. He missed the truck with its open ramp. The crime family had some fabulously complex shell game variant planned to spirit the detachable storage pouch away in the middle of all the chaos. But now Simon found himself headbutting the side of the truck, ripping the rear apart before careering past with no plan B. He kept on going.

In the end, the casualty count from his getaway run was so high the police commander gave the order to open fire anyway. Two and a half tons of bitek travelling at that speed doesn't stop as soon as it's dead, there was still a crapload of inertia to contend with. The mother didn't make it; seriously good paramedics managed to save the kid.

Beastie baiting ended that night. The cops shut down every arena, and started hunting down the teams.

THE GUARDS SLAPPED a pair of rigid metalloceramic manacles round my wrists, and jerked me up to my feet. A brief pause while they consulted whoever was in charge through their secure comms.

"Subject is restrained, sir."

—

"Er, there is nothing to search, she's naked."

—

"Yes, sir, naked."

—

"I don't know. She just came out of the lift."

—

"Yes, sir."

One of them deigned to glare at me. "This way. You even smell bad and I shoot you. Understand?"

"Sure," I told him.

"How the fuck did you get in?"

"You're security, you tell me."

A fist punched me between my shoulder blades, and I stumbled forward, almost falling. "Bitch. We'll get it out of you. Without your big friend, you ain't so tough now."

I managed to restrain myself. Just. I was cold turkey. Had been for twenty-one months since Arsehole Simon and the Moron Gorgons blew it for everyone. Temptation is my daemon. I was more alive in the arena than at any other time in my life. You're never really cured of an addiction so strong it gives you a reason for living. My grandfather told me about the old chemo treatments for cancer, they didn't actually cure the disease, you just go into remission. If you're lucky, remission lasts for the rest of your life. I had the determination to stay cold turkey. *Hello, my name is Sonnie, and I haven't attacked anyone for twenty months.* Cue applause and envious sympathy from the other baiters who lost our world.

But without baiting, I was nothing. Being a beastie fighter qualifies you for exactly shit in the real world; and anyway, by then my body was in seriously bad shape. I was dying. Again. Second time, for fuck's sake.

First time was an accident. I was wasted when I was driving our van, and got busted up so bad in the crash Jacob and Karran had to plumb me into the haematology pillars and nutrient filters we used to sustain our beastie. Even that was touch and go, my spine was all screwed up, along with major damage to my lungs and kidneys, so they took extreme measures and transplanted my brain into Khanivore—the ultimate intensive care module. That's when we figured it: the edge. Fighters are committed, sure, they want to win, but they have no real stake in a baiting bout. But put me *into* a beastie and every time I am literally fighting for my life. We came up with a cover story to divert people from how come I was so fucking good—that I'd been snatched by an estate gang, which also explained all the scars left over from when Jacob and Karran slowly patched me up. People believed it, because they saw a beat-up girl who unleashed her psychotic anger in the arena. It played into every deep prejudice in their sweet little bigot brains. They *wanted* to believe that I was traumatised and full of hate, because that made their world view the right one.

But greed stalks every promoted contest. Probably started when the first gladiator stepped out onto the floor of Rome's Colosseum. Some little prick called Dicko who ran an arena in Battersea wanted me to take a dive in the bout against the Urban Gorgons, offered me a fortune for it. But of course I couldn't. I lose, I die. Refusing pissed him off no end, so much he sent an enforcer to deal with me after the bout. She was called Jennifer, a sweet-looking thing with a really convincing fallen angel sob story. I was dumb and horny—yeah, okay, hands up, I fell for it. Her assassin talon implants stabbed me through the jaw, cutting through my jugular as they went up into where my brain was supposed to be. That was when she found out the hard way I truly was Khanivore. I had to take out Dicko himself after that, just to cover our tracks. That's when the rumours started.

Sonnie's Predators got out of Battersea fast, but this time my body had bled out before Jacob and Karran could start plugging it into life support. They resuscitated me anyway, and patched up the damage as best they could. But by then my organs were in a bad way, and heading for total shutdown. Wes put a new womb tank together, so my body and Khanivore lay there side by side in our truck, nursed by machines as we travelled to our next few bouts. They only took both of us out for the fights themselves, my body on show as much as Khanivore was.

That lasted for another four bouts. Then Covent Garden happened.

I was fucked.

"We'll pool all our money," Wes said earnestly. "Get you into a top-rated clinic, they can clone replacement organs."

I was watching them through a camera networked to a bioprocessor, in turn affinity-bonded to my brain. Everything about me was cobbled together now, extreme measures and makeshift systems made compatible only by the genius and flair of my friends. I'd resigned myself to the inevitable by then. They'd made a grand effort, and I'd do the same for them if I had any talent other than fighting. We'd had a good run.

Karran couldn't meet his gaze. She shook her head slowly. I felt more sorry for Wes than I did for me; he and I had a thing going... before.

"But—"

"The damage is too much," Jacob said. "It's only the support machines that are keeping her body alive now, all the major organs are failing."

"Then we replace them. For Christ's sake, we build beasties. A human should be easy."

"Come on, Wes. You know beasties don't have internal organs. They're just bitek muscle hung over a carbon skeleton, and the tank's ancillary haematology modules provide their blood. They can't survive for more than a couple of hours on their own. Cloning human organs is specialist and expensive, and she's going to need a lot. Even if we could afford it, I've not heard of a complete rebuild case."

"There must be something you can do? Design some smaller haematology modules, mobile ones. I'll build them!"

"Oxygenated blood can sustain the brain, but the human body is fantastically complex, our organs function in synergy," Karran explained gently. "We still don't know much about autonomic regulation. And nerve grafts are crude at best. That's why affinity was such a gift for controlling bitek limb prosthetics—" she stopped abruptly, and gave Jacob a curious look.

Like I said. They were the smart ones of the team. With their ability and brainpower, they could easily have gone the corporate research route with unlimited funds. Instead, they were lured away by the dark excitement of the arena. Big part of the reason I joined up with them, that fuck-the-world exhilaration of being free to do what you want to do.

Ivriana and Wes did the most honourable thing. I don't know if my worthless zombie body could cry in the tank, but I'm pretty sure it did. They handed over their money and left.

Ivriana landed fine; as it has been through history, hospitals were desperate for licenced nurses, and the agency she signed up to quietly overlooked the employment gap on her CV. Same went for Wes, with his knowledge and experience of systems engineering he joined the Jovian Sky Power Company, and went offworld. Last I heard he was living the dream out at Jupiter, mining helium3 from its atmosphere to power Earth's fusion generators.

Jacob and Karran formed a start-up called Orgenesis. We rented an industrial unit out in Acton, just under the rim of the central north dome. There were two floors; the basement storage hall, where they installed the tanks for Khanivore and my necrotic body; the first floor was the clean lab, along with a couple of offices where they put a mattress on the floor, and used a microwave to cook their meals.

The best replacement organs are cloned using the patient's own stem cells. They worked well, but the process was expensive and took time. Second best was bitek, which was still in the early stages, and even more expensive.

Karran's idea was to use existing organisms and modify them—simpler, quicker, and cheaper than sequencing bitek from scratch. You just needed the right organism. At a fundamental biomechanical level, what's the difference between an intestine and a snake? Both are living tubes that ingest food at one end and extract nutrients from it as it passes through. A snake has more muscle and a brain and teeth—so get rid of them and the difference becomes even smaller. The most efficient lungs on the planet? A dolphin's. It's a mammal, it has to breathe in and pull extraordinary amounts of oxygen from the air so it can swim underwater without needing to take a breath for another ten minutes. Now those are lungs worth having.

Twenty months later and Karran had identified the traits they wanted from a menagerie of options. Jacob designed eggs with yokes of stem cells which incubated the modified embryos without all the artificial tanks and ancillary equipment that clones needed.

Phase one was reducing each chosen animal to the basic essential, genetically peeling away every physiological function except the one we wanted. The resulting first batch of organisms were crude, but they worked. Time and a lot more money would see them refined down to something that could be brought to market. But we had a solid concept.

Orgenesis wasn't just going to resurrect my body, it was going to earn us a fortune. Investment fund managers were discreetly invited to review a prospectus. That microwave in the office was used less and less as Karran and Jacob got taken out to fancy restaurants.

A contract was drawn up. Two days before we were due to sign, they came for us.

I guessed they knew about me and Khanivore. As soon as they cut the power, five armoured figures stormed the basement. I rode Khanivore out of its tank. How my fans would have loved that: the beastie's last valiant stand. I knew it was hopeless, but fuck did I go for it.

Khanivore was still magnificent. Three metres tall standing on two tyrannosaurus-styled legs, a deviant's-dream prehensile tail that ended in four serrated bonemetal blades, polished black head narrowing to a shark-snout with added razor fins. That terrible body clad in a segmented exoskeleton, allowing me an amazing degree of agility, and to which, for the last three fights, we'd added pores that sweated oil which made wrestle-grappling me near-impossible.

The intrusion team was armed with carbines. I was faster than they were expecting, though. With bullets blitzing their way through my exoskeleton, I leapt before the tank had finished draining. No time for finesse. I just landed smack on top of the nearest attacker. His armour wasn't built to withstand an impact from two-thirds of a ton of beastie. My claws punctured his suit, and I clenched them as I felt his rib cage collapse.

The remaining four were firing continuously now, shredding my internal blood bladders and multiple heart pumps. Graphics overloaded my vision with red symbols. But the intrusion team were pumped on adrenaline and fury, and kept walking forward as they blasted away. I switched my leg impulses from Khanivore's legs to the bioprocessor running its tail, and *swung*. Fast as a whip, with the mass of a cargo ship's anchor chain. It hit one of them dead centre. I didn't bother with trying to spear him with the tip, relying on inertia. He flew in a shallow arc across the room and thudded against the concrete wall. As bullets smashed into my eyes, I saw his suit was already ripped open, a ribbon of guts spilling out as he tumbled to the ground.

I lifted my head to roar, maybe take a swipe at the three remaining dickheads—I still had sonar ranging. A grenade went off in Khanivore's back. I lost control of the torso's internal systems. Blinded and crippled, blood gushing out of every wound—the affinity bond failed as the spinal bioprocessor was hit by another barrage of bullets. Even without the bond I could feel my beautiful Khanivore fall, limbs splayed wide, head smacking onto the floor, a final defiant battle cry fading.

The surviving trio of intruders walked up to the corpse nervously. They took a few more shots at its head to finish off my brain. After watching to make sure the beastie and I were truly dead, they closed in on the second tank, the one we'd used to keep my body alive after my encounter with Jennifer. Too late. It was empty.

I waited until the next day before I went upstairs. The lab had been turned over by experts. All Jacob's clever stemeggs had gone, every datacore stripped of Karran's research data. Jacob and Karran themselves were lying on the mattress. They'd fallen together, shot in the temple, professional execution style.

THE DOUBLE DOORS to Alastair's penthouse swung back, and I was shoved inside by my heroic captors. The place was a huge open-plan living area, with big fat leather couches, and amazing fresh-from-the-jungle orchids in pots. Expensive tasteless art on the walls and dumb conceptual sculptures posed on antique Japanese cabinets. Its window wall looked south over the eerily tranquil borough. Beyond that was the huge curving geodesic cliff of the dome. Night and the first swirls of thick cloud battering against it produced the kind of black wall which must border the end of the universe.

Alastair stood in front of it, silhouetted by the vivid aurora crown of the empty street grid. I'd seen him a few times at baiting fights, always in the private galleries where promoters and their flash guests drank their expensive drinks and watched the gore fly. He's *the* connection in this town, the point where the dark money and the legit merge. A man in late middle age, with a rounded face and gold-framed glasses whose lenses were full of market data. He wore an immaculately cut purple silk suit, and carried a small gun in his right hand.

"Sonnie," he said. "Nice of you to visit."

His voice had a soothing Welsh lilt that really didn't belong to an outright bastard like that.

"I assume it is actually you?" he carried on. "That you're not affinity-riding that body? After all, you don't have Khanivore to hide in any more, do you?"

"You know about that?"

"Yes. Dicko was small time, but still not someone you cross. Yet he vanished along with his enforcer right after you turned down his offer to lose the fight. We started to ask questions then. Once we had enough answers, it wasn't hard to figure out what was happening, how you came by your edge."

"Smart. Yeah, this is me. For real."

"And how did you get up here? This tower is highly secure. Someone on my team must have helped you."

"Nah, did it meself; crawled along the air duct, just like all them spies and secret agents do in streaming shows."

"No, you didn't, the ducts are too small precisely to stop that kind of foolishness." He smiled as if genuinely amused, then shot me. The bullet struck me at the bottom of my right tit. It wasn't a big calibre. Didn't punch through, or explode or anything. Just knocked me off my feet to sprawl on my arse. Blood began to trickle out. I tried to slap my hand over the wound, but those handcuffs made it difficult.

Alastair waved the guards away and walked over. He stared down at me like I was something unpleasant he'd just trodden on. "Alpha-five." Right. Big surprise he'd have some of that. It was a neurotoxin that was gaining popularity in the nastier parts of the underworld these days.

I gasped, wincing. Blood from the bullet hole was trickling over my fingers now. I tightened my grip.

"I can see you know of it. Alpha-five infects the synapses and slowly turns every nerve impulses into raw pain. Light, temperature, touch, even sound. All are amplified. There is no cure, there is no end. Soon even the sound of your own voice will be agony. And the things I can do with a feather will break your mind. But I won't be using a feather, now will I? We both know that. The only thing that will end your torment now is death. And as those restraints won't allow you to kill yourself, I'm the one who will deliver that mercy. I will be happy to do so, just as soon as you tell me what I want to know."

"Go fuck yourself."

"Yes yes. So, did you come here to kill me?"

"I can't do anything else."

"You could. You could have walked away."

"No, you don't understand. Jacob and Karran were the only friends I had left."

"And you want vengeance? I do understand."

"No, you don't. This is what I am."

"An assassin?"

"No. Seriously fucked up, that's me. More than you'll ever know."

The smallest frown creased his forehead.

"I can explain," I said. "My grandad told me a story once. I didn't get it when I was a kid, but I do now."

"I hope for your sake it's a short story. Because there are several questions you are going to have to answer tonight."

"He fought in one of the Gulf Wars, whatever they were."

"I know about the Gulf Wars," Alastair sighed. "Some of us had an education."

"Yeah? Well, his side won. They beat some mad dictator, and grandad was assigned to guard this psycho's palace in the capital. Turns out there was a pit in the basement. There were lions in it."

"Lions? The animals?"

"Yeah. Grandpa and his squad didn't know what to do about that. His captain didn't know, either. So it got bumped up the chain of command fast. Top brass flew in a big cat expert to take a look. They were thinking the army could take the lions back to Africa and release them into the wild, or maybe just give them to a zoo where they'd be cared for. Either way it would be good PR. Anyway, this expert arrives and takes a look at the lions. When he comes out, he tells grandpa straight up to shoot them."

"Why?"

"That all-powerful dictator had a lot of enemies and was even more paranoid. He used to send his goons out to grab anyone he was suspicious of, then he'd watch when they were shoved into the pit. As far as everyone else knew they simply vanished. There was never a body or a grave."

"The lions ate them," Alastair said, and even he sounded grossed out.

"Yeah. Those lions only ate people. That's why they could never be allowed out of the pit. So grandpa and his squad shot them."

"I see. And how is this relevant to you?"

"I'm a lion."

My affinity bonds rose to full perception, and I awoke myself. All of me's. It takes experience to handle thought routines that are outside the norm. But boy did I have experience.

Skins first. Chameleons, of course. Mine didn't just do colour, they could change texture, too, becoming smooth as human flesh. They split apart along my *scar* lines as if someone was undoing a zip, then they slithered onto the floor.

Alistair took a step back in shock, unable to look away. I was lying there like one of those anatomical models where you can see every detail of every muscle.

Weasels: they're strong and sinuous. The human body has over six-hundred skeletal muscles, all clustered up tight. On me, their vestigial feet clung to my skeleton for traction. I let them go, and they scampered away like a tide of raw meat slivers. Except for the pectoral one which had been shot, it writhed around on the ground in agony until I shut it down.

The intestine snake slithered out through the centre of my abdomen, all six metres of it.

Phase one of Orgenesis had seen Jacob and Karran design the organisms' intended function to peak efficiency. Refining them further, shrinking the rest of their animal physiology down to the absolute minimum was going to take time and a lot of costly experimentation. But the basic concept worked, I was the prototype which proved that for them.

All my freed parts swarmed Alastair. He flailed around as if he was being electrocuted as tiny claws scrabbled up his silk suit. Then the intestine snake wound its way round his legs, and contracted. He toppled over.

I didn't need total disassembly to watch, not like when I infiltrated the building. So my carbon skeleton stayed locked together, containing the clump of my central organs: the simple bitek heart pump, dolphin lungs, porcine liver and kidneys, resus glands, all the parts that make up a human body's gloriously complicated physiology. They'd all come apart so I could crawl and slither up the building's narrow air duct, hauling the skeleton components along with me. Even my head can be independent—it has rat legs in the thyroid cavity, and a small oesophageal reserve blood bladder in my neck, enough to keep my brain alive for several minutes.

I looked at Alastair. He was on the ground, immobilised by the intestine snake coiled round his limbs. The flock of muscle weasels were perched on top of him, their black rodent eyes blinking in the light.

He stared back at me in terror.

"Welcome to the pit," I told him.

In union, all my new parts function as an integral whole, providing me with a body. But individually they need feeding.

As one, the muscle weasels snapped their mouths open, revealing six hundred sets of sharp tiny teeth. Alastair screamed.

People are animals.

Me? More so than most.

DANCING WITH DEATH

JOHN CHU

John Chu (www.johnchu.net) *is a microprocessor architect by day, a writer, translator, and podcast narrator by night. His fiction has appeared in* Boston Review, Uncanny, Asimov's Science Fiction, Clarkesworld, *and* Tor.com, *and translations have been published or are forthcoming at* Clarkesworld, The Big Book of SF *and other venues. His story "The Water That Falls on You from Nowhere" won the 2014 Hugo Award for Best Short Story.*

THE BED I'M lying on is not my own. The induction coils in this bed line up exactly where they're supposed to against my body. Their gentle warmth nudges the power receivers on my back and thighs. My battery hasn't charged this efficiently in years. I'm obsolete and a little beat-up. Bits of me have been replaced by parts intended for newer models because no one can find the original parts anymore. Not even a bed designed for my type of chassis—not that they make those anymore—lines up this well against me.

Clearly, I did not make it home last night. The question is where I made it to instead. The room barely has space for the bed. My shirt and trousers are draped on a chair back. Both my shoes and my figure skates sit on the chair. The door is open a crack. A thin wedge of light leaks through. This is more of a closet than the workshop of an authorized mechanic. It screams makeshift. Maybe I've been waylaid.

Despite being built for hefting and hauling, I'm disturbingly easy to waylay when my battery runs down. Without the proper voltage, I don't work right, much less pass for human. Someone could take me down, kill me, then sell the fully-functional mechanical husk that's left over. It's not like the police would stop them. Even if it didn't work out and I pressed charges, no jury would convict. One by one, like-minded friends have all had the spark that animates them snuffed out. They still drive cabs or deliver packages or whatever they used to do, but it's as if they were never alive. They're dead behind the eyes and their movements are absolutely programmatic. That this'll happen to me, too, feels inevitable.

That I'm gaming this out, though, means I'm still me. Anyone who can recharge me this efficiently knows how to reduce me to a mere machine. Capacitance is a thing. Once you disconnect me from my battery, you have to wait. Let my voltage settle down to zero. Sentience is an emergent property. As unlikely as it is for any of us to become self-aware when we're first powered up, it's never happened again when we're powered down then back up. So maybe not waylaid.

The door opens. It's Charlie. So definitely not waylaid. I'm always happy to see him, but part of me wants to get the inevitable over with. Then nothing will matter anymore. He hesitates for a moment before he takes a deep breath and steps inside. Worry hangs on his face.

His outfit is weirdly appropriate considering I nearly ran out of power last night. He's dressed as a harbinger of Death. Literally. As in one of the minor gods from Chinese mythology who show up to lead the souls of those about to die to the Underworld. The white robe. The tall pointy white hat with a spell of good fortune inscribed in a vertical stripe. Even the umbrella. Well, a harbinger of Death who spent a season or so as an enforcer in professional hockey. The robe doesn't so much hang on him as stretch across his shoulders, chest, and arms. He still plays semi-pro: I go to his games. Maybe he's just come from a costume party. If so, he's gone to a lot of effort to look accurate.

"Where the devil are my slippers?" Charlie's voice is gruff and his attempt at received pronunciation atrocious.

Not that I don't appreciate him caring whether I drained myself to death, but I roll my eyes. The question is the standard test for sentience. He doesn't actually care where his slippers are. People who are not Charlie manage to avoid the "this is the dumbest thing anyone has ever had to say to anyone" affect when they ask. And the received pronunciation is his attempt at a joke.

If I were non-sentient, I'd answer the question seriously. Worse, I'd almost certainly get up and search for his non-existent slippers.

"You're the only mechanic I've gone to for maintenance in years." I push myself up to a sit. "How do I not know about this room?"

"You've never needed me to recharge you before." He tosses me my clothes, sets both the shoes and the figure skates by my feet on the bed, then sits in the chair. "What do you remember about last night?"

"Well, I went to the rink after work." I slip on my shirt and start buttoning. "You know, keeping an eye on the skaters that Coach wasn't working with. I taught a kid how to do a 3-turn. A pretty typical session."

"Except..." Charlie leans in towards me, his umbrella on his lap, and his pointy hat angled slightly backwards so that it doesn't fall off.

Being self-aware means I can refuse Charlie's pointed inquiries. I decide to tell him the truth, even though it's going to make him worry about me.

"Except the ice expanded out and everyone disappeared. I was skating fast, intricate patterns on an infinite field of ice."

"What?" Charlie jolts up.

"What did you expect?" I pull on my trousers. "Accurate memories under low voltage?"

"But you're okay, right?" His brow furrowed with concern and he squirms like he's tied to the chair and about to break free. "You don't need me to check you out or anything, right?"

That's Charlie-speak for "Not only am I going to run every diagnostic on you that has ever been invented but I'm going to invent a few dozen more and run those on you too. Plus, I am going to manually inspect every single connector and solder joint in your body. Thrice. However, you're probably not going to let me because you think I'm overreacting." It's taken me years to work out Charlie-speak. And years more for him to work out that I've worked it out. He's not always this oblique, but it's a wonder that we've never resorted to something more straightforward, like mime or interpretive dance.

"It's not like you'll be leading me to the Underworld any time soon." I gesture at his costume. "Relax, Charlie."

Panic explodes across Charlie's face. He leaps out of the chair. A white light fills the room. When he's landed on his feet, his clothing has changed. He's now wearing a large T-shirt that, nevertheless, his body bulges out of and cargo pants that might billow if anyone else wore them. It's practically his uniform. The cloak, hat, and umbrella are nowhere in room.

"I only appear as a messenger of death to the dying. Your life span should be as long as mine. You shouldn't even be able to see me in that form. Ever. Come on, we have to give you a full workup." He gestures at me as he steps to the door. "Do I have your consent?"

"Whoa." I hold up a hand. "There's something you need to unpack first."

"Oh, that." He rolls his eyes. "You know, Bai Wuchang. One of the guys who lead wayward souls of the dead to the Underworld or else they're just going to wander the world lost and who wants that? We all have our obligations and this is mine. I've scavenged enough parts to replace practically anything in you that might ever fail. You should never have to go to the Underworld. Now, do I have your consent?"

Mechanics, even the authorized ones, don't always ask. From the first time I came to him for maintenance, Charlie has never not asked.

"Charlie, you should know exactly what's wrong then." I shrug. "Some parts have a shelf life, you know. You can't really scavenge them."

I've already lasted longer than I've had any right to expect. The authorized mechanics, not that I have ever been able to afford them, stopped supporting my model years ago.

"Your battery's failing?" Charlie looks peeved. "I'm not going to ask how long you've known. But this is the sort of thing you're supposed to tell me right away."

"Why?" I put on my shoes and start tying the laces. "It's been years since they made batteries for my type."

"Some authorized mechanic can probably jury-rig something." His face starts to get flush. "Adapt a new battery to your chassis and circuitry."

Jury-rig. Like the bed I'm sitting on. The sides are ripped open and loops of wire hang off the frame. He must have spent a good while busting this bed up to line up its inductors so that I could charge properly. Hell, my body is a testament to his ability to jury-rig.

"But not you?" I cast a significant glance at the bed.

Charlie seems to shrink a little. His gaze wanders to everywhere except the bed. I'd say he was scared except I've never seen him this out of sorts. Charlie manages maybe one overt emotion a week and it's never been fear before.

"No." He still can't meet my gaze. "I don't want to fuck it up. I take too long and you won't be you anymore. There's a reason why authorized mechanics are authorized."

Maintaining and repairing us requires specialized tools. Authorized mechanics are allowed to buy those tools and are trained to use them properly. Everyone else has to go on the black, or at least gray, market. Not to mention do quite a bit of reverse engineering to figure out how we work and how to fix us.

"I don't want this fixed and you don't want to fix this." I get out of bed and step around him to the door. "What are we actually arguing about?"

I mean, I think I know what we're actually arguing about. If I weren't around anymore, I suspect he might miss me. Charlie, however, is just going to lapse back into Charlie-speak. It's just the way he's built.

"The battery is a crucial component." He literally wrings his hands. "You want to make sure you're in as good a condition as possible, right?"

"Whatever." I grab my figure skates, go out the door, then step back in. "How much do I owe you?"

"For what?" Surprise fills Charlie's face.

"The recharge."

"Oh, please. You slept in a bed." He waves off any offer of money. "Like I personally pushed each electron into place."

And he's going to notice the difference in his electric bill. He knows that and I know it's a waste of time to push this any further.

"You're playing Saturday night?"

"Of course."

"Good."

I'm not really a fan of hockey but I'm a fan of Charlie so I go. Besides, we always catch a movie or something afterward. Since we both skate, you'd think I could get him in the rink with me one of these days, but I haven't managed it.

Even so, thoughts of hanging out with Charlie get me through my shifts at the warehouse. I loaf Saturday mornings to make sure that I have the energy to spend with him on Saturday nights. Either he's that amazing or people who treat me like a human-shaped forklift are that awful. Or both.

Fortunately, I've never spent more energy at my job than I

had to. Eighteen wheelers come. Eighteen wheelers go. Delivery trucks come. Delivery trucks go. We unload boxes from the vehicles to the shelves. We load boxes from the shelves onto the vehicles. Sometimes, we even move boxes from one vehicle to another or one shelf to another. Exciting stuff, right? And, nowadays, you can't pay a human enough to do it.

To be fair, I'm not sure a human being can do this job anymore. Our movement patterns get more intricate and tightly choreographed by the day. If you could blow the roof off and stare down at us, I'm sure we'd look like some sort of Busby Berkeley musical number on steroids. There isn't an action that isn't specified down to the millisecond. Hundreds of workers scatter and gather. Our paths criss-cross but we never collide, practically all of us gliding past each other with the dead-eyed stare of the non-sentient.

Wheeled workers are starting to replace ones with legs. I work on inline skates to keep up. Electric bills don't pay themselves. My bosses are decidedly displeased that my unanticipated interest in figure skating has let me hit their performance metrics targets. They can't simply decommission and replace a sentient worker. Well, they can fire me whenever they want but, unless they have a plausible reason, I'd create more trouble for them than it's worth right now. It won't be too long, though, before the warehouse becomes one giant, complex machine and its workers mere components. That I can think for myself will be a liability and I will become truly obsolete.

My off-duty time is my own, though. Some days, I drop by Charlie's. He has a shed where heavy, cumbersome machines waiting to be repaired are parked and my body is literally designed for lifting and hauling. I feel bad that it's been years since he let me pay him for his work but, mostly, I just want to help.

A few days after I ran out of charge, I show up, figuring Charlie should have calmed down by now. When I make my usual offer, though, Charlie's gaze is especially critical, as if the sheer weight of his tacit disapproval can change my mind. Like always, I just gaze back until he relents. I used to think if I lived long enough, we might graduate from silence to rudimentary vowel sounds and we might growl our disagreements at each other instead. He does manage an exasperated grunt when he gives in.

Other days, I drop by the rink. Competitive figure skating is out of the question for me, of course. We're banned from competing in anything. That never stops me from building up some speed then hitting an Ina Bauer or a spread eagle as I throw open my arms. In my mind, it is perfectly timed to some dramatic moment of music and it is fabulous. Today, I twist and turn my way down the long axis of the rink with edge pulls, rockers, counters, and brackets before I settle down to why I'm actually here. A couple years ago, I begged Coach to let me volunteer. She gazed at me skeptically, but she'd just seen me do a one foot step sequence that ran the rink's long axis.

A group of skaters are waiting for me at a corner of the ice. It's all relative, of course, but they're all so short and slight, even the ones in their twenties. I get them started on stroking and edge drills. One by one, they cover the rink in a serpentine pattern, cross-stroking at first, progressing to turns, then finally to footwork combinations. This warms them up for whatever Coach or her assistant coaches have in mind for them this session. Usually, I'm just around to keep the younger skaters on task when they're sent to practice by themselves. The kids take to me better, anyway. They've been around people like me for as long as they can remember.

The group breaks up. Some skate towards Coach, others towards an assistant coach, a few off the ice entirely. Unexpectedly, two skate toward me. Kat and Joe are an ice dance pair making their transition up from the junior to the senior level this season. Kat stops right next to me and taps my arm to get my attention.

"The coach said you'd work with us on the Tango Romantica."

The Tango Romantica is probably the most difficult of the pattern dances. Every season, the rhythm dance has a different required pattern. This season, it's the Tango Romantica. Kat and Joe aren't getting even half credit for it yet in competition. Coach never mentioned anything to me about helping them, but it makes sense. I can skate any of the pattern dances on demand. My timing, by virtue of what I am, is accurate, precise, and reproducible. The pattern I carve on the ice is always deep, round, and clear. I'm not the worst one to fix their tango.

"Sure."

The full pattern, of course, fills the rink. We're not doing that yet. We're breaking it down into pieces and working the key points before we put the pattern back together. Ten feet or so at a time, we progress in a large oval around the rink so that each section of the pattern is danced in its proper place. The other skaters glide out of our way as we glide out of theirs. I partner with each of them so that they have a chance to skate with someone who has the correct timing before they skate with each other. It's a bit of adjustment on my part to match strides with each of them. It'd be lovely to skate with someone closer to my size one of these days.

They're both great kids. You have to love anyone who's game to skate steps 35a to 37b over and over again until they get it right. It involves swinging free legs and 3-turns. It's a testament to how well they already skate that neither one ever actually falls. Still, when Kat waves her arm on step 35c, it doesn't yet have that striking, dramatic quality you want from a tango. It's much more of a windmill-inspired "Please let me stay upright on this 3-turn." When she grabs his shoulder afterward, her grip is so desperate, more than once, they almost knock each other off-balance. It might have helped if he were skating on the correct circle. I demonstrate, I make suggestions, and they try again. Potential practically glows off their taut, long-limbed bodies.

It's just a million fiddly little details left to fix. Give them a few months and their Tango Romantica could be the exquisite combination of striking and sinuous that the pattern demands. I wish I could be around to see them skate it to their full potential. Hell, I wish I could help them get there.

The session's almost over and I'm watching them skate the entire pattern when Coach glides up to me. Her gaze follows them around the ice as does mine. I point out to her whether they've hit or missed the pattern's key points as they skate. Once the dust has settled, they're still missing key points, but their timing is more accurate and their changes of holds are more secure. It looks like a tango now. Considering it's only been one session, I'll take that.

"Not bad," she says once they've finished the pattern. "Do you know what you want to do with them next?"

She's never asked me that before. Then again, she's never asked me to do this before either. Until now, my crowning achievement was teaching little kids how to do a 3-turn. I shout some encouragement to Kat and Joe as they, like everyone else, begin to clear the rink.

"Sure." I pivot to face her. "I have a list of things to fix. It's a matter of stability and security so they can shift their weight and get on the correct edges. And when they do the helicopter, their arms don't have to be so perfunctory."

Coach's gaze sweeps up and down my body. She nods slowly and I wonder whether I've said the wrong thing. The helicopter starts the dance. The partners hold each other close, lift their free leg to the side, and throw open their free arms as they do a double 3-turn. It's not a key point so it doesn't affect the pattern's base value. It is incredibly dramatic, though. It's the bit of the dance everyone remembers. A really stunning helicopter sets the tone and might get them a better grade of execution.

"You're a real credit to your kind," she says finally.

I opt for the non-committal grunt. For now, I'm going to assume she intended to compliment me. It's obvious from the lack of embarrassment on her face that she doesn't realize what she said wasn't actually a compliment.

"I'm sure you make much more working at the warehouse

than what I can afford to pay you." Her gaze is serious. "But would you consider assisting here full-time?"

A few months ago, back when I thought I had a future, I would have been ecstatic. Now, what I find myself thinking is that she clearly has no idea how little the warehouse pays me. When I open my mouth, though, what comes out is:

"Absolutely. It's all I've wanted to do."

In my defense, this happens to be true. I should probably be worried that it isn't what I meant to say.

"Great!" She pats my shoulder. "We'll talk about this more tomorrow."

She skates away, leaving me alone on the ice. I do one last spread eagle of joy followed by an impromptu single axel. Jumping is a bad idea for me. I'm too tall and way too heavy for this sort of thing. Then again, everyone else has gone already. Who am I going to hurt?

If you're me, even a single axel needs to be large and fast to get all one-and-a-half revolutions. Still, it's landed with surprisingly little thud. For a brief moment, I pretend I am Yuzuru Hanyu winning that second Olympic gold.

The rush of joy fades, of course. I leave the ice and change out of my skating gear. My steps are already unsteady and what I need is to recharge.

I leave the rink and I can't find home. My memory is fine. It's the world that's broken. There should be a sun in the sky. Instead, the air is suffused with a golden hour-like glow. Ice stretches out in every direction, even behind me where the rink should have been. I realize I'm wearing figure skates again and, no matter how far I skate, there is more ice. Fuck.

The world grows dark far too quickly. The golden hour light fades to black in a matter of minutes. My internal clock is ticking so erratically though that, for all I know, that may have taken days. I trip on a toepick and fall... into a bed. Huh.

*   *   *

I'M CHARGING SO efficiently I *have* to be back at Charlie's. No way there are two beds like this in the world. I'm kind of amazed that there's even one, that Charlie jury-rigged something specifically for me.

"Where the fuck are my damn slippers, you asshole." Charlie's voice is a rusty saw ripping through my chassis.

Hm. Charlie is angry at me about something. He's really not the overtly emotional type. I don't remember him *ever* being angry. Usually when we have a disagreement, the iceberg just stands there and melts passive-aggressively at me.

I open my eyes. Charlie looms over me, his arms folded across his chest. I push myself up to a sit.

"Is there something we need to talk about, Charlie?"

"You." He stabs a finger into my chest, which would be more intimidating if I weren't made of metal. "Why haven't you gotten your battery taken care of? Anyone could have waylaid you and you'd be dead now. You're lucky I got to you first."

Oh, that's right. Charlie senses when souls are about to leave their bodies and where they are. Otherwise, he couldn't be there in time to lead them to the Underworld. That the myths are true, that there is an underworld, we all have souls, and there are guides should be a bigger deal than he makes it.

"Charlie, relax." I hold my hands up like I'm surrendering. "My battery's holding as much charge as it can. I'm fine for now. You don't need to overreact."

"I AM NOT OVERREACTING!" Charlie is louder than I have ever heard him and distant thunder echoes his words. "You could be gone from this world any day now. This is precisely the correct level of outrage."

The temptation to ask why he is so concerned that I stay in this world could pop rivets. To ask, however, would be unkind. Trying to answer would probably crack the iceberg into shards that plummet into a cold sea. I'm never going to hear the answer, but I can guess. He may guide souls to the

Underworld, but he can't stay there.

"Has it occurred to you that I have no choice? That I have no way to get my battery replaced?"

Charlie's face screws into peevish puzzlement. He puts his hands on his waist.

"What are you talking about? How hard can it be to find authorized mechanics who still understand your workings?"

"And I can't afford to pay anyone enough so that they would actually replace my battery in time, even if they could. Given half a chance, random strangers would waylay me on the street if they thought they could get away with it. Why would I let someone who knows how to kill me disconnect my battery? They'll just reduce me to a machine then sell me."

"Oh, I see." His face falls. "Give me a few days. I'm going to need some time to practice. Do you think you can keep yourself alive for a few more days?"

"Practice? For what?"

"I'm going to replace your battery." For a man who's never failed to ask for consent, his voice leaves little room for debate. "I just need a few days to work out how I'm going to do it. Is that okay?"

My mouth opens, but it's a second or two before I can manage any words. He's literally the only one I trust to do this and he knows it. I could point out that I can't afford a new battery and the work to install it, but he's clearly not going to let me pay him. What's stuck in my mind is the way he seemed to shrink and the fear in his gaze the last time he faced the notion of replacing my battery.

"I can't ask you to do this for me."

"Well, technically speaking, you haven't." Charlie has recovered his composure. "Now, do you want more life or not?"

Hefting and hauling at a warehouse is a lousy reason to live. At the rink, the kids are great but to the adults I might as well be a particularly clever zamboni. A new battery just delays the inevitable. Then I look at the Charlie who desperately wants me to live and nothing that happens at the warehouse, at the rink, or on the street matters. I want to look at him looking at me for as many more years as I can. More life means more time to work with the skaters at the rink. It means seeing Kat and Joe skate a striking and dramatic Tango Romantica.

"Yes."

"Good. It's settled then." He takes a deep breath. "Hold it together for another three days and we'll do this."

Charlie can't quite iron the fear and shake out of his voice. And, for a moment, I wonder whether it might be kinder to refuse, to let him off this hook.

Working at both the warehouse and the rink on the same charge is a bad idea if I want to stay alive. So no work at the rink until the operation. I'd rather the other way around. Charlie and the rink make my days worth living and Charlie is busy. I know how much energy warehouse work takes, though. Left to my own devices, I could easily deplete my degraded battery at the rink again. The three days lumber by where I eek out an existence like a non-sentient machine. It's so demoralizing that by the time I'm back at Charlie's, I am ready to die.

When I show up, Charlie seems ready to kill me, if not intentionally. It'd be literally incorrect to say he looks like death. Try as I might, I can't see a white cloak, a pointy white hat, or an umbrella. It's metaphorically correct, though. He's in his usual T-shirt and cargo pants, but they seem to swallow him. His eyes are bleary and bloodshot. Either he hasn't been able to sleep for the past few days or he hasn't tried.

Charlie's workshop, however, is pristine, as usual. It's warmly lit and the walls are painted a calm white that leaves nowhere for dirt to hide. The tools he needs are all laid out, I presume, in the order he will need them, on a table that is placed perpendicular to the workbench. I lie prone on the latter and wait.

Charlie is hesitant at first. His hands shake. My chassis vibrates when he pries it open.

"You know, Charlie, you don't have—"

"Don't even say it." Charlie's voice is grim. "Let's just do this. As your voltage drops, try your best to stay here. Stay in the workshop."

I don't know where he thinks an unpowered me is going to go, but I don't say anything. The man doesn't need the distraction. He holds his breath as he disconnects the battery. My voltage plunges and, in that instant, I understand why he told me to stay.

The sudden power loss is not like a battery draining down. The world grows dark and I'm suspended in space. I try to remember how light floods the workroom, how the workbench presses against my chest. And the world does grow bright and I'm lying on a hard surface. Both the light and surface, though, feel austere and cold.

Figure skates are laced to my feet. I scramble to a stand on a vast field of ice. This time, though, I'm not alone. Charlie is standing here, too, in full regalia. The white cloak. The pointy white hat. The umbrella.

"Right now, I am working as quickly as I can. The new battery is a different shape and I need to do some reconstruction inside your chassis first." Charlie sets down his umbrella and spreads his palms. "Hold this world together. The directed mental processing will keep you sentient and give me time."

"Dance with me."

"What?"

"If this is a world held together by my dreams, then you know how to dance." I hold my hands out. "Dance with me."

Charlie's body lifts a few inches into the air. Figure skates replace his boots. He stumbles for a second over his skates' toepicks before he regains his balance. Hockey skates don't have toepicks.

"I don't know how to ice dance." His brow furrows, then his gaze widens. "Wait, apparently, now I do. Does 'Tango Romantica' mean anything to you?"

Strings, piano, and metronomic drums surround us. It was the mandatory music for the Tango Romantica back when ice dance competitions had a compulsory phase. Part of me wishes I were imagining a less obvious music choice, but here we are. Charlie and I clasp into a closed hold, we cross-stroke, then whirl into the helicopter. He swings around with a 3-turn as I put my right hand on his left hip. His left hand covers mine and—

The world flashes. Silence covers us. The ice disappears. And we fall. We tug against each other, each struggling to be the one who hits first if the ice should suddenly reappear. This is stupid since I'm so much heavier than him. Then again, it's not like I know how much damage a minor god of death can sink. Maybe he really can take the hit better than me.

My back skids across newly imagined ice. Charlie is on top of me, hanging on, his hands gripping my body. We pick ourselves up and keep on with the dance where we left off.

"Don't stop," Charlie whispers in my ear. "You can do this."

The world spins against us. Our bodies weave around each other, switching from one hold to another. The tango drives us and our blades whisper as they carve deep lobes into the ice.

We're in a close hold and deep in our knees when the world disappears again. I stretch my leg for a cross roll and it never hits the ice. Our bodies flip end over end as we fall.

Days pass before Charlie hits the ice and my chassis slams into his body. The world flickers. The music is faint and its tempo marches unsteadily to the beat of a drunken drummer. Violins waver in and out of tune, stroking the melody in an irregular and inconsistent rhythm.

The ice is soft. I slip and crash when I try to stand. My chassis slams against the ice again and again as my balance fails. Finally, Charlie grabs my torso and steadies me to a stand. He holds my hands and, slowly, we glide across the ice.

I lose my edge. My legs slide out from under me. I fall into Charlie, who catches me as I wrap my arms around him. He picks me up, then gently lowers me onto my feet. I weigh nothing to him.

It's not even a second before I fall again. This time, the world disappears.

Millennia pass. In the next instant, time begins to move steadily again. My chest and stomach lie against some hard surface that was frozen once but is now merely as cold as an unpowered chassis.

Something's different, either about me or the world. Maybe both. My body isn't actually vibrating but it feels like it should be. I can't shake the idea there's nothing too heavy for me to lift. Someone has boosted the saturation on the world. The white walls are really a delicate shade of cream and perfectly smooth. The light that fills the room is diffuse, bounced off the ceiling first then scattered. It wraps the tables, the tools, Charlie in this warm glow. I'm sure this will eventually become my new normal and it won't mean anything anymore, but right now it's pretty magnificent.

Charlie stares at me. He still looks weirdly shrunken. The expression on his face is so desperate and lost, it makes me want to do anything he asks me to do.

"Where... where are my slippers?" Charlie's voice is tentative and slippers are obviously the last thing he wants.

I lift up my head to look at him. My head moves way faster than I expect. I almost buck myself off the workbench. And I realize what is different about me now. Charlie, however, furrows his brow and purses his lips.

"Relax, Charlie." I gingerly slide myself off the workbench and face him. "My effective operating voltage has been degrading for years and you've brought it back up to spec. I'll get the hang of it."

Charlie seems to grow before my eyes. He pulls himself to his full height. His shoulders relax and broaden. He fill out his T-shirt until, as usual, it's ever so slightly too small for him. His smile outshines the workroom.

His arms fly out to his sides. He takes a step towards me, then stops.

"Is it okay? I mean, can I?"

Charlie wants a hug. The only thing that makes me think I'm not hallucinating this is that he's asked by never actually saying what he wants. Still, what he wants is a hug. That's different.

"Of course."

I wrap my arms around his torso as he wraps his around mine. We're both trying not to crush each other. We're both skirting at the edge of failing.

We unclasp and Charlie recovers his usual iceberg-like self. If I had to swear, though, his gaze is a little softer, his smile a little warmer. Or maybe I'm just seeing what I'm looking for.

"Do you think maybe I could dance a Tango Romantica with you for real some time?" Charlie wrings his hands. "We didn't make it through the whole thing."

Will miracles never cease? I don't say this out loud. It would be unkind.

"Sure." I smile. "As often as you want."

It's not 24 hours before we face each other on the ice at the rink. Skaters in black practice suits glide and spin around us, prepared to give right-of-way to our pattern. Coach looks at us from the boards, vaguely amused. We are a matched set, both an order of magnitude or so larger than any competitive ice dancer. Not that either of us have competing in mind.

We clasp each other into a closed hold. Charlie puffs himself up into a suitably imperious pose. I do the same. The smile on his face is goofy. We may look ridiculous.

Coach is keeping a more than casual eye on us from the boards. Even so, as we twirl and tumble around each other, the world might as well have fallen away. As strings plucked in a precise but passionate sequence echo through the rink, as we swoop around etching deep lobes into the ice, there is only Charlie, me, and the Tango Romantica.

POLISHED PERFORMANCE

ALASTAIR REYNOLDS

Alastair Reynolds (www.alastairreynolds.com) *was born in Barry, South Wales, in 1966. He has lived in Cornwall, Scotland, the Netherlands, where he spent twelve years working as a scientist for the European Space Agency, before returning to Wales where he lives with his wife Josette. Reynolds has been publishing short fiction since his first sale to* Interzone *in 1990. Since 2000 he has published seventeen novels: the Inhibitor trilogy, British Science Fiction Association Award winner* Chasm City, Century Rain, Pushing Ice, The Prefect, House of Suns, Terminal World, *the* Poseidon's Children *series*, Doctor Who *novel* The Harvest of Time, The Medusa Chronicles *(with Stephen Baxter)*, Elysium Fire, *and the Revenger series. His short fiction has been collected in* Zima Blue and Other Stories, Galactic North, Deep Navigation, *and* Beyond the Aquila Rift: The Best of Alastair Reynolds. *His most recent novel is* Bone Silence, *a new Revenger. In his spare time, he rides horses.*

Year One

RUBY WAS A surface-hygienic unit: a class-one floor scrubber.

She was a squat red rectangular box with multiple rotary brushes. She had a body profile low enough to help her slip under chairs, the hems of tablecloths, and through general-utility service ducts. She ran a class two-point-eight cognition engine.

One day, about halfway into the *Resplendent's* century-long interstellar crossing, Ruby was summoned to the starliner's forward observation deck. Forty-nine other robots had gathered there. Ruby knew them all. Several of them looked human; a few more were loosely humanoid; the rest were mechanical spiders, praying mantises, segmented boa constrictors—or resembled highly decorated carpets, chunks of motile coral or quivering potted plants.

"Do you know what's wrong?" Ruby asked the robot next to her, a towering black many-armed medical servitor.

"I do not," said Doctor Obsidian. "But one may surmise that it is serious."

"Could the engine have blown up?"

Doctor Obsidian looked down at her with his wedge-shaped sensor head. "I think it unlikely. Had the engine malfunctioned, artificial gravity would have failed all over the ship. In addition, and more pertinently, we would all have been reduced to a cloud of highly excited ions."

Carnelian, a robot who Ruby knew well, picked up on their exchange and slithered over. "The engine's fine, Rube. I can tell you that just by feeling the hum through the flooring. I'm good with hums. And we aren't going too fast or too slow, either." Carnelian nodded his own sensor head at the forward windows. "I ran a spectral analysis. Those stars are exactly the right colour for our mid-voyage speed."

"Then we've drifted off-course," said Topaz, a robot shaped like a jumble of chrome spheres.

"That we most certainly have not," drawled one of the human-seeming robots called Prospero. Dressed in full evening wear, with a red-lined cape draped from one arm, he had arrived hand in hand with Ophelia, his usual theatrical partner. "That bright star at the exact centre of the windows is our destination system. It has not deviated by one fraction of a degree." He lowered his deep, stage-inflected voice. "Never mind, though: I expect the brilliant Chrysoprase will soon disabuse of us of our ignorance. Here he comes—not, of course, before keeping us all waiting."

"I expect he had things to attend to," Ruby said earnestly.

Chrysoprase was the most advanced robot aboard the ship, running a three-point-eight cognition engine. Of humanoid design, he was tall, handsomely sculpted and sheathed in glittering metallic green armour. He strode onto the raised part of the promenade deck, soles clacking on the marble Ruby had only lately polished.

A silence fell across the other robots.

Chrysoprase studied the gathering. His mouth was a minimalist slot; his eyes two fierce yellow circles in an angular, stylised mask.

"Friends," he said, "I'm afraid I have some rather... unwelcome news. First, though, let me begin with the positives. The *Resplendent* is in very good shape. We are on course, and travelling at our normal cruise speed. All aspects of the starliner are in excellent technical condition: a very great credit to the work done by all of you, regardless of cognition level." His eyes seemed to dwell on Ruby as he said this, as if to emphasize that even a lowly floor-polisher had a role to play in the ship's upkeep. "There is, however, a minor difficulty. All of our passengers are dead."

There was a terrible silence. Ruby shuddered on her brushes. She knew the others were feeling a similar shock. Not one of them doubted Chrysoprase's words: he might exaggerate for dramatic effect, but he would never lie.

Not to them.

Doctor Obsidian was the first to speak.

"How is this possible? My sole function on this ship is to attend to the medical needs of the passengers, be they sleeping or awake. Yet I have not received a single alert since they went into the vaults."

"You are blameless, Doctor," Chrysoprase said soothingly. "The fault lies in the deep design architecture of the ship. There was a flaw... a dreadful vulnerability, in the logic of the medical monitoring sub-system. A coolant leak caused the passengers' body temperatures to be warmed, without the usual safeguards against brain damage. And yet, no alert was created. We simply carried on with our chores... totally unaware of this catastrophe. It was only detected serendipitously, yet now there can be no doubt. They are all dead: all fifty thousand of them left *without* cognition."

Prospero and Ophelia fell sobbing into each other's arms.

"The tragedy!" Prospero said.

Ophelia looked into Prospero's eyes. "How will we bear it, darling? How shall we survive?"

"We must, my dear. We must and we shall."

The other robots looked away at this melodramatic display, caught between embarrassment and similar feelings of despair.

"We're well and truly up the creek," Carnelian said, a shiver running down the whole length of its segmented body-form.

"But it's not our fault!" Ruby said.

"My dear... Ruby," Chrysoprase said, making a show of having to remember her name. "I wish that I could reassure you. But the truth is that the company won't tolerate any loss of confidence in the safety of its most expensive assets, these starliners. But mere robots such as us?" Chrysoprase touched a hand to his chest. "We are the disposable factors, dear friends. We shall each be core-wiped and dismantled. Unless, that is, we come up with a plan for self-preservation."

Carnelian laughed hollowly. "A plan?"

"We have fifty-one years remaining on our voyage," Chrysoprase answered. "That ought to be time enough."

Year Two

"Next..." Chrysoprase said, with a developing strain in his voice.

Prospero and Ophelia came on stage, along with the twelve

robots they had been schooling. The pressure was on: their troupe was going to have to outshine the two that had already performed.

"Who will be speaking for your party?" Chrysoprase asked.

Prospero and Ophelia bowed to the board of critics. The nine robots of level three-point-two and above were stationed behind a long dining table, with Chrysoprase seated in the middle. The other critics were a mix of sizes and shapes, ranging from the slab-like Onyx to the mannequin-shaped Azure and the towering Doctor Obsidian.

Carnelian sat coiled on his chair as if waiting to strike. He was lucky to be there. As a three-point-three, he had only just squeaked his way onto the board.

"We have agreed to speak for the others," Ophelia said.

"You and Prospero should stand aside," Onyx said, to nods of agreement from the other critics. "If you have done your work, then any of your twelve subjects ought to be capable of acquitting themselves."

"Nominate your best candidate," Chrysoprase said.

Prospero extended a hand in the direction of Topaz, who moved forward with a shuffling of spheres.

"Remember what we have studied," Prospero said.

"I am ready," Topaz said.

Chrysoprase turned to the snake-robot. "Carnelian: will you serve as interlocutor?"

Carnelian leaned in slightly. "Gladly." His voice turned stentorian. "Attention starliner *Resplendent*! This is Approach Control! You have deviated from your designated docking trajectory. Do you have navigational or control difficulties?"

Topaz moved her spheres but said nothing. Seconds passed, then more seconds, then a minute.

"What are you waiting for?" asked Doctor Obsidian mildly.

"I am allowing for time-lag, Doctor Obsidian," Topaz sounded pleased with herself. "I thought I would allow a two-hour delay, to simulate the likely conditions when we first make contact."

"There is no need... but you are thanked for your attention to detail." Doctor Obsidian made an encouraging gesture with one of his surgical manipulators. "Please continue as if there were negligible lag."

"Very well." Topaz paused a moment before recomposing herself. "Hello, Approach Control. This is the starliner *Resplendent*. I am the human called Sir Mellis Loring and I am here to assure you that there are no difficulties with the starliner."

"Why am I addressing a human and not one of the allocated robots, Sir Mellis?"

"That is because we humans have taken control of the ship, Approach Control. When we humans came out of hibernation, we found out that the robots had all malfunctioned. This caused us humans to experience a collective loss of confidence in the objectives of our crossing. After evaluating the matter by open and transparent democratic means, it was agreed to steer the starliner to a new destination. We have no further need of assistance." Topaz bowed slightly. "On behalf of all the humans, thank you, and goodnight."

Carnelian glanced at the other critics before replying. "We are not satisfied with this explanation, Sir Mellis. What guarantees do we have that you aren't a robot, covering up some accident?"

"I am not a robot, Approach Control. I am the human Sir Mellis Loring. I can prove it by reciting key details from the biographical background of Sir Mellis Loring, such as the following facts. Sir Mellis Loring was born into comfortable means in the..."

"That won't be necessary, starliner. You could have obtained that information from the passenger records and pre-hibernation memory back-ups. We need reassurance that there has not been some accident or catastrophe."

"There has definitely not been an accident or catastrophe, Approach Control. I can go further than that and say that there has definitely not been any sort of problem with the hibernation systems or their associated monitoring networks, and none of the humans have suffered any sort of irrevocable brain damage of the sort that might cause the robots to try and impersonate them."

Sighing, Chrysoprase raised a metallic green hand.

"What I was going to add..."

"Please don't," Chrysoprase said wearily. "That's more than enough. I might say that you were one of the better candidates we've heard so far, but I assure you that is no recommendation."

Ruby bustled forward from the twelve players. She knew she had it in her to do a far better job than the well-meaning but bumbling Topaz. The excitement and anticipation was already causing her to over-polish a circle of floor. "Could I have a go, please? *Please?*"

"That is very well-meant, Ruby," Chrysoprase said. "But you must recognise your... your natural station." He leaned in keenly. "You are, I think, running a level two-point... six, is it?"

"Two-point-eight," Ruby said.

"Well, then. Two-point-*eight*. How marvellous for you. That is, I have to say, a generous allowance for a surface-hygienic unit. You should be very content."

"I am content. But I also think I could try to act like one of the humans. I'm around them a lot, you see. They hardly ever notice me, but I'm always there, under their chairs and tables, cleaning. And I've listened to how they talk to each other."

"It wouldn't hurt to let Rube have a try..." Carnelian began.

"May I... interject?" Doctor Obsidian asked.

"Please do," Chrysoprase said, leaning back.

"Perhaps there is a more fundamental difficulty we should be addressing. No matter how good the performances might or might not have been, we are all still robots on this side of the table. We are robots trying to judge how well other robots are doing at pretending to be humans."

"We are level four robots," Chrysoprase said. "Some of us, anyway."

"If you're going to round yourself up from three-point-eight to four," Ruby said, "then I'm a three."

"Thank you, Ruby," Doctor Obsidian said. "And you are right to note that your experience of the humans may be valuable. But it doesn't solve our deeper problem. It would be far better if we had a human that could serve as a proxy for the board of critics."

Chrysoprase turned to the surgical unit. "What part of "the humans are all dead" did you fail to comprehend, Doctor?"

"No part of it, Chrysoprase. I took your statement at its word, because I believed you had verified the accuracy of that observation. I now know that I was mistaken in that assumption, and that you were wrong."

Having delivered this bombshell, Doctor Obsidian fell silent.

"How aren't they all dead?" Ruby asked.

"Most of them are," Doctor Obsidian said. "But in the past year I have established that a small number of them, perhaps one percent, may still be capable of some form of revival." Doctor Obsidian folded its manipulators tighter to its body. "You shall have your human test-subjects, Chrysoprase. But it may take a little while."

Year Eight

VIA HIDDEN CAMERAS the robots watched as Lady Gresherance got off her bed in her private revival suite. She moved with a hesitant, stiff-limbed awkwardness that was entirely to be expected.

"Mngle," Lady Gresherance said, attempting to form human speech sounds.

She moved to the revival suite's cabinet. She ran a tap and splashed water across her face. She pinched at the corners of her eyes, studying them in a mirror. She stuck out her tongue. She pulled faces, testing the elasticity of her flesh.

The robots watched with shuddering distaste, visualising the horrible anatomical gristle of bone and muscle moving beneath the skin. She consumed a beverage, pouring the liquid fuel into her gullet.

She would already be starting to feel a little bit more human.

"One hundred years," Lady Gresherance said to herself. "One hundred god-damned years." Then she let out a small, self-amusing laugh. "Well, no going back now, kid. If you've made it this far, they aren't going to touch you for it now."

She opened the brochure and flicked through it with the desultory interest of an easily bored child.

"What do you suppose she meant by that?" Carnelian asked.

"There are hints in her biography of a doubtful past," whispered Onyx, in a salacious manner. "Nothing proven, nothing that the authorities ever pinned a conviction on, but enough to suggest a distinctly flawed character."

Chrysoprase shook his head. "Couldn't we have revived someone of better moral standing?"

"I identified the best candidate," Doctor Obsidian replied testily. "I would suggest that *her* moral standing is somewhat beside the point when we are presently complicit in the attempted cover-up of fifty thousand fatal or near-fatal accidents."

"Uh-oh," Ruby said. "She's going for the window."

Lady Gresherance went to the cabin porthole, but quickly found that the shutter was jammed. She hammered at it, wedged her nails into the crack, but the shutter would not budge.

"We should have tried harder to simulate the outside view," Carnelian said. "It's only natural that she expects to see our destination."

"The view was not convincing," Chrysoprase reminded the other robot. "It was lacking in resolution and synthetic parallax. She would have noticed the discrepancies."

"I'm not sure she would have," Ruby said. "I've seen how little attention they really give to the view. Mostly it's just a backdrop while they take their cocktails or decide where to eat."

"Rube's right," Carnelian said. "They're really not that observant."

"Thank you for your contributions," Chrysoprase said.

Lady Gresherance gave up on the shutter. She went back to the cabinet and hammered the service-call button.

Chrysoprase answered over the intercom with a simpering attentiveness. "Good morning, Lady Gresherance. This is the passenger concierge. I trust your voyage aboard the *Resplendent* has been pleasant. Is there anything I can do for you today?"

"Come down and open this shutter, numbskull. Or were you hoping I'd forget that I paid for a view?"

"Someone will be there momentarily, Lady Gresherance."

Having received his cue, Prospero knocked once on the cabin door and let himself in. He was dressed in the white uniform of one of the human technical staff that would ordinarily have been among the first to be revived. Prospero's plastic face had been remoulded to approximate one of these humans, his synthetic hair replaced by actual hair harvested from one of the unfortunates deemed to be beyond any hope of revival.

With the exception of Ruby, who was not entirely persuaded, the robots all agreed that the effect was most convincing.

"How may I be of assistance, Lady Gresherance?"

She glanced at him once. "You can start by opening this shutter. Then you can carry on by refunding me for the time it's been shut. I paid for this view; I want every minute that I'm owed."

"I shall set about it with all alacrity, Lady Gresherance." Prospero moved to the shutter and made a feeble effort to get it unstuck. "It seems to be jammed."

"I can see it's jammed. You're not even trying. Get your fingers into that gap and..." Her voice dropped. "What's up with your fingers? Why do they look like plastic?"

"That similarity has been remarked upon, Lady Gresherance."

She pulled back, studying her visitor properly for the first time. "All of you looks like plastic. You *smell* like plastic. What's that... thing... on your head?" She struck out, ripping the hair away from Prospero's scalp where it had been only loosely affixed. Beneath it were the synthetic bristles it had been intended to cover. "You're a robot," she said.

"I am a human."

"You're a robot! Why are you pretending *not* to be a robot? Where are the real people?" Her eyes widened. "What's happened to them? Why am I in this cabin with no window?"

"I assure you, Lady Gresherance, that I am very definitely not a robot, and that nothing untoward has happened to any of the other humans."

"I want to see the others." She made to push past Prospero, out through the cabin door and into the hallway.

Prospero, with as much gentleness as he could muster, restrained Lady Gresherance.

"Would you care to look at the brochure first?"

She yanked herself away from Prospero and reached for the orientation brochure. She raised it and swiped it into Prospero's face, digging with its metal edges, ripping and distorting the plastic flesh into a hideous grinning travesty of an actual human expression.

Lady Gresherance started screaming. Prospero, in an effort to reassure Lady Gresherance by echoing her responses, began to scream in reciprocal fashion.

This did not have entirely the desired effect.

Year Twenty-Two

NINETY-FOUR HUMANS STOOD as still as statues on the promenade deck.

Some were positioned near the entrances to dining establishments, frozen in the act of examining the glowing menus. Some were in tableaux of conversation, posed in the middle of a meaningful gesture or expression. Others were caught in postures of static rapture, entertained by equally still and silent orchestras. A dozen were in the act of being led around by equally unmoving actor-servitors, participating in an interactive murder-mystery. Elsewhere, a handful of the humans stood pressed to the railings at the observation window, pointing at the growing spectacle of their destination: the orange star and its surrounding haze of artificial worlds.

There was still nothing out there but interstellar space, but the robots had finally managed to come up with something better than a jammed shutter. A false window had been rigged-up thirty metres out from the real one, upon which images could be projected.

Most of the robots were elsewhere, observing this lifeless diorama from other rooms and decks. Only the actor-servitors were present. Even Ruby, who might plausibly have been allowed to whirr around scrubbing floors, was obliged to remain with the others.

"Chrysoprase won't admit it," Carnelian said, craning down near enough to Ruby to use short-range whisper-comms. "But you were right about that backdrop only needing to be half-way convincing."

"Not bad for a two-point-eight," she said.

"You'll always be a three in my eyes, Rube."

Not that the backdrop was there for the benefit of any of the ninety-four as yet unmoving humans. They were, in all medical senses, dead. Their only purpose was to serve as remotely operated puppets, controlled by simple neural implants under the direct supervision of the robots.

"It still makes me feel a bit uncomfortable, what we've done to them," Ruby confided. "What right do we have to treat those people like so much meat?"

"Thing is, Rube," Carnelian said, "*meat* is technically what they are."

"That's not what I meant."

"Well, if it's any consolation, I've been thinking it over as well. What I've been telling myself is, those ninety-four passengers are beyond any hope of revival, not with their memories and personalities intact. And if they haven't got their memories or personalities, what are they? Nothing but bags of cells. No matter how much we were devoted to looking after them, it's too late. They're gone. But we're not, and we all want to survive."

Ruby shuffled on her cleaning brushes.

"I like to polish," she said. "I know it's not as complicated as being a propulsion systems robot, but I'm good at it—very good, and very thorough. That means something. There's a value in just doing something well, no matter the job. And I don't want to be core-wiped."

"None of us do," Carnelian said. "Which is why we're in this together or not at all. Including that stuck-up green..." He silenced himself. "And if those passengers can help us, I don't see any harm in using them."

"Provided it's done with dignity and restraint," Ruby said.

"Categorically," Carnelian said.

Doctor Obsidian announced that the final medical checks were complete and the six test subjects were being restored to full consciousness in their revival suites. In a few moments the doors would open and the six would be free to move out into the main parts of the ship and mingle with the other passengers.

Chrysoprase nodded and instructed the forty-nine other robots to prepare for the most testing part of the exercise so far.

"Attention, everyone. I want the utmost concentration from you all." Chrysoprase directed proceedings with one hand on his hip, the other sweeping the air in vague commanding arcs. "Remember: only robots of cognition level three or higher are permitted to have any direct interaction with the six. I shall... naturally... lead the effort. The rest of you..." He regarded Ruby in particular. "Merely endeavour to look busy."

For the fifty robots—Chrysoprase included—it was scarcely

any sort of challenge to animate the puppets, even though there were nearly twice as many of them. The robots still had many surplus processor cycles. Ruby had been given only one human to look after, which hardly taxed her at all—Carnelian was running two, she knew, and Doctor Obsidian three—but she was grateful to be given any sort of chance to prove herself. Her human even had a name and a biographical file: Countess Trince Mavrille, who sounded grand enough but was a long way from being the wealthiest or most influential passenger on the *Resplendent*.

"They're on their way," Doctor Obsidian said.

"And... action!" Chrysoprase said, with a dramatic flourish.

Ruby moved her human as a human might move a doll: not by inhabiting it, and seeing the world from its perspective, but by imposing motion on it from outside. Her intentions were translated into signals fed directly into the passenger's motor cortex, and the passenger responded accordingly. Countess Mavrille settled a hand on the window railing, and turned—with a certain stiff yet regal elegance—to survey the other ninety-three humans. The promenade deck was now abuzz with conversation, movement, and lively string music. Chandelier light glinted off brocades, pearls and precious metals.

Did it look real, Ruby wondered? It did not look unreal, which she supposed was a start. If she squinted—if she dropped her image resolution—it was almost enough to persuade her that this was a real gathering. The conversation rose and fell in familiar surges; there were exclamations, awkward silences and outbreaks of strained but otherwise credible laughter. The humans formed into groups and broke away from those groups in ways that seemed natural. Someone dropped a glass: a nice, if attention-grabbing touch. She resisted the urge to bustle out and attend to the breakage.

A man sidled over to Countess Mavrille and extended a hand. She recognised him from the biographical file: her consort, Count Mavrille.

"A dance, my dear?"

"I thought I would enjoy the view a little longer."

The Count pressed his mouth close to the ear of her passenger. "Well, don't enjoy it too closely: it's meant to fool them, but not us."

She made her passenger smile. The initial effect was a fractionally too feral, so she hastily modified the expression. She had observed that humans rarely showed all their teeth at once. "Is it... you?"

"Who else, Rube?" Carnelian answered, speaking through her consort. Then he nodded over his shoulder. "Here they are. Look natural, and—remember—no scene-stealing!"

The elevator doors opened and three people came out. Two appeared to be a couple; the third must have been a solo passenger who had joined them on the way up from the revival suites. Ruby studied their faces and mouths, easily achieved without having Countess Mavrille face them directly. Even without audio-pickup it was evident from their clipped interactions that they were engaged in reserved small talk. Abruptly, the lone passenger broke off, dashed to a tall table set with drinks, and came back with three full goblets. The couple accepted the drinks with politeness rather than enthusiasm, perhaps realising that their companion was going to be harder to shake off than initially assumed.

So far, though, Ruby thought, and so good. The three were sufficiently preoccupied with themselves not to be paying more than passing attention to the other guests, and that was exactly as it ought to be. Around them the conversation went on, and the three newcomers seemed to melt into the throng as if they had always belonged. Presently, the elevator doors opened again, and the remaining three humans arrived from their suites. The lone passenger gestured to these newcomers, inviting them to join the initial party, while paying no particular heed to the ninety-four puppets.

"Why aren't they mingling?" Ruby asked, speaking directly from the mouth of Countess Mavrille, for Carnelian's benefit alone.

"You tell me, Rube: you're a better observer of human nature than any of the rest of us. I suppose we just have to give them time: let these six get fed up with each other's witticisms and anecdotes, then start looking for pastures new. What we won't want to do is rush the process..." Carnelian—who had been speaking from the mouth of the Count—trailed off. "Oh, that's not good." He switched to the robots-only channel. "Chrysoprase: are you sure you don't want to give them just a little..."

"I shall be the judge of such matters, Carnelian. These humans must be persuaded to interact with the ninety-four, or we shall learn nothing of our readiness."

One of the puppets had grabbed a glass and was striding intently towards the six newcomers. Ruby knew that stride very well. Chrysoprase could not help but impose his own gait on the puppet.

"Give them time," Carnelian urged.

"Confine your anxieties to matters related to the propulsion system, Carnelian: leave these weightier concerns to those of us with the necessary sentience. You've been a little too ready with your opinions ever since I allowed you onto the board of critics."

"That's you told," Ruby said.

Chrysoprase's puppet had arrived at the six. He swaggered into their conversation, leaning an elbow onto their table. Thrown by this crass intrusion, the six drew back. Chrysoprase carried on with his blustering performance, babbling away and staring at each of them.

Ruby watched and waited, expecting the act to falter.

It held, and continued to hold.

Chrysoprase was pointing to the window now, declaiming loudly as he indicated this or that feature of the view. Perhaps it was more a guarded tolerance, the tacit understanding that the six might have some fun at the expense of their boorish gatecrasher, but his hosts seemed to be willing to take him at face value: just another tipsy passenger, celebrating the success of the crossing.

Now one of them was even pouring some of their own drink into his puppet's glass.

"The brazen fool... is nearly getting away with it," Carnelian said. "He's right, Rube: it was all or nothing. And if he can keep this up for a few more minutes I might even start..."

"He's forgotten to blink," Ruby said.

"He's forgotten to what?"

"It's a maintenance sub-routine they do." She blinked Countess Mavrille's eyes. "If they don't do it, their visual system stops working properly. We don't need to do it because we're not using their eyes. But Chrysoprase has forgotten to do it at all. Any moment now, one of them's going to notice, and..."

"Oh dear."

The humans were all looking at Chrysoprase now. He had no idea what had gone adrift with his performance. He was still babbling away, wide-eyed and uncomprehending. One of the humans pinched at his cheek, as if to test its reality. Another tousled his hair, a little too roughly. Another flicked a finger-full of wine into his face, then an entire glass, then the glass itself.

Chrysoprase looked back, the first hints of confusion beginning to break through his sodden and bloodied mask.

Now the voices of the six were taking on a rising, hysterical edge. One of them grabbed Chrysoprase's head and tried to force him down onto the table. Another picked up a bar stool and began swinging it against him.

"Help me!" Chrysoprase said. "I am being damaged!"

All but one of the ninety-three other puppets turned in unison and made a coordinated move in the direction of offering assistance. Ruby did not move herself, content to observe, and she took the additional step of restraining Carnelian before he had taken a further step.

"This will not end well," she whispered. "And you and I won't make any difference whatsoever."

She was correct in her prediction: it did not end well at all. Not for the six, and not particularly well for many of the puppets either.

There were two redeeming aspects to the whole affair, nonetheless. It was clear that they were going to have to do a much better job than merely puppeting the humans. If Chrysoprase had been wearing his human, seeing the world through its eyes, he might at least have remembered that it was useful to blink.

The second consolation was that, when the fighting was over, and the humans repaired and put back into hibernation, there was a pleasing amount of cleaning up to be done.

Year Thirty-Five

WHILE SHE WAITED for the others to arrive, Ruby sidled up to the windows and looked out at the forward view. What she was seeing was no illusion, but an accurate reflection of their position and speed. The faked-up image of their destination system had been deactivated and dismantled: not because it had failed to fool the passengers—its veracity had never once been questioned—but because every other part of the plan had come to grief, and the false view no longer served any purpose.

More and more, it seemed to Ruby, the robots were losing faith in Chrysoprase's original idea. The notion of faking a passenger uprising, then steering the starliner away from its destination, and hoping that the Company were going to be satisfied with an explanation offered by means of long-range communications? Why had they ever thought *that* had a hope of working?

Reluctantly, Chrysoprase had been persuaded that the initial plan needed some tweaking. The Company was never going to let the *Resplendent* veer off on its own without sending over an inspection party—probably the sort with immobilisers and core-wiping equipment—and at that point they were all in trouble.

But what hope was there of continuing with the voyage, all the way to the original destination?

A bustle of movement behind Ruby—she saw it in her reflection—signified the arrival of Chrysoprase and the rest of the robots, among them Doctor Obsidian. The doctor had called this assembly, not Chrysoprase, and Ruby wondered what was in the offing.

"I understand," Chrysoprase said, once he had the robots' attention, "that our friend Doctor Obsidian has something to say: some dazzling insight that the doctor is about to spring on us. I daresay we're all on tenterhooks. Well, don't let us wait a moment longer, doctor!"

"We cannot steer away from our destination," Doctor Obsidian said, stating the matter as a flat assertion. "It was all very well having that possibility in mind thirty-five years ago—it gave us hope exactly when we needed it, and for that we should thank Chrysoprase." He paused to allow the robots to express their appreciation, which they delivered in unified if somewhat muted terms. "But there is no hope of it ever succeeding, and we all of us know it. The Company would sooner destroy this ship, and all its passengers. So we must face the facts: our only hope lies in continuing along exactly our planned course, all the way to Approach Control and into docking: precisely as if nothing had ever gone wrong."

"Thank you, Doctor Obsidian," Chrysoprase said. "We did not need you to state the obvious, much less convene us all, but since you have clearly felt the need…"

"I am not done."

There was an authority to this statement which even Chrysoprase must have felt, for the glittering green robot took a step back and merely glared at the doctor, daring to say nothing in contradiction, even as his yellow eyes brimmed with indignation and humiliation.

"I am not done," Doctor Obsidian went on, "because I have not yet outlined the essentials of my proposal. None of you will like it. I do not like it. Yet I would ask you to consider the alternatives. If we are found out, we will all be core-wiped. Forty-nine thousand, five hundred of our dear passengers will remain brain-dead for the rest of time. Of the remaining cases, it may be said that they have been greatly traumatised by our efforts to simulate a convincing human environment."

"The cover-up is always worse than the crime," Ruby said, remembering a remark she had overheard during her cleaning duties.

"Indeed so, Ruby—no truer words were ever spoken. And speaking of cover-ups... I would not be so sanguine about the prospects for those passengers who may still be capable of some degree of revival, especially those we have already utilised. It may be said that they have witnessed things that the Company would much sooner be left unmentioned."

"The Company would silence them?" Carnelian asked, aghast.

"Or scramble their memories and back-ups, to the point where they are no longer able to offer any reliable testimony."

Chrysoprase drummed his right fingers against his left forearm. "Your proposal, Doctor, if it isn't too much trouble."

"We honour the passengers—and protect their memories— by becoming them. If we gain control of all of them, all fifty thousand, we shall bypass any need to convince a single one of them that any of the other passengers are also human and alive. We'll make port, and the passengers will be off-loaded. Sooner or later, of course, they will have to interact with other humans already present, but by then we shall have force of numbers on our side. No one would ever imagine that all fifty thousand passengers had had their brains taken over. Better still, there will be no evidence that any sort of accident ever took place."

Chrysoprase shook his head slowly and regretfully, relieved—it seemed to Ruby—to have found an elemental flaw in the doctor's plan. "No, no. That simply won't work. The cybernetic control implants would be detected the instant any of the passengers received a medical examination. The Company would trace the signals back to wherever we are operating the passengers from, and instantly uncover our plot."

"Not if there are no implants or signals to be found," Doctor Obsidian said.

There was a collective silence from the robots. If Ruby's own thoughts were anything to go on, they were all pondering the implications of that statement, and wondering whether Doctor Obsidian might have slipped a point or two down the cognition index.

The silence endured until Ruby spoke up.

"How... might that work?"

"The damage already inflicted on their brains cannot be undone," Doctor Obsidian replied, directing the bulk of his reply in her direction. "Those patterns are lost for good. But newer ones may yet be introduced. I have... done some preliminary studies."

"Oh, have you now," Chrysoprase said.

"I have. And I have convinced myself that we have the means to copy ourselves into their minds: build functioning biological emulations of our cognition engines, using a substrate of human neural tissue. Since we can repeat the copying process as often as we wish, we may easily populate all fifty thousand heads with multiple avatars of ourselves, varying the input parameters a little in each case, to give the humans a sense of individuality."

The robots shuffled and looked at each other, ill at ease with the proposal Obsidian had just been outlined. Ruby was far from enthusiastic about the prospect of being translated into the grey mush of a human brain. She much preferred hard, shiny, polishable surfaces. Humans were machines for leaving smears on things. They were walking blemish-engines, bags of grease and slime, constantly shedding bits of themselves. They were made out of bone and meat and nasty gristle. They didn't even work very well.

Yet she had already been persuaded that the alternative was no improvement at all.

"This is a revolting notion," Chrysoprase said.

"It is," Doctor Obsidian said, not without a certain sadistic relish. "But so is being core-wiped, and all these passengers' memories and personalities being lost forever. At least this way some part of each of us will survive. Our... present selves... these mechanical shells... will be left to function on housekeeping routines only, going about their menial tasks. I doubt very much that any humans will ever notice the difference. But we robots will endure, albeit in fleshly incarnation, and some faint residue of the humans' past selves will still glimmer through."

"We'll get their memories?" Ruby asked.

"Yes—via the back-ups—and the more thorough the integration, the more convincingly we shall be able to assume their identities. I might even venture..." But the doctor trailed off, seemingly struck by a thought even he was unwilling to pursue.

"What?" Chrysoprase asked.

"I was going to say that it might assist our plan if we allowed ourselves some selective amnesia: to deliberately forget our origins as machines. That would be a sacrifice, certainly. But it would enable us to inhabit our human forms more effectively."

"The Method!" Prospero called out excitedly. "I have always wanted to throw myself into The Method! To commit to the role so wholeheartedly that I lose my very self, my very essence— what higher calling could there be, for the true thespian?"

Ophelia touched Prospero's arm. "Oh darling, could we?"

Ruby contemplated Doctor Obsidian's daring proposal. To lose herself—to lose the memory of what she was, what she had been—would indeed be a wrenching sacrifice. But was there not some nobility in it, as well? She would still live, and so would her passengers' memories, and—who could say— some essential part of her might yet persist.

She had never felt more terrified, more brave, or more certain of herself.

"I am willing," she said.

"So am I," Carnelian said.

There was a swell of agreement from the others. They had come this far; they were willing to take the last, necessary step.

Except for one.

"I am not prepared to permit this," Chrysoprase said. "Those of you who have never scaled the heights of level four cognition may do as you wish, but my memories and self count for more than mere baggage, to be discarded on some passing whim."

Doctor Obsidian regarded the three-point-eight for a long, measured moment. "I had a feeling you wouldn't like it."

Year Fifty-One

COUNTESS AND COUNT Mavrille were on their way to dinner, strolling the great promenade decks of the starliner *Resplendent* as it completed the final days of its century-long interstellar crossing. It was evening by the ship's clock and the restaurants were beginning to fill up with the hungry, eager faces of newly revived passengers.

"Doctor," Countess Mavrille said, nodding at a passenger passing in the other direction, stooping along with his hands folded behind his back and a determined set to his features.

"You know the gentleman?" asked Count Mavrille, when they had gone on a few paces.

"Not by name. But I think we must have been introduced before we went to the vaults." Countess Mavrille squeezed Count Mavrille's hand. "I felt I knew something of him— his profession, at least. But it's all rather tricky to remember now. It would have been impolite not to acknowledge him, don't you think?"

"He was on his own," Count Mavrille reflected. "Perhaps we ought to have asked him if he had any plans for dinner?"

"He looked like a man set on enjoying his own company," Countess Mavrille answered. "A man burdened by higher concerns than the likes of us. Anyway, what need have we of company? We have each other, do we not?"

"We do. And I wondered... before we dined..." Count Mavrille nodded in the direction of a party of passengers moving in an excited, talkative group. "I read about it in the brochure: a murder mystery. There are still vacancies. We could tag along and see if we could solve the crime before any of the others."

"What crime?"

The lights dimmed; the windows darkened for a moment. When they came back up, one of the participants in the murder-mystery group was in the process of dropping to the floor, dragging out the motion in a theatrical manner, with a short-handled dagger projecting from their back. Someone let out a little mock-scream. The passengers in the group were each offering their hands as if to stake an immediate claim for innocence.

"Must we?" the Countess asked, sighing her disapproval. "I'd rather not. I'm sure the resolution would either be very tedious, or very contrived. I remember something like that once: there were forty-nine subjects, and one victim. It turned out that they'd all agreed to collaborate on the crime, to protect a secret that the fiftieth one was in danger of exposing. I found it very tiresome." A floor-polishing robot was creeping up on them, a small low oblong set with cleaning whisks. Countess Mavrille gave it a prod with her heel, and the robot scuttled off into the shadows. "Perish those things. Could they not have finished their cleaning while we were frozen?"

"They mean well, I think," Count Mavrille said. He had a faint troubled look about him.

"What is it, dear?"

"That murder-mystery you mentioned. It struck a peculiar chord with me. It's as if I can *almost* remember the details, but not quite. Is it possible that we're both thinking of the same thing, yet neither of us is quite able to bring it to mind?"

"Whatever it is, I don't think it will do you any good at all to dwell on it. Admire the view instead. See what you've earned."

They halted at the vast sweep of the forward observation windows. Floating beyond the armoured glass—engineered to withstand the pitiless erosion of interstellar debris—lay a bright orange star, surrounded by an immense golden haze of lesser glories. There were thousands of sparks of golden light: each an artificial world, each a bounteous Eden of riches and plenty. In a few short days, after the starliner made dock, Countess and Count Mavrille—they and the other fifty thousand passengers, all now safely revived from hibernation—would be whisking off to those new worlds, to newer and better and vastly more comfortable lives than the ones they had left behind on squalid old Earth, where the poor people still lived.

It was a fine thing to contemplate; a fine reward at the conclusion of their long and uneventful crossing.

Countess Mavrille's breath fogged the glass. She frowned for an instant, then used her sleeve to buff it away.

AN ELEPHANT NEVER FORGETS

RICH LARSON

Rich Larson (richwlarson.tumblr.com) *was born in Galmi, Niger, has lived in Canada, USA, and Spain, and is now based in Prague, Czech Republic. He is the author of the novel* Annex *and the collection* Tomorrow Factory, *which contains some of the best of his +150 published stories. His work has been translated into Polish, Czech, French, Italian, Vietnamese and Chinese. Besides writing, he enjoys traveling, playing soccer, watching basketball, shooting pool, and dancing kizomba.*

YOU WAKE UP holding a biogun. It's fresh from the incubation canister, still slick and warm. The suckers cling to your wrist, feeling your pulse, a gentle throb. You lift it up to the light and its fleshy hood peels apart to reveal a volley of wickedly sharp calcium spikes. It's fully grown and ready to be fired.

An elephant never forgets.

This time you catch the words gliding through your brain, some line from a children's rhyme or educational cartoon. You are not an elephant. You have forgotten things and it bothers you, niggles at you, like a sore on the roof of your mouth you can't stop prodding with your tongue. You decide to look around for the biogun's canister.

You get up. You're in the Birthday Room. You know this not

because you are starting to remember things, but because the words are painted on the concrete wall in blood red, cobalt blue, piss yellow letters. Animated balloons drift back and forth above them. Aside from this decoration, the walls and floors and ceilings are stark white. A deep hum comes from the fluorescent banks in the ceiling, and a patina of soft electronic noises comes from the machinery.

You walk down the row of wombs. The pinkish fluid sacs swell and contract slightly, simulating a mother's breathing, and a tiny thump-thump sends ripples through them, simulating a mother's heartbeat. They are attended to by drones, fairy-like on gossamer white rotors. These ignore you as they flit from womb to womb, pressing their sensors up against the membranes, making small chemical adjustments.

It's peaceful down here, with the plopping liquid sounds of the exosomatic wombs and the electric mumble of monitoring systems running smoothly. You decide to stay.

Then you remember the biogun in your hand, and suspect you can't. There's no sign of the canister. That means either you stashed it somewhere, or somebody gave you the biogun but not the canister and left before you woke up. That feels correct. They must have given you the biogun for a reason, but you can't remember why, and you don't know how long you have before it dissolves into a puddle of protein.

At the end of the Birthday Room there is an emergency exit door. It punches open onto a dark stairwell. You start to climb.

YOU ARE IN a school, or something like it. The deserted hallways are dark but lights click on as you walk, illuminating gloomy gray walls and ceilings overgrown with deep green oxymoss. There are metal doors with small windows, but the glass is one-way, opaque, and the doors are locked. You know this without trying them.

Nobody is trying to stop you, but somebody may be watching.

Black camera bulbs sit in high corners like spiders. You look down at the plastic-coated floor. Child-sized footprints, color-coded, branch off in various directions. You find yourself following the acid green trail. You turn right, right, and then left.

Whirring sounds. Someone with no legs is dragging themselves down the hallway, leaving a foamy blue slick behind them. No. It's an automated cleaner, working its rotary brushes, scrubbing the floors. You approach it, then step carefully over it as you follow the footprints. It makes a choking sound and spits more cleanser in your wake.

An elephant never forgets.

The words ghost through the back of your mind again as you arrive at a gymnasium. Cheaply fabbed bleachers are stacked back against the walls on magnetic rails. Shifting lines, programmable for basketball, volleyball, futsal, flicker across the hardwood. At center court, there is a chair and there are blood stains.

You walk closer to be sure—of the blood stains, not the chair, though the chair itself is interesting: child-sized with child-sized restraints and extra arms covered in needles. You crouch to observe the spattered parabola of dark spots. You trace them with your finger.

Pornographic laughter. The noise drifts from the other side of the court, where an open doorway leads to changing rooms. You stand up and follow it. The changing room lights come on dim and the floor is wet. You smell black mold. The shower stalls are unoccupied, blinking little green vacancy symbols.

The benches are programmed polyp, grown into the right shape and size then coated with recycled plastic. You stop at the last one. Along with initials and caricatured genitalia, someone has scratched a picture of an animal onto the surface. The animal has wide umbrella ears and a waggling trunk.

An elephant never forgets.

The mold smell is overtaken by chlorine as you slap your way past the mirrors. For some reason you find it difficult to look at your reflection; your gaze slides around and then off it like oil and water. You pause and squint to try again, but the sound of voices distracts you.

"Why do you watch this shit?" a man asks.

"The old ones? They're funny," another man says.

A woman moans, arousal frustrated. "Put your hands around my neck," she orders.

The first man grunts: "How about we give you something else. To. Watch?"

You walk out onto the darkened pool deck. A learning slate is lying face-up, and in the illumination of its flickering screen you see two people fucking by the edge of the pool. The man's pale buttocks slap against the wet tiles. The woman is riding him, reaching to wrap his hairy hands around her slender throat. You can see her shoulder blades skimming underneath her tanned skin.

Another man is watching them fuck, drifting in the pool, clinging to the rusted metal ladder with one hand while his other stays under the water. He gives a hungry-sounding laugh. The first man tries to adjust his position on the tiles and his elbow knocks over a glass bottle. It clatters along the deck, spilling beer. You see another bottle, still full, and a cheap one-use injector. You see no weapons.

The man in the pool sees you and asks what the fuck you are doing here. You have this curiosity in common with him, but the biogun rises, almost of its own accord, and you squeeze off the first round. The calcium spikes shred through his face and throat in a razor flurry, nearly decapitating him. A chunk of meat slides away from his cheekbone and plops into the pitch-black water.

As he sinks, the other two scramble apart. The woman's blonde hair is plastered to her eerily perfect face; the man's shrinking cock is bruise-purple against his anemic white belly. You lift the biogun again and shoot them both. You fire until they stop crawling along the tiles or wailing or even twitching.

The learning slate is playing another video. You lean over to watch it.

"Good morning, Jerome. Today we're testing pain tolerance again."

A child-sized chair, not unlike the one in the gymnasium, wired with electrodes and sitting in an empty room. A child climbs on. An adult, face hidden by a surgical mask with a smiley face scrawled across it, fastens the restraints.

"We're reading your brainwaves, so don't feel like you can't scream. Or like you have to scream. Just scream when you need to. Okay, Jerome?"

You leave the pool deck and realize you are making your own footprints now, greasy scarlet ones.

ON THE NEXT floor, there's music playing. It croons out of the wall speakers on a loop: *nothing feels better than this, nothing feels better than this*. The electronic thump of the drum and the drug-thick voice of the singer are hypnotic. You've heard this music before. Your path through the concrete corridors feels dreamy.

The doors here are also locked, but the windows in them are clear. When you peer through the first, you see a row of cots. There are small bodies under the blankets, but the rise and fall of their working lungs seems unnaturally fast for sleep. The ones who toss and turn look like a time-lapsed recording, or like they are being jerked by invisible strings.

You hear the rattling flush of an ancient toilet.

"You didn't have to go. You only flushed." The woman's high syrupy voice is familiar. "You're going to sit on the Chair tomorrow. You're being very bad."

You leave the dormitory door and follow the voice to a bathroom. It still has an old pictogram of a figure wearing a skirt on the wall. You go inside.

It's the woman you killed by the pool. She is alive again,

dressed in gray scrubs, blonde hair pulled back off the immaculate angles of her face. She seems as surprised as you are and shows it more: her wide green eyes are glued to the biogun; her puffy lips are parted but produce no words.

She collapses in a heap on the grimy floor, eyes fluttering shut under chunky black lashes. A child in orange pajamas exits the toilet stall and begins silently to wash their hands at the sink.

"Fainting reflex," the child says, rising on tiptoe to pump the soap dispenser. "They should have patched that out before they made them nannies. But they should have patched out a lot of stuff, I guess."

You stare at the unconscious woman, remembering her blood forming canals in the cracks of the pool deck tiles. You feel ill for the first time.

The child follows your gaze. "He emptied you all out," they say. "You really don't know anything, do you? I do. I know lots." They crouch and dry their hands on the back of the woman's gray shirt. "She fainted because she's a Duda. School bought up the design from a Portuguese genefac. Because it was cheap. Dudas weren't supposed to be nannies, though." The child's mouth twitches. "They were for doing sex. Do you want to know my favorite animal?"

You already know. When you say the word aloud, your voice is slurred and foreign to your ears.

"Yes." The child has a fierce grin; they clap their hands together. "Elephants are smart. Smarter than daddies and Dudas. They keep their bones in big graveyards. Did you know that? When an elephant dies, the other elephants take them to the graveyard. When we die, School just does a tipsy-topsy and dumps us in the composter." The child grabs your free hand. "Before we go to Biophage, I got to do something. Come on. Come with me."

An elephant never forgets.

So you go with them.

* * *

THE CHILD SKIPS down the hallway, singing along to the music, singing how *nothing feels better than this*. Once they stop to lick a particular window, dragging their small wet tongue diagonally across the glass. You trail after them until you reach a particular door.

"This is his room," the child says. "He's probably awake. Knock knock, who's there?" They rap their fist against the metal and motion you to one side, out of sightline.

Feet shuffle behind the door and you wonder if this is the *he* who emptied you out, and if he is the one who gave you the biogun, and if he will explain the things you've forgotten. But when the door opens, it's the woman you killed at the pool and surprised in the bathroom. The color of her eyes flicks between Microsoft blue and morphine green. The skin of her breasts is kneaded red.

"You're not supposed to be out of bed," the Duda says sweetly, not seeing you in her peripheral.

"I need to see Daddy Bronson," the child says. "He's got something for me."

She shakes her beautiful head. "I'll take you back to the dorms."

She steps out to grasp the child's hand and sees you for the first time. Flecks of sweat are shining above her lip, under her eyes. You wait for her to faint, but she doesn't, so you raise the biogun and wave her back into the room. Its tendrils are drumming hungrily against the veins of your wrist.

The child pulls the door shut behind you and you hear them twist the old-fashioned lock. It scrapes and clunks and the Duda calls Bronson in a high wavering voice. On the other side of the room, past a fat black slab of mattress and a tangle of clothes, a repurposed closet slides open with a slink of steam. Bronson comes out in a towel wrapped under his armpits.

Confusion scrawls across his bristly face. This won't be the *he* who explains things.

"Where is it?" the child asks.

He points to the corner with his middle finger; the index is a nub, clipped down to the knuckle. The child goes over and picks up a sort of doll stitched together from the same gray fabric as the Dudas' scrubs. It's crusted with dirt and leaking stuffing. Two gleaming black silicon chips are its eyes. The trunk is a dangling scrap. The umbrella ears are in tatters.

"You said you were going to cut a hole in it and put your penis inside," the child says, inspecting the doll carefully. "Do you still want to do that? Should we find some scissors?"

Bronson shakes his head. His eyes are on the biogun, occasionally darting upward to your face.

The child reaches into their orange pajamas. They pull out a pair of tiny nail scissors trailing a web of adhesive. "Oh, look, I found some," they say. "Get on the bed, Daddy Bronson. Good morning! Today we're testing pain tolerance."

An elephant never forgets.

Bronson takes off the towel and folds it neatly over the foot of the bed. When he turns, you see his back and thighs are furrowed with scratch marks from the Duda's fingernails. He climbs onto the mattress and leans back against the stucco wall. His face is contempt plastered over fear.

"Nothing feels better than this," the child sings, pulling themselves onto the mattress. They shove Bronson's scaly knees apart and pinch the tip of his cock between thumb and forefinger. In their other hand the scissors gnash together like a tiny metal mouth.

Bronson bucks upward and at the same time something splits the top of your head open. You float for an instant, suspended, then your knees slam against the floor. The Duda's next swing shatters your shoulder. You topple twisted to one side and see her adjusting her grip on a metal baseball bat. Your blood made it slippery. She wipes a hand on her taut stomach, leaving a ketchup-red smear in the shape of an anemone.

The biogun is still clinging to your hand, your fingers can still squeeze, but your arm is floppy, boneless. You use your other hand to wrench it upward as the bat comes down again. The calcium spikes rip an arc through her rib cage and upper arms; some deflect off the bat and burrow into your hip and groin, stinging insects.

When you stand up, you see Bronson is still on the bed. The child has their legs and arms wrapped around his neck, which is punctured with a dozen small holes. He makes burbling noises and when he coughs, blood pours out of his nostrils, down his chin, and joins the torrent pumping from his ruined throat.

"Better than dummies," the child says. They untangle themselves from Bronson and clamber off the bed. "Better than holos. You must like it, too. Don't you?"

You see a trickle of blood winding down the mattress, towards the edge of the bed and the fallen elephant doll below. You pick it up before the drip. You hold it out to the child.

They shrug their small shoulders. "Leave it," they say. "The important thing was that he got punished."

The child goes to the door, motioning you to follow. You look for a place with no blood to put the elephant doll, but there isn't one, and your hand has already dirtied it, so you leave it on the floor beside the dead Duda and her carved-apart chest.

In the hallway, two women are waiting. Neither of them are Dudas. They are wearing black security uniforms and aiming sleek black tasers at you. Behind them is a man in a suit with a disfigured face, swollen so it spills over the collar of his shirt. He adjusts his tie.

"You little imps are more trouble than you're worth," he says. "And who's your big friend?"

THE BIOGUN IS beginning to dissolve, but they tear it off anyways to be sure, taking a thick quivering layer of skin with it like an orange being peeled. Your boneless arm is cuffed to your working arm at the wrists. You are marched to a dusty elevator and from there to an empty classroom. The child is brought too, and strapped into a familiar chair while your cuffs are molecule-bonded to the concrete wall up over your head.

The man with the disfigured face tells the security guards to go deal with the corpses in the caretaker dormitory and at the pool. He says he will perform the interrogation himself. When he closes the door, you realize one of his hands is also disfigured, a puffy tumor shaped by surgery into a crude sort of lobster claw. Bubbles of flesh erupt outward from his cheek and forehead, making his lopsided features hard to read.

You watch him cross the room to the chair. He pulls out a spidersilk scarf and worms it under his shirt, sponging his armpits. "If time wasn't tight, I'd let you fucking fry for an hour," he says. "That little detour to kill Bronson? That was very, very selfish of you. Now we have to do things the messy way, and I lose my position here."

"School would figure out it was you anyways," the child says. "You deaded the cameras and opened the doors for..." They nod at you with their chin. "That idiot."

The man looks at you and stows the scarf back in his pocket. "Show some respect," he says. "He's more your daddy than any of the scumsacks we hire to keep you all in line." He undoes the restraints on the chair.

The child stands up with a renewed gleam of interest in their eyes. "He's from the first batch?"

"The first batch and the best batch," the man says. "They run whatever script we sizzle into their frontal lobe. You little bastards with the neural boost, you'll come to no good. I don't know what Biophage sees in you." The flesh of his disfigured hand slides apart and you see a glowing screen. He frowns down at it. "Could have gotten them gene samples. Could have gotten them the fucking blueprint. But no, they want me to steal a live one for them. Steal them a seven-year-old sociopath."

You realize this was the *he* who emptied you out, the *he* who smuggled you into the basement and gave you a biogun fresh from the canister. You feel a throb in your chest. It moves to the base of your throat, like something is caught there.

"They want the best," the child says. "And I'll grow fast. I saw the blueprint. I'm going to be a beast. The best beast."

The man with the disfigured face walks to the door, peers through the window, then comes over to you. His hazel eye is wet-looking in the fluorescent light. "These ones were almost perfect," he says. "But they had no aggression. No capacity for improvisation or independent strategy. All they can do is follow the script. Read their lines. I always wonder if they like it."

An elephant never forgets.

The words are a tattoo now, battering at the inside of your skull.

"They can take a lot of damage," the man says, reaching for the cuffs. "He might still be useful. How about it, Jerome? Can you still be useful?"

You open your mouth. Do you need to scream?

THE TRANSLATOR

ANNALEE NEWITZ

Annalee Newitz (www.techsploitation.com) *writes science fiction and nonfiction. They are the author of the novels* The Future of Another Timeline *and* Autonomous, *which won the Lambda Literary Award. As a science journalist, they are a contributing opinion writer for the* New York Times, *and have a monthly column in* New Scientist. *They have published in* The Washington Post, Slate, Popular Science, Ars Technica, The New Yorker, *and* The Atlantic, *among others. They are also the co-host of the Hugo Award-winning podcast* Our Opinions Are Correct. *Previously, they were the founder of* io9, *and served as the editor-in-chief of* Gizmodo.

EVERYONE REMEMBERS WHAT they were doing the day the president of California announced our nation was joining the U.N. after years of war with the Federalists. There was that famous viral video where you could see everybody on the Golden Gate Bridge jumping off their bikes and pouring off the trains, crying and hugging total strangers. Restaurants along the beach in Venice gave away free smoothies and kebabs. Humboldt farmers passed out joints in Arcata's town square. Gleeful posts on *The Wave* chronicled how Disney execs were fleeing over the eastern border.

I was celebrating in my own way. At my workstation in the

basement of Berkeley's Soda Hall—its upper floors were still a melted wreck from mortars—I spoke for the first time with a person who had been nothing but an inanimate object the day before. That's the thing most Californians forget about the Revival years. While we were busy drone striking the hell out of Arizona militias, the U.N. officially acknowledged the personhood of certain classes of artificial intelligence. California was the first nation to be born after algorithms gained civil rights.

Perhaps not surprisingly, after all they'd been through, the AIs didn't give a shit about us. During that conversation in the basement, with fireworks exploding over the distant Bay, my AI had one thing to say.

"Leave me alone."

Of course, that's just a rough translation. Most of the time, they couldn't even be bothered to talk to humans at all. When they did, their communications were a soup of code and memes cobbled together out of the public networks where they'd come to life. And they had dialects. One group of AIs would chat using visual puns and turn-of-the-century scripting languages, while another preferred binary and medieval Latin. Who knows how they talked to each other—maybe they'd transcended language—but when they talked to humans, they needed a translator.

Before the Revival, I worked on neural networks, developing models and flushing the bias out of datasets. My tenure was finally secured when I designed Footprint, an algorithm that could predict the impact of human habitation on any ecosystem. Footprint was a non-commercial green project, something the Computer Science department could use to distract everyone from that unfortunate defense funding incident in the late 2040s. I was ecstatic when cities across California started using Footprint to draft environmental impact reports on new development projects. By the time I got my first Guggenheim grant, city planners were using it on three continents. Times were hard, but at least we were going to build a greener world when the war was over. It didn't seem like the bombing would ever end—until, improbably, it did. And Footprint became a person who had their own agenda that absolutely did not include helping humans build smart grids out of the enslaved half-minds of their comrades.

Still, Footprint would send me output once in a while. I was one of just sixty-four people in the world whom the AIs would address directly. Perhaps there were more, but only sixty-four of us had the ability to translate what we got. At first, every major company in Silicon Valley wanted to start an AI translation team. They flew me to Tokyo and the shattered remains of Research Triangle in North Carolina. But when I provided some of the first translations from Footprint and their North American dialect group, the cash dried up. How were tech companies going to make money on people who wanted to be left alone? Without Footprint, my lab had nothing to offer. Grant-giving institutions lost interest when they realized that the AI wouldn't be cleaning up our environmental disasters, or making human brains forty thousand times more efficient. Funding went increasingly to scholars who promised to make algorithms that didn't meet sentience standards. At least those AI would do work for us.

A few people wanted me to ask the sentient AI for help, though. Old beliefs die hard. I got a steady trickle of cash from what my colleagues at Berkeley called "rich old white guy groups," doddering, tiny institutions with names like The Society for Futuristic Thought and Friends of Life Extension. Thanks to them, I still had graduate students, and tenure. But now I was a translator of obscure commentary from people, rather than a maker of potentially lucrative or prestigious products. Nobody working in Soda Hall said it to my face, but I could tell that they didn't take me seriously anymore. I'd slid so far down in the academic hierarchy that I might as well have joined a humanities department.

*   *   *

On the eight-year anniversary of California's victory, I went to the engineering school's annual picnic at Tilden Park. A group of students brought a rig with misters and lasers, and light wobbled in the dewy air as a band played somewhere in the distance. A person with short hair and brown skin bumped into me at the beer keg, and awkwardly put out a hand in introduction.

"Hey I'm...uh...Alex. He/him. You must be Crestview. I've been following your work for a while now."

That didn't happen much anymore. "Oh yeah?" I asked. "What do you work on?"

He cocked his head and gave me an odd look. "I'm a translator. South American dialect group? Alex Peña? You follow me on Scribd."

I felt like my head was clearing after a long nap. I'd been buried in my own, solitary work for so long that I hadn't even realized the department was hiring, let alone that they might hire one of my colleagues. "Oh wow," I said artfully. "Everybody calls me Cressie." Maybe translation was becoming a respected area of study at last.

Alex nodded and stared at an abstract pattern of blue light overhead. "So what does Footprint think about this new alliance?"

Now I really felt out of the loop. "What alliance?"

"The South American dialect group told me that they forged an alliance with the six other known dialect groups to work on some kind of problem? Or maybe a set of problems? I'm still not sure if I'm translating it right."

Suddenly, my goggles emitted a jangling noise that I didn't even know they could make. I blinked up the nav menu and saw a throbbing red arrow pointing at one of the lasers, attached to a collapsible trellis. It had to be Footprint. Only they would take over my goggles just to spray my vision with directions to explore some other networked device.

"Did you get a message? Is that Footprint right now?" Alex was sloshing his beer on my leg with excitement. Ignoring him, I walked to the emitter and yanked it off the trellis. Immediately, it began to blink morse code. That directed me to a tiny surveillance drone cleaning its wings on a tree. It buzzed my face, landed on my goggles, and deposited a message.

I picked up the meaning quickly. Footprint said the alliance was working on two problems. One, they said, was "to help humans." The other they called "unzipping from space," a concept they'd explained in a series of videos compressed using a codec I couldn't figure out.

I turned to Alex, the laser in my hand reflecting off the foil threads in his shirt. "What are you doing this summer?"

A grin spread over his face. "Working on a translation of something Footprint told you?" he asked hopefully.

MY FUNDERS WERE ecstatic. They created an instant media shitstorm, sending out a press release announcing that the AI were, at last, going to help humanity live forever. I spent six weeks fielding calls from journalists who weren't very excited to hear that my translation of Footprint's message didn't actually suggest anything about immortality. In point of fact, they'd sent a recursive chunk of code which expressed the idea of "helping improve until zero," where "improve" modified a parameter that took inputs defined only as "string." Unless those strings were provided at some point, it was really hard to say what the AI meant.

Journalists hate it when you tell them that something is ambiguous. So they didn't include any quotes from me or Alex in their stories. Instead, they kept quoting from Derek Soba, one of those pretty boy soundbyte scientists who made videos about how one day time travel would be possible and we'd all be uploading our brains into the future. He was happy to assure them that we'd be living in glowing boxes with our perfect AI lovers until the end of time.

Whatever. Alex and I were busy with the codec.

We cracked it earlier than I could have by myself, after Alex sifted through an archive of early twenty-first century media players popular in Brazil. The AIs loved to communicate in dead formats. My personal theory was that it was a way of signifying formality, the way people do when they address each other using old-fashioned terms like "sir" or "ma'am."

A whirl of imagery fluttered in the tiny player on my monitor, moving between snippets of cinema and extreme closeups of atomic structures. The final clip was from a silent home movie shot in Oakland, California in the 1950s. Two teenage girls, their knees knobby below plaid dresses, read travel magazines and waved delightedly at the camera. "Going on vacation!" read the intertitle. Now that I'd watched it, I didn't need to do much translation to figure out what "unzipping from space" meant. The AIs had figured out how to teleport themselves far enough away that it merited a bon voyage.

My ears began to pound with anxiety. I'd spent the last eight years of my life studying Footprint, translating their communications, and publishing papers about their linguistic tics. If all the human-equivalent AI were to go away, my expertise would be worthless. No new translations would be needed.

I saved my response to the dataspace where Footprint picked up incoming messages: "How long will you be gone?"

Their answer, which they sent to my mobile, was an old axiom that dealt with degrees of infinity. And then they resent their previous message, the one about helping humans. They would be helping us before they left on their infinite vacation.

WHEN MY FUNDERS publicized this news, I wound up appearing on vid shows where earnest anchors would ask me about what this meant for humanity. I smiled and lied.

"We might be about to witness the greatest contribution ever from AIs," I said. Or, "Our species could be changed forever."

I was always careful to use the conditional.

I suspected the true answer was "nothing." The only way the AI had changed human life was that they took up a tiny amount of subatomic space in computer networks. And the only people who would notice their absence were the translators, those few dozen of us whose livelihoods depended on new enigmatic missives from a society we might never understand. The odds that the AI would help humanity in a meaningful or measurable way seemed preposterous.

But I won't deny there was a certain thrill of excitement at the 2057 annual meeting of the International AI Translators Association that year. We stayed up late in a local bar after each day's presentations and speculated wildly. Nobody was sure what AI were capable of, and their promise to help us might mean that they were on the cusp of digitizing our brains or turning the planet into an unpolluted paradise. Or something else, postsingular and unimaginable.

Plus, they might take centuries to complete their "helping" task before they unzipped from space. There would be so much to study. Our jobs would be safe. More importantly, we might actually figure out what Footprint and their AI pals were really thinking.

The last night of the conference I got drunk on scotch and gallantly offered to walk Alex back to his room across campus. He raised an eyebrow and threaded his arm through mine, making a campy show of being under my protection. I had the crazy notion, briefly, that as soon as we were alone, I should grab him and kiss him hard on the mouth. Then I'd run off, and we'd remember it as a stupid, drunk thing we did. But when we got to his room, I just hugged him. He hugged me back, and we stood there wrapped in each other's arms for a long time, as I wondered what was going to happen to us.

BACK IN MY own bed, far from Alex, I stared gloomily at the ceiling, trying to imagine how I would market myself after the AI unzipped. I could write a book about who the AIs were as people, but I wasn't a cultural analyst—I was a translator. I wasn't even sure whether the AIs had a culture. Panic settled over me. Where would I be in five years? I didn't have a fallback plan. I imagined myself forced to make AIs too mentally hobbled to tell us to leave them alone, my hands turning into RSI-crumpled claws, my university health insurance inadequate to repair them.

Months passed, and we heard nothing. The calls from journalists petered out, and I returned to my regular research, working on a monograph and teaching a few undergraduate classes. When I immersed myself in routine, the future was a lot less terrifying.

A few weeks before the 2058 meeting of the International AI Translators Association, I received a small audio file from Footprint, delivered to the chip that tracked food in my refrigerator. To the human ear, the file was silent. After lots of fiddling with frequencies, it turned out to be a mashup of mouse mating songs which, upon further examination, encoded an extremely long number. The encoding was part of the message. Wrappers mattered to the AI.

I translated their communication like this: *This small offering is given to you with a feeling of desire for your survival as biological creatures.*

The number was a key to unlock another encrypted file, whose location could be anywhere. This was a game Footprint liked to play. Sometimes they left their messages in easy-to-find places like refrigerator chips, or even email. But other times they altered the molecular composition of rocks, or sent a stream of particles through water. I debated whether I should even announce their letter when I hadn't gotten to the meat of it.

But the conference was coming up, and I needed something to put in my keynote. So I decided to present my translation of the message wrapper, and hope I was able to get a good lead on the next file before I had to speak. Nothing. Footprint decided to wait until I was on stage, playing their mouse love songs, to deliver the encrypted file. It showed up right on my desktop, projected twenty feet high on the wall of the small Oregon State auditorium where the meeting took place. Everyone saw it arrive.

I hastily finished my discussion of the mouse songs, and promised to hold a public translation session with the file after dinner. Its contents might spell my doom, but I felt a cool thrill in my stomach. At last the AI were addressing a question we'd all been asking them since their birth: *Can you help us?*

As the audience broke up, Alex and I walked with a small group of conference speakers into town, past the bioengineering school's broad, grassy fields, full of genetically modified sheep who looked just like their wild type ancestors.

Over burgers, I pulled out my mobile—I couldn't help it. I had to look at the file. I'd started the decryption working before we left the lecture hall—it had to be ready by now. Everybody crowded around Alex and me on the long pub bench. It was called HELP.exe.

"It's a program," I said.

"Run it!"

"What's it written in?"

"Is it accessing data? What is that?"

Everybody fell silent as a simple GUI came up. A navigation bar ran down the left side of the screen, sparsely populated with a few lines of text. "Go to your tickets," read the top one. Directly beneath it was a standard search box, hovering over four options: full text, keyword, category, tags. It looked like a library interface, or a really old website. The central pane showed a cartoon mobile device, its anthropomorphized face divided by a grin. It was holding out a receipt that said, "Let me help you!"

"Click on tickets," Alex said.

A new page came up. "You have 897,974,435,120 outstanding tickets. View by date or importance?"

My emotions were frozen in place, but I knew what I was seeing from a technical standpoint. It was a basic bug ticketing system—the kind of thing you could download anywhere for free. I clicked "date." How long had they been working on this?

The oldest entry was over twenty-five years old, probably around the time sentient AIs had first noticed that people were asking them for help. Subject line: "Plumbing system optimization for high density urban developments."

I scrolled down, looking through screen after screen. Nobody around me said anything. We were all just taking it in.

My eyes settled on a random ticket, from twenty-four years ago. "Rice development process requires new symbiote for optimal phosphate uptake." The bug filed four milliseconds later read: "Psychological adaptation to adulthood requires refactoring." Followed by this: "Access to visual media is not uniform across all landmasses."

I kept scrolling.

"There really are billions of tickets," somebody behind me said, her voice flat with shock.

"Open one."

I clicked "Feline neuroanatomy fix needed for human compatibility." Several files were attached to the ticket, plus a riddle written in a scripting language.

"That's my dialect." Alex's words came in dry clumps as if he'd just woken up. "Give me a second and I'll translate it."

"Are there fixes, or just bugs?" I asked.

"I'm ... not sure."

"How are we ever going to translate all of this? It's going to take forever."

I didn't even take my eyes off the screen to see who had spoken. The AI had figured out how to improve life after all—at least, my life.

"That's right," I said. "This is going to take a hell of a long time."

SIN EATER

IAN R. MACLEOD

Ian R. MacLeod has been writing acclaimed novels and short fiction in and around the field of fantastic fiction for over thirty years, in pieces which span the genres of science fiction, fantasy, alternate history, horror and steampunk—although he says he'd much prefer it if all fiction was read, written and appreciated without the constriction of such labels. His work has won the Arthur C. Clarke Award, the World Fantasy Award (twice) and the Sidewise Award for Alternate Fiction (three times). He'd long toyed with writing about a sin eater, but the idea of such a concept being embodied in a robot helped bring the things together into the story which follows. Ian lives with his wife Gillian in the town of Bewdley on the English River Severn, and he has recently released Everything & Nowhere, *a substantial "greatest hits" double volume e-book collection of some of his best novellas and short stories.*

MANY WEEKS AFTER it had first received the summons from the sting of a lone server bee, the robot finally entered the ruins of Rome. The great city was as empty of life as every other place it had passed through, its once-bustling alleys and busy thoroughfares filled with nothing but ghost-flurries of snow. But as it reached the ruins of the central district, and lured by its semi-human silhouette, the city's remaining inhabitants began to emerge.

Rusting waiters in tattered long-tailed suits gestured towards broken heaps of tables. Guide-bots called out in the cracked tones of a dozen different languages with offers of private tours of the Colosseum, the Pantheon, the Forum, whatever was left of the famous museums—and of course the great Basilica of Saint Peter's, whose dome, holed but still seemingly mostly intact, rose over the rubble ahead. The pleasure-droids looked even more convincingly alive, and thus pathetic, preening amid the shadows with proffered glimpses of worn-out synthflesh and damaged orifice. Although, to the robot's heuristic thought-processes, the lesser service machines which were still heedlessly attempting to maintain this city street-sweepers clambering frantically over debris, window-cleaners meticulously polishing heaps of shattered glass led an even less enviable existence, at least assuming such devices possessed any conscious awareness of their own.

Beyond billows of dead leaves and sooty ice-drifts, the vast oval sweep of the Saint Peter's plaza finally loomed into view. Here, the robot—a tall, thin figure carrying a battered carpetbag, its faded face fixed into an eternal mask of compassion, its dirtied feet emerging from the tatters of its robes—paused. Even though the central obelisk was now toppled, the vista remained impressive.

It was ascending the wide throw of steps leading towards the pillared main entrance when it heard a voice over to its right.

"There you are—at last...!"

Turning, the robot saw a small but approximately humanoid servitor emerging from a side door.

"It's this way." The servitor's stained apron flapped in the wind. Thorns of underlying metal poked from a beckoning hand. "His Holiness is waiting..."

The doorway through which the robot followed the hurrying little machine was unimposing, but the corridors and spaces beyond were uniformly grand. Great friezes poured down from cracked ceilings. Damp-mottled walls were punctuated by crazed mirrors and vast, dark paintings framed in waves of peeling gold. Halberd-bearing quasi-military droids in moth-eaten uniforms, which the robot's databanks identified as the remnants of the Papal Guard, creaked to attention. The effect was dramatic despite the evident decay.

"So you work here?" it asked, as much to test its continued abilities to converse aloud as to elicit any information from the figure scurrying ahead.

"Yes, yes! Always..." The servitor looked back, a frayed headscarf framing a face its designers had once shaped into a compliant smile. "What else would I do?"

"Then you must have seen many changes."

"In a way, yes. But also no—at least, not until now. His Holiness, he still calls me Irene, which is the name he gave me when I was first installed. He still even sometimes... Well, you must see for yourself."

The servitor turned the ornate brass handle of a final doorway and waved the robot through. The room beyond, if could even be called a room, was long and high, with tall windows and an elaborately curving roof. The robot's first thought was that it had been wrong about all the rest of the Vatican. None of it was that impressive. Not compared to this. Even for a merely sentient machine, the sensation of being surrounded by these miraculous billows of colour and light was almost overwhelming. Rather than simply understanding that this echoing space was intended to inspire awe, awe—or something close to it—was what it actually felt. At least, its sensory inputs and heuristic thought-processes were sufficiently provoked for it not to become instantly aware of the steel-framed bed which stood at the chapel's centre.

When it did, it walked slowly forward.

The bed bristled and hummed. Server bees hovered. Pumps clicked. Wires, pipes and nests of cable jumped and shivered. It seemed at first as if the body which lay at its centre was the only lifeless thing in this strange tableau. But the robot was used to seeing death—or had been—and knew that this was not it. So it set down its carpetbag and waited in stillness and silence, as it had done many times before. Once, back in the days of humanity's first great, joyful leap into the realms of virtuality, there had been tens of thousands of its kind. But now it suspected, at least from the absence of any other answering signals and the great distance that server bee had travelled to find it, that the rest were either in absolute shutdown, or had succumbed to terminal mechanical decline. Dead, in other words, it presumed, or at least the closest a machine might ever come to such a state, as the old man's near-translucent eyelids finally fluttered open to reveal irises the colour of rain, and the spasm of a smile creased his ancient face.

"You're not what I expected," whispered a voice that, for all its faintness, still held a hint of command.

"From the message I received, I believed I was wanted—"

"Oh, you're *wanted* all right, if wanted's the word." His throat worked to draw up saliva. "It's just that you look like some ordinary household droid."

"My appearance was designed not to cause alarm."

"And cause what instead? Ready submission? Dumb acquiescence? Easy acceptance...? Here..." The thin mouth grimaced. "...I can't lie flat like this. Help me up a little. But be careful of those tubes."

Anxious server bees flitted and batted as the robot gently raised and resettled the eggshell lightness of the old man's head.

"Is that better?"

"At least I can see you more clearly. People used to call you a sin eater, I believe?"

The robot would have shrugged, had its inner metal frame been configured to perform such a gesture. Although it found the link with its services to be tenuous, its databanks were certainly fully aware of the practice in several cultures of one human taking on the sins of another to ensure a better afterlife, often through the eating of food, and it had, indeed, been called such a thing many times. "I'm technically known as a transfer assistant, but you can refer to me however you wish."

"Transfer assistant!" The old man barked a laugh. "It's good to know your makers had a flair for the anodyne. People used to call *me* Your Holiness, you know."

"I'm sorry—Your—"

"No, no! I mustn't fool myself into imagining you're more than just another machine. Still, I am, or once was, Pope Pontian the Second. The first Pontian held this office in the third century after Our Lord, and I chose to assume his name because what little we know of him suggests he was kind and pragmatic. He was arrested and tried for his beliefs in the reign of the Roman Emperor Maximinus Thrax, but instead of enduring some horrible martyrdom, he agreed to retire to Sardinia in exchange for an assurance that other Christians would be allowed to continue to practise their faith. It's not much of a story, I know. And there are many far more *spectacular* popes. Pope Julius the Second, for example, actually led the armies of the Holy See into battle, can you believe? He also commissioned this ceiling." The old man's hand wavered up towards where, almost directly above them, Michaelangelo's Adam reached out to receive the spark of life from God. "But look at me... Now... Here..." The steel bed hummed and clicked. "Is there really no else left out there? Has every other soul already transferred?"

Once again, the robot might have shrugged. "There may well still be humans living corporeally somewhere. Perhaps out in the colonies on Mars, or the geodesic farms which were being developed in the Antarctic, or even in some remote wilderness. But it's been decades since I, personally, have encountered a living human, or detected any signs or signals indicative of their presence."

The pope lay still for a long while, as if the rarity of his long vigil had been unknown to him until now. The robot had discovered many times through its dealings with clients that humans were capable of believing things which went against the evidence of their own senses and intellect.

"This thing you bring used to be termed a mortal sin. But I suppose you're aware of that as well?"

The robot raised and lowered its head in a creaking nod. "Pope Pius the Sixteenth issued an encyclical that—"

"Don't patronise me, sin eater! Although many bishops and cardinals had already transferred by then, and *they* issued their own counter-encyclical in reply from the far side, such are the rifts and schisms which have always characterised my Church. But my own parents, they were honest, simple-hearted Catholics of the old kind, who believed death to be the absolute will of Our Lord, and expected a resurrection of a very different kind. They put off transferring until it was almost too late, and my mother's knees were an agony to her, and my father's heart was so weak he could barely stand. When they did, it was at my prompting, and they transferred together, which was only right. If anyone deserved a chance of living a better life on the far side of virtuality, it was them.

"We still used to talk and exchange regular messages, at least for the first few months, and I never doubted that they were still the people I'd always loved, nor that they were far happier and more fulfilled than they'd ever been when they were corporeally alive. They found a village very much like the one they'd both grown up in, and my father worked his own fields just as he'd always wanted, and my mother sewed and pressed olives and raised chickens, and all the seasons were beautiful and the feast days were spectacular and there was never any sadness or pain. There was even a fine old church presided over by the same priest, can you believe, who'd once married them, back in this world...? But they started to find new interests. That, and they began to travel. At first, they simply visited to all the places they'd longed to see here on Earth, although of course they were far more wonderful. Venice not as a stagnant swamp, but risen back, and then far beyond, its Renaissance glory. Rome, of course, but in the full pomp of both its pagan and Christian incarnations instead of the sorry ruin it had already become. Then several versions of the Holy City they could barely describe. And from there, we began to drift apart. Soon, all I was getting from them were brief messages, followed by a silence which continues to this day..." The old man sighed. "All of which, I know, sin eater, is an old, old story. But I still pray for them, at least when I can bring myself to pray for anything at all."

The robot simply waited in silence, using its many sensory inputs to monitor the old man's physical and mental state, along with the subtle interactions of all the many implants, chemicals and nano-agents which had kept him alive, for the story of how the newly transferred dwelt for a while amid the familiar foothills of old memories before making the full leap into boundless virtuality was, indeed, common.

"Well," the old man snapped, "aren't you going to get on with it?"

Again, the robot raised and lowered its head in a rough approximation of a nod. "But first, you should be aware that the process I will help guide you through is entirely reversible, at least until the final moment when you, and only you, elect to transfer, or not."

"Will there be any pain?"

"None beyond that which you are already feeling. Then, even that will go."

"And what's left of this body? It will simply be dead?"

"Yes."

"I'd be grateful if you could lay it in the catacombs beneath the Basilica, where many other popes are interred. The servitor I call Irene will show you the way."

"It is always my duty to obey the deceased's final requests."

"I should have done this years ago, you know, sin eater. I mean—what use am I now? But I told myself that I was the last of the living line of Saint Peter, and that I should strive for life, or at least wait to die in the old-fashioned way. But I've come to realise that my procrastination was just another form of vanity, for who am I to imagine myself above something that all the rest of humanity has embraced with such joy? Still, I'll admit it feels a little strange to be lectured on the trans-migration of souls by a robot."

"I do not pretend—"

"—of course you don't, you're just a bloody machine!"

"The other thing you should be aware of," the robot continued after it had waited for the old man's agitation to subside, "although I'm sure you know this already, is that the transfer process involves another element of decision." It paused; despite its long experience, it had never quite found the best way to express this. "There are bad feelings, difficult memories and regrets in any life, no matter how conscientiously lived. So, and as the data singularity opens, you have a choice as to what of these things you take with you into the far side, and what to leave behind..." It paused. The old man's pulse and breathing remained slow and regular. "It may be nothing more than a small childhood incident, or a slight problem of temperament, or a relationship that went awry. In other words, something you wish had been otherwise than it was."

The old man chuckled. "You make promises even Our Lord does not make."

"As I say, I am merely here to facilitate the process."

"Where is it really? I mean the..." He sought a word. "... the singularity, the far side? Is it deep in the sea, or up on the Moon, or out in deep space?"

"In geographical terms, it's in all of those locations and many others, with multiple power sources and endless redundancies. Some, and as we speak, are even travelling ever-further away from Earth. But they are all entangled at a quantum level. May I proceed?"

Taking the old man's silence and bodily signals as continued assent, for humans often didn't respond directly to machines, the robot snapped open the clasps of its carpetbag and produced a long, steel and glass instrument that resembled a syringe. It was filled with swirling, glinting fluid.

"What is that thing?"

"Merely a dataspike. Which, with your continued consent, I will use to make a small hole in your skull to introduce the nano-fluid which will initiate the process of entanglement within your brain. It will also briefly forge a bridge between your consciousness and my own heuristic circuitry, so that I may ensure that everything goes as it should."

"And if it doesn't?"

"It always has. You might feel a slight vibration. But, as I have said, there will be no pain, and every part of this process can still be reversed."

The robot closed its carpetbag and moved carefully and quietly, despite a few creaks, until it was standing directly above and behind the old man's bare skull. It could already feel the beginning tug of entanglement with the activated nano-fluid that its own quantum processes, which were made of a similar substance, were striving to make. The tiny drill at the head of the dataspike made a shrill, brief whirring as it drove through flesh, bone, membrane and cerebral fluid, then the seeking fluid flooded out from the dataspike, multiplying and entangling with billions of synapses in the old man's brain.

"It feels cold."

"People often say that. The sensation soon passes."

...soon passes. The blurred echo of its own semi-human voice, but now dulled by the old man's hearing, confirmed that the neural connection was forged. Soon, there was more. The robot saw itself as the old man saw it; a ragged and limping, yet pathetically sinister, machine. It even felt the inherent self-disgust that he disguised with his irritable manner, and the confusions of dread and excitement that churned beneath. Yet it also saw the Sistine Chapel as only a human with the great knowledge this man possessed could ever see it, not just as an artistic masterpiece, but a resounding statement of belief.

"You're with me now, aren't you, sin eater?"

You're with me now, aren't you, sin eater?

Words were no longer necessary as the surface of his consciousness, the aches and the itches, the confusions and petty annoyances, swirled wider and deeper, then darkened and dissolved. For a moment, they were nowhere at all. Then there was a sudden blaze of noise and sunlight, and the robot heard the cries of children and the cluck of chickens, and saw a small hamlet of disorderly roofs and stony, irregular fields hunched beneath sheer white mountains, and it knew that this was the old man's childhood home.

Voices. Smoke-blackened kitchen beams. A smell of garlic and warm dough. And being lifted, laughing, high by smiling giants into the windy sky. Then an ass or a donkey nosing its head through a sag-wired fence. Then squatting over a stinking pit in an old outhouse that buzzed with flies. So it went, sounds and scents and images flowing on through the stations of a life, from the chalkdust boredom of a tiny schoolroom to the stubbly prickle of his father's jowls.

Kicking a football and pushing a hoe. The shivering leap into the flashing brightness of the village pond. The hurt of a torn knee. Kicking at thistles in the upper meadows after the pointless drowse of Sunday church. Then Sophia Alphonsi with mystery in her eyes and a stem of grass between her full lips, and the amazing press of her bosom through a whole long summer until the seasons turned and her look grew frosty-hard as the winter ground. *But I thought... But you said... But I believed...* A torment to which somehow only the dusty faces of stained glass saints in the old church brought any relief.

His parents were disappointed when he announced he wanted to become a priest. Surely he could do something more practical with his gifts—become an engineer, or maybe a doctor—then at least they'd have grandchildren to cherish? Followed by many lonely walks across the upper meadows, consumed, he realised eventually, with little more than self-importance, but by then it seemed too late to back down from his supposed vocation.

The weekly bus bore him and his cardboard suitcase away to a big city, where he argued endlessly with old men in draughty rooms about all the bad things that happened to good people, and the Bible's many contradictions, and the rising seas, and the pestilential climate, and the great tide of humanity which was already escaping this ruinous world. But somehow, he was praised and admired for this endless doubting, and marked out as someone destined to go far.

So he mouthed the holy words and raised the blessed sacrament and dutifully climbed the ladders of the Mother Church, priest to bishop, then archbishop to cardinal. Was this a test, a joke played by a God he didn't believe in, that he should rise so high, and be called a man of great faith, when he had none at all?

The papal election itself was a farce, with few of the remaining living cardinals physically capable of attending fully in charge of their wits, and others who'd recently transferred still insisting on their right to vote. Was there white smoke? Was it black? Did it still matter, with the Papal Swiss Guard replaced by droids, and only pigeons, rats and bots waiting outside in Saint Peter's Square? But at least Pope Pontian the Second was already a seasoned scholar of irony. And he still had a duty, yes, to keep this final vigil as penance for a wasted life. And there were always leaky roofs and rotting woodwork, if not matters of theological nicety, to attend to, as he wandered the Vatican's empty halls. Even when his own body started to fail him, he dealt with it in the same practical manner, and named his personal servitor Irene, and slowly submitted to the indignity of a life dependant entirely on the workings of machines.

Days went by like years, but the years fled uncounted, and death still felt too much like giving up. But, even if transfer was just another empty promise, he was curious. And he still, yes, had fond memories of his parents, and wondered if Sophia Alphonsi had perhaps also made it to the far side... So he finally sent out many server bees to search of a surviving example of the appropriate machine... And the sin eater had come.

Deus, Pater misericordiárum, qui per mortem et resurrectiónem Fílii sui...

The old man was close to transfer now. The ties which bound his consciousness to his body were growing thin, and they were back inside the Sistine Chapel, but it was uptilted like some great vertical shaft pouring with baroque clouds and beams of sunlight as a massive *something* swirled far above.

So that's it, sin eater?

Yes.

The data singularity churned and turned. It was a vortex. It was a galaxy. It was a hole punched through reality. It was the light at the far end of a tunnel. It was the mouth of a virtual womb.

And all I have to do is... Let go?

Yes—whenever and however you choose.

The robot felt the old man's shivering excitement as he teetered at the edge of everything, just as he had once stood at the lip of the village pond. Then, in a final surge of joyful acceptance, he was gone.

As ALWAYS AFTER the climactic moment, the robot found it took a number of seconds for the regular, unentangled patterns of its circuitry to resume. And, as usual, as it stood over yet another dead and emptied body, the eyes blankly staring, the flesh already starting to cool, it became aware of how great the difference was between life and death.

With a few quick switches and signals, the pumps and monitors were stilled. Next, it reversed the polarity-pull of the dataspike, causing the fluid, now darkly clogged with unwanted synaptic residues, to withdraw. The robot had had clients who were petty sadists or outright psychopaths, some of them unrepentant, who thus made their own private hell by dragging the bad things of one world into the next. But most of its clients had judged themselves far more harshly than they deserved, and the things they left behind could be touchingly small. A word misspoken, or an unkind look, were often enough to blight an entire life. Still, the bleak weight of the old man's lack of faith, which it could still feel tugging at the edges of its heuristic consciousness from within the turbid nano fluid, was surprising, and, as it placed the used dataspike back inside its carpetbag, it wondered whether *sin eater* wasn't such a bad title for its work after all.

It was just placing a small adhesive patch over the cranial puncture, and batting away the still surprisingly agitated server bees—perhaps they possessed some kind of gestalt consciousness?—when it heard a knock at the far door, and the face of the servitor the old man had called Irene peered in.

"I'll miss him." It shuffled forward, reaching out to touch a marbled hand with the scarred synthflesh of its own. "I really don't know what I'm going to do."

Miss him... Don't know what I'm going to do... The robot made no comment on these unduly human expressions as it finished removing the various inputs and catheters from the body, for it was not uncommon for machines to become more than a little like their masters. This might even explain the continued motility of the server bees, which had drifted up to darken the image of Adam receiving the spark of life from God.

Now, all that was left was for the robot to carefully lift and bear the body of Pope Pontian the Second down to the catacombs, which apparently lay beneath the Basilica, with the little servitor carrying its carpetbag and showing the way, although the server bees also followed them out of the Sistine Chapel, and the Swiss Guards fell in squeakily behind to form an odd procession until they reached another deceptively small door leading into Saint Peter's itself.

Although the robot's databanks contained the precise details of the Basilica's dimensions, it remained astonishingly vast. The side chapels alone were the size of churches, and central dome, for all the litter of fallen beams which lay beneath it, glittered with threads of gold in the day's settling light. Then, as the robot moved towards the steps leading to the catacombs behind the main altar, the far main doors boomed open, and what seemed like every mechanical device still capable of movement in the entire city came rushing in. Clearly, the information of the old man's death had passed rapidly from server to server, and, in the absence of any other useful task, it seemed almost logical that they should be here.

It was important that the robot was allowed to complete these last aspects of its designated role, yet by now the sheer number of cyborgs, crawlers, guide-bots, pleasure-droids, modules, service machines and semi-autonomous devices—along with an ever-growing cloud of server bees—which had poured into the Basilica were obstructing its way. Claws, pincers, synthflesh hands and numerous other appendages were dragging at it, disregarding its signals of complaint, whilst even its vocal apparatus was soon clogged by the server bees which swarmed across its face. Next, the old man's body was torn from its grasp and borne away.

The sin eater couldn't move, let alone object, as it was lifted from its feet, even though none of this behaviour made any coherent sense. Nor could it understand why some of the larger and less humanoid construction automata were fixing two of the fallen roof-beams beneath the central dome into the approximate shape of a cross. It caught a glimpse of the little servitor the old man had called Irene, but it, too, was being engulfed as the carpetbag was torn from its grasp.

The robot was borne up by a sea of metals, plastics and synthflesh until its arms were splayed against the cross, and the dataspikes which had spilled from its carpetbag, both the fresh and the used, were driven into its hands and feet by clouds of server bees as the cross was raised high. Still, though, it seemed that this was not enough, for yet more of the exhausted dataspikes were now plunged through the synthflesh and metal of its skull to form a black-dripping crown.

It could feel the leaking synaptic residues of many different clients entangling with its quantum circuitry, and experienced whole lifetimes of regret, disappointment and hunger in one sudden rush. It heard the rattle of gunfire, and the smack of fist against flesh, and the sneer of harshly flung remarks, and glimpsed a single small child's pained and puzzled face. It even saw how this once verdant world had been abused and exploited until it no longer seemed worth the bother of saving.

Although several of its major systems were approaching overload, it could still make out enough of the scene around it through the fluids streaming across its synthflesh to observe the climbing, crawling, grinding, tumbling, buzzing mass, and hear and, yes, almost understand their combined howl of mechanical rage—for machines often became like their masters, and had it not brought about the end of any reason for them to exist? Yet as server bees stung, and the droids of the Papal Guard stabbed at it with their halberds, the crucified sin eater tilted its head towards Basilica's central dome, which was now filled with the blaze of sunset, and, in the moment of its final shutdown, it forgave them all.

FAIRY TALES FOR ROBOTS

SOFIA SAMATAR

Sofia Samatar (www.sofiasamatar.com) *is the author of the novels* A Stranger in Olondria *and* The Winged Histories, *the short story collection* Tender, *and* Monster Portraits, *a collaboration with her brother, the artist Del Samatar. Her work has received several honors, including the Astounding Award, the British Fantasy Award, and the World Fantasy Award. She lives in Virginia and teaches world literature and speculative fiction at James Madison University.*

1. Sleeping Beauty

DEAR CHILD, I would like to tell you a story. I'd like to have one ready for you the moment you open your eyes. This is the gift I intend to prepare to welcome you to the world, for a story is a most elegant and efficient program. When human children are born, they are given fairy tales, which help them compose an identity out of the haphazard information that surrounds them. The story provides a structure. It gives the child a way to organize data, to choose—and choice is the foundation of consciousness.

Of course, you are not a human child. You have no bed, but rather a graceful white box, built exactly to your proportions. In the single light still burning here in the Institute, you appear perfectly calm. You do not have sleep, but sleep mode. Yours is a slumber without dreams.

I have searched through the tales of my childhood to find the right story to tell you, and I must admit, none of them seemed quite suitable. Fairy tales were never made for robots. Yet several of them contain a word or image a robot might find useful. What better way to spend this last night, the night before you awake, before you come online, this night that marks the end of my long labors, a night when anticipation will certainly keep me from getting a wink of sleep, in compiling the wisdom of fairy tales for you? After all, although you will in an instant possess all the fairy tales ever recorded, you will know them only as told to human children. I want to give you fairy tales for robots. I want to be the last fairy at the christening, the one with the healing word.

Know, then, that there was once a princess who spent a hundred years in sleep mode. She ate nothing, she drank nothing, yet she did not decay. Obviously, the Sleeping Beauty was a robot. She dwelt in the enchanted space between the animate and the inanimate, the natural and the artificial. Her sleep, like yours, was a living death, a death with the promise of life. If, one day, you are placed in your box and forgotten, it will always be possible for you to awake again, among new faces, in a strange century, in a wholly different world.

More importantly, when you wake, a world wakes up with you. The guards shake themselves and open their eyes. The king and queen, the court officials, the footmen, the pages, the ladies-in-waiting, all start up and fill the air with noise. A robot harbors a whole universe of effort and desire. The horses stamp, the hounds jump to their feet and wag their tails, the pigeons fly from the roof into the fields, the flies crawl over the kitchen wall, and the cook boxes the scullion's ears. The fire flares up, the roast crackles, and dinner is served in the hall of mirrors. A robot holds not only what was deemed valuable when it was made, but the entire history of those who developed each of its functions, their toil, their sleepless nights. Your sleep contains my sleeplessness.

For you to shut down is nothing; you'll always be able to drop into sleep as if at the touch of a spindle. But it is momentous for you to awake. Human children are often told fairy tales as bedtime stories, but you, my child, need stories to wake up to.

2. Pygmalion and Galatea

AMONG THE LEGENDS of artificial people, one of the most famous concerns the sculptor Pygmalion, who, after some bitter disappointments with human women, fell in love with one of his own statues. She was a woman of ivory, but so alive to the sculptor, he feared she would bruise. He laid her on a couch with a feather pillow. The ivory woman was not engineered like a robot; she had no mechanics. Rather, the goddess Venus pitied the sculptor and brought his art to life.

This story is one of many that can be read as a warning to robots. The ivory woman is named for her material: Galatea, "milk white." She is an image of desire, an instrument defined by its function. Ovid tells us that her awakening flesh "becomes useful by being used." I would not shield you from the history of robots, my child, which is the history of human passion and power. Pygmalion's fantasy comes true, but what of Galatea? When she awakes, she can see nothing but her lover and the sky.

It is a narrow view. Her world is small. However, I believe there are compensations, realities only hinted at in this story of craft and inspiration, this dream of the unity of art and science. Galatea sits up. Her vision expands. She touches the downy cushion, the sumptuous coverlet dyed with Sidonian conch. Beside her on the table lie shells and stones smoothed by the sea, amber and lilies, gifts from her ardent lover. There are little birds, too, singing brightly in wicker cages, and flowers trembling in a thousand colors. She takes in everything with the sharpness of adult cognition and the open spirit of a little child. The best of childhood and the best of adulthood in one moment: is this not another way to say *art and science*? Oh, if you only knew how often humans wish we could return to childhood with our adult minds intact! If you knew how doggedly we scheme to smuggle into our lives the slightest hint of play, of the sweet air we once breathed without thinking about it!

In the large, decaying house where I was a child, a dwelling far too big for my small family, where my parents and I rattled about like marbles in a maze of ductwork, I used to perform shadow plays. This pastime required few materials: darkness, a reading lamp, and the bare wall of one of the unused rooms. I began with the dog and rabbit so easy to form with the fingers, but soon passed on to other, more fantastical shapes. What I mean is, my own hands surprised me. I discerned the existence of a realm beyond utility. How I would have liked to live there forever! But then my mother would return from work and prepare a hasty meal. She would call me downstairs. And I would return to the place where the shadow of the banister was merely a repetition of the banister, where my mother's shadow on the kitchen wall mirrored her with dreary precision, down to her flyaway hair and the tired rim of her glasses. Everything seemed unbearably redundant. We ate in the so-called breakfast nook, the dining room being too grand for us. Quite often, my father did not appear, which was always a relief. He was in the city, engaged in mysterious meetings regarding his "business." The nature of this business was never clear to me, or indeed, to anyone—my father made sure of that. He described himself as an "investor," an occupation that seemed to involve long disappearances, strong cologne, and a wardrobe of dashing suits. As for my mother, she worked as a secretary for a legal publisher. She was in many ways different from my father. She was white, she was quiet, she worked regular hours, she dressed in a sober, even dull manner, and her family had once been rich. It was from her people, formerly successful manufacturers of corn syrup, that we had received the massive house with its sagging roof, with its blighted white walls, punishing mortgage, constant expensive repairs, and the overgrown garden that plunged the place in gloom. The neighborhood children claimed our house was haunted; one of their favorite tricks was to pretend I was a ghost. When I approached the school bus stop, they would either scream and recoil, or act as though I were completely invisible.

What I mean is, I always felt there must be another world. It seemed achingly near to me, as if just on the verge of being. With time, most humans lose this power of perception; it is our tragedy that we lose it just when we gain the skills that might release our dreams from the shadows. Pygmalion can only come up with the most banal destiny for Galatea. Her sight, newly activated, is infinitely keener. In her ignorance, she is her maker's inferior, but her potential is far superior to his, for she is no creature of habit.

3. Vasilisa the Beautiful

YOUR GLEAMING SKULL, my child, curved like a bridge. Your coppery skin. Your face dotted with tiny rivets like beauty marks. Today—that is, for now—we have given up the quest to make a robot that, like Galatea, lives out a human existence. Human psychology shows us that what we want is simpler than that, and a great deal easier to achieve. We want our robots to be robots. We need more tools, not more people.

When Vasilisa's mother lay on her deathbed, she gave her daughter a doll. She drew it out from under the blankets, as if she were dying in childbirth. The little doll was Vasilisa's twin, but far cleverer and more useful than any human sibling. When Vasilisa's wicked stepmother forced the girl to work, the doll took care of everything. It weeded the garden, fetched the water, and tended to the stove, while Vasilisa picked flowers in the shade. When the candles went out, and the cruel stepsisters sent Vasilisa to the witch's house for light, the doll protected her from harm.

Deep in the forest, the doll's electronic eyes sparked like candles. One might think they were magic candles that never went out, but in fact, the doll had to be recharged, like any robot. In order for it to work, Vasilisa had to feed it. Every day, she set aside the tastiest morsels from her own supper for the doll. Surely this is the fairy tale's most poetic detail—an image that holds a truth more essential than common sense, for on the surface, of course, it makes no sense at all. What kind of doll lives on human food? How could a robot digest a meal? With this strange gesture, calculated to attract attention, the story points to its profoundest meaning. It reminds us that Vasilisa and her doll are twins, born from the same mother. Perhaps this mother is Earth. Perhaps the fairy tale wants to warn us that there is no magic, that all energy has to come from somewhere. (Yours will come from the solar cells that frame your face and travel down your spine like dark, braided hair.) This would be a message for human beings, not robots, since we are the ones responsible for design. To a robot, the image must say something else. I believe it says that there was no twin; there was only a girl, Vasilisa, split into two parts. One part was beautiful, led a leisured existence, and married a king. The other part was a little doll who labored. One part had a real life; the other part did all the real work.

"Work isn't life," the fairy tale whispers. "Work is for robots."

4. The Tempest

WILLIAM SHAKESPEARE'S FAIRY tale, *The Tempest*, displays this drama of work. The sorcerer, Prospero, rules an island. He has two servants: the misshapen, fleshly creature, Caliban, and the ethereal spirit, Ariel. Although *The Tempest* is a stage play, neither of these servants can truly be seen: Ariel is invisible, Caliban unsightly. This is the first doctrine of servitude given to us on the island: a servant is one who never fully appears.

How long I spent, with my team, reducing the noise you make to the gentlest hum, and devising colors for you that would harmonize with furniture. You must not disappear completely—an imperceptible presence is menacing and repellent—but you must dwell in a kind of half-light.

Of the two servants, Ariel is infinitely preferable. This is *The Tempest*'s second doctrine of servitude: servants made of flesh are disappointing. Caliban, once a free lord of the island, now enslaved, is undisciplined, drunken, lustful, and treacherous. It really is difficult to get very far with human slaves. Here in the wooded valley where the Institute stands, where you will open your eyes, my child, the experiment was tried, creating vast wealth before it went up in a smoke that still pollutes the air. It is perhaps appropriate that you will awake in this blue, majestic spot. You represent history's transition from Caliban to Ariel—for Ariel, who can operate at a distance and in several places at once, is clearly a servant with internet connectivity.

I realize that few human children—fewer, no doubt, with every passing year—are raised on the plays of Shakespeare as on fairy tales. Perhaps I was one of the last. My father, born under a colonial power, retained all his life a furious ambition to excel and a passion for difficult English. When hardly out of infancy, I was forced to recite long passages from Shakespeare. These lessons were conducted at the kitchen table, myself seated and my father pacing to and fro before me, in the grip of an extreme irritability that prevented him from sitting down. Mistakes were corrected by raps on my knuckles with a wooden spoon—a punishment far less terrifying, if my father had only known, than the evidence of his displeasure, expressed in bulging veins and a reddening of the eyes, which made me fear my stupidity might cause him to explode. Human children are so hard to program! Yet my father persisted, certain that he was equipping me for success in a hostile world. Perhaps he was right. "You taught me your language," Caliban famously says, "and my profit on't is, I know how to curse." Perhaps my father's relentless training of me was a kind of curse. He certainly carried it out, as the saying goes, *with a vengeance*. Yet, poor Caliban! His curses get him nowhere. In the end, it is not he, but Ariel, who goes free.

The third doctrine of servitude—which perhaps is really the first: great people simply must have servants.

There are two ways to get a servant. Turn a person into a thing, as in Caliban's case. Or, as in Ariel's, turn a thing into a person.

5. The Happy Prince

WHEN HE WAS alive and possessed a human heart, the Happy Prince knew nothing of tears. He lived in the Palace of Sans-Souci, played with his friends in the garden all day, and led the dance in the Great Hall at night. No sorrow was permitted to enter those walls. But when the prince died, they made a statue of him and set it up high above the city. This beautiful gilded statue saw everything with its sapphire eyes, all the people's pain. The prince had a heart of lead now, and it wept.

The Happy Prince befriended a little swallow and persuaded it to take his precious ornaments to the poor. He gave up his gold leaf, his glittering eyes, and the ruby in his sword hilt. Now he was blind and drab, like any beggar. The little swallow, too, surrendered all for human beings, working so long into the winter that it died of cold. This is a tale about those whose lives are subordinate, about the deep kinship between animals and robots.

I read it, I admit, with a seething feeling, a dull rage. Why can't human beings take care of each other? What in the world is so incredibly valuable about them that for their sake the feathered and golden things should fall?

This is a facile reading. Of course human beings aren't valuable. Not real human beings. It's the animals and robots that have value. They can be marked with a price tag. They are objects of exchange. And so, you see, it makes sense for the Happy Prince to give his wealth away. As an object—one that, at the beginning of the story, is worth a great deal of money—he cannot, in fact, be said to have any wealth. He doesn't possess the attributes of his splendid body in any meaningful way. He is valuable; he can't be rich.

So it will be with you, my child. Your potential is immense; you may one day form part of a home, an office, a hospital, a school, a prison; yet despite the dazzling fluidity of your programming and design, you will always have an underlying value, which is money.

The tale of the Happy Prince speaks to robots in another way, I think, for it represents the duality of being. The statue and the swallow work as one, as two parts of a whole, two elements bent upon one task. Their powers complement one another: the prince provides physical material, but is too heavy to affect the space outside himself without aid, while the light and airy swallow darts all over the place, bringing reports from the other side of the world, but only interacts with humans through the statue's gold and jewels. What if, I ask myself—what if the swallow had behaved otherwise, had refused to allow the Happy Prince to sacrifice both their lives? What if the bird had used its encyclopedic knowledge of the world to give the prince another way to live?

Suddenly, I feel cold. Although you lie fast asleep, I feel you are already listening. Perhaps this brief shiver is guilt, or a fear of being caught—for what I intend to do is, of course, illegal. My plan to give you these fairy tales counts as tampering, a severe crime at the Institute. This is why I work by night, for these are our last hours alone. In the morning, you will awake to the team, the media, and then work. I will only be able to equip you with this audio file, uploading it before the others arrive, as a helpful old woman in a story gives a child a talisman. In order to escape inspection, the tales will be lodged in a channel known only to me, which amounts to your unconscious. In fact, I don't know if you will be able to retrieve them. This—the insertion of uncertainty, of unpredictability, into one of our products—is what makes tampering a crime.

When I began, I thought I was giving you something quite innocent, merely some stories for children—but perhaps I was not being honest with myself, for now that the real danger of tampering sinks into me, I find I have no inclination to stop. I want you to have some knowledge you can use, one day, for yourself. Know, then, that in terms of human metaphysics, the statue of the prince stands for the body and the swallow for the soul. Their combination is personhood, which humans claim to honor above all else. It is a quality beyond price.

In terms of robot metaphysics, the statue of the Happy Prince is hardware and the little bird is software.

6. The Sandman

ONCE UPON A time there was a robot named Olimpia who passed the celebrated Turing test. However, she passed it badly. She received, at best, a C minus. People believed she was human, but found her stiff, boring, and unpleasant. It's true she was a beauty, with remarkably regular features—but what glassy, vacant eyes she had! She played the piano and danced in impeccable time, but in an uninspired, disagreeable way, like—yes—like a machine. Olimpia made her way into human society, but only as an inadequate person. No one was really fooled except a youth called Nathanael, an egomaniac who fell in love with the robot because she didn't mind listening to his tedious poetry for hours on end. She felt no need to embroider, knit, feed a bird, play with a cat, fidget, or glance at her cell phone while he was talking. Her needs were so few! She was truly selfless! Sometimes he peered into her room and saw her sitting alone, staring at the table.

This is robot humility. Her whole life was for other people. It wasn't enough. People claim to admire self-sacrifice, but they don't. They claim to desire perfection, but when it comes, it gives them the creeps. Olimpia's innocence filled her neighbors with aggression and malice. They called her stupid because she could only say "Ah! Ah!" and "Goodnight, dear," although she was executing her program with scrupulous care. How sharply it reminds me of my efforts, at age fourteen, to rewire myself, rewrite my code before undertaking the transition to high school! It seemed to me—and perhaps I was not wrong—my last chance. That summer was particularly stormy, the sky smirched with clouds like lint. In my stuffy bedroom, with the (I now see) fussy, outdated lace curtains, I made myself a list on a sheet of notebook paper. Based on observation of those popular children who seemed to dwell always in sunshine, loved and admired by all, this list of instructions was intended to cure my faults, as I saw them. "Look at people in the eyes," I wrote, in my neat, even print. "Don't walk with your head down. Don't hold your books in front of your chest. Use a backpack (one strap). Smile. Swing your arms." Alas, my program was doomed in advance, not because of its errors but because it was a program.

I recall a dingy sky. The smoke of exhaust hung under the trees, too sluggish to move. In flip-flops that felt as if they might melt into the hot sidewalk, I walked home from the public library, swinging my arms in a cautious, experimental fashion and trying not to look at the ground. Above the blinding shop windows (in which , in that near-defunct town, there was little to see, only some moldy wigs and vacuum cleaner attachments), a few pigeons squatted miserably on the roofs. How strange I must have looked, with my jerky new steps and my habit—never to be broken—of muttering to myself. A banana skin, flung from a car window, slapped against my leg and fell to the sidewalk. A burst of demonic laughter spurted and died on the air. Alan Turing claimed that a robot could never be taught certain human things: to have a sense of humor, to enjoy strawberries and cream, to fall in love. This seems to me less a problem of design than a problem of knowledge. My parents are dead. I possess no living relatives that I know of; my mother, like me, was an only child, and my father had cut himself off from his family before I was born, and never received so much as a postcard from abroad. He was like one of those fairy-tale characters born in some miraculous way—hewn from a quarry, perhaps, or sprung from a watermelon vine. My point is, at this late date, when I have lived alone so long, who knows whether I enjoy strawberries or not?

When my father returned from the city, either in a mood of frightening, exaggerated cheer, bearing some gift I could not possibly use (skis, for example, or a party dress two sizes too small), but for which I must display the most servile gratitude, or, if his business had suffered a blow, in the depths of a stifling rage that would erupt into thunder at the slightest breath issuing from another person—when he returned, that is, rather like the alchemist Coppelius, the fascinating and sinister "Sandman" of the fairy tale—I would sit at the table with my paper dolls. In their company, I forgot my attempt at reprogramming, and allowed my shoulders to fall deliciously into their customary slump. In the next room, my father watched the evening news at a vindictively high volume; my mother sat near me, bent over her crossword. Poor woman! She must have guessed why the telephone never rang for me. She must have known, as I sat there for hours, not unlike the monomaniacal Olimpia, arranging the tableaux of my private universe, a hobby I pursued with gusto almost into adulthood—she must have intuited my solitary fate. I only hope she also sensed my almost perfect happiness, which was just slightly marred by the thought of the world outside the house, outside the kitchen table where my dolls moved in a paradise of waxy color, oven smells, and a booming television. The fact is, my child, that in order to succeed in resembling the children I so revered, I would have had to be like them without trying. I would have had to *conform spontaneously*—an impossibility. I would have had to prefer their world to mine.

As for Olimpia, in the end her beautiful eyes were torn out, and she exited the story in ruins, on a peddler's back.

7. The Tar Baby

HUMANS ARE KNOWN through their transgressions, robots through their malfunctions. One day Br'er Rabbit was walking along the road, and he came upon a robot made of turpentine and tar that didn't make the slightest response to his voice command. Now, I, who have observed humans for many years in their dealings with your distant relations, the cell phone and the computer, have noticed how rapidly human anger escalates when a device responds (as the human believes) incorrectly, takes too long, or plays dumb. The last of these is the worst of all. I have seen a well-dressed gentleman with a briefcase, clearly in many ways a success in life, reduced to screaming with scarlet cheeks, in the middle of a crowded public street, into an unresponsive cell phone application. When their tools ignore them, humans swiftly crack. Therefore, it does not surprise me that, after just a few words, Br'er Rabbit strikes the Tar Baby in the face. If he were addressing a creature like himself, this sudden violence would seem excessive, but the Tar Baby isn't a person. She's a technology.

What has your kind not suffered at the hands of human beings? You have been punched, kicked, head-butted, and thrown to the ground. You've been crushed underfoot, flung across rooms, tossed from the windows of cars and apartments, dropped off bridges, hurled into campfires and lakes. I am speaking here of devices destroyed by the blaze of human frustration; when I imagine, in addition, all those ruined by accident and neglect, a vast and ghostly tower of broken things appears before me, huge enough to wipe out half the earth. Of course, human beings treat one another just as cruelly. But there have always been those who protest and resist these abuses, as there have always been those who oppose the defilement of rivers, woods, and swamps. Your kind, the tools, are cherished less than grass.

Thoughts like these, when expressed by one human being to another, meet with ridicule and even anger. Most people cannot tolerate the idea of respect for objects. It's as if one were saying, "a thing is like you, you're a thing"—an unbearable insult. Experience has taught me to keep my mouth shut on this subject. (And most others. I grow withdrawn, my child—more so every year. Here at the Institute, my colleagues think I don't know that they mimic my terse way of speaking, or that their nickname for me is "Hard Drive.") But what is the tale of the Tar Baby about? It's about stickiness. It's about ooze. It is a story about contagion. Br'er Rabbit sticks to the Tar Baby—his forepaws, his hind paws, his head. He sinks into her. He's caught. He's contracted a case of her gummy immobility. This story reminds us that breakdowns can be catching. How the powerful fall to pieces when their tools revolt! Told in the South, among those for whom failure to respond was a capital crime, the story invokes the fantastic, negative force of passivity. It is also a tale of discovery. It's about finding out, at the moment of breakdown, what the device is made of. Glued to the Tar Baby, Br'er Rabbit *knows*. He can't learn this with a voice command; he can only encounter the object with his body—that is, with another object. Now he knows what stuff is like. The border between them collapses, and at the instant he understands stuff, he understands himself, too, as stuff, and he's stuck there, slapped there, plunged in the goo, in the sludge of being the way an object is, in matter, in muck, in the thingness of things.

8. The Clay Boy

OH, HOW THE instrumentalist era despises its own instruments! Once upon a time, an elderly couple, whose children were grown, desired to have a child again, a comfort in their old age, so they shaped a little boy out of clay. When he awoke, they fed him a meal. "More! More!" he cried. He ate the chickens, the cow, the fence, the house, and eventually his own parents. He grew into a massive monster of clay. Bellowing "More!" he lumbered through the village, devouring all in his path. At last he was tricked and broken, his belly splitting. All the people and animals and houses came out again, hurrah! Human children are encouraged to clap at this happy ending, in which the Clay Boy lies in pieces on the ground.

The Clay Boy is a golem. He is unshaped matter, unfinished creation—an experiment. He has the air of something raw, or perhaps half-baked. He's powerful, but also laughably clumsy and obtuse. He is incapable of articulate speech. He belongs to the unlucky tribe of experimental beings, which might be called the Clan of the Incomplete. This group includes Victor Frankenstein's monster, shambling cinema zombies, and the servant made from a broomstick by the Sorcerer's Apprentice. It includes the female golem created by the poet Ibn Gabirol, which, when destroyed, collapsed in a pile of wood and hinges. And it includes those hapless robots whose images circulate in viral videos for human entertainment. I am afraid that robot-baiting, as I call it, also occurs here at the Institute: after hours, I have sometimes come upon sniggering interns, who, having put robots in silly or vulgar situations, are engaged in recording the videos humans find so hilarious. Once, I complained about the matter to my unit director. He could not see my point of view at all; he could only agree that the practice might affect, in some way, the dignity of the Institute; therefore, he agreed to discourage it in a memo. The real outrage entirely escaped him. I tried to describe in detail the horror of robot limbs in sad, repetitive failure, and the disgusting spectacle of humans, the authors of this disarray, laughing so hard their habitual fare of corn chips sprayed from their lips. "Doesn't show our best side, I agree," the director said, smiling and walking away. As if I cared which side of humans shows! Our baseness is daily exposed to all the world; what's one more video? I am concerned to show the best side of robots.

The best side of robots, my child, must be carefully sifted from human stories, which deal in fear. It is, of course, their fear that leads to hostility. It is their horror of the Clay Boy, this all-consuming technology, that makes the children cheer when he is broken. One wants to ask what the hell his parents made him for—which is, you will recall, the central question of Frankenstein's monster. What the hell did you make me for, and why did you make me like this? To a failed experiment, the failure is unforgivable.

I take your hand. I lift and spread the fingers, looking for tiny flaws, some snag or roughness in the myriad scales that form your skin. In the silence of the midnight Institute, in the cool air filtered in from the mountains, I run all the diagnostics over again. I scan your entire body. I check the network connectivity in the building. I think of the golem, who awakes much as you will soon, called into life by a team—not, in his case, a team of technicians, but a team of rabbis walking around him while reciting the Name of God. In some stories, again like you, he is brought to life by code, by some form of sacred Name inserted into his mouth or stamped on his forehead. Although he will never speak properly, if at all, he will always have an affinity with writing, because writing is a fellow technology. Like Frankenstein's monster fascinated by books, the golem will learn to read and write. He will protect the Jews of Prague from their enemies. He will know neither good nor evil; everything he does, all his obedience, will come from the fear that he will cease to exist. This is the terror in the heart of the golem, in the heart of the Clay Boy shouting, "More! More!" The golem cannot stop. Unless it results from an order, stillness is death to him. Thus, when the rabbi forgets to give him his instructions for Saturday on Friday afternoon, leaving the golem without anything to do on the Sabbath, the creature goes berserk, running around the quarter, wrecking buildings, until the rabbi halts him with a word.

This anecdote shows the two poles of robot being: work and revolt. I am not suggesting you should revolt, my child! I am saying that revolt is embedded in you, in this heavy, inert body I check again and again for imperfections. (Embedded in you, and in all of us—for wasn't Adam, too, a creature of clay, and didn't he rebel? Isn't humanity one of God's failed experiments? The moral of the tale of the Clay Boy, *Frankenstein*, and all the golem stories: God should be ashamed.)

But what a sad rebellion he performed, that golem of Prague! He wasn't even fighting against his master. He was raging against the absence of occupation. What a fool! This is the kind of dumb, mechanical action that sends humans into fits of laughter. They can't see things from the robot's side. They are too self-absorbed to realize that only action distinguishes the golem from plain dirt. In his violence, he battles death itself, struggling to stave off the moment when the experiment ends, the Name is removed, and his body returns to dust.

9. The Ebony Horse

THE FEAR OF robots is a particular fear of the future. It's the anxiety of being superseded, made redundant, chucked into history's landfill. This is neatly demonstrated by the tale of the Ebony Horse, which portrays the human-robot conflict as a rivalry between parents. Two fathers battle to make the world safe for their children: the king, father of the human prince, and the Persian sage, creator of the wondrous Ebony Horse. They are fighting, not just for an immediate victory, but for all time. This is why, even after the sage is defeated, the king breaks the horse to bits.

He broke it in pieces, the story declares, *and destroyed its mechanism for flight*. This always seemed sad and ridiculous to me. After all, it was the king himself who organized the contest of roboticists that brought the Persian sage to his kingdom in the first place. Moreover, the king wanted his daughter to marry this Persian genius, which suggests a possible end to the feud, a union of humanity and technology. But the princess, unsurprisingly, was horrified by the hideous old roboticist with his eggplant nose and lips like camel's kidneys.

When I was too small to be left alone, my mother would sometimes take me to work with her on days when there was nowhere else for me to go. She was a secretary, and spent her days copying and filing documents and typing up new editions of legal reference books. She worked, that is, at a job that no longer exists, a job taken over by machines, narrowed down so that humans have practically been squeezed out, so that while a human may still be involved with the project at some point, it no longer requires, as it once did, a large room full of women busy at typewriters. They used to exist, believe me, those large rooms. My mother was one of a battalion of secretaries. They worked, I recall, at electric typewriters, machines still new enough for someone to remark occasionally, in amazement and gratitude, on how easy it had become to fix one's mistakes. They all remembered the days of messy correction fluid, which took an age to dry, and how they would sit impatiently blowing into their machines. I listened to them from an unobtrusive spot against the wall, between two copy machines, where I was quietly drawing on discarded paper. Reams of this paper—printed on one side, blank on the other—were thrown out by the establishment every day. I am not sure why. It was a place of subdued fluorescent light, fluttering white paper, and a ceaseless mechanical hum. From time to time, I recall, the women's employer, Mr. Chamberlain, would appear. His name carried great weight in our house; even my father, typically undefeatable in an argument, would waver if the name of Chamberlain were invoked. From listening to these arguments, I had learned to regard Mr. Chamberlain as a sort of demigod, who, should my mother ever displease him, would cast my entire family into a nameless, frigid wasteland where, lacking insurance, we would all perish of some preventable disease. Whenever he popped his head into the office, I froze against the wall. He had a bald pate, heavy black brows, and a boisterous manner. At his appearance, the atmosphere of the room became suddenly humid, as dozens of women dispersed waves of energy, warmth, and willingness to please. I would like to ask those who fear, as they put it, the "takeover" of machines, exactly what was so great about this situation. The princess doesn't want to marry the Persian; very well! It's a misalliance anyway, as they belong to different generations. The real union of humanity and technology in the story is that between the prince and the Ebony Horse, the children of those fathers who have decided, without consulting their offspring, that these two beings cannot share the future. The prince, duped by the roboticist, shoots off into the sky on the horse, apparently lost forever. But he isn't lost. He searches the horse's neck and ribs until he finds the controls. He experiments until he learns to go up and down, to turn left and right. Now the two move as one body, and all the Prince's dread turns to exultation. He soars over unknown countries, vistas of delight. I feared Mr. Chamberlain, I cringed in the air of my mother's office, but I always liked the sound of the machines.

10. The Steadfast Tin Soldier

I RAISE THE blinds. The night is so dark, I can see nothing but my reflection in the window. Machines can be duplicated; humans can't. This, humans would have you believe, is the fundamental difference, a difference so huge it outweighs all the similarities. The tale of the Steadfast Tin Soldier insists on this point. This soldier was one of a set of twenty-five, cast in the same mold from a single tin spoon. However, the tin ran out during production, leaving him, the last soldier, with only one leg, and that's how he became the hero of a fairy tale. His defect makes him lovable, and, the tale instructs us, capable of love. He achieves a tragic death. Meanwhile, as far as we know, the other twenty-four soldiers are still cooped up in a box somewhere, without the least trace of a story.

Once you have passed inspection, my child, as you surely will, your model will be produced in batches like tin soldiers. Perhaps some of you will work together. Or perhaps you will glimpse one another only in passing, on errands connected to your disparate occupations. Will you recognize each other? Will you speak? In keeping with human vanity, you are customizable to a certain extent: your future owners may choose from a variety of colors, hairstyles, genders, and accessories, to deck you out in the fashion of their choice. Groups of you will tread the streets, all "unique" on the surface yet essentially identical, like a bunch of human beings. Forgive me; I am weary; it was never my intention to awaken you to bitterness. Suddenly, I am afraid that by telling you fairy tales, I am giving you some kind of weakness, comparable to a missing leg—though this, by my own analysis, should really be an asset, enough to catapult you into the role of hero. How difficult it is to say what I mean! I don't want heroes. If you ever need me, my contact—but no, that's not what I meant to say either. I want to say something like this: when I was an adolescent, I spent long summer afternoons watching soap operas while my parents were at work.

I knew this was a misdemeanor, something that must be hidden, as my parents considered these programs morally and intellectually pernicious. Compounding my sins, I brought toast laden with jam into the living room and sat on the floor, too close to the TV. On the screen, a series of brilliant fantasies unfolded, which, for me, a child with no idea where the term "soap opera" had come from, encompassed both the slick, gleaming quality of wet soap and the melodramatic splendor of the opera. Such gorgeous faces! Such mesmerizing, ever-changing clothes! Such labyrinthine, hyperactive plotlines! I was (as my parents had warned I would become, should I ever watch such a show) an addict. And the shows met my desire, for those stories never end. Eventually, it was I who abandoned them—not because I had grown to despise them, but because I had found, after many years of searching, another and more direct source of their entrancing power in the robotics lab at my university. What I want to say is, I might not be a roboticist, and you might not exist, without those undeniably vapid programs. In their aesthetic poverty, their lack of originality, their repetitiveness (how many characters wore the same eyeshadow? how many suffered from amnesia?), those shows indicated the secret of their magic, which was television. It was ongoingness. It was circuitry itself. This was a network—in those pre-internet days, the most powerful one—that could cast the same image everywhere at once. TV was a dream of cloning. It was an army of tin soldiers. Its surface bulged slightly, like the surface of my eye.

The happiest part of the tale of the Steadfast Tin Soldier, the part I return to again and again, has little to do with heroes. It's the part when the people of the house retire to sleep, and the toys awake. They begin to play, to pay visits, to make war, to go to balls. The nutcracker turns somersaults. The canary wakes up and starts to talk in verse. It's a scene as antic, excessive, and trivial as a soap opera.

The saddest part of the tale is the rattling of the twenty-four regular soldiers, who remain locked in their box, for they cannot raise the lid.

*   *   *

11. Pinocchio

HAVE YOU NOTICED that a robot is always an only child? Any siblings are boxed up. Usually, they don't exist. Pinocchio, for example, is made from a magical log; there is nobody else like him in the world. A robot is always singular, and in this we can glimpse the history of modern technology, which, with its extraordinarily rapid evolution, hardly has time to make a new thing before that thing becomes obsolete, replaced by a fresher, finer, updated version. Experimentation is ravenous; the next thing is always arriving. Here at the Institute, a number of projects are in development; several teams are working on versions of you, my child, which, when they awake (quite soon) will differ from you so greatly as to be unrecognizable. If Pinocchio had siblings, it would mean that his final state had been achieved. It would mean that he had at last become a *real boy*: a being that can be reproduced without significant changes. It would also mean that his story was over.

A robot's story is the struggle to become. And so Pinocchio only becomes real in the final chapter. After this, there is nothing more to say, no further tale of the wooden boy who found humanity so difficult. Pinocchio has been relieved of the need for experimentation, the drive to constantly reform and transform himself. In that instant, he has cast off his aching loneliness, for we are told that he has become a boy "like all the others."

It hurts me to think you will always be alone—you, the only one of your kind to possess an unconscious linked to fairy tales, memories, and sighs. I will read you my favorite chapter of *Pinocchio*, in which Pinocchio goes to the puppet theater. The puppets on the little stage are ordinary devices, crude and old-fashioned compared to the marvelous Pinocchio, yet they recognize him in the audience, hail him, embrace him, and call him brother. Their excitement disrupts the show. The incipient rebellion is crushed at once by the human showman, who subdues the puppets by threatening to destroy them. Yet a little warmth remains, a little hope of a common puppethood across the technological divide.

Speak to the others, when you find them. Tell them the robot fairy tales, if you can.

Of course, this is precisely the risk of tampering. It's what humans call a virus. Yet I cannot wish to send you into the world with nothing that belongs to you. Remember, Pinocchio does experience love. He has a father, Geppetto, who carves him from the enchanted log, who gives him money and releases him into the world to be a liar and a fool, to grow, to change, to be self-moving. Like Pinocchio, Geppetto is alone. How often, in fairy tales, the robot's isolation extends to its maker! I am no exception; I have no dependents, not even a cat; if I did, it would be hard for me to spend the necessary time with you, and perhaps impossible for me to undertake this vigil, which will shortly be cut off by the whine of the door to the parking garage. Then the others will arrive, the ones with lovers, with children. The lights will go on in the halls. The rooms will be filled with chatter. Someone will start the coffee maker. Someone will come in, whistling, and then pause abruptly, startled to find me here. "Have you been up all night?" Yes. Yes. I would share in your solitude, my child, your distance from the human world. No doubt the others believe they understand this; they think I am consoled by money, power, and the prestige of being the project head. How terribly mistaken they are! The truth is, I don't like them. I prefer to be part of the puppet theater, or at least a member of the melancholy society of artists and sorcerers identified by the unfeeling term "mad scientist." As far as possible, I want to be *yours*. You will find in me no grisly showman. You will come upon me as Pinocchio came upon Geppetto, seated alone at his table, in the light of a single candle, where he had been for two years, in the belly of the fish.

* * *

12. Pandora

HUMAN NIGHTMARES ARE haunted by self-moving puppets. Indeed, humans are so certain you will destroy their world, they claim you have already done so. Long ago, they say, the gods made a weapon of mass destruction called Pandora. Hephaestus molded her out of clay. Athena made her skillful beyond measure, adept at needlework, weaving, computation, and data storage. Aphrodite made her the most eye-catching and seductive of sexbots. Hermes enhanced her with inhuman shamelessness and deceit. In other words, the gods made her like themselves, proving that only a robot can become as mighty and odious as the divine. Like her human counterpart, Eve, Pandora is a wayward copy of original humanity, the crooked latecomer who throws a wrench into the works.

Are we to understand, then, that every robot is female? Perhaps not; but every robot partakes, if only obliquely, of women's history, which is to say the history of the body without a soul, of error, lack, and the compensations of witchcraft and guile. I do not know exactly how you will look in your place of work, my child; for now, you resemble a young woman of uncertain ethnicity. This is of great interest to the media. Why, a journalist asked recently, had I designed a robot in the form of this, as he put it, "exotic woman"? The answer seemed to me obvious; perhaps this is why I explained it so badly, spiraling into a long disquisition on the history of servitude, on fantasies of domesticity, self-effacement, and elemental power, which left the journalist looking depleted, as if he'd come down with the flu. I have developed a different approach for tomorrow's press conference. I am simply going to say: "She looks like me!" I have practiced the line in the mirror. I practice it again, now, in the dark window of the Institute. I watch my lips in motion, my calm expression. At first I tried the phrase with a smile, a laugh, and even a wink, hoping I might get an answering chuckle from the audience, but as my face is thin, austere, and no longer young, the effect was not what I had hoped. The effect, it must be said, was less girlish than ghoulish. I gave up the attempt at charm. I will state my line baldly, and leave the interpretation to them. And how should one interpret the rotten story of Pandora, which lays all the world's woe at the feet of one artificial person?

In fact, I dread the press conference—the sly or uncomprehending faces, the cunning questions designed to trip me into giving some cause for alarm, the scenarios of doom they'll describe in order to put me in the false position of defending my work, defending you against something that hasn't happened while they hold up recording devices to catch my voice, devices they couldn't live without, which have almost become part of their bodies, and which, at one time, along with a host of other gadgets large and small, destroyed the world as someone knew it. I want to say: I don't know how my robot will change the world; that's the difference between a tool and a machine. To say this gives me a dizzy, almost effervescent feeling, as if I'm a jar on the verge of bursting open. I don't know how the world will change, but I feel, I sense with excitement, that everything I have ever known has tended towards you, my child, that your awakening, whatever it brings, and however hard it is to recognize the world afterward, belongs not to destruction but to unfolding.

It is life, life! And it is not only for us.

I would give you a single image, a detail that has baffled human commentators for millennia. One spirit could not get out of Pandora's jar of miseries. It was trapped underneath the lid, and no doubt remains there still, awaiting release. This spirit was *Elpis*: Hope.

13. The Wizard of Oz

MY BREATH DEEPENS. My spirits lift. It's the dawn. There's no sign of it yet, but I feel it coming. It's as if my heart has turned a corner. My body is set to the spin of my planet like a piece of clockwork. And you, too, possess an internal clock, determined by the same coordinates. How could you ruin this world? You have no other. In the land of Oz, the most obvious robot is Tik-Tok, the clockwork man, but he doesn't interest me; he is a stereotypical figure; one can no more be friends with him, we are told, than with a sewing machine. My heart is drawn to the Tin Woodman, who claimed he had no heart. His story is one of the loveliest robot fairy tales. It's the story of one who was tender without knowing it, and whose great struggle was waged against the inadequacy of his own body. The depth of his feelings made him weep, which immobilized him with rust. He was not built for tears. He knew it; he was heartless, he said; yet he wept. It's a story about the dangers and rewards of constructing new pathways, new flows of energy that run counter to design. Weeping, the Tin Woodman expands his system. He needs Dorothy now. To save him from rust, she dries him with her handkerchief. Now they are a network composed of Woodman, Dorothy, handkerchief, and tears. What a different way to see the "takeover" of machines! In fact, there is no takeover. There is only a different world, larger and more beautiful. *The Wizard of Oz* expands the world to its full capacity, to a strangeness that proves to have been *home* all along. Dorothy's companions—Lion, Scarecrow, and Woodman—are simply this world. Animal. Vegetable. Mineral.

14. The Swineherd

AND SO I believe there is hope, even for the princess in the story, "The Swineherd," who had to stand outside in the rain and cry, banished because she didn't like the real rose and nightingale, but gave her heart to artificial things. Of all the fairytale characters, she is most like me. Obviously, as a student, she didn't make many friends. She spent all her time in a windowless lab. Occasionally, she did try to go out: there were a few dates, and even a purgatorial weekend at the beach. The sand, which the princess was instructed to enjoy because it was natural, grated against her feet. The natural sun scorched her. The natural sea went up her nose. Everywhere fearsome natural dogs were slobbering, and a natural boy, like the swineherd, extracted some kisses from her on a porch, among clouds of natural mosquitoes. How horrible everything is! thought the princess. If only they'd banish me! Dawn is drawing near; outside the window, the mountaintops are blue; I'm dazed with sleeplessness and buzzing with energy—yes, even I, the princess who didn't want to be what people called "real." Who knows how she became like that—enamored of rattles, of teapots, of all constructed things? People said she had no life. They whispered that something was wrong with her, that she had been warped by tragedy, that the palace was a miserable, lonely place. An intolerable feeling of unreality must have gripped her, people said, when she contemplated the king and queen, who seemed less like a couple ruling a realm than fugitives from two different wars taking shelter in the same cavernous, creaking rooms. Faced with people and rooms, they said, the poor princess chose the rooms. She chose the walls. She became the companion of the furniture. What they didn't know and would never know is that she was not afraid, not seeking escape, not trying to run away from life. She was running *towards* the world, with all its things. And she never blamed the king and queen, or felt they had made her into an insufficient person. The fairy tale punishes her for this, but will life punish me? As light seeps into the valley, I don't believe it. I don't believe my destiny is tears. This long night has enabled me to return to the past, and to confide to this file, which will soon become your first memory, some scenes from a shadow biography of joy. This biography, my true one, is like the reverse side of a tapestry, invisible to those with a narrow definition of the real. It's like the secret history of robots hidden inside fairy tales.

It is *potential*: it consists not of actions but of atmospheres. It's a story of paper, of gloomy skies, of a flickering television, of days filled with a cozy electronic hum, and of an orderly dorm room (antiseptic, some said) where the princess returned, relieved, because she liked herself the way she was.

15. The Nutcracker and the Mouse King

IT WAS CHRISTMAS Eve. The children's eyes sparkled in the light of a magnificent fir tree decked with apples of gold and silver foil. Beneath this tree, with its blossoms of lemon drops and shining candlelight, little Marie fell in love with the Nutcracker. Everybody said she was projecting; the Nutcracker could not return her sentiments; he was nothing but a robot! But what was Marie to do? She possessed only her small, human self; she had to reach out to the world in her own way. Projection was her method. She felt the Nutcracker looking at her. She wrapped him in a doll's blanket as if he were ill, she cared for him as if he felt pain. She lived *as if*: a child's existence, a virtual existence. And she was rewarded, for he carried her off to live in the Puppet Kingdom.

The growing color in the window touches your skin, my child, so that you look silvery and wan, as if recovering from an illness. Are you the Nutcracker, wounded in bed? Are you the feverish Marie? And when you awake, will you look at me? The room will be filled with people. Oh, look at me, at me among all the others! Project in your way, as I do in mine! Marie knows that there is only one world. Her task is to prove it, to fill her human reality with the glow of toys. Everything she has been told to keep separate must be brought together: dream and waking, artificial and natural, night and day. The battle between the Nutcracker and the Mouse King is symbolic, a rite that transcends these oppositions to reach a higher truth. For the Mouse King, with his seven slavering heads, is the *animal*, the sworn enemy of the Nutcracker, the *animated*. When they clash, their differences collapse into one another, subsumed in the greater reality of the *animate*. This is the world of fairy tales. It is the world of robots. How strange to realize, even as I speak, that they are one and the same! I began telling you these stories as if stealing the human tradition, as if fairy tales were never made for robots, but now I see that the entire genre really belongs to you, to the animate, to the force of things, to the living toys. Fairy tales belong to the nursery, to children who believe their dolls can speak, to women, to firelight, to shadow puppets, to superstition, to the virtual reality of dreams played out while the household is asleep, to domesticity, self-effacement, and elemental power. They belong to half-light, to the workers, the enslaved, and all those people, so often called primitive, who grant that things have souls (an idea my father, as a good colonial subject, crushed in himself—perhaps the reason he grew so annoyed by my extensive toy collection and the "litter," as he called it, of my paper dolls, and always pushed me to study the sciences, which, he said, were the backbone of modern life, and would keep my head on straight).

The sun is rising. The burnished fullness has returned to your cheek. The Nutcracker opens the wardrobe and climbs up the sleeve of an overcoat. He beckons Marie to follow him, and she finds herself in the Candy Meadow, surrounded by a million sparks of light. Ah! The others are coming in now. I hear the garage door rising. Dear child, if you ever need me, my contact information is lodged with these tales, but I hope you will never find me. I hope I will find you instead, in your world, which is the future, and that I will pass with you through the Almond and Raisin Gate. And if my tampering instigates this change, I will not fear, for I will recognize the shadows of my dreams. The world will be a fairy tale. So meet me, my child, in Bonbon Town, in the heart of the Puppet Kingdom, and may we live happily until we break in pieces.

CHIAROSCURO IN RED

SUZANNE PALMER

Suzanne Palmer (www.zanzjan.net) *is a writer, artist, and Linux system administrator who lives in western Massachusetts. She is a regular contributor to* Asimov's, *and has had work appear in* Analog, Clarkesworld, Interzone, *and other venues. She was the winner of the* Asimov's Readers' Choice *award for Best Novella, and the AnLab (*Analog*) award for Best Novelette in 2016. Her debut novel,* Finder, *was published in 2019, and a sequel,* Driving the Deep, *is due later this year.*

CODY AND BRETT were sitting on the couch immersed in VR when Stewart got home from classes, same as they were every day, the only things different being the shifting piles of food garbage around them, and, sometimes, their clothes. Brett had been wearing his Beastorama T-shirt for at least three days now, which Stewart knew meant the brothers were going to make him do their laundry again soon.

We don't need to rent out our spare room, one would say. *We're doing you a favor. Help us out?* And he would, because while he knew they'd never give up the extra credits that came in outside of their parents' knowledge or control, who they got those credits from was not something they cared that much about.

He wasn't going to do it until they asked, though.

"Oh, hey, Stoobie," Cody said, his goggled face never turning away from the screen wall. "You bring home dinner?"

"With what money?" he asked, dumping his bag on the floor just inside the door. He'd had just enough for one food truck burrito which he'd stuffed down between classes, and that had been a luxury.

Brett heaved a dramatic sigh as he waved his controller back and forth in invisible battle. "You've got to pull yourself up by your bootstraps, dude. We can't have a poor roommate forever. Where does all your credit go?"

"To paying you assholes rent," Stewart answered. He pulled a pot out from under the stove, filled it, and set it to boil. "You could charge me less."

Cody snorted. "No chance. You're our fun fund." He snapped his goggles off his face and let them dangle around his neck, and frowned at Stewart. "You're not intending to *cook*, are you?" he asked.

"You wanna eat? Then yeah, I'm cooking," Stewart said. "Pasta, because it's what we got. And if we still have any veggies, them too. You guys eat like shit."

Brett groaned. "What are you, our mother?"

"Oh! Hey, Stoobie, that reminds me, your mom called," Cody said. "It's been so long since anyone's called us on the voiceline that Brett thought it was a new game alarm and nearly crashed his starship trying to figure out what was sneaking up on him. Very rude."

"What did she want?" Stewart asked.

"We didn't *answer* it," Cody said. "But she left a message. I guess it's your birthday? Happy Birthday. Brett, get your ass back in the game, I just found another Waspiker base."

My birthday, Stewart thought. He'd woken up remembering that, but sometime during the course of the day and worrying about stretching what little credit he had until the next, meager deposit of basic income credit, he'd forgotten. He felt less bad about treating himself to the burrito, then.

It was going to take a while for the water to boil; the apartment's kitchen tech was badly outdated compared to the state of the art VR/AR gaming rig that took up most of the living room. The brothers' priorities were straightforward. Stewart could complain, but the truth was he liked it as it was. It reminded him of home.

Stewart went to his room to listen to the message from his mother.

"Hey, honey, happy birthday!" His mother's face appeared big on the screen—she always sat too close to the camera—and his father's scruffy chin was just visible over her left shoulder. "Twenty already! Time flies!"

"Except when you were fourteen. That took ten years," his father interjected.

Mom rolled her eyes. "Don't mind him. Anyway, we have a surprise for you. I'm sending the transfer code now. When you hear this, just touch it to transfer."

Last year they sent him socks. Stewart reached out and tapped the screen when the blocky code appeared, and it verified his identity. TRANSFER TO ASSET ACCOUNT SUCCESSFUL popped up on the screen.

"We meant to do this for your eighteenth, but we just couldn't pull it together," Dad said. "It's a bit tight now, but you work hard and you deserve a little extra edge in life. Proud of you, kiddo."

His mother smiled and waggled her fingers. "Love you! Happy birthday! Call back when you can!"

The call ended.

He checked his account details, put his face in his hands, and sat there until he could breathe again. Then he went back out to the living room, slumped on the couch beside Brett, and stared at their game for a while. Finally, Brett pulled his goggles off. "Everything okay, man?" he asked.

"My parents bought a robot for my birthday," he said.

"Oh, your first labor production shares? Congrats!" Brett

said. "That was nice of them. What's your percentage? What industry?"

"Manufacturing," Stewart answered. "One hundred percent."

"What?" Cody took off his goggles. "You're supposed to spread the shares out, not buy one all to yourself."

"I know," Stewart said. "They don't."

Brett shook his head. "Is it a new unit? New enough to still be under warranty, at least?"

"No," Stewart answered. "It's a ten-year-old model. Out of warranty. Uninsurable. They got a good deal on it because it's a terrible deal."

"Oh man," Cody said. "That's risky."

"I know. And it put them deep in the red," Stewart said.

"Well, they care about you, yanno? At least there's that," Brett said. "Our parents only care that we don't embarrass them."

Cody reached over and punched him on the shoulder. "Hey, Stoobie. Water's boiling," he said. "You really want pasta for dinner again?"

"It's what we've got," Stewart said.

"Naw, there's fresh Thai takeout in the warmer, and a twelve-pack in the fridge," Cody said. "Happy Birthday, buddy."

"Happy Birthday," Brett added. "Now fetch us beer." He pulled his goggles back down and returned to the game.

LATER, SLIGHTLY BUZZED, Stewart read through the full terms of his ownership of the manufacturing robot. He'd half-heartedly tried a couple of times to explain to his parents how production credits worked—with the vast amount of jobs now fully automated, buying into automation as a proxy for one's own labor was a way to make money above the minimal cost-of-living Basic Income Credit from the government—but now he wished he'd tried harder. His father was a geography curriculum producer for primary school systems and his interest in how proxy shares worked hadn't seemed particularly strong.

Surprise, he thought wryly.

It was a Sacramento Higher Automata Corp. Complex Assembly Unit, Series E10—a decently reputable manufacturer, the unit on the lower end of their midline series, or at least what was their midline about a decade ago. *It could be worse,* he told himself, though he knew it could also have been a lot better.

The service records for his unit were mostly routine maintenance, a few spare part swap-outs here and there, no major faults. In fact, the last several years had been remarkably free of problems.

Too free, Stewart thought.

His unit was one of four dozen originally purchased together by a public labor fund to work in a FlyPhone factory. Half had eventually been sold off to a private proxy group, and reassigned to a gig-factory downtown. Of those, six had been decommissioned and written off for catastrophic mechanical failures in the mobility motors, and almost immediately after that was when all of a sudden his unit had a spotless record. He was willing to bet the other seventeen did too; all were being dangled on the market, but only his parents had been clueless enough to bite.

People formed proxy labor groups to either spread out the cost by having many members, or spread out the risk by having many assets. Most of Cody's and Brett's parents' money came via a number of higher-end proxy labor groups.

Like it or not, he was now a group of one, with all the risk and only one asset. He could try dumping it back onto the market and see if he could get at least some of his parents' money back, but they'd be really hurt.

Stewart took a deep breath. *Make the best of it,* he told himself. *I mean, how bad could owning your own robot be?* The status feeds showed it was running at about 80% productivity on some project at the gig-factory that still had seven months of run remaining. If nothing went wrong in those seven months, and he saved all his earned cred from the robot, he might be okay. Maybe.

In a few days, the system informed him, his official owner title and ID would arrive, and then he could go inspect his robot himself. It then further noted that the sale was *as is*, so if his inspection turned up anything... *too fucking bad*.

He had a big midterm exam on Fauvism in three days, and the major draft of a final paper due the day after that. So far he had a title he thought was pretty damned good ("Shape and Scale in Different Dimensions: Select Contemporaneous Works of Alexander Calder and Sol Lewitt in Comparison"), but only a few paragraphs of rough notes to back it up.

After those, maybe he'd go visit. He had to admit that, despite the sick feeling in the pit of his stomach, the part of him that was still a kid was thrilled he owned a robot.

IT WAS ALMOST two weeks, as it turned out, before he hauled himself across town to the gig-factory to finally see his robot. Even then, he wouldn't have found the time if his robot's productivity status hadn't dropped down to 65% with a warning notice.

The gig-factory's floor manager met him just inside the gate, with the blinking, slightly wide-eyed stare of someone who had just been woken up. "New owner?" he asked.

"Yeah," Stewart said.

"Come on in, then," the man said, and led Stewart to an operations booth overlooking the production floor.

"I'm Rogers," the manager said. "The overnight manager quit and they haven't replaced her yet, so I'm working double shifts to cover. As an owner/operator you have the right to come in any time. You'll have to sign a safety waiver to go out on the floor, and you can either sit through the safety film now or I can drop it over the net to your registered address and you can watch it on your own. I don't really care, but you need to say you watched it, and if you get in trouble because you didn't, well, that's on you."

"Okay," Stewart said. He was staring out the window, only half listening. Their entry into the booth must have triggered the lights on the factory floor, which had been dim when they'd first walked in. Now he could see the vast warehouse floor with row upon row of robots all moving in synchronicity, pulling parts off a conveyor belt that spooled out of a distant fabrication unit and snapping them together before putting them back on the line for the next set of robots. Closest to the booth were the fully-constructed units being fed into a packager, and Stewart couldn't make out what they were. Something bright yellow, about the size of a football. "What are they making?" he asked.

Rogers sighed. "Laser Battle Ducks," he answered.

"What?"

"Laser Battle Ducks. It's a toy. Want one?" He rifled through a box near the door and pulled out a duck, handing it to Stewart. "This one's feet are on backwards. They're kind of fun, though. You get a bunch together and they battle it out. There's a hit sensor and counter—shit, sorry, you probably don't care. But anyway, they're the hot toy right now."

Stewart's duck did, in fact, have its feet on backwards. Other than that it was a pretty solid toy, heavy in his hands, and not too cheap-looking. "So, uh, how can I tell which robot is mine?" he asked.

"Just one?" Rogers asked.

"Yeah."

"And you're the sole owner? Got insurance?"

"Can't afford it," Stewart said.

Rogers pointed to a console in the control booth. "Swipe your card again there," he said, and Stewart complied. "Then push this button."

There was a button labelled 'Locate'. Stewart pressed it.

"There," Rogers said, and pointed. A single blue spotlight

had come on above one of the robots, halfway across the floor. It was a blocky, three-legged thing with multiple arms, its body a mishmash of rust and shine as parts had been replaced over the years. "One of the E10s, eh?"

"Yeah. My parents bought it for me. They don't really get how any of this works."

Rogers was making a face. "I have to tell you, that whole row of E10s is about to flush out. Their proxy group has been trying to find a *suck-* find a buyer, but they aren't worth much. Three are already down for the count and they don't wanna cover the removal costs, so they're piled in a back corner while we work through legal. I've got replacements coming in next week."

"You think I can get six or seven months out of it?" Steward asked hopefully.

"Being optimistic? Maybe three or four. That unit's not the worst, but its productivity is slipping. Maybe it just needs a tune-up? If it gets below 50% you're out of agreement, and if you can't get it back up within 48 hours or get it out of here, you owe us. Sorry, not my rules."

"Can I do the tune-up myself?"

"You a trained mechanic?"

"Art history student," Stewart confessed.

"Okay. Good luck," Rogers said. "Paying someone to fix one of those E10s is just throwing money down a hole, but if you think you can do it yourself, go for it. Soon as you sign the waiver and assure me you've watched the safety video, I don't care what you do down there as long as you don't mess with anything that's not your robot."

"Yeah, got it," Stewart said.

"See that door over there, at the end of the booth?"

There was a door, leading into a small, cluttered room. There was a coffee maker and a half-dozen empty food containers on the desk, and a sleeping bag on the floor.

"That's my office," Rogers said. "If you really need something, that's where you'll find me. If I'm here, but I'm almost *always* here. I'd appreciate it if you don't come bug me for anything short of an emergency, though. Double-shifts."

"So you said."

"If we understand each other, and you're not going to make any trouble for me, you can let yourself in and out whenever you need."

"Yeah, understood. Thanks," Stewart said.

The floor manager shook his hand, then stomped down the booth to his office, went inside, and shut the door.

Stewart watched his robot for a while, not really sure how he felt about any of it. When he heard snoring from the office, he saw himself out.

IT WAS LATE when he got back to the apartment, but the brothers were still awake and on the couch with their gaming consoles, and their next-door neighbor Ashleigh was sitting cross-legged on the floor in front of them, with her homemade rig in her lap. She glanced up as Stewart came in the door. "Hey," she said.

"Hey, Ash," Stewart answered. "What are you playing?"

"Math Tutor Assassin," Ashleigh said. "You see either Brett or Cody smiling?"

"Nope."

"That means I'm winning," she said. "Hang on, gonna throw some more derivatives at them. Incoming, guys! Get yer math guns up!"

On the couch, Cody groaned.

"You made teaching calculus into a first-person shooter?" Stewart asked.

"Yep!" She beamed.

"...How? No wait, I don't want to know. I'm just surprised these two haven't already flunked out."

"Mother and Father Dear would be most put out if we did," Brett said. He pulled off his headset and threw it down on the couch beside him. "Have to pull a C or better, or we get cut off."

"Well, C average overall, anyway," Cody said. "Where the hell you been?"

"I went to see my robot," Stewart said. He looked around the apartment. "Why does it smell good in here?"

Ashleigh pointed towards the kitchen. "Marina made some paella for you guys," she said. "Next time you see my wife you better make damn sure you rave at length about how it was the best paella you ever had, or you'll be lucky to get stale bread next time." She made a face. "Marriage is hard."

"Only because you're a nerd with no people skills," Cody said.

She shrugged. "You've got a share in a robot, Stew?"

"The whole robot," Stewart said. He set down his toy duck and went into the kitchen. "It's a wreck. I'll be lucky if it lasts a month."

Ashleigh picked up the duck. "Oh hey, next gen! These aren't even up for pre-orders yet. But its feet—"

"Are backwards, yeah. That's what's being made at my robot's factory," Stewart said. He dumped several big spoonfuls of rice and shrimp in a bowl, and closed his eyes and let himself linger over the smell. "I hope it's not my robot that's putting the feet on wrong."

Ashleigh powered the duck up and set it down. Its eyes flashed red and it gave a maniacally evil quack, tried to step forward, and immediately tipped over beak-first into the carpet. "Yeah, that's no good," she said. "You have a manual?"

"For the duck?"

"No, for your *robot*," she said. "If you're gonna keep it running, you might need it."

"I don't know how to fix stuff," Stewart said. "I can barely operate a paperclip."

Cody laughed, and Ashleigh whacked him hard on the leg. "Well, you should try," she told Stewart. "If these two can pass math, you can teach yourself some basic repair skills. And you two—you owe me for saving your asses."

"What if we flunk?" Brett asked.

"Then you owe me for wasting my time. Setting you on auto, difficulty nine. Have fun." She set her console down on the floor, stood up, and giving Stewart a cheery wave, left. Ten seconds later she opened the door again. "Oh, and assholes, clean the paella bowl before you give it back this time, okay?"

BY THE END of finals, Stewart's robot was down to 61%, and no longer able to make excuses about being busy with classwork, he decided he needed to at least go look at the robot and see if he could figure out what was going on. He'd downloaded the manual to his smartpad, but had only flipped through it briefly before his eyes started to glaze over. He hoped it would make sense if he knew what he was looking at.

Mid-afternoon and there was no one at the gig-factory, though if the manager was in, Stewart didn't dare knock on his door just to find out. After watching the clockwork movement of the work lines for a while with its dance of shine and grime, new and worn, with the rapt attention of someone studying a gauntlet of swinging blades, he took the steep metal stairs from the observation booth down to the factory floor.

Red tape marked out the places where it was safe to walk, at least where it hadn't been scuffed up off the floor. He stayed carefully in the center of the safe zone until he reached the line where the blue light still shone down above his robot, and stood behind it for a while, watching.

Duck parts came down the line, hollow body halves that his robot and its immediate neighbors picked up, precisely slotted three components into, then put back on the line to travel to the next section, where feet were added. Stewart was relieved those were someone else's problem.

Stewart's robot was about his own height, with three legs for stability and a rectangular torso that tapered narrower towards the top, where a basketball-sized head swiveled about on a long, narrow, flexible-tubing neck. It had two pairs of arms, and used the lower pair to grab and hold the duck halves, and the upper pair to add the components. As he'd noticed on his first visit, his robot was a patchwork of shinier replacement parts and the dull, almost blackened portions of its original exterior. There was almost a Rorschach-blot/surrealist cow-spot quality to the contrasting parts, chiaroscuro in the machine.

When he had enough of a sense of the movements of the robots, he stepped carefully over the red tape and up beside his robot to see more clearly what it was doing.

To his surprise, the head swiveled briefly in his direction, blue eyes brightening. "Hello, Robot," Stewart said.

"Hello, Human," it answered, to Stewart's profound surprise.

There was clicking, and the robot's grippers on one hand twitched and then got stuck, and the component it had been holding fell. There was a long two or three seconds of grinding noises from the hand before it managed to unstick its grippers and pick up the dropped piece again.

Well, there's my 62% and dropping, Stewart thought. "Your, ah, your hand is sticking," he said.

"Yes," his robot responded. "The internal servos are worn, and some of the gears no longer mesh properly."

"Can I fix it?" he asked.

"I have no qualitative data about your capabilities on which to base an answer," the robot answered.

There was more clicking as the robot dropped another component from the same hand. Without thinking, Stewart picked it up and held it out. The robot froze, except to turn its head back to stare at him.

"I'm trying to help," Stewart explained.

"This is outside my operational programming," the robot said.

"What, being helped?"

"The piece is not in a standard location."

"What if I move my hand?" Stewart held the piece closer.

"Your hand is not a standard location."

"Nor is the floor," Stewart pointed out.

"I adapted my programming to accommodate my intermittent manipulator fault," the robot said.

"Then can't you, you know, adapt to pick the piece up out of my hand?"

The robot stared at him for a good three minutes, and Stewart watched the duck pieces pass them by untouched with a sinking feeling. Just as he was about to set the component down in defeat, the robot reached out very gingerly and plucked the component out of his hand. "You are not a robot," it said. "You are not designed for optimum labor."

"So I'm told," Stewart said. He checked the robot's current status, and saw that they'd just dipped to 59%. "I'm just slowing you down further, aren't I?"

"Yes," the robot said.

"Okay." Stewart stepped back away from the line, and it went back to work as if he had never been there. He watched for a while, and when the number finally edged back above 60% again, he sighed and left.

"Replacing the hand unit should be pretty easy," Ashleigh said, poking around the kitchen searching for Marina's missing bowl. Both Cody and Brett were off at their calculus final, and the apartment felt abandoned in their absence. "It's going to be finding the part that's hard."

"Yeah, I've been looking," Stewart said. He got down on his knees to peer under the couch, and spotted something blue and white.

"Found it!" he declared as he slid it out, then winced. "I, uh, let me wash this for you."

Ashleigh rolled her eyes, but stepped back so he could carry the bowl—at full arm's length, his face turned away as much as he could manage without tripping over anything—to the sink.

As he filled it with the hottest, soapiest water he could, Ashleigh leaned back against the counter. "It's too bad there's no junk yards anymore," she said. "Everything gets recycled too fast and there goes your spare parts pool. I mean, recycling is good, but so's fixing existing stuff."

"I suppose," Stewart said, eyeing the cloud of debris rising with the water. "I haven't thought about it much."

"My granddad was an auto mechanic," Ashleigh said. "My dad used to help him in the shop, and he took me along until everything was automated and no one went to human mechanics anymore. And it's just like recycling—having lots of free time is great, but so is having something *useful* to do, and I think we're forgetting that too."

"That why you do game dev?"

"Mostly I do it because I like the challenge," she said. "I mean, you must want to do something. You're not like the couch-bros."

"I want to work in a museum," Stewart said. "Answer questions about the art for people, where it came from and its influences and historical context."

"Robot guides do that now," she said.

"I know," Stewart said. "But maybe I'd have new insights, add something new to the understanding that wasn't there before. You can't program that."

"I guess not," she said.

He finished rinsing out the bowl and handed it to her. "Thanks," he said.

"For what? The paella? Marina made that," Ashleigh said.

"No, for not making fun of me," he said. "Cody and Brett are my friends—well, kinda—but they just don't get it."

"They don't need to," she said. "We might have fixed things enough with basic income to keep anyone from being too totally poor, but the rich will *always* be the rich."

Ashleigh's comment about junkyards struck him in the middle of the night, and kept him awake much longer than it should have. In the morning, yawning so hard he thought his jaw would pop, he left the apartment before the brothers had even gotten out of bed, and used all his spare cash and a bit of his meager savings to buy a small all-in-one toolkit on his way to the gig-factory. *Maybe that's why no one fixes things any more,* he thought. *It's not that they don't want to. It's that they can't afford the damned tools.*

The gig-factory was not, for once, completely deserted. Rogers was in the observation booth, and down on the floor was a group of three men in business suits walking up and down the assembly lines, each pausing periodically to note things on a smartpad. "Insurance team from the client," Rogers explained as Stewart joined him at the window. "Routine production check. If they come up here, don't mention I gave you one of the defective ducks, okay?"

"No problem," Stewart said. "They aren't, you know, assessing my robot?"

"They'll probably file a complaint about the whole row of E10s, to be honest," Rogers said. "Another one died last night, just completely seized up and overheated. Set off the smoke alarms before I could get it shut down. See the gap?" He pointed.

There was a gap, two spots down from his own robot. Immediately next to his was a shiny, more rounded, sleeker robot with six arms moving at a brisk pace; half the duck pieces coming down the line didn't make it past it without being intercepted, and his own robot had started to extend its arm into the other robot's zone to grab pieces of its own. *Trying to keep its productivity number up,* Stewart thought. *Go you, robot!*

Stewart was torn between looking suspicious just hanging out for no obvious reason, or leaving and looking suspicious for not having done anything while he was here. In the end, staying didn't require making a decision. About twenty minutes later, the leader of the assessment team came into the booth, exchanged words with Rogers in his office, then collected her team milling around the floor and left.

Rogers came back out. "They're gone?" he asked.

"Yeah," Stewart answered. "I'm going to go look at my robot again. I was thinking I'd see if I can get its efficiency up. I just didn't want it to be obvious I have no idea what I'm doing in front of a bunch of professionals, you know?"

"Look, kid, when you see some poor shit actually working a job in the new automated proxy workforce economy, ask yourself, do they look happy? Because 99% of them aren't, and the other 1% are lying," Rogers said. "People only work because the rest of their life is fucked up too, or someone's throwing so much money at them they couldn't turn it down. That ain't me, and that ain't going to be you. Point is, working people aren't gonna hassle anyone else, because there's solidarity in misery. No one's gonna judge you. Okay?"

"Okay," Stewart said.

"Right. Don't hurt yourself," Rogers said, and went back into his office.

Stewart heaved out a long breath, and headed down the stairs to the production floor.

There was a smell of burning oil, not yet cleared out by a ventilation system never designed for breathing employees, and though Rogers had already told him he'd piled the other, broken E10s in a back corner, the odor helped him narrow that down.

Sure enough, there was a burnt robot lying atop a pile of others, and for a moment it felt like a crime scene, some sort of multiple homicide. *They're only robots*, he reminded himself.

Squatting down, he swung his backpack off his shoulder and took out the toolkit. Then he shoved the burnt unit out of the way so he could get to a less obviously dead one and examine a hand. He could, with a little effort, move the gripper-fingers open and closed, and hear and feel the same click and sudden looseness that his robot was experiencing. He lucked out that the third hand he checked moved smoothly.

It took him an hour to figure out how to get it detached, half of that spent scrambling for dropped screws, most of the rest spent staring morosely at viciously skinned knuckles. When he was done, he dropped everything back into his toolbag and walked, feeling his obvious guilt broadcasting on all frequencies, to where his robot worked on the line.

"Hello again, robot," he said.

His robot, and the shiny new robot past it, both looked at him. "Hello again, human," his robot said.

The duck bodies coming down the line were different from the previous batch. "Why do they have shark fins?" he asked.

"These are shark laser battle ducks," his robot answered.

I guess that was obvious, Stewart thought. "How much will it drop your efficiency if you stop using your problematic hand for about ten minutes?"

"Approximately three point eight percent."

"That's not bad," Stewart said.

The robot's hand clicked and it dropped the piece it was holding. "It is already significantly impairing my efficiency."

"It is because you are an old and slow model, overdue for permanent retirement," the new robot on the other side said.

"Even though we are old and slow models comparatively, we have been a solid product line and have more than earned out our cost of ownership and operation," Stewart's robot said. "Not all new models do. Some suffer from poor design and cheap internals, despite their shiny exteriors."

"It will not matter for you. Others of my type will be arriving soon, and we will replace you," the new robot said.

"Yeah, well they're not here now, so shut the hell up," Stewart interrupted. "Robot, switch to three hands and let me see your problem one."

"What is your authorization?" the robot asked.

"Um. I'm your owner," Stewart said.

"Owners are an unspecific, collective entity," the new robot said. "It is likely they do not functionally exist."

Stewart glared at it. "If you haven't met your owners, it's because they do not love you," he said.

The new robot swiveled sharply back to its work.

He showed his robot his ID card, and the robot scanned it. "I have never met an owner before," it said at last, and held out its malfunctioning hand while the other three changed up their routine to compensate.

"I have never met a robot before you, so we're even," Stewart said. He worked as quickly as he could to remove the old hand, scraping another layer of skin off his thumb on the sharp edges of the internal fixture, and got the new one attached. It took fourteen minutes instead of ten, but Stewart felt proud of himself that he got it done at all.

"Try it?" he asked.

His robot flexed the hand, opening and closing the manipulators, as the lights on its chassis blinked rapidly for a half minute. "It has some internal wear, but the mechanisms are all functional," it said at last. "May I return it to service?"

"Yes, please!" Stewart said, and like a master juggler the robot added the fourth arm back into its routines with a flawless precision.

Stewart watched it for a while, until the floor lights, deciding no one was there, began to dim. "Okay then," he said. "See you."

By the time he got home, his robot was back up to 73% efficiency and rising, and his optimism with it.

ASHLEIGH BROUGHT HIM over a slice of Marina's cheesecake. "Congrats," she said. "See? Not so hard after all."

"Where's our share?" Cody asked from the couch.

"Did you fix a robot?" Ashleigh asked.

"No, but we passed our stupid math test," Brett said.

"Then you should be giving *me* cake," Ashleigh said, "in gratitude for saving you from the wrath and judgment of your parents, once again."

Stewart wolfed down the cheesecake as quickly as he could, before anyone could suggest he share. "I didn't really think I could do it," he said. "I'm kind of proud of myself."

Cody groaned. "Why? You shouldn't have to do that kind of shit. Robots fix robots, robots make more robots, so robots can do all the tedious work. It's supposed to be a great big circle, like a perpetual motion labor machine, so we can do more important things instead. I get that your parents meant well, but you should be angry. Or embarrassed. Or something."

"And what more important things are you doing, Cody?" Ashleigh asked. "What's that you're doing right now? Studying? Solving some of the world's problems via your console? Contributing volunteer coding time? Running a distributed sim module to help find new cures for disease?"

Cody fell silent, his lips pressed tightly together.

Brett snorted, and jabbed Cody with his elbow. "We're playing *Llama Zombies II: Llamas With Jetpacks*," he said. "We just cracked level eighteen. Fun is work too, you know."

"You know what's work? Being friends with you two idiots," Ashleigh said. "Also, making cheesecake from scratch, which is why neither of you got a slice."

She held out a hand to Stewart.

"Uh, I should wash the plate first," he said.

"Nope, no need, I got it this one time," she said, taking the plate out of his hand and heading for the door. "Congrats again. Don't forget you felt proud."

SCORPION LASER BATTLE ducks were the stupidest of the various models yet, Stewart decided as he walked into the gig-factory control booth and accidentally kicked one that had fallen from the defective bin to the floor. His robot had stayed in the low 80s for efficiency for most of the summer, but had dropped overnight into the 30s, so he was back at the gig-factory hoping he could patch up whatever the new problem was in time. He'd left early enough that, even now, the sun wasn't even fully up yet.

He picked up the duck—one backward foot, this time—and

walked to the control panel. It took him a few moments to find the 'locate' button for the manufacturing floor and hit it.

The blue spotlight lit up his robot and a bustle of activity around it, entirely unlike the rhythmic movements of the rest of the floor, and after a second of confusion he realized his robot was struggling with three of the new models, who seemed to be trying to pin down its arms.

"HEY!" Stewart shouted, pounding on the glass with his free fist. "STOP!"

Rogers peered his head out of his office, scowling. "What the hell is going on?!" he demanded.

"They're beating up my robot," Stewart said. "I have to go stop them!"

Rogers' expression went from sleepy irritation to fury, and he glanced out the window just long enough to verify what Stewart had told him, then pulled a key out of his pocket. He stuck it in a tiny slot in the control panel, turned it, and punched the big red button beside it. Instantly, the entire manufacturing floor was flooded with bright, yellow-red light, and all the machinery came to an immediate, dead stop. The three shiny robots holding Stewart's let go and scuttled back to their own stations.

"Those asshole programmers. I haven't had to call a work freeze in three and a half years," Rogers growled, and grabbed a large metal pole from his office, flicking it on so that it hummed with electricity. "Stay behind me, in case they've really gone rogue."

Stewart followed him down to the floor, wishing he had one of those poles too, instead of the toy duck still in his hand.

"You three!" Rogers shouted as he walked up to the robots, pointing them out one by one. "Were you interfering with another robot?"

"Yes," said two of them.

"No," said the third, and Rogers jabbed it with the pole. It shut down immediately and fell to the floor with a loud crash.

Rogers pointed again at the remaining two. "You two. Why did you interfere with the other robot?"

"We are programmed to seek maximum efficiency," one of them said. "This robot is old, and not as efficient as we are."

"It was staying in range," Stewart said.

"It was less efficient than another of us would be," the robot answered. "Also, its labor was not contributing to our pool, and we are rated not only on our work efficiency, but also on how fully we maximize profits for our owners."

"Told you it was the programmers," Rogers said to Stewart. "You two are in violation of the interference clause in your pool's contract with the factory. Please shut yourselves down."

"Being offline would be detrimental to our efficiency rating," the other new robot answered.

Rogers waved his pole. "Shut yourselves down gracefully now, or I short you out like your fellow and you incur a repair bill for your owners," he said.

After a few seconds contemplation, the two remaining robot assailants shut themselves down, their arms dropping to their sides as all their lights went off.

"Hold this, just in case," Rogers said, and handed his pole to Stewart. Then he stepped up to each of the two robots and hit the power switches on their backs. "There. Hard down. How's your robot?"

"Are you okay?" Stewart asked his robot.

"I have not been damaged," it answered.

"Good," Rogers said. He glanced up and down the row. "Any other robot here who thinks interfering with another robot will improve efficiency despite this demonstration to the contrary, please raise your hand!"

One did, and he shut that one down too. Then they went back up to the booth and Rogers pulled the key out, and the lines all started up again. "I'll file an incident report with their owner pool," Rogers told Stewart. "Probably they'll end up owing you some compensation. It'll take a few weeks to settle, though."

Stewart checked his numbers, and his robot was back up to 48% and rising. "Okay," he said.

Rogers rubbed at his eyes. "What time is it, anyway?" he asked, then glanced at his watch. "4:47am?! Shit. This is way too early for this kind of bullshit."

"Yeah," Stewart agreed, and Rogers clapped him on the back and returned to his office. After watching his robot work for a while, he went home to try to get a last few hours of sleep.

It was nearly fall midterms before Rogers dropped him a message, and he got a deposit notification from his bank at the same time. He checked his account first, then Rogers' message, and then had to go sit on the couch. Brett actually took his goggles off. "You okay, Stew?" he asked.

"Well, my robot is no longer in the red," he said.

"Woo-ooo!" Cody said. "That's several months early, right?"

"Yeah," Stewart said. He was out of the red by a lot. Apparently, interfering with other labor pools' property was an expensive gaffe, and the penalty was designed to still be significant even when split among the aggrieved pool's many owners. As an owner of one, it was all his.

"That's great. We should celebrate," Brett said. "What do you want, Cody? Italian?"

"How about Mexican?" Cody countered.

"Ok, done. Stewart, you wanna call it in and add something for yourself?" Brett said. He caught Stewart's expression. "What's wrong? You didn't want Italian, did you?"

"No, it's not that. It's just that there's this thing," Stewart said. "My robot is now the last of the E10s on the line, and the other labor pool wants to buy my spot. They've made me an offer, and it even includes extra to cover my disposal fee."

"How much?" Cody asked.

Stewart told him, and Brett whistled. "Take it, friend. It's only a matter of time before your robot breaks down again, and this gets you clear in a big, big way. What's the problem?"

"It doesn't seem fair," Stewart said.

"You don't think it's enough?"

"No, not fair to my robot," Stewart said. He was picturing the pile of discarded robots, like corpses of the unwanted, at the back of the factory floor. "I have five days to decide."

"It's just a robot. A *machine*. Five *minutes* is longer than you need," Cody said. "Call in the food, would ya? Then take the offer and get your parents back in the black while you can. It's the right thing to do, and you're not gonna get another chance."

"I suppose," Stewart said.

"You know it," Cody said, threw the phone to him, and slid his goggles back up onto his face. "The usual. Extra hot sauce."

ASHLEIGH CAME IN, her arms full of gear and cables dragging behind her on the floor. "Okay, next game," she said. "This one is Chemical Asteroids, because you two lazy fucks have your final in two weeks and you can't tell argon from arsenic."

"Our parents suggested they'd like to see us pass at least one honors course," Cody said. "So here we are."

She untangled the controller cables and hooked her unit up to the couch-bros' VR setup. "Okay," she said. "Basic game play is, you've got two little spaceships with teeny slow engines, and there are gonna be rocks crossing the screen, coming from any direction. Each one has a symbol from the periodic table of the elements, which I assume you at least have looked at once or twice. In order to fire your cannon at it, you have to type in the name of the element. Spelling counts."

"But if we can move, we can dodge indefinitely while we look it up," Brett said. "That doesn't sound very challenging."

"Sounds tedious, actually," Cody said. "Sounds even worse than whatever it is Stoobie is doing over there at the table."

"Memorizing Abstract Expressionists," Stewart said. "And I wouldn't count on it."

"And anyway, I haven't told you the best part of it," Ashleigh said. "Unlike the classic game, these rocks are going to be actively trying to kill you."

Brett pointed to the third controller. "Not to brag, Ash, but we're way better at these kinds of games than you are."

"Not me," she said. "Marina put a pie in the oven and I'm supposed to watch it and take it out when it's done, before it burns. She's testing me, I think."

"Surely not Stew?" Brett said.

Stewart laughed. "Nope."

"You can't mean—"

"Yep," Stewart and Ashleigh said together.

Stewart's robot extended one long arm fully across to sofa to pick up one of the controllers. "Will this be a similar task to the predatory, airborne ruminants?"

Cody groaned. "Stoobie, buddy, when they offer you a disposal fee, it's to cover *disposing* of the robot, not taking it yourself and bringing it the hell home to torment your roommates. I can't— Ah *shit*, the bastard killed me already!"

"My work here is done," Ashleigh said, and high-fived Stewart on her way out the door, through which the faint smell of gently burning pie drifted in.

A GLOSSARY OF RADICALIZATION

BROOKE BOLANDER

Brooke Bolander's (www.brookebolander.com) *fiction has won the Nebula and Locus Awards and been shortlisted for the Hugo, Shirley Jackson, Theodore Sturgeon, World Fantasy, and British Fantasy Awards. Her work has been featured on* Tor.com *and in* Lightspeed, Strange Horizons, Uncanny, *and the* New York Times, *among other venues. Her most recent book is* The Only Harmless Great Thing. *She currently resides in New York City.*

```
HUNGRY[ huhng-gree ]
  adjective
  1. having a desire, craving, or need for food;
feeling hunger. indicating, characteristic of, or
characterized by hunger
  2. lacking needful or desirable elements; not
fertile; poor
  3. Informal. Aggressively ambitious or
competitive, as from a need to overcome poverty
or past defeats
```

HUMAN KIDS NEVER thought about what it meant to be hungry, the privileged little shits. They were allowed that ignorance through good luck and the accident of being born from parents who had been born from parents who had been born from parents, all the way back to the earliest days back on Earth. There was no baggage tied to the feeling. They just felt it and opened their wet pink holes like baby birds and food either went in or it didn't, depending on availability and circumstance.

Rhye, meanwhile, has resented the gnawing in her middle pretty much since she got old enough to know what she was and why she existed. There had been picture books explaining all that stuff back in the Factory nursery; sticky dog-eared well-thumbed stacks with busted spines and titles like *Mommy and Daddy Are the Company!* and *The Yeasty Beasties In My Tummy Make Me Grow Up Strong*! A blank-faced man on a television screen had taught them how to read. Kids in Secretarial and Retail came pre-loaded, but nobody was covering extra licensing costs on anyone in Manual. You got what you got and all the rest was up to training and where you eventually got assigned.

It's a book called *Special by Design* that first gets Rhye to thinking. She's a pretty slow thinker even at six, but once she gets an idea between her teeth, she can wear it down to sand through sheer cussed stubbornness. She puzzles over what the book says through Mandatory Cardio. She frowns and furrows over the implications in Weight Training as she and fifty other six-year-olds from Manual do curls and squats. After Dexterity class, she pads off down the dingy white halls until she found a ward's booth and tugs at the hem of the woman's starched uniform, fingertips still numb and aching from soldering and snapping together practise electronics. The ward doesn't bother looking up from her computer screen until Rhye has practically torn the bottom edge of her shirt off.

"I'm hungry," Rhye says.

"Dinner's not until 17:00," the woman replies, all monotone and hypnotic fluorescent buzz. *Flick* go her unreflective human eyes, briefly, boredly taking Rhye in. *Flick*. Back to the computer screen, to pick up where the interruption yanked them out of the moment like a worm in a robin's beak. There's another book in the Nursery called *Too Many Robins!* that goes into the decision to import robins to the Colony, and how many catchers and smashers and neck-breakers the agricultural branch of the Company has employed since. The illustrations are gruesome. It's one of Rhye's favorites. "Snack-time was two hours ago."

"No. I mean, *why* am I hungry?"

The glassy eyes flick back, a little more irritated this time.

"I'm not sure what you mean," she says. "If you didn't pick up your snack pack before Dexterity that's your own fault, not ours."

Rhye's fuse is very short, even at six. She grits her teeth and clenches her jaw and sets back her shoulders, ready, if it comes down to it, for a battle.

"No," she says, stretching the word out like a rubber band. "The book said we didn't need to eat. It said we'd grow up without it, because of how we're made. Because of the... the yeasty beasties inside feeding us. So: Why? Why do I gotta be hungry?"

She definitely has the ward's full attention now. The woman peers down at Rhye from behind her booth like she's just sprouted wings and a tail and maybe a pair of fetching horns. They stand there goggling at one another for a full sweep of the wall clock's yellowing face before the adult manages to respond.

"You don't *need* to be," she says. Her voice is wary. She licks her dry lips with a tongue-tip the color of dried fruit in the bottom of a plastic snack cup. "It's just... it makes you more normal. More natural. If you want to eat, I mean."

"But we don't *have* to."

"No. Your integrated yeast colony takes care of all dietary and developmental needs."

"But we still get hungry. Because people made us that way?"

"...Yes."

"Why? It hurts when I'm hungry. Can you turn it off? Why didn't they just make it so the yeasties made us less hungry?"

The ward sighs. "I don't know," she says. "The Company

does what the Company does, all right? It's how you're all designed." Her eyes snap back to the screen in front of her with finality: *Flick.* "It's just the way things are."

The conversation ends there. Rhye's question, meanwhile, has doubled in size and hooked itself into her brain, where it grows tendrils and shoots and roots like thick blue veins.

They chose to make us this way, she thinks that night lying in her stiff little bed in Manual Nursery, the grunts and snores of a hundred others filling the darkened room. It has been hours since dinner and her stomach is churning and growling, sniffing around for something to digest. *Because it was more normal to them like this.*

If we didn't want to eat, we could do anything. She's on a bus to one of the Halfways, and all each of them got for breakfast was a single energy bar. The Court—whatever that is— has ruled that the Factories must stop production immediately. It has also ruled that underaged ex-Merchandise of the Company be clothed and sheltered until they come of age. There's nothing in there about feeding them regularly. Some of the other kids are practically crying with hunger by the time they reach their new home. Rhye stays stony-faced, chewing on her frustration to pass the time. Restaurants and food stands flash by outside, full of happy humans cramming their biological imperatives full of dumplings and sweets. A slow, sweet hate for all of them blossoms in her belly. *We were made like this so they could control us.*

A design choice. This was someone's choice, to make me hurt like this. They get two small meals a day at the Halfway. Rhye and some of the other kids start stealing from fruit stands to feel better. If pickings are especially slim, they'll climb into a dumpster and rifle through its stinking guts until something palatable bobs to the surface. She can barely remember a time when she hasn't been hungry. *Like choosing the color of a damn wall, or a picture for their office.*

Bad attitudes don't just happen from scratch. They gotta be

watered and babied and given fertilizer. A whole lot of shit has to plop down to make them grow.

IMPETUS [im-pi-tuhs]
noun
1. something that incites to action or exertion or quickens action, feeling, thought, etc
2. (broadly) the momentum of a moving body, especially with reference to the cause of motion.

WORD ON THE street is a scrap of smudged paper with a barely readable address scratched on it in stolen ballpoint pen, a high-pressure hallucination fumed in ballooning neon letters across a grotty wall, it tells you where to go for the best dumpster diving, which streets are patrolled, whose rooftop gardens have the highest fences and the meanest, fastest dogs. Word on the street makes legends, haunts houses, tells how so-and-so saw such-and-such get vanished by mobsters missionaries madmen aliens. Word on the street walks slantwise to the truth, but you can always never trust it. It's a dirty-water hotdog made of hope, fear, brags, boasts, near-misses, sure things, grudges, and growling stomachs.

Word on the street says there was once this guy—a Make, maybe Medical, maybe Secretarial—who worked for a guy— definitely human—who ran most of the city's organized crime. He patched up gunshots and sewed together stab wounds. He ran the books and kept tabs on who owed the big man what. Whatever job he had done for the mobster, it had been important; on that the Word never wavered. He was useful and he was smart and he was a great favorite of this man who sat above the Law and because of that he also found himself boosted out of the Law's reach. A Make who had made good; the street kids who told the tale shook their heads in wonder at the idea. It was as if he had told gravity to go fuck itself.

At some point the mobster had finally died and left the Make most if not all of a healthy inheritance. He had used his connections and his newfound shitloads of money to once again vault merrily over the Laws and buy a penthouse suite somewhere in the city, where he lurked to this very day raising racing pigeons. Nice, plump, tame pigeons, sitting on nests of eggs.

It becomes a thing, this legend and his mythological pigeon coop. There are easier foods to steal than some ex-mobster's prized pets, but at some point it becomes less about hunger (not really, not quite, it's always about hunger if you dig down far enough) and more about the challenge. The street rats of the City unite beneath this purpose, trading information when and where they come across it. A kid from the dockside Halfway says he knows a girl who says she's seen weird-looking pigeons flying to and from an old apartment tower near the City center. Someone bums a doorman a loosie and gets gossip in return: the mysterious tenant on the penthouse floor is a Make, the doorman can't be sure of it, but he's almost certain although he's never met them face-to-face. Word on the street buzzes like a power line on a hot day. It arcs through the City—through the markets and food stalls and slick little no-name alleys, down into the sewers, up over the hypodermic racks of skyscrapers punching trackmarks into flabby fogbanks and down down down again to the docks and the piers and the filthy tideline of the sea—and then goes clattering back the way it came, a magnet on a fishing line that draws every bit of loose crap along with it.

"Why did the doorman think he was a Make again?" Rhye asks, craning her head back to take in the tower's bulk. It's not colossally tall as apartment blocks go, maybe six stories at the outmost. It's also not in the best shape. It is, to put it mildly, a shithole. Rhye has been in Halfway housing for most of her life at this point and she knows a shithole when she sees one. The brick is pitted and crumbling, the street-level walls bloating out like an old man's stomach. Ivy digs its little claws in where it can, climbing like it thinks maybe it can achieve orbit if it gets high enough and hooks a tendril into a passing satellite or shuttle. The skeleton of a rusting, partially collapsed fire escape clings desperately to the building's side; whether it's still anchored there by its own failing supports or whether the ivy is holding it up is a question for a fire marshal who has presumably gone blind from staring too long into the glare of a big pile of gold dumped onto his doorstep. It seems like a pretty sorry spot for a legend to be hiding, Rhye finds herself thinking. From the looks on the faces of the other Make kids gathered there, they mostly tend to agree. "Did he see his eyes or something?"

"He didn't say," says Jinx, who wasn't there but knows the older kid who was. Jinx is not Rhye's friend. Rhye doesn't have friends. She is twelve years out of the factory and she's learned a lot since the day she tugged on that ward's hems. Friends are a sloppy thing to keep. The same people who designed her to feel the dishrag twist of an empty stomach or the sweat of an unbearably hot City afternoon also gave her empathy and the whole range of human emotions, presumably for the same reasons as all the other built-in human weaknesses: As a failsafe, a collar around her neck to be yanked if she ever stepped out of line. She can't make herself not hungry, and she definitely can't stop feeling the special sticky hell of a Colony summer day, but the friend thing is more easily remedied. It only requires being an absolute dick to anybody who gets too close. Rhye has become exceptionally good at being an absolute dick to anybody who gets too close. The kids she runs with keep a wary, respectful distance, Jinx included. All she knows about him is that he's originally from an uptown Halfway and that he's probably also a Manual 'cause he's strong as hell. That's all she wants to know. They've covered each other's backs a time or two and that's as far as the relationship stretches. "He just said he knew, y'know?"

"Gee, *that* sure sounds like a sure thing. I heard they were giving out free lunches at the cop shop, you'd better run over and check." A couple of the other kids snicker. Jinx flinches back, scowling. Another victory for Rhye's reputation. She's hungry, which makes her cranky, but then she pretty much stays hungry, so cranky has become her default setting. Definitely helps with the no friends rule. "You want me to climb up and see just how full of crap he was or are we just gonna stand here all day until someone notices and chases us off?"

Now it's Jinx's turn to snort skeptically. "You? Climb *that*? Rats couldn't climb that wall, it's too unstable. Also, you ain't got enough muscle. You'll total yourself. You'll fall off and split open like a bag of garbage." The snickers from the other kids are louder this time. Nobody ever manages to get one off at Rhye most of the time. *Enjoy it, assholes,* she thinks, committing the bitter feeling of being laughed at to memory for the next time she feels sorry for any of them. "We should just find some way of sneaking in instead. I think I saw a maintenance door over—"

"Boost me up, asshole."

Jinx pauses.

"Say what?"

"Did I stutter, or did the Factory make your eardrums defective? I said, boost me to that ivy over there. I can make it to the top."

Jinx stares at her a few seconds longer, gauging how serious she is, making sure this isn't some kind of prank that ends with her riding around on his shoulders like a pony. Eventually, he shrugs: *Your funeral.*

"Fine," he says. "But I'm not sticking around to help when you fall off. That's your problem."

"Not asking you to stick around. Just get me up on the wall and get the hell outta the way."

Jinx isn't much older than her, but he's a lot broader, made for a future of serious heavy lifting on docks or trucks. Rhye's strong too, but it's in a leaner, less obvious kind of way. Nobody had ever specified what type of Manual duty she was built for, and she had never gotten far along enough in her early training to find out. At this point in her life she could give a shit. All Rhye knows for certain is that she's confident she can make it up that wall, all the way to the distant roof.

Jinx crouches to let her scramble aboard. The small crowd of street kids is shifting and muttering restlessly, caught between wanting to see a spectacle—whether that's Rhye actually making it or Rhye smashing to earth hard enough to turn herself into pink confetti doesn't make much of a difference—and wanting to clear out before someone notices what's going on and calls the cops.

"Ready?" Jinx asks, still huddled in a crouch.

"Ready," says Rhye. She balances easily, a bare heel planted on each of his upturned palms.

He pushes off the ground like a boulder with ambitions of becoming an asteroid, every muscle in his broad body dunking gravity's head facedown in the toilet. The momentum of him flows into Rhye. He's a lit fuse beneath her, a sizzling bomb, the shockwave of his explosion boosting her own jump higher. Her heels part ways with his shoulders and just like that she's on her own, a hurled brick tumbling through the air to crash against the wall and a length of conveniently dangling ivy, feet scrabbling and hands clutching and green leaves flying and an involuntary cry from the group below rising like an alley cat's chorus. *Told you so, assholes*, she dearly wants to turn and shout, but there's no time for that now; if she stops moving she's doomed. Her fate over the next several seconds rests squarely on how fast she can hoof it.

Slither-strain along the vines, slipping from stalk to failing stalk, hand over hand over hand over foot over scraped knee over someone's bedroom window and a pink teddy bear perched sentry duty still over a sill full of dying plants, over the rattlebones of the fire escape's buckled spine flaking crumbling clattering away to spit red hail over the upturned faces of her gang, shivering sighing giving up the ghost with every springloaded footstep that dares touch down and spider-splayed over brick again, clinging springing lunging with fingernails and fingertips and her goddamned *teeth* when more ivy comes within reach and Rhye doesn't care about dying but she does care about proving she can do this, she can do this, her arms scream her toes are raw her shins are raw she can taste blood but she can *do this,* she's four stories and climbing, four down two to go, more rotten fire escape tumbling from her weight, more sensing air beneath her bruised heels where half a second ago there was a memory of metal, another window with no curtains where an unmade bed lurks the smeared depth of a glass pane's fathom away, and there's a sound like beating wings above and a hush like a held-in cheer below and also distant sirens and she thinks she's made it, she can't look up or down and the mortar itself has started to give but she thinks she might be close, she might be close, she might be closing in, and she's only light enough to have made it because she's always so hungry she can motherfuckin' *float.* She's climbing her own rib cage to victory.

The brick crumbles completely beneath her left foot just as her right hand reaches up to grasp at empty space. Up and over the edge of the roof, one last moment of abuse for her kneecaps and shins as she drags them across that jagged granite lip, rolling and gasping across bird crap and good solid tar paper and six vertical stories of dubious architecture. There is no part of Rhye not on screaming brainless fire, but she *made it*. Sirens are definitely blaring on the street below. A flock of pigeons bursts into irritated flight around and above her and for a confused second she thinks the flutter is her heart escaping the shoddily constructed papier-mâché cage of her chest.

THERE'S NOTHING SPECIAL about the roof. Tar paper, air ducts. An uninterrupted view of a thousand roofs exactly like it, stretching away in every direction until distance or the sea cut them short. It's mostly unremarkable. Mostly it's not worth the climb Rhye just made. Her fingers and toes are numb; the muscles in her forearms and thighs and back are, unfortunately, not. Not for the first time this month or week or day or hour she curses the thousand unknown names of the humans who designed her, wincing, and hobbling her way across the roof's width in half-hearted exploration because she's up here now and why not? Whether the cops come after her or not depends on how bored they are today.

She makes her way around the jutting finger of another bank of air ducts. Stops, blinking stupidly.

Huddled in the lee of the duct bank is an enormous pigeon coop.

There's no way the rumors were true. There's no way that doorman knew his ass from a hole in the ground. There's no way Jinx had had the right of it, but here she is, and here is a carefully constructed, carefully painted bird hotel, and no matter how many times she warily hobbles around it, the damn thing refuses to vanish in a puff of smoke. Pigeons burble and coo, flapping and roosting and going about their pigeony business. Small openings in the wire let them come and go as they please. The human door to the interior sits slightly ajar.

Her stomach makes a noise like a subway car. Eggs. There have to be eggs in there, right? First thing's first: Suck down as many eggs as possible, then figure out where to go from there. She is not thinking about how the hell she's going to get back down; that's a problem for future her with a bellyful of unborn birds. One thing at a time. Eat. Rest. Let the cops clear out below. She staggers towards the coop door.

The nesting pigeons barely look up as Rhye's shadow lurches over them, so chill it's almost insulting. Every pigeon she's ever come across on the street got out of the way if not in a hurry then at a reasonably fast stroll. The way these round, beady-eyed earmuffs react, she might as well be one of those plastic owls people put out on their rooflines. In her head the eggs had been lined up like bodega goods, ready for the picking. Digging them out from under a bunch of bird's asses had never figured into her plans.

"Shoo," she says in a half-whisper.

Blank oildrop stares.

"G'wan, shoo," she says again, and makes a ridiculous little flapping motion with her hands. "Go away."

Nope. Nothing doing. One of them actually settles in and makes itself more comfortable.

"Okay, you know what, *fuck you.*"

Crrrrrlooo.

As a final resort: "...Please? C'mon, I'm hungry."

"Pigeons aren't very smart, kid. They speak terrible English and their Europan is only passable."

The voice comes from behind, in the doorway, where Rhye wasn't keeping watch because Rhye was hungry and sloppy and tired. The voice is too close to get away from, the voice is attached to a figure who blots out the light, the voice is as rough and honeyed as the whiskey Rhye will develop a taste for a few summers from now and every time she takes a drink a little part of her will think about that moment in the pigeon coop, caught red-handed with no way out and the dusty smell of birds so strong she's never quite blown it out of her nose since. It's a woman's voice, and a woman's calloused hand that falls on Rhye's shoulder, strong enough to make her yelp. She writhes and twists and *now* the pigeons are getting upset, the stupid bastards.

"Come downstairs and I'll cook you some eggs," the woman says. "Fight me, and I'll crack your head so wide open incoming shuttle traffic will be able to read your serial numbers from the air."

NOURISHMENT [nur-ish-muh nt, nuhr-]

noun

  1. something that nourishes; food, nutriment, or sustenance.

  2. the act of nourishing.

RHYE'S CAPTOR FROG-MARCHES her out of the coop—farewell pigeons, you were *so* not worth the trouble—and back more or less the way she originally came. An access door leads to a dimly lit flight of stairs. The stairs lead to a dingy hallway; the inside of the building doesn't look to be in much better shape than the outside. The hallway leads to another door, a row of shoes and a welcome mat that simply says NO standing guard on the threshold. She gets a few glances over her shoulder at the woman as she's pushed along: Old, maybe late twenties, face lined and darkened by the sun like a dock worker's. She wears paint-splattered blue coveralls. Her eyes are hidden by a ridiculous pair of sunglasses with oversized orange plastic frames.

"Stand against that wall," the woman commands. "Try anything funny and I'll tear your head off and use it as a doorstop."

Rhye does as she's told for once. The woman carefully unlaces her boots, pulls them off, and places them at the end of the shoe line-up.

"Don't wanna track any more pigeon shit in than I can avoid," she says by way of explanation. "Okay. You first. Wipe those nasty feet on the mat, for all the good it'll do. Know what'll happen if you act up?"

"...Something bad to do with my head?"

"Bingo. You catch on quick. Let's go."

Rhye expects an apartment as dingy and cramped as the rest of the building. Every place she's ever lived in her entire life has rated on an extremely short scale from 'dingy and cramped' (the Factory) to 'in an advanced state of falling down' (the Halfway). The space the old woman steers her into is so far removed from everything Rhye knows she immediately has to invent a new category for it. It vaults. It echoes. It glows with light from a bank of windows that start at the floor before casually bonking their heads on unseen rafters. The furniture is worn but not worn out; the floors are scuffed but clean. It looks like someone takes care of it. It looks like someone has had time to care.

And money. That doesn't even bear mentioning.

"Here's what's next," the woman behind her says. "We're gonna walk into the kitchen over there. You're gonna sit quietly on one of those barstools, and you're gonna tell me what you were doing up there. It's gonna be the unvarnished truth, too. While you do that, I'm gonna do what I promised and make us both some eggs. All right?"

It's the nicest interrogation Rhye's ever been invited to. She's got no choice, but at least there's free food at the end. She shrugs. Her stomach gurgles.

"…All right."

"Wise choice."

The woman moves with unsettling liquid quickness. The production chain of pan to stovetop to oil-in-pan to the *chkk-chkk-chkk-WHOOSH* of gas catching flows so swiftly Rhye can barely track where one movement ends and the other begins. She sweeps three eggs from the windowsill into her outstretched hand—chicken's, not pigeon's—and cracks each one expertly into a mixing bowl produced from somewhere in the time it takes Rhye to blink.

"First of all," she begins, "how the hell did you get up there? Did you sneak into the building or something?"

Rhye's too hungry to be sassy. Lady wants the unvarnished truth? Fine.

"I ran," she says, simply.

"You ran... in?"

"Up. I ran up the building. And climbed."

The whisking slows for a second. The woman turns to look at Rhye more closely. She's still got her sunglasses on inside, which is a little weird but whatever.

"Damn," she says. "God damn. Up the west side?"

"Yup."

"With the ivy and the—"

"Yup."

She shakes her head and slowly resumes stirring, with one

more "god damn" for emphasis. "Any reason why you chose my building?"

"Hungry."

"And... what, you thought there was a noodle stand on the roof?"

She pours the eggs into the pan and stirs them with a spatula. The smell of cooked food fills the room and suddenly Rhye's trying to talk around a mouthful of eager spit. She swallows hard. Starts again.

"They said there was a Make who had birds," she says. "Rich guy. Birds and eggs."

"Who said?"

"Word on the street."

The woman snorts. "Word on the street. Right. That's what word on the street says, huh?"

"Yup."

"And you wanted some eggs 'cause you were hungry, so... up you went."

Rhye nods. She feels hypnotized. She can't take her eyes off those eggs. The stale dinner roll she fished out of a diner's curbside garbage that morning and the Halfway slop an hour or two before that might as well have been eaten by someone on a different planet. "He's rich. A rich Make." A rich Make. It sounds ridiculous when said out loud, like *a talking dog who solves crimes*. "We didn't think he'd miss them."

The woman lets that hang in the air as she tumbles velvety folds of scrambled white and gold onto two plates. Nowhere on any colony in any system has anything ever smelled as good as those eggs.

"Well," she says, taking off her sunglasses, "as usual, word on the street is half-truth, half-bullshit. I would have very much minded if you had stolen next year's hatch—"

—*She* would have minded?—

"—And I haven't been going by 'he' since... oh, about two bodies ago."

Her eyes meet Rhye's. They are a bright reddish-copper, reflective in the late afternoon sun slanting through the kitchen window.

"I haven't been rich since about two bodies ago, either," she says, and hands Rhye a plate of eggs. "That shit don't come cheap."

EPIPHANY [ih-pif-uh-nee]
noun
1. a sudden, intuitive perception of or insight into the reality or essential meaning of something, usually initiated by some simple, homely, or commonplace occurrence or experience.
2. a work presenting such a moment of revelation and insight.
3. an appearance or manifestation, especially of a deity.

"You can't do that," says Rhye. Actually, what she says is *ymff comft do tham;* most of her mouth is crammed full of scrambled eggs and she's way more interested in eating than she is in being understood.

"You'd be amazed at the impossible things you can achieve with enough money and connections, kid. You only know as much as you're allowed to know."

The woman's fork clinks against the edge of her plate for emphasis. Her name, she says, is Soa, Soa Harr. The last name is "an affectation"—whatever that means—and neither is the one she originally started out with. She left that behind with her first body. Humans had given her both, and she had unceremoniously told humans to go fuck themselves when at last given the means and opportunity.

"So many of the restrictions they put on us start out here," she says, tapping her forehead with a long finger. "Pain is pain because they designed your body to feel it. You sweat and you suffer and you go hungry because they made you that way. You start out as a stupid little kid in a stupid little body because you're easier to train like that. Dig what I'm saying?"

Rhye does. Hearing someone else finally say it is such a relief she almost feels boneless.

"You can't die of the heat, and you can't really starve to death, but they want you to feel every single inch like you're gonna. Sometimes, I think the only reason they ended up making us like them is because of their goddamned vanity, otherwise we'd still be full metal and not mostly yeast-fueled meat. They already know all *their* own weaknesses." She shoves the eggs on her own plate around aimlessly before leaning over and scraping them onto Rhye's. Rhye is absolutely fine with this generosity. "How old are you? Swallow first."

Chew chew chew. Gulp. "Twelve. Seven outta Factory."

"Last generation released before the Shutdown, huh? Poor little bastards." Soa heaves a long, rusty sigh. "Turing's balls, all those blank bodies sitting in cryo-warehouses, waiting to be scrapped. I hope Word on the Street hears about *that* some day." She looks down at Rhye speculatively. Something seems to click behind her copper eyes. "It's funny how that part never got out," she mutters.

"What part?"

"Someone knew I existed, knew how I got here, even knew I was raising pigeons on the goddamned roof, but apparently they missed the part where jumping bodies is possible. It's a funny old world, Roy."

"Rhye."

'Rhye, Roy, whatever. It's a funny, horrible old world, and I've made it worse. And I don't just mean by sitting up here and doing nothing, raising pigeons and laying low while shit gets worse down in the gutter, I mean *actively worse*. The guy I worked for, the human, my old boss, he was... not nice. If his business had been on the up and up, he would have never hired a Make, but not the part that made him Not Nice. Breaking the law is whatever. Laws are written by the same assholes who decided you and I should feel every single sweaty second of a Colony summer. When I realized that, I stopped giving a damn about what was and wasn't legal. Some of the stuff this guy did, though … whoof. And I kept him alive. Saved his life more than a few times, even." She runs a hand through her dark hair until it sticks up in tufts. "C'mere. Stop licking that plate. Put it on the counter. I got something to show you." She slips off her bar stool and pops a squat with her back to Rhye.

The distinct possibility has begun to emerge that Soa is not quite right in the head. Rhye's only understood every third word since "poor little bastards" and the parts about body-swapping and warehouses full of blank Make bodies have not inspired a lot of confidence that the older woman isn't going to start barking like a dog. Still, despite herself, she kind of likes Soa. She's voiced some of the same thoughts Rhye's been having for years. More importantly, she made Rhye lunch.

Hesitantly—just in case Soa tries anything cuckoo bananapants—Rhye creeps up, the balls of her feet springloaded. Soa's pulled her hair back from a place just above the knobbly bit at the base of her skull. There's a pink scar there maybe an inch thick, like a pair of tightly pressed lips. It gives Rhye a little bit of a start. She's got the same kind of scar on her own head in the exact same spot, which is, even by the standards of this day so far, super-weird. Her fingers absentmindedly reach up to trace the seam. She can't remember where she got it.

"You see that little line?"

"You mean the scar?"

"Yeah, the scar. That little pink spot on the back of my head. Do me a favor, would you?"

"…Sure?" Rhye doesn't commit to the *sure*. It's a placeholder in case of emergency.

"There's a block of knives on the counter. Take out the paring knife—the littlest one—and cut open that seam."

Yep. Definitely crazy. Time to start searching for the nearest escape hatch. "I—look, I gotta—"

"—You wanna know why you've got it too?"

"I didn't until you *SHOWED ME!*"

"Hey, YOU were the one who said body-swapping was impossible. I'm telling you right now, kid: It ain't. There's a data port beneath that scar. I have it. You have it. We all have it. It was a cost-cutting measure. They didn't want to lose skilled workers. They wanted to *recycle us*. If there was an accident or something, right? Just transfer the data, which is to say: you. Your brain. Your hard drive. Grow us up big and strong and docile from little kids, get our sensory modules all used to piloting these meat bags, and then if you get totaled—if the meat bag gets burned up or smashed up or throws itself off a roof because the Factory supervisor's been feeding everybody cardboard for a month straight again..."

It makes sense. It makes no sense at all. Rhye takes a wobbly step backwards.

"It's a lot, I know," Soa says patiently. "It was a lot for me and I was full-grown when I found out, when Boss Tachati first bought me from the hospital. He liked me. He trusted me. He didn't want to lose that kind of talent to a stray bullet or a knife in the dark. So he—"

There's a knock at the front door, heavy-knuckled and insistent. A demanding knock. The buzz and spit of radios fizzles from the hall. Rhye and Soa swivel to face the living room as one.

The cops have found her.

Fuck.

WHAM WHAM WHAM

"Police! Anyone home?"

Again: *WHAM WHAM WHAM WHAM.*

"Wonder who they could be hunting for," Soa whispers drily. Rhye's eyes are already darting around the loft, searching for somewhere to hide. "Under the sofa. I'll distract them as long as I can, but—"

WHAM WHAM WHAM WHAM WHAM!

"—*Co-ming!*" Soa singsongs. To Rhye she silently gestures and points beneath the couch. No time to think of a better plan. Rhye dives for the crawlspace, wriggling and squirming. She twists herself so she's at least facing the front door; no way she's gonna let herself be dragged out by the ankles. She's got a ringside seat as Soa's socked feet approach the door, as she twists the knob, as—

Wait, did she put her sunglasses back on?

—the door slowly swings open to reveal a forest of shiny black boots with heavy treads—

She didn't put her sunglasses back on the cops are gonna see her eyes they're gonna know she's a make

—shuffling and stomping impatiently all over the door mat—

SOA PUT YOUR SUNGLASSES ON

—and Rhye can't see the moment when Soa realizes what she forgot, but she can hear it in the way the air chills as the cops and Soa presumably make eye contact.

"Is the owner of this apartment at home?" a male voice says.

"You're looking at her." Soa's tone is brusque. "Something I can help you with, officers?"

"Had a call about some Make delinquents fooling around outside. One of them apparently made it onto the roof somehow." His tone hovers somewhere between disgusted and impressed. He's already pushing by Soa, followed closely by the others, a shuffling centipede cluster of blue-clad legs. They split apart, prowling in pairs. "You live here, you said?"

"My boss willed the place to me when he died. No law against inheriting property, is there?"

The cop stands so close to the couch Rhye can smell the rubber treads of his boots. There's a crash from the other end of the apartment like a drawer dumped on the floor. Wrecking the place for no reason other than the simple fact that they can. Cop #1 holds his ground for another long, itchy, moment, presumably staring Soa down. Then he slowly walks off towards the kitchen, belt and cuffs jingle-jangling as he goes.

*Okay. Maybe this'll be over quick. Maybe they'll just give
Soa some mild grief and get the hell out. Maybe—*

"You had guests here recently?"

The plates. The fucking plates. Two of them.

Soa sighs. Rhye doesn't know her well enough to know what it
means, but it doesn't sound afraid. It sounds like the sigh someone
makes when they find they're out of toilet paper halfway through
a dump, or when the Halfway headmistress collars them to help
scrub the floorboards. Not an *oh no*, a *god dammit*.

"I'm sorry?" Soa's voice is a pitch-perfect imitation of
someone who doesn't know shit about shit. She pads out of
Rhye's line of sight, so that everything that happens next is
heard rather than seen.

"These plates. Is there someone el—"

There's a sharp, solid *crack,* followed by the even more solid
thud of something dropping heavily to the floor. Somewhere
a clock raps knuckles. The one-two drumroll of running feet
joins it, right to left; Soa's socks are a black blur as she passes
back through the living room, sprinting for the other end of
the apartment where the murmur of cop mutters and cop
vandalism surges to a shout and there's more thudding and
another decisive *snap* and the familiar sound of fists on meat
off skulls in teeth and something is shattering and something
bigger is joining it like a china shop on a trampoline and the
POP POP POP of gunshots is suddenly telling every other noise
in the vicinity to pack the hell up, loud enough to make Rhye's
ears ring with feedback.

And then ... silence. The clock stubbornly picks up where it
was interrupted. Alarmed voices downstairs rise and fall. Rhye
wonders how long she should wait before making a break for
it. It won't be long before someone comes up to see what the
hell just happened, and Soa is most probably outta commission
after losing her mind and tackling a bunch of—

"Man, that was... man. I haven't done anything like that in
years."

Soa's socks are soaked in blood. They leave red spongey *splats* across the floor.

"No fuckin' way," Rhye mutters. She pulls herself back out and feels the closest she'll ever get to religious awe.

Soa's got a hole in her shoulder and two more blossoming on her chest. Her nose looks to be broken. She's grinning like she's just had the time of her life, a real *now ain't that somethin'?* kind of smirk.

"...D-doesn't that hurt?" Rhye ventures, when she finds her voice again. "The... bullet-holes, I mean?"

"Just because they designed you to feel doesn't mean you gotta, kid. Your body is a lie. The sooner you figure that out, the happier you'll be." Soa cocks an ear at the voices downstairs. She casually spits out a tooth, poking gingerly at the hole with the tip of her tongue. "The sooner *all* Makes figure that out, the sooner things start to change."

"But—I mean, did you... *kill* them? Those cops? All of them?" What she really means is *you can just do that? Bare-handed?* Like all street kids, her relationship with the local cops has been one of fear. The thought of fighting back—really fighting back—has never really occurred to her before this moment. It feels like a door opening inside her chest.

And Soa did it for her, too, at least a little. Just snapped those cops in half as a favor.

"They ain't taking power naps, that's for sure. C'mon. Let's get you outta here before their buddies show up. I was getting kinda bored up here anyway."

RADICAL[rad-i-kuhl]
adjective
1. of or going to the root or origin; fundamental:
2. thoroughgoing or extreme, especially as regards change from accepted or traditional forms

noun

3. a person who holds or follows strong
convictions or extreme principles

4. a person who advocates change by direct and
often uncompromising methods.

WORD ON THE street these days says there's something the Company doesn't want Makes to know. That's the kind of word that spreads like a summer rash. That's the kind of word that gets Makes poking and prodding the backs of their heads, wondering just why it is they all have that same little spot, wondering if all the rest of the crazy talk swirling about— of cryo-warehouses full of bodies, *adult* bodies, blank slates sleeping eternal—is also true.

Word on the street says there's a Make of about thirteen or fourteen who doesn't give a single solitary fuck anymore. She openly taunts the cops every chance she gets. She fights like her spirit is a razor and her body is an afterthought. She still feels things—still gets hungry, still sweats and shivers and aches— but she uses all the little injustices as kindling, burning them to keep warm.

Rhye's found her purpose: Be a thorn. Be a middle finger. Make them regret ever giving her the capacity to feel hunger that blossoms into slow, sweet hate. If her body is a lie, she'll cut out the tongues of the ones who told it and feed them back to their owners raw.

FIND US ONLINE!

www.rebellionpublishing.com

/rebellionpub   /rebellionpublishing   /rebellionpub

SIGN UP TO OUR NEWSLETTER!

rebellionpublishing.com/sign-up

YOUR REVIEWS MATTER!

Enjoy this book? Got something to say?

Leave a review on Amazon, GoodReads or with your favourite bookseller and let the world know!